GUARDIAN ANGEL

Also published in Large Print from
G.K. Hall by Sara Paretsky:

Burn Marks
Blood Shot
Bitter Medicine
Indemnity Only

GUARDIAN ANGEL

Sara Paretsky

G.K.HALL &CO.
Boston, Massachusetts
1992

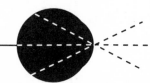

**This Large Print Book carries the
Seal of Approval of N.A.V.H.**

Published in Large Print by arrangement with
Delacorte Press, Bantam Doubleday Dell Publishing Group, Inc.

G.K. Hall Large Print Book Series.

Printed on acid free paper in the United States of America.

Set in 16 pt. Plantin.

Library of Congress Cataloging-in-Publication Data

Paretsky, Sara.
  Guardian angel / Sara Paretsky.
    p. cm. — (G.K. Hall large print book series)
    ISBN 0-8161-5541-0 (hc). — ISBN 0-8161-5542-9 (pb)
    1. Large type books. I. Title.
  PS3566.A647G83 1992b
  813'.54—dc20   92-17881

For Matt and Eve
(Eva Maria, that is,
the once and future princess)

"Tread softly, because you tread
on [their] dreams."
—*W. B. Yeats*

Thanks

Dan Paretsky, World's Greatest Vet, provided valuable information on Peppy's condition. Norma Singer and Loretta Lim, both registered nurses at Cook County Hospital, used one of their rare days off to give me a tour of the hospital. They explained its intricate workings in detail and showed me the pride they have in their own very difficult jobs. Norma Singer helped solve the problems that beset Mrs. Frizell in this novel.

Madelyn Iris, from Northwestern University's Center on Aging, was most helpful on questions of guardianship, city and county emergency services, and the procedure used to appoint someone as an elderly person's guardian. This book accelerates the timetable for that procedure, but the process described here is depressingly close to reality.

Rob Flater showed me where to start research so I could grapple with the skullduggery this novel discusses. Jay Topkis killed an impertinent dragon that was trying to spray fire in my direction.

An expert on mechanics—both quantum and otherwise—worked out the technical problems in Chapter Fifty.

This novel is a work of fiction. As is always the case, none of the people or events detailed here is based on anything except the distortions of reality caused by an overheated, morbid imagination. And as is also always true, any mistakes in the text are due to my ignorance, sloth, or stupidity, not to the advice of the experts I consulted.

Bonnie Alexander and Mary Ellen Modica made it possible for me to return to work. Without their help I might never have been able to do so again. Diann Smith made the connections for me, as she has done for Chicago women for thirty years. Professor Wright and Dr. Cardhu supported my spirits through long months of pain.

Chicago
May 1991

Contents

1

Sex and the Single Girl

Hot kisses covered my face, dragging me from deep sleep to the rim of consciousness. I groaned and slid deeper under the covers, hoping to sink back into the well of dreams. My companion wasn't in the humor for rest; she burrowed under the blankets and continued to lavish urgent affection on me.

When I covered my head with a pillow she started to mew piteously. Now thoroughly awake, I rolled over and glared at her. "It's not even five-thirty. You can't possibly want to get up."

She paid no attention, either to my words or my efforts to dislodge her from my chest, but looked at me intently, her brown eyes opened wide, her mouth parted slightly to show the tip of her pink tongue.

I bared my teeth at her. She licked my nose anxiously. I sat up, pushing her head away from my face. "It was this indiscriminate distribution of your kisses that got you into this fix to begin with."

Happy to see me awake, Peppy lumbered down from the bed and headed for the door. She turned to see if I was following, making little whimpering

1

noises in her impatience. I pulled a sweatshirt and shorts from the heap of clothes near the bed and padded on sleep-thickened legs to the back door. I fumbled with the triple locks. By that time Peppy was whimpering in earnest, but she managed to control herself while I got the door open. Breeding shows, I guess.

I watched her down the three flights of stairs. Pregnancy had distended her sides and slowed her progress, but she made it to her spot by the back gate before relieving herself. When she was finished she didn't take her usual tour of the yard to drive away cats and other marauders. Instead she waddled back to the stairs. She stopped outside the ground-floor door and let out a sharp bark.

Fine. Let Mr. Contreras have her. He was my first-floor neighbor, part owner of the dog, and wholly responsible for her condition. Well, not wholly—that had been the work of a black Lab four doors up the street.

Peppy had come into season the week I left town on the trail of an industrial sabotage problem. I arranged for a friend of mine, a furniture hauler with steel thews, to run her twice a day— on a short leash. When I told Mr. Contreras to expect Tim Streeter he was deeply wounded, although not, unfortunately, beyond words. Peppy was a perfectly trained dog who came when she was called, didn't need to be on a leash; and anyway, who did I think I was, arranging for people to come walk her? If not for him she wouldn't

2

get any care at all, me being gone twenty hours out of twenty-four, I was leaving town, wasn't I? Just another example of my neglect. And besides that, he was fitter than ninety percent of the young jerks I brought around.

In a hurry to take off I hadn't heard him out, just agreed that he was in terrific shape for seventy-seven, but asking him to humor me in the matter. It was only ten days later that I learned that Mr. Contreras had dismissed Tim the first time he showed up. The results, if disastrous, were utterly predictable.

The old man met me dolefully when I returned from Kankakee for the weekend. "I just don't know how it happened, doll. She's always so good, always comes when she's called, and this time she just tore away from me and headed down the street. My heart was in my throat, I thought my God, what if she gets hit, what if she gets lost or kidnapped, you know, you read about these labs that hire people to steal dogs off the streets or out of the yard, you never see your dog again and you don't know what happened to her. I was so relieved when I caught up with her, my goodness, what could I ever have said to make you understand—"

I snarled unsympathetically. "And what are you going to say to me about this business? You haven't wanted to spay her, but you can't control her when she's in season. If you weren't so bullheaded you would've admitted it and let Tim run her. I'll tell you this much: I'm not going

3

to spend my time looking for good homes for her damned offspring."

That brought a spurt of his own temper, which sent him back to his apartment with an angry slam of the door. I avoided him all day Saturday, but I knew we had to make up before I left town again—I couldn't leave him in sole charge of a litter. Anyway, I'm too old myself to enjoy bearing a grudge. Sunday morning I went down to patch things up. I even stayed over on Monday so we could go to the vet together.

We brought the dog in with the angry tension of the ill-assorted parents of a wayward teenager. The vet cheered me no end by telling me that goldens sometimes have as many as twelve puppies.

"But since it's her first litter it probably won't be quite that large," he added with a jolly laugh.

I could tell that Mr. Contreras was delighted at the prospect of twelve little black-and-gold fur balls; I did eighty-five all the way back to Kankakee, dragging out my business there as long as possible.

That had been two months ago. Now I was more or less resigned to Peppy's fate, but I was much relieved that she seemed to be doing her nesting on the first floor. Mr. Contreras grumbled about the newspapers she shredded in her chosen spot behind his couch, but I knew he would have been unbearably hurt if she'd decided her den was in my apartment.

4

This close to her due date she was spending almost all her time inside with him, but yesterday Mr. Contreras had gone to a Las Vegas Night that his old parish was running. He'd been involved in the planning for six months and didn't want to miss it, but he called me twice to make sure Peppy hadn't started into labor, and a third time at midnight to check whether I'd written down the phone number at the hall they'd rented. That third call was what was giving me malicious pleasure at her trying to wake him before six.

The June sunshine was bright, but the early morning air was still chilly enough that my bare feet grew too cold to feel the porch floor. I went back inside without waiting for the old man to get up. I could hear Peppy's muffled barks continuing as I kicked my shorts off and stumbled back into bed. My bare leg slid over a wet spot on the sheet. Blood. It couldn't be mine so it had to be the dog's.

I pulled my shorts back on and dialed Mr. Contreras's number. I had my knee socks and running shoes on before he answered, his voice hoarse beyond recognition.

"You guys must have had a good old time last night," I said brightly. "But you'd better get up and face the day—you're about to become a grandfather again."

"Who is this?" he rasped. "If this is some kind of joke you oughtta know better than to call people at this time of morning and—"

"It's me," I interrupted him. "V. I. Warshawski.

5

Your upstairs neighbor, remember? Well, your little dog Peppy has been barking her head off outside your door for the last ten minutes. I believe she wants to come inside and have some puppies."

"Oh. Oh. It's you, doll. What's that about the dog? She's barking at my back door. How long have you left her outside? She shouldn't hang around out there barking when she's this close to her time—she could catch a chill, you know."

I bit back various sarcastic remarks. "I found some blood spots in my bed just now. She may be getting ready to whelp. I'll be right down to help you get things in order."

Mr. Contreras started in on a complicated set of instructions about what I should wear. These seemed so pointless that I hung up without ceremony and headed back outside.

The vet had stressed that Peppy didn't need any help with her delivery. If we got involved with her while she was in labor or picked up the first-born puppies it could cause her enough anxiety that she might not be able to handle the rest on her own. I didn't trust Mr. Contreras to remember in the excitement of the moment.

The old man was just shutting the back door on Peppy when I got down to the landing. He gave me a harassed look through the glass and disappeared for a minute. When he finally opened the door he held an old workshirt out to me.

"Put this on before you come inside."

I waved the shirt away. "This is my old

6

sweatshirt; I'm not worried about what I may get on it."

"And I ain't worried about your stupid wardrobe. It's what you've got underneath it I care about. Or what you ain't got underneath it."

I stared at him, astounded. "Since when do I need to put on a bra to look after the dog?"

His leathery face turned a dull crimson. The very thought of female undergarments embarrasses him, let alone hearing their names spoken out loud.

"It's not because of the dog," he said, agitated. "I tried telling you on the phone, but you hung up on me. I know how you like to go traipsing around the house, and it don't bother me any as long as you're decent, which generally speaking you are, but not everybody feels the same way. That's a fact."

"You think the dog cares?" My voice went up half a register. "Who the hell else—oh. You brought someone home with you last night from the gambling den. Well, well. Quite an evening for you, huh?" Normally I wouldn't be so vulgar about someone's private life, but I felt I owed the old man a lick or two after all the snooping he'd done on my male visitors during the last three years.

He turned a deeper mahogany. "It ain't what you think, doll. It ain't like that at all. Fact is, it's an old buddy of mine. Mitch Kruger. It's been a real struggle for him, making ends meet since him and me retired, and now he's been tossed out on his rear end, so he come home crying on my shoulder last night. Course, like I told him, he wouldn't have to worry about his rent if he didn't drink it first. But that's neither here nor there. Point is, he's never exactly kept his hands to himself, if you know what I mean."

"I know just what you mean," I said. "And I promise that if the guy feels inflamed by my charms I will put him off without breaking his arm—in deference to our friendship and his age. Now, put your jacket away and let me see how Her Serene Dogginess is."

He wasn't happy about it, but he grudgingly let me into the apartment. Like mine, it had four rooms arranged boxcar style. From the kitchen you went into the dining room and then into a little hall that fed the bedroom, bath, and living room.

Mitch Kruger was snoring loudly on the living room couch, his mouth hanging open under his bulbous nose. One arm was flung over the side so that his fingertips trailed the floor. The top row of his thick gray chest hairs peeped out from the edge of the blanket.

Ignoring him as best I could, I crouched next to the sofa, under the shadow of his malodorous socks, and peered around the back to look at Peppy. She was lying on her side in the middle of a heap of newspapers. She'd spent most of the last few days shredding these, building a nest over the stack of blankets Mr. Contreras had folded for her. When she saw me she turned her

8

head away, but thumped her tail once, feebly, to show there were no hard feelings.

I got back to my feet. "I guess she's okay. I'm going upstairs to make some coffee. I'll come back in a little while. Remember, though, you've got to leave her alone—no going back there and trying to stroke her or anything."

"You don't have to tell me how to manage the dog," the old man huffed. "I guess I heard the vet as good as you; better, since I took her in for a checkup while you was out doing God knows what."

I grinned at him. "Right. Got it. I don't know what she makes of your pal's buzz saw, but it would put me off my feed."

"She ain't eating," he began, then his face cleared. "Oh, I get you. Yeah, I'll move him into the bedroom. But I don't want you in here looking on while I do it."

I made a face. "Me, neither." I didn't think I could stomach the sight of what might lie below the fringe of greasy chest hair.

Back in my own place I suddenly felt too tired to cope with making coffee, let alone assuaging Mr. Contreras's expectant-father anxiety. I pulled the bloodied sheet from the bed, kicked off my running shoes, and lay down.

It was almost nine when I woke again. Except for the twittering of birds anxious to join Peppy in maternity, the world was quiet beyond my walls, one of those rare wells of urban silence that give the city dweller a sense of peace. I

9

basked in it until a squeal of brakes and furious honking broke the spell. Angry shouts—another collision on Racine.

I got up and went into the kitchen to make coffee. When I moved here five years ago this was a quiet blue-collar neighborhood—which meant I could afford it. Now rehab mania had hit. While housing prices trebled the traffic quadrupled as cute shops sprang up to feed the gentry's delicate appetites. I only hoped it was a BMW that had been hit, not my own beloved Pontiac.

I skipped my exercise program—I wouldn't have time to run this morning, anyway. Conscientiously donning a bra, I put my cutoffs and sweatshirt back on and returned to the maternity ward.

Mr. Contreras came to the door faster than I'd expected. His worried face made me wonder if I should go back up for my car keys and license.

"She ain't done nothing, doll. I just don't know—I called over to the vet, but the doc don't come in till ten on Saturdays and they told me it wasn't an emergency, they couldn't give me his home number. You think you should call and see if you can make 'em?"

I grinned to myself. A real concession, if the old man thought there was a situation I could handle better than he. "Let me look at her first."

When we passed through the dining room to the hall I could hear Kruger's snores coming through the bedroom door.

"You have any trouble moving him?" A major altercation could have gotten the dog too agitated for easy delivery.

"My first thought was for the princess, if that's what you mean. I don't need any criticism from you; it don't help me right now."

I swallowed my tongue and followed him to the living room. The dog was lying much as she had been when I went upstairs, but I could see a dark pool spreading around her tail. I hoped that meant progress. Peppy saw me watching but made no sign. Instead she tucked her head underneath her body and started washing herself.

Was she all right? It was all very well to say not to interfere with her, but what if we let her hemorrhage because we didn't realize she was in trouble?

"What do you think?" Mr. Contreras asked anxiously, mirroring my own worries.

"I think I don't know anything about birthing puppies. It's twenty of ten now. Let's wait till the guy comes in—I'll go get my keys just in case."

We had just decided to make a pallet for her in the car so we could rush her to the clinic when the first puppy slid out, smooth as silk. Peppy attacked it urgently, washing away the afterbirth, using her jaws and her forepaws to settle it next to her. It was eleven before the next one appeared, but then they started coming every half hour or so. I was beginning to wonder if she would fulfill the vet's prophecy and have a dozen. But around three o'clock, after the eighth little creature squirmed its way to a nipple, she decided to stop.

I stretched and headed to the kitchen to watch Mr. Contreras fix her a big bowl of dry dog food mixed with scrambled eggs and vitamins. His absorption in the process was so complete that he didn't respond to any of my questions either about his Las Vegas Night or Mitch Kruger.

I figured I was an unneeded third at this point. Some friends were playing softball and making a picnic over by Montrose harbor and I'd told them I'd try to join them. I undid the bolts to the back door.

"What's up, doll? You going someplace?" Mr. Contreras paused briefly in his stirring. "You run along. You can be sure I'll look after the princess a-okay. Eight" —he beamed to himself— "Eight and she did it just like a champ. My, oh my."

As I closed the back door a horrible noise came from the old man. I was halfway up to my apartment before it hit me: he was singing. I think the song was "Oh, What a Beautiful Morning."

2

Black Tie Optional

"So you've become an obstetrician?" Lotty Herschel mocked me. "I've always thought you needed a backup profession, something with a more reliable cash flow. But I wouldn't recommend obstetrics these days: the insurance would overwhelm you."

I flicked a thumbnail at her. "You just don't want me muscling in on your turf. Woman reaches the top of her profession and can't bear to see the younger ones scrambling up behind her."

Max Loewenthal frowned at me across the table: that was about as unfair an accusation as I could make. Lotty, one of the city's leading perinatalogists, always had a spare hand to stretch out to younger women. Men too.

"What about the father?" Max's son Michael quickly changed the subject. "Do you know who it is? And are you making him pay child support?"

"A good question," Lotty said. "If your Peppy is like the teenaged mothers I see, you won't get many dog biscuits out of the father. But maybe his owner will help out?"

"I doubt it. The father's a black Lab who lives up the street from us. But I can't imagine Mrs. Frizell helping care for eight puppies. She's got five dogs of her own and I don't know where she gets the money to feed them."

Mrs. Frizell was one of the stubborn holdouts against the gentrification of my stretch of Racine. In her eighties, she was the kind of old woman who terrified me when I was small. Her wispy gray hair stuck out from her head in uncombed elflocks. Summer and winter she wore the same

13

array of faded gingham dresses and shapeless sweaters.

Although her house badly needed painting, it wasn't falling down. The concrete front steps and the roof had both been replaced the year I moved into my coop. I'd never seen any other signs of work on the place and vaguely assumed she had a child somewhere who took care of the most pressing problems. Her yard apparently didn't come under that heading. No one ever cut the rank, weed-filled grass in the summer and Mrs. Frizell didn't seem to mind the cans and cigarette packs that people tossed over the fence.

The yard was a sore spot with the local block development committee, or whatever my upwardly mobile neighbors called themselves. They didn't much like the dogs either. The Lab was the only purebred; the other four were mutts ranging in size from a large, off-white Benji replica to something that looked like a walking gray earmuff. The animals were nominally fenced in, except when Mrs. Frizell walked them on a tangle of leashes twice a day, but the Lab in particular came and went as he pleased. He'd jumped the four-foot fence to mount Peppy, and presumably other dogs as well, but Mrs. Frizell wouldn't believe angry callers who told her so. "He's been in the yard all day," she would snap. And somehow, with that telepathy that exists between some dogs and their people, he would miraculously appear in the yard any time she opened the door.

"Sounds like a problem for the Department of Health," Lotty said briskly. "An old woman alone with five dogs? I can hardly bear to think about the smell."

"Yes," I agreed, but not wholeheartedly.

Lotty offered dessert to Michael and his companion, the Israeli composer Or' Nivitsky. Michael, who made his home in London, was in Chicago for a few days to play a concert with the Chicago Symphony. Tonight he was giving a solo recital at the Auditorium as a benefit for Chicago Settlement, the refugee assistance group. It had been a favorite charity of Max's wife, Theresz, before she died nine years ago; Michael was dedicating tonight's recital to her. Or' was playing the oboe in a concerto for oboe and cello she'd written in Theresz Loewenthal's name.

Or' refused dessert. "Prepremiere butterflies. And anyway, I need to change." Michael was already superfine in tails, but Or' had brought her concert gown with her to Lotty's— "That way I can pretend it's just an ordinary evening as long as possible and enjoy my dinner," she'd explained in her clipped British English.

While Lotty bustled out to fasten the back of Or's dress, Michael went down with his cello to fetch the car. I cleared away the dinner plates and put water on for coffee, my mind more on Mrs. Frizell than on Or's premiere.

I'd refused to sign the neighborhood petition demanding that she cut her grass and chain the dogs. A lawyer who'd rehabbed the house across the street from her wanted to take her to court and force the city to remove the dogs. He'd been around, trying to drum up support. My building was pretty evenly divided—Vinnie, the tight-assed banker who lived on the ground floor, had eagerly signed on, as had the Koreans on the second floor; they had three children and were worried about dog bites. But Mr. Contreras, Berit Gabrielsen, and I firmly opposed the idea. Even though I wished Mrs. Frizell would neuter the Labrador, the dogs weren't really a menace. Just a minor nuisance.

"The puppies worrying you?" Max came up behind me as I stood lost in thought over the kitchen sink.

"No, not really. Anyway, they're living with Mr. Contreras, so they won't be under my feet. I hate to find myself cooing over them with his enthusiasm, because getting them all back and forth for shots and everything else is going to be nightmare enough. And then finding homes for them, training the ones we can't give away—but they are adorable."

"I'll put a notice in the hospital newsletter if you like," Max offered. He was the executive director at Beth Israel, where Lotty sent her perinatal patients.

Or' swept into the kitchen as I was thanking him, resplendent in soft coal crepe that clung to her body like soot. She kissed Max on the cheek and held out a hand to me.

16

"Good to meet you, Victoria. I hope we'll see you after the concert."

"Good luck," I said. "I'm eager to hear your new concerto."

"I know you'll be impressed with it, Victoria," Max said. "I've been listening to the rehearsal all week." Michael and Or' had been staying with him in Evanston.

"Yes, you are an angel, Max, putting up with our swearing and screeching for six days. Good-bye."

It was only six o'clock; the concert didn't begin until eight. The three of us ate poached pears with almond cream and lingered over coffee in Lotty's bright, spare living room.

"I hope Or' has done something palatable in Theresz's honor," Lotty said. "Vic and I went to hear the Contemporary Chamber Ensemble play an octet and a trio of hers and we both left with headaches."

"I haven't heard the piece played through properly, but I think you'll be pleased. She's done some very painful work on this—examined the past in a way that many contemporary Israelis don't want to." Max looked at his watch. "I think I must have prepremiere butterflies as well, but I'd like to get an early start."

I was driving. Max had lent his car to Michael and no sane person would let Lotty chauffeur them. Max graciously took the small backseat the Trans Am offered. He leaned forward to talk to Lotty over the seatback, but once we were on

Lake Shore Drive I couldn't hear them above the engine. When I turned off at Monroe and stopped at the light between the Inner Drive and Congress, I could make out snatches of the conversation. Lotty was upset about something to do with Carol Alvarado, her nurse and right arm at the clinic. Max didn't agree with her.

The light changed before I could make out what the problem was. I turned down Congress toward Louis Sullivan's masterpiece. Lotty whipped her head away from Max to admonish me sharply on the speed at which I'd taken the corner. I looked at Max in the rearview mirror; his mouth was pinched into a line. I hoped the two weren't planning a major quarrel in honor of the evening. And anyway, what possible disagreement could they have about Carol?

At the half-circle connecting Congress with Michigan Avenue we ran into a jam. Cars heading to the south underground garage were snarled with those trying to stop at the theater entrance. A couple of cops were frantically directing traffic, whistling people away as they tried pulling up to the curb in front of the Auditorium.

I pulled over to the side of the road. "I'll let you two out here and go park—we'll never be on time if I try to get across here."

Max handed me my ticket before unwinding himself from the backseat. Although I'd put a blanket down to cover Peppy's traces I could see red-gold hairs clinging to his dinner jacket as he climbed out. I made an embarrassed face and furtively looked at the skirt of Lotty's tailored coral gown. It held a few hairs too. I could only hope her annoyance kept her mind off her clothes.

I made a sharp U, ignoring an outraged whistle, and zipped the Trans Am back up to Monroe and the north garage. It was only half a mile from there to the Auditorium, but I was wearing a long skirt and high heels, not the best garb for jogging. I slid in next to Lotty in the box Michael had given us just as the houselights went down.

Looking austere and remote in tails, Michael came onto the stage. He opened the evening with Strauss's *Don Quixote Variations.* The theater was full—Chicago Settlement had become a trendy charity for some reason—but it wasn't a music-loving crowd. Their whispered conversations created a background rumble and they kept applauding at the pauses between variations. Michael scowled at the breaks to his concentration. At one point he replayed the final thirteen bars of the previous section, only to find himself interrupted again. At that he made an angry gesture of dismissal and played the final two variations without stopping for air. The audience applauded politely, although not enthusiastically. Michael didn't even bow, just walked quickly from the stage.

The next performance evoked greater response: the Chicago Settlement Children's Choir performed a set of five folk songs. The choir held rigorous auditions and the children sang with a beautiful clarity, but it was their appearance that brought down the house. Some PR genius realized that native garb would sell better than choir robes, so bright dashiki and velvet Afghan jackets gleamed next to the embroidered white dresses of El Salvadoran girls. The audience roared for an encore and gave a standing ovation to the soloists, an Ethiopian boy and an Iranian girl.

During the intermission I left Max and Lotty in the box and strolled to the foyer to admire the costumes of the patrons—they were even more colorfully decked than the children. Perhaps left to themselves Lotty and Max would sort out their disagreement. Lotty's ferocity creates periodic sparks in all her relationships. I didn't want to be privy to whatever conflagration she had going with Carol.

On my way out of the box I caught my heel in the threads of my skirt. I wasn't used to moving in evening clothes. I kept forgetting to shorten my stride; every few steps I'd have to stop to disengage my heel from the delicate threads.

I'd bought the skirt for my husband's law firm's Christmas party during my brief marriage thirteen years ago. The sheer black wool, heavily shot with silver, didn't compare with Or's custom-made gown, but it was my own most elegant outfit. With a black silk top and my mother's diamond drops it made respectable concert attire, but it lacked the dramatic flair of most of the ensembles I saw in the foyer.

I was particularly fascinated by a bronze satin

dress whose top resembled a Roman breast-plate—except that it was slit to the waist. I kept trying to figure out how its wearer managed to keep her breasts from spilling out into the middle. Starch, maybe, or Scotch tape.

When the chimes sounded to announce the end of intermission, the woman in the breastplate moved toward me. I was thinking that the diamond choker didn't go with the dress—that it was just a chance for someone with Trump-like ideas of female adornment to display his wealth—when my heel caught once more in my skirt. I twisted around to free myself as a man in a white dinner jacket hurried toward us from the other end of the foyer.

"Teri! Where've you been? I wanted to introduce you to some people."

The light, authoritative baritone, with its faint undercurrent of petulance, startled me so much that I lost my balance and fell into the path of another diamond-encrusted woman. By the time she'd disengaged her spikes from my shoulder and we'd exchanged frosty apologies, Teri and her escort had disappeared into the theater.

I knew that voice, though: I'd woken to it every morning for twenty-four months—six months of sweetly tormented eroticism as we finished law school and studied for the bar, and eighteen of simple torment after we married. It was as though by wearing my best outfit from those strange days I had conjured him up.

Richard Yarborough, his name was. He was a

partner at Crawford, Mead, one of Chicago's giant firms. Not just a partner, but a significant rainmaker in a place whose clients included two former governors and the heads of most of Chicago's contributions to the Fortune 500.

I only knew these facts because Dick used to recite them at breakfast with the awe of a cathedral guide displaying his reliquaries. He might have done so at dinner, too, but I wasn't willing to wait up to eat with him at midnight when he had finished salaaming to the prestige gods for the day.

That kind of summed up why we'd broken up—my not being impressed enough with the power and money he was wallowing in and his suddenly expecting me to drop everything and be a Japanese wife when we finished law school and started working. Even before our formal split, Dick had realized that a wife was an important part of his portfolio and that he should have married someone with more clout than the daughter of a beat cop and an Italian immigrant could ever carry. It wasn't my mother's Italianness that bugged him, but the taint of immigrant squalor that clung to me. He'd made that clear when he began accepting invitations to Peter Felitti's Oak Brook estate while I was doing Saturday duty at women's court— "I made your excuses, Vic, and anyway, I don't think you have the wardrobe for the kind of weekend the Felittis are planning."

Nine months after our final decree, he and Teri

Felitti were married in a fanfare of white lace and bridesmaids. Her father's financial prominence made the nuptials a major news item—and I couldn't resist reading all the details. Which is how I knew she was only nineteen at the time, nine years younger than Dick. He had turned forty last year; I wondered if Teri at thirty-two was starting to look old to him.

I'd never seen her before, but I could understand why Dick thought she was a better ornament for Crawford, Mead than I'd been. For one thing, she wasn't sprawled on the floor as the ushers were closing the aisle doors; for another, she didn't have to sprint, holding up her dirty hem to avoid her high heels, to get inside ahead of them.

3

Feeding Frenzy

I dropped back into the box just as Michael returned to the stage with Or'. Hearing my panting, Lotty turned to me, eyebrows raised. "Did you need to run a marathon at intermission, Vic?" she muttered under cover of the polite smattering of applause.

I made a throwaway gesture. "It's too complicated to explain now. Dick is here, my old pal Dick."

"And that set your pulse racing like this?" Her astringent irony made me flush, but before I could come up with a snappy rejoinder Michael started speaking.

In a few simple sentences he explained the debt his family owed the citizens of London for taking them in when Europe had become a hellhole in which they couldn't survive. "And I am proud that I grew up in Chicago, where people's hearts are also moved to help those who—because of race or tribe or creed—can no longer live in their native lands. Tonight we are going to play for you the debut performance of Or' Nivitsky's concerto for oboe and cello entitled *The Wandering Jew*, dedicated to the memory of Theresz Kocsis Loewenthal. Theresz supported Chicago Settlement most ardently; she would be moved to see the support you give this important charity."

It was a rehearsed speech, delivered quickly and without warmth because of the coldness of the audience. Michael bowed slightly, first in the direction of our box, then to Or'. The two seated themselves. Michael tuned his cello, then looked at Or'. At her nod they began to play.

Max was right. The concerto bore no resemblance to the atonal cacophony of Or's chamber music. The composer had returned to the folk music of Jewish Eastern Europe to find her themes. The music, forgotten for five decades, came to life in fits and starts as cello and oboe made tentative passes at each other. For a few poignant minutes they seemed to find each other

24

in a measured antiphon. The harmony shattered abruptly as antiphon turned to antagonism. The instruments fought so fiercely that I could feel sweat on my temples. They built to a frantic climax and broke off. Even this nonmusical audience could hold its breath when they paused at that peak. Then the cello chased the oboe from terror to peace, but a horrible peace, for it was the repose of death. I gripped Lotty's hand, not making any pretense of dashing away my tears. Neither of us could join in the applause.

Michael and Or' bowed briefly and disappeared from the stage. Although the clapping continued for some minutes, with more enthusiasm than had greeted the *Don Quixote Variations*, the response lacked the vital spark that would have shown they'd got the point. The musicians didn't return, but sent out the children's choir for the set that concluded the concert.

Like Lotty, Max had been shaken by his son's recital. I offered to get the car at once, but they felt they had to stay for the reception.

"Since it's in Theresz's honor, it would look strange if Max wasn't there, especially as Michael is his son," Lotty said. "If you want to leave, though, Vic, we can take a cab home."

"Don't be ridiculous," I said. "I'll keep an eye out for you—you give me a signal when you're ready to go."

"But you might see Dick again—could you stand the excitement?" Lotty strove to steady herself with sarcasm.

I kissed her cheek. "I'll manage."

That was the last I saw of her for some time. The minute the concert ended a crush of people poured into the stairwells. When Max, Lotty, and I finally struggled into the upper foyer, we were immediately separated by the throng. Instead of fighting my way through the mob to rejoin them I went to the balustrade and tried following their progress. It was hopeless: Max tops Lotty's five feet by only a few inches. I lost sight of them within seconds of their reaching the main floor.

During the second half, caterers had set up shop in the lobby. Four tables, formed into an enormous rectangle, were covered with staggering amounts of food: shrimp molded into mountains, giant bowls of strawberries, cakes, rolls, salads, platters of raw oysters. The shorter sides of the rectangle held hot dishes. From my perch I couldn't make out the contents very clearly, but thought egg rolls and chicken livers jostled next to fried mushrooms and crab cakes. In the middle of the two long sides, white-capped men poised carving knives over giant haunches of beef and ham.

People were stampeding to get at the spread before it vanished. I noticed Teri's bronze breastplate in the first surge toward the shrimp mountain. She was riding in Dick's wake as he snatched shrimps with the frenzy of a man who feared his just share would be lost if he didn't grab it fast. While stuffing shrimp into his mouth he talked earnestly to two other men in evening garb, who

26

were plunging into the oysters. As they slowly moved toward the roast beef in the middle they punctuated their conversation by stabbing at olives, crab cakes, endives, whatever lay in their path. Teri bobbed behind, apparently talking to a woman in a blue gown whose surface was tightly covered with seed pearls.

"I feel like Pharaoh watching the locusts descend," a familiar voice said behind me.

I turned to see Freeman Carter—Crawford, Mead's token criminal lawyer. I grinned and laid a hand on the superfine broadcloth of his jacket. Our relationship went back to those days when I used to bob along behind Dick myself at the firm's social functions. Freeman was the only partner who ever talked to the womenfolk without showing what a big favor he was doing us, so I'd started turning to him for my own legal needs those times the system looked like mangling me.

"What are you doing here?" I demanded. "I wasn't expecting to see anyone I know."

"Love of music." Freeman smiled sardonically. "What about you? You're the last person I'd look for at a hundred-and-fifty-buck function."

"Love of music," I mimicked solemnly. "The cellist is the son of a friend—I'm sorry to say I'm freeloading, not supporting the cause."

"Well, Crawford, Mead seems to have adopted Chicago Settlement as a pet. All partners were encouraged to buy five tickets each. I thought

27

it would be collegial of me to join in—make it my last gesture of goodwill to the firm."

My brows went up reflexively. "You're leaving? Since when? What will you do?"

Freeman looked cautiously over his shoulder. "I haven't told them yet, so keep it to yourself, but it's time I went into practice on my own. Criminal law has never been important at Crawford—for years I've known I should cut the ties—but there are so many perks in a big firm that I just coasted along. Now the firm is growing so fast and so far away from the work I think is important, it just seems to be time to go. I'll notify you officially—notify all my clients—when I'm actually on my own."

A few clumps of people stood around talking, not wishing to head into the melee below. Freeman kept looking at them to make sure he couldn't be overheard and finally changed the subject abruptly.

"My daughter's here someplace, along with her boyfriend. I don't know if I'll ever see them again."

"Yeah, I was wondering the same about the couple I came with. They're not very tall—I'll never find them if I head into the scrimmage.

"I wondered what brought Dick here. I'd have put refugees down near the bottom of the list of people he'd shell out for, kind of near women with AIDS. But if the firm is pushing Chicago Settlement I suppose he's out in front leading the cheers."

Freeman smiled. "I'm not going to comment on that one, Warshawski. He and I are still partners, after all."

"He's not the one bringing in the business you don't like, is he?"

"Don't sound so hopeful. Dick's done a lot to revitalize Crawford, Mead." He held up a hand. "I know you hate the kind of law he practices. I know you love driving a beater and sneering at his German sportscar—"

"I no longer drive a beater," I said with dignity. "I have an '89 Trans Am whose body still gleams despite my having to keep it on the street instead of in a six-car garage in Oak Brook."

"Believe it or not, there are days when Dick wonders if he made a mistake—if you're doing things the right way, not him."

"I know you haven't been drinking, because I can't smell it on your breath—so it must be something you put up your nose."

Freeman smiled. "It doesn't happen often, but the guy did think enough about you to marry you once."

"Don't get all sentimental on me, Freeman. Or are you thinking there are days when I wonder if he's doing it right, 'stead of me? How many women are partners at Crawford now? Three, isn't it, out of a roster of ninety-eight? There are days when I wish I made Dick's money, but there's never a time when I wish I'd put myself through what a woman has to do to make it in your kind of firm."

Freeman gave a placatory smile and tucked my hand under his arm. "I didn't come here to alienate my feistiest client. Come on, Saint Joan. I'll clear a path to the bar for you and get you a glass of champagne."

In the few minutes we'd been talking the shrimp mountains had disappeared and most of the strawberries were gone. The haunches of beef seemed to be holding their own. I scanned the crowd as we strolled downstairs but couldn't make out Lotty or Max. Teri's bronze dress had disappeared too.

I tried staying close to Freeman, but as we hit the ground floor this proved impossible. Someone cutting between us got my arm separated from his. After that I followed the close-cut gold hairs along his neck for a few twistings through the mob, but a woman in pink satin with trailing butterfly wings needed a yard's clearance and I lost him.

I moved with the eddies for a bit. The noise was intense, echoing off the marble pillars and floor. The sound filled my head with a white roaring. It became impossible to concentrate on any outside goal, such as looking for Lotty; all my energy had to go to protecting my brain from the swells of noise. No one could possibly carry on a conversation in this lion's den—they all must be shouting simply for the pleasure of adding to the uproar.

At one point the jostling moved me close to the food tables. The men behind the haunches

30

stood expressionless in their little island, only their hands moving as they sliced and served. The shrimp had vanished, as had all the hot food. All that was left besides the meat—now close to the bone—was the picked-over salads.

I dove back into the tide and began fighting my way across the current to the theater. Some fancy elbow-work brought me to the columns separating the aisle doors from the foyer. The crowd thinned there; people who were trying to talk could get their heads close enough together to hear one another. Michael and Or' were huddled with five or six serious looking people. I moved past without speaking in case these were major donors, and escaped into the body of the theater.

Dick was standing immediately inside the door on my right, talking to a man of sixty or so. Even though I knew he was here, seeing him so close made my heart skip a beat. Not romantic enthusiasm, just a jolt—kind of like losing your footing on a glassy floor. Dick seemed jolted to—he broke off a smooth phrase mid-word and gaped at me.

"Hi, Dick," I said weakly. "I never knew you were a cello enthusiast."

"What are you doing here?" he demanded.

"I've been hired to sweep the theater. I have to take what work I can get these days."

The sixtyish man looked at me with blank impatience. He didn't care who I was or what I did as long as I got out of there fast. He was also oblivious of the children's choir: free from the responsibility of looking angelic they were chasing each other through the seats, shrieking wildly, throwing rolls and bits of cake at each other.

"Yes, well, I'm in the middle of something, so why don't you start work on the far side." Dick wasn't above a little humor as long as it wasn't at his own expense.

"Are you wheeling and dealing?" I tried to infuse my voice with humble admiration. "Maybe I could watch you and get a few pointers, move up to toilet scrubbing or something."

A flush rose in Dick's closely shaven cheeks. On the verge of spitting out a curt insult, he turned it into a bark of laughter. "It's been what—thirteen years? fourteen?—and you still know the shortest distance from your mouth to my goat."

He grabbed my shoulder and moved me toward his partner. "This is Victoria Warshawski. She and I made a big mistake in law school by thinking we were in love. Teri's and my kids are all going to have to work for five years before I'll let them think about marriage. Vic, Peter Felitti, chairman of Amalgamated Portage."

Felitti held out a reluctant hand—because I was his daughter's predecessor? Or because he didn't want me interrupting high-level finance? "I don't remember the details of your settlement. You been paying ever since for your sins, Yarborough?"

I squeezed Felitti's fingers with enough force to make him wince. "Not at all. It was *my* alimony that bought Dick his stake in Crawford, Mead. Now that he's launched on his own, though, I'm trying to get the court to let me off the hook."

Dick made a face. "Must you, Vic? I'll be happy to swear all over town that you never asked for a dime. She's a lawyer," he added to Felitti, "but works as a detective."

Turning back to me, he said plaintively, "Are you happy now? Can Pete and I finish our conversation?"

I was extricating myself—from Dick's arm as well as the conversation—with what grace I could when Teri came in, the woman in beaded blue satin close on her heels.

"There you are," the woman in blue said gaily. "Harmon Lessner wants to talk with you two especially. You can't sneak off and do business now."

Teri eyed me narrowly, trying to decide if I was a business encounter or a sexual competitor. Champagne had added a rosy glow beneath her foundation, but late as it was her makeup was still perfect: the eyeshadow on the lids where it belonged instead of meandering around her face; her lipstick, a subdued bronze that was an understated version of her dress, fresh and glossy. Her chestnut hair, pulled into a complicated knot, looked as though she had just left her hairdresser's. No frizz, no stray strands creeping down her neck, marred the effect.

By this time of night, without looking in a mirror, I knew that my lipstick had vanished and that such styling as I had given my short curls was long gone. I wanted to think I had the more interesting personality, but Dick wasn't interested in women with personality. I felt like telling Teri not to worry, that she had looks and they would win the day for her, but I sketched a wave at the four of them and moved on to the far door without speaking.

When I finally found Lotty it was past midnight. She was alone, shivering in a corner of the outer lobby, her arms hugging her.

"Where's Max?" I said sharply, pulling her close to me. "You need to get home, get to bed. I'll find him and go get the car."

"He left with Or' and Michael. They're staying with him, you know. I'm all right, Vic, really. It's merely that the concert stirred up old memories. They started to haunt me while I waited. I'll walk with you to the car. The fresh air will do me good."

"Are you and Max having a fight?" I hadn't meant to ask, and the words came out abruptly.

Lotty made a face. "Max thinks I'm behaving badly about Carol. And maybe I am."

I shepherded her through the revolving door. "What about her?"

"You didn't know? She's quitting. It's not that I mind that. Well, of course I mind it—we've worked together for eight years. I feel bereft, but I wouldn't try to stop her moving on, trying new

34

opportunities. But it's why she's quitting. It drives me mad that she lets that family of hers run her life—and now—and Max says I have no empathy! I ask you!"

During the drive home she spoke determinedly about the concert, and what pungent remarks Theresz would have made over the collection of nonmusical parvenus who had flocked to her memorial concert. It was only when I dropped her at her door that she let me get the conversation back to Carol.

"What is she doing? You don't know? She's going to stay home and nurse some damned cousin of that morbid mother of hers. He's got AIDS and Carol feels it her duty to look after him."

She slammed the door with a snap and swirled through her front door. I felt the chill fingers of depression creep into my shoulders. Poor Carol. Poor Lotty. And poor me: I didn't want to be caught between them. I waited until the lights came on in Lotty's living room and put the Trans Am back into gear.

4

Rye on Eggs

I slept badly that night. The thought of Lotty, shivering in the dark over her dead family, brought back the nightmares of my mother's final illness. I would approach Gabriella's bed through the maze of tubes and oxygen that shrouded her only to see Lotty's face propped against the pillows. She stared at me blankly, then turned away. I felt wrapped in gauze, unable to move or speak. When the doorbell rang, forcing me back to consciousness, it was a relief to wake up.

I had been crying in my sleep. The tears glued my lids together and I moved unsteadily to the door as the buzzer shrilled again. It was the upper bell, the one right on my door, not in the outer lobby. I couldn't see clearly enough to make out the person on the other side of the peephole.

"Who is it?" I called hoarsely through the edge of the door.

I put my ear against the jamb. At first all I could make out was senseless gabbling, but finally I realized it was Mr. Contreras.

I undid the bolts and opened the door a crack. "Just a minute," I croaked. "I need to put on some clothes."

"Sorry to wake you, doll, I mean it's nine-thirty and all and usually you're up and about by now, but you must've got in late and of course I turned in early, being done in by getting Her Highness through—"

I slammed the door on him and stomped off to the bathroom. I took my time in the shower. If something had gone seriously wrong with Peppy he would have come right out with it. This was doubtless by way of a minor emergency: one of the pups wasn't nursing or she'd rejected the old man's offering of ham and eggs.

Before going down I made myself a cup of strong coffee and swallowed it in great scalding gulps. It didn't make me feel rested and refreshed, but at least I could navigate the stairs.

Mr. Contreras bounded out as I rang his bell. "Oh, there you are. I was beginning to think you'd gone back to bed and I didn't want to bother you none. I thought being as how you was out with the doc last night it wouldn't be such a late evening, but you must've run into someone else you knew."

His incessant burrowing into my love life sometimes brought me to the screaming point. Lack of sleep moved me to irritability faster than usual.

"Just once, as a noble experiment, could you pretend my private life is private? Tell me how Peppy is and why you had to come wake me up."

He threw up placatory hands. "No need to get your tail in a knot, doll. I know you got a private life. That's why I waited till nine-thirty. But I wanted to make sure I had a chance to talk to you before you took off for the day, that's all. Don't be so shirty."

"Okay, I'm not shirty." I tried to keep my voice calm. "Tell me how Her Serene Doggedness is doing. And how are the little ones?"

"Everyone's a-okay. The princess is a champ, you don't need me to tell you that. You wanna see her? Your hands are clean, ain't they?"

"I just scrubbed myself squeaky clean inside

and out and these are fresh jeans," I said solemnly.

Mr. Contreras led me into his living room. Peppy was still stretched behind the sofa, but the old man had cleaned up her nest, giving her a fresh stack of soft sheets to lie on. The eight fur balls were squirming at her nipples, squeaking a little if one got pushed aside by another's greed. Peppy looked at me and thumped her tail to show we were still friends, but her total attention was on her babies, too blind and helpless to survive without her.

"Every now and then she gets up to go out, but only for thirty seconds, then it's back to her station. What a champ. My, oh my." Mr. Contreras smacked his lips. "Of course, I feed her regular, just like the doc said, so don't you go worrying about her."

"I'm not." I knelt cautiously next to the nursery and stuck my hand slowly behind the couch, giving Peppy time to growl me off if she wanted to. She watched warily as I stroked her babies. I longed to pick one up—their tiny bodies would just about fit in the palm of my hand—but didn't want to alarm her. She seemed relieved when I stood back up.

"So where's the fire?" I asked. "Your old buddy steal Clara's silver or something?" Mr. Contreras's dead wife had left behind a pair of candlesticks and a silver salt shaker which he never used but couldn't bring himself to pass on to his daughter.

"No, nothin' like that. But I want you to talk to him. He's got something on his mind that he's acting awful cute about. I don't have time to figure out what he's driving at. Besides, it ain't good for the princess to have him drinking around her babies, and then snoring all night on the couch right over her head the way he does. I need to get him out of here today."

"I can't get the guy into A.A., my friend."

"And I ain't asking you to. Crying out loud, you jump to conclusions faster'n a flea trying to reach the dog."

"Why don't you tell me what the problem is, then, instead of dancing around it—listening to you is like hearing a mosquito buzz away for an hour while you wonder where it's going to land."

"There's no call for that kind of language, cookie, no call at all. You don't mind my saying so, but sometimes you're a little bit fresh."

I rolled my eyes but bit back a snappy retort. At this rate I'd be here all day and I didn't have a day to spend on it.

"What seems to be troubling Mr. Kruger?" I asked primly.

Mr. Contreras scratched the back of his head. "That's what I can't exactly figure out. I thought maybe you could talk to him, being as you're a trained investigator and all. See, him and me used to work together out at Diamond Head—you know, the engine makers on Damen down by the river. Then we retired, but we picked the wrong year to do it, back in seventy-nine when inflation was so rough, and our pensions, which seemed good enough at the time, couldn't keep up. I wasn't so bad off, because I owned my house, and then when Clara died I bought this place, but Mitch kind of outdrank his, and he also don't have my luck at the track. Or more to the point, he don't have my self-control." He started for the kitchen as though that explained everything.

"Sorry," I said. "I'm short on sleep and can't make the connection."

Mr. Contreras stopped to look at me in exasperation. "So he needs money, of course."

"Of course," I agreed, trying to keep a sharp edge out of my voice. "What's he doing to get it that has you so worried? Holding up 7-Elevens?"

"Of course he ain't, doll. Use your head. Would I let someone like that into the building here?" He stopped a minute, sucking his cheeks in. "Trouble is, I don't know what he might be doing. Long as I've known him, which is a *long* time now, Mitch's always had some scheme or other going. And now he thinks he's got a way to make Diamond Head put him back on the payroll."

Mr. Contreras snorted. "I ask you! It isn't even as if any of the guys we used to know was still there. They're all retired or been kicked out or whatever. And between you and me, he wouldn't have been kept on the last three years if we hadn't had such a tight local. But nowadays? With the shape he's in and guys half our age pounding

40

the sidewalks looking for machine work? But he's making a big old mystery out of it, so I thought of you. Where there's a mystery, you like to be poking your nose into it."

Something about the story didn't ring quite true to me. I rubbed my eyes, hoping to bring life into my fuzzy brain.

"What is it you really want to know? Why do you care if Kruger's panhandling out at Diamond Head?"

Mr. Contreras took out his giant red handkerchief and rubbed his nose. "Mitch and me grew up together down in McKinley Park. We went to school together, we ran with the same gang, fought the same guys, all that stuff. We even signed our apprenticeship papers the same day. He ain't much, but he's about all I got left from that time in my life. I don't want to see him make a goddam fool of himself in front of the bosses. I'd like to know what he's up to."

He spoke in a fast, mumbly voice that I had to strain to hear, as if he were embarrassed to admit sentiment or affection for Kruger. I was touched by both his feelings and his awkwardness.

"I can't promise you anything, but at least I can talk to him."

Mr. Contreras blew his nose with a final flourish. "I knew I could count on you, doll."

He'd left Mitch Kruger in the kitchen reading the *Sun-Times,* but when we got there the back door was open and his friend was nowhere in sight. A plate of fried eggs, cold grease glistening on them, sat in front of the newspaper. Kruger had apparently eaten a few bites before something made him decide to take a hike.

"He has got problems, hasn't he?" I said affably.

Mr. Contreras's generous mouth set in a hard line. "I told him a hunnert times he can't go off and leave the door open. This ain't some high-priced suburb where the people coming in your back door are the same ones you'd invite in through the front if you thought of it."

He stomped over to bolt the door, then opened it wide. "There you are, Kruger. I went and got my neighbor, see if she could understand what you're driving at. She's a detective, like I told you—Vic Warshawski. All you had to do was sit on your butt and eat your eggs and wait for her. That too much to ask?"

Kruger smiled fuzzily. It was obvious that he'd walked down to Frankie's Shortstop Inn on the corner for a few quick ones. By the smell it was bourbon, but it could've been rye.

"Told you to mind your own business, Sal," Mitch mumbled. It took me a moment to remember that my neighbor's first name was Salvatore.

"Don't want any detectives butting their noses into my affairs. No offense to you"—Kruger nodded at me—"but detectives mean cops and cops mean union busting."

"If it ain't just like you to get so stewed you

Mr. Contreras switched his frown to me but didn't try to stop me when I walked out the back door to go up to my own kitchen. As I made some fresh coffee I thought briefly about Kruger. I couldn't get myself excited about his broad hints of malfeasance at Diamond Head. He'd been mooching around hoping for some kind of hand-out and would be too ashamed to admit that. If they gave him a brush-off he would exaggerate his grievance with a drunk's paranoia, talking about a revenge that would never materialize.

Maybe someone at Diamond Head was siphoning off inventory, or tools—it wouldn't be the only plant in Chicago where that happened. But if he thought he could blackmail them into cutting him in on some penny-ante deal, it was just typical drunken mush. And it was more likely that he'd imagined the whole thing.

5

Just a Neighborhood
Lynch Mob

By the time I finished my exercises and started to jog up Belmont it was past eleven. The heels of my running shoes were so worn down that I had to move slowly on concrete to save my knees. The sides had frayed, too, and weren't giving my ankles good support. Someone who runs as much

as I do should buy a new pair every four months.
These had gone seven and I was trying to stretch
them to nine. My share of Peppy's vet bills had
eaten away my spring discretionary money; I just
didn't have ninety bucks to spare for a new pair
of Nikes.

Most of the people I'd gone to law school
with would have been at work for three hours
or more by now. And most of them, as Freeman
Carter had implied last night, didn't have to
defer a new pair of Nikes because their stupid
neighbor let the dog off the leash while she
was in heat.

I stopped in front of Mrs. Frizell's house to
frown at the cause of my financial woes. The
black Lab and the earmuff had been in back,
whining and scratching at the door, but when
they heard me they raced to the front to bark
at me. Inside the house I could see two other
noses push underneath the ratty shade to join
in the barking.

"Why don't you do something useful?" I
scolded the Lab. "Get a job, do something to
support the family you started. Or go steal me
a pair of running shoes from Todd Pichea over
there."

Pichea was the lawyer who wanted the neighborhood improvement association to take Mrs.
Frizell to court. His frame house had been re-
stored to a state of immaculate Victoriana,
painted an eggshell tan with scalloped trim in
bright reds and greens. And the yard, with its

early-flowering shrubs and tightly manicured turf, enhanced the raffishness of Mrs. Frizell's weed bin. It was only perversity that made me prefer the old woman's place.

The Lab wagged his tail in genial agreement, barked at me a few times, and returned to the back. The earmuff followed. I wondered idly where Mrs. Frizell was; I'd half expected her to appear behind the noses in the front window, shaking an angry fist at me.

I did my five miles to the harbor and back and forgot about the woman and her dogs. In the afternoon I forced myself to do some routine assignments for regular clients. Daraugh Graham, my steadiest and best-paying customer, called at four-thirty. He wasn't happy with the credentials of a man he wanted to promote. He wanted information on Clint Moss by the next afternoon, which made me grind my teeth—but quietly. Besides Peppy's bills and new running shoes I had payments on the Trans Am and my apartment to keep up.

I wrote what information he had about Moss onto a form and labeled a manila folder with a dark red magic marker so it would jump out of the desk at me in the morning. That was the best I could do for the day. As I typed up bills for the two jobs I'd finished the phone rang again. I was tempted to let it go, but heightened consciousness of my fiscal state made me answer it. Carol Alvarado was on the line. I wished I'd let it go.

"Vic, can I come over tonight? I need to talk to you."

I ground my teeth again, this time more audibly. I didn't want to take sides in her struggle with Lotty: it was the easiest way to lose both their friendships forever. But Carol pleaded, and I couldn't help remembering all the times she'd supported me when Lotty was threatening to take a stripe out of me for bringing in either myself or a client for repairs after a dust-up. I had to accede, and as gracefully as possible.

Carol arrived at eight, bringing a bottle of Barolo. Out of her nurse's uniform and in jeans she looked small and young, almost waiflike. I opened the bottle and poured out a couple of glasses.

"Here's to old friendships," I saluted her.

"And to good friends," she responded.

We chatted idly for a few minutes before she brought up her personal business. "Has Lotty told you what I mean to do?"

"Stay home to nurse your mother's cousin?"

"That's part of the story. Guillermo's been very ill, pneumonia, complications, and he's been at County, where they don't exactly have the resources for round-the-clock care. So Mama wants to bring him home, and of course I'll help her look after him. With good care, skilled care, we can probably get him back on his feet, maybe for a while anyway. Lotty thinks I'm abandoning her and throwing myself away. . . ."

Her voice trailed off and she rubbed the rim

of her glass. It was thick, chunky Woolworth's stock and didn't make the highpitched hum that crystal would produce.

"You couldn't take a leave of absence instead of quitting?"

"The truth is, Vic, I'm sick of that clinic. I've been doing it day in and out for eight years and need a change."

"And staying home to nurse Guillermo will be the relief you're looking for?"

She flushed a little. "Can't you say what's on your mind without sarcasm? I know what you and Lotty think—that at thirty-four I should divorce my mother and make a life for myself. But my family isn't a millstone for me the way it might be for you or Lotty. And anyway, didn't you come close to being murdered, looking out for your aunt Elena last year?"

"Yeah, but I sure hated doing it." I played with a loose thread on the easy chair. Another thing I could do if I'd gone to a high-end law firm: buy new living room furniture. "I helped nurse my mother when I was fifteen and she was dying of cancer. And my dad, who died of emphysema ten years later. I'd do it again if I had to, but I couldn't give that kind of care to someone who wasn't important to me."

"That's why you're a detective, Vic, not a nurse." She held up a hand as I started to speak. "I'm not sacrificing myself, believe me. I'm burned out at the clinic. I need a change. That's what Lotty can't understand: she puts so much of herself, so much energy, into those patients that she can't see why someone else wouldn't want to. But being at home, wrestling with one medical problem, it will give me time to think, to decide what I should do next."

"And you want me to sell that to Lotty?"

I didn't blame Carol for wanting to leave the clinic. I'd burned out at the Public Defender's office after five years, and Carol's work was much more intense than mine had ever been. But of course, Lotty felt betrayed. She had no family to speak of—a brother in Montreal and her father's brother, Stefan, were her only relatives to survive the Second World War—so she couldn't understand the calls family make on you. Or maybe she had some hidden resentment of those lucky enough to have families making demands on them?

My doorbell rang before I could chase that unpromising thought further. I looked through the peephole at Mr. Contreras's face. Opening the door, I felt my blood begin to boil.

"Sorry, doll, I know you don't like to be bothered when you have company, but—"

"You're right. I don't. And I can't even remember the last time you didn't come huffing up ten minutes after my guests arrived to see who's here. Look. Carol Alvarado. Not a man after all. So go back downstairs and give it a rest, okay?"

He put his hands on his hips and looked a little ugly. "You have been way out of line lately, Vic. I mean way out, how you been talking to me.

50

If I left you alone like you're always claiming to want it, you'd be dead now. Maybe that's what you want, for me to leave you alone and let you get drowned in a marsh or let someone put a bullet through you."

Yes, he'd saved my life all right, and that meant he thought he'd acquired property rights in it. But looking at his angry stare, I couldn't say something that would hurt him so painfully. I couldn't bring myself to apologize, but I asked in a milder tone what had brought him up to the third floor.

He frowned for another few seconds, then decided to let it go. "It's that lawyer up the street, that Pichea. He's downstairs trying to get a posse together, and of course Vinnie Buttone is only too happy to sign on. I was sure you'd want to know about it."

"Posse to do what?"

"To get the county to come for the old lady's dogs. He says they've been creating a nuisance for twenty-four hours and no one's answering her bell."

I remembered wondering why she hadn't come to her window this morning. "Isn't the boy worried about Mrs. Frizell?"

"You think something's happened to her?" His eyes grew large in his weather-beaten face.

"I don't think anything. She might not answer her door because she knows it's Pichea and he's a pain in the tail. On the other hand, she might be unconscious in the bath. I think before we get the county to haul her dogs away we ought to see where she is and what she has to say.

He trailed behind me when I returned to the living room to describe the situation to Carol. "I'm going to see if something's wrong with her. I know I've just been lecturing you against succoring the world—but I would appreciate on-the-spot medical expertise if she's had a stroke or something."

Carol gave a twisted smile. "You going to break and enter for a stranger, V.I.? Then I guess I can come along and give her mouth-to-mouth if she needs it."

The police had confiscated my professional picklocks a number of years ago, but during the winter I'd acquired some new ones—billed, of course, as "state of the art"—at a security conference out at O'Hare. Tonight might be my first chance to use them. The thrill was less than overwhelming: the razor edge of excitement that comes from chasing and being chased seems to diminish with age. I stuck the picklocks in a jacket pocket and went downstairs with Mr. Contreras and Carol.

"Hi, Todd, Vinnie. Getting the lynch mob together?"

The two looked enough alike to be brothers— white men in their mid-thirties with blow-dried, carefully cut hair and square, conventionally good-looking faces now flushed in righteous anger. My neighbor and I had enjoyed, if that's the word, a rapprochement while he'd been having an affair with a set designer I liked. But when Rick left him, Vinnie and I went back to a more natural hostility. So far I hadn't found anything that brought me closer to Todd Pichea, even for an afternoon.

Hovering behind Pichea were a couple of women I recognized vaguely from the block. One was a plump blonde in her fifties or sixties, wearing black stretch pants that revealed the sags of time. The second woman made the pair an ad for "Then and Now on Racine Avenue." Her spandex leggings hugged a body toned to perfection in a gym. The diamond drops in her ears showed up the clunkiness of the older woman's faux pearls, and the impatient frown marring her perfect complexion contrasted sharply with the other's expression of plain worry.

Pichea's scowl deepened when he heard me. "Look, Warshawski, I know you don't give a damn about the value of your property, but you ought to respect the rights of others."

"I am. I do. It's been a while since I studied constitutional law, but isn't there at least an implication in the Fourth Amendment that Mrs. Frizell has the right to be secure in her own home?"

Pichea tightened his lips into a thin line. "As long as she isn't creating a public nuisance. I don't know why you have such a hot spot for the old bag, but if you lived across the street and had those damned dogs keeping you awake you'd change your tune fast enough."

"Oh, I don't know. If I knew you were on her case I could probably bring myself to tolerate the barking. You work for some big downtown firm, you've got a lot of connections in the courts, and you want to use all your muscle to smash some helpless old woman. She's been living here a long time, you know—forty or fifty years. She didn't try to stop you coming in and ruining the street for her. Why don't you engage in a little reciprocity?"

"That's the thing," the older woman broke in in an anxious voice. "Hattie—Harriet—Mrs. Frizell—has never been an easy neighbor, but she minds her own business as long as you mind yours. Only, I'm kind of worried, I haven't seen her since yesterday morning, so when I saw this gentleman ringing her bell I went over to see what the problem was—"

"Ruining the street? Ruining the street?" The woman in spandex barked sharply. "Todd and I improved this rattail block. We spent a hundred grand fixing up that house and yard—they'd look like her place if not for us."

"Yeah, but you're disturbing her peace, trying to force her out of her home, put her dogs to sleep, whatever."

Before the argument could escalate further, Carol put a hand on my shoulder. "Let's go see if the lady's home and awake, Vic. We can sort out who's done the most harm to the street later."

The older woman smiled gratefully at her.

54

"Yes. I'm kind of worried. Only, she can be rude if you bother her, but if we all went together . . ."

Our convoy moved slowly to the front sidewalk. "I'm giving her fair warning," Pichea said to Vinnie. "The next time those dogs are out barking past ten I'll see her ass in court."

"And that will make you feel like a real he-man, I suppose?" I shot over my shoulder.

Pichea gave a contemptuous laugh. "I can understand why you're so worked up: you're scared you'll end up alone and crazy at eighty-five, with nothing but a bunch of flea-ridden dogs to keep you company."

"Well, Pichea, if you're an example of the available talent, I'd rather be alone till I'm eighty-five."

Carol grabbed my arm and hustled me up the street. "Come on, Vic. I don't mind you dragging me into your business, but don't make me listen to this crap. I could lean out my back door and hear it in the alley if I were interested."

I was sufficiently abashed to ignore Pichea's follow-up comment—an ostentatious whisper to his wife that I needed a good lay—but not sorry I'd picked up the cudgels to begin with. In fact, I kind of wished I'd given him a good punch in the sternum.

6

Down and Out on Racine Avenue

As soon as Pichea and I stopped brangling we could hear the dogs. The Lab was filling the night with a deep-throated baying; the earmuff responded with a higher-pitched antiphon, and the three inside were providing a faint accompaniment echoed by the rest of the dogs on the street. Behind us even Peppy interrupted her nursing with an occasional bark. So maybe Mrs. Frizell wasn't the most wonderful neighbor in the world. But why couldn't the Picheas have stayed in Lincoln Park where they belonged?

When we opened Mrs. Frizell's front gate the Lab rushed over and jumped up at me. I grabbed his front paws before he could knock me off balance.

"Easy, guy, easy. We just want to see if your mistress is okay."

I dropped his legs and went up the shallow steps to the door. I knocked my shin against an old metal chair and swore under my breath. Fortunately Mr. Contreras had remembered a flashlight. He shone it on the door while I worked the locks.

"Stupid jerks are afraid of the dogs. Afraid of

being caught breaking and entering with you. That lawyer's the kind of management creep you got to watch out for: can't do his dirty work for himself, gets on the phone and hires someone to do it for him."

"Yeah," I grunted. "Hold the light steady, okay?"

The lock should have taken me thirty seconds, but the Lab kept rushing at my legs until Carol managed to grab him by the scruff and hang on to him. After that I only had to contend with Mr. Contreras's moving the light as he emphasized his contempt for Todd and Vinnie. It was a good five minutes before I finally felt the simple latch click back.

As soon as I opened the door the other dogs, who'd been barking and scratching on the other side, came pelting out at us. Behind me I could hear a sharp yell from one of the guys, and then a yelp from one of the dogs.

"Did you see that?" I couldn't tell if the angry squeak belonged to Todd or Vinnie. "That damned mutt bit me."

"Will the perpetrator step forward for a dog biscuit and a medal?" I said, but under my breath.

The stench in the house was so bad that I wanted to get in and out as fast as possible. I took the light from Mr. Contreras and shone it around the entryway, hoping to find a light switch. The inside dogs had been relieving themselves by the door and I didn't want to step in the mess. I couldn't see a switch, so I got as clear a look as possible at the dimensions of the urine and did a standing broad jump across it.

"Mrs. Frizell! Mrs. Frizell! Are you home?"

Her neighbor, who'd hovered on the front walk while I worked on the lock, came in with Carol, clucking her tongue and making worried sounds in her throat. The dogs rushed past us, spattering our legs with urine.

"Mrs. Frizell? It's me, Mrs. Hellstrom. We just want to see if you're all right."

Mrs. Hellstrom found a lamp inside the living room door. In its feeble glow I finally saw a wall switch for the hall. It had been a long time since Mrs. Frizell had felt the impulse to clean anything. Dust had disintegrated into a thick coat of dirt; our damp shoes turned it to mud. Even through the stench and the chaos, though, it was clear that the only place the dogs had been relieving themselves was by the door. She looked after them even if she didn't care about herself.

I followed the Lab up the stairs, playing the flashlight on the threadbare carpet, choking and sneezing on the dust I kicked up. The dog led me to the bathroom. Mrs. Frizell was lying on the floor, naked except for a towel clutched to her side.

I turned on the switch but the light was burned out. I called the news down to Carol and knelt down to find Mrs. Frizell's pulse. The Lab, energetically licking her face, growled at me but didn't try to bite me. Just as Carol and Mrs. Hellstrom joined me I felt a faint flutter.

"Bruce," I heard Mrs. Frizell say faintly as I backed away. "Bruce, don't leave me."

"No, honey," Mrs. Hellstrom said. "He won't leave you. You're gonna be okay now—you just took a bad fall."

"Can you get me a better light, Vic?" Carol said sharply. "And call 911. She's going to need a hospital."

I shoved my way past the other dogs crowding into the doorway and found the old woman's bedroom. As I went in I tripped and fell over the piles of bedding on the floor. I supposed they were for the dogs, although I had assumed they would sleep in bed with her. I unscrewed the twenty-watt bulb from the naked gooseneck lamp by the bed and took it back to the bathroom.

"Blankets, Vic, and get that ambulance," Carol said sharply, not looking up.

"Mrs. Hellstrom? Can you bring some blankets while I hunt for a telephone?"

Mrs. Hellstrom was glad to be useful, but clucked again in dismay when she saw the blankets. "These are so dirty, maybe I ought to go home and get something clean."

"I think it's just important to get her warm. She can't get much dirtier than she already is, lying on that floor all day."

Downstairs I found Mr. Contreras trying to clean up the worst of the mess by the front door. "You found her, doll? She alive?"

I gave him a brief report while I hunted around for a phone. I finally found an old-fashioned

59

black model buried under a stack of newspapers in the living room. The dial was stiff but the phone was still connected. So she was at least in touch with reality enough to pay her bills.

I called the emergency number and explained the problem, then went to the kitchen to find something to use as a cleanser. It seemed important that Todd Pichea and Vinnie not know the dogs had been defecating in the house. Although anyone who thought about it would know they'd have to. Even the best trained dogs can't hold on to themselves for twenty-four hours.

I took the dogs' water dish and a bottle of Joy so old the detergent had hardened in it. I dug a spoonful of soap out, mixed it with water, and started scrubbing with some kitchen towels I found in the back of a cupboard. The kitchen was as bad as the front hallway, so I emptied the dogs' food dish and dug some soap into it for Mr. Contreras. By the time the paramedics arrived, escorted by a couple of blue-and-whites, we'd cleaned up the worst of the mess. The stretcher bearers wrinkled their noses against the clouds of dust as they climbed the stairs, but at least they wouldn't be able to report a heap of dog shit to the city.

"You her daughter?" one of the cops asked as the medics brought Mrs. Frizell down.

"No. We're all neighbors," I said. "We just got concerned because we hadn't seen her for a few days."

"She got any kids?"

"Just one son. He lives in San Francisco, but he comes to see her every now and then. He grew up here but I don't really know him; I never can remember his first name." That was Mrs. Hellstrom.

One of the medics leaned over the stretcher. "Can you tell us your son's name, honey? Or his phone number?"

Mrs. Frizell's eyes were open, but they were unfocused. "Bruce. Don't let them take Bruce away from me."

Mrs. Hellstrom knelt clumsily next to her. "I'll look after Bruce for you, honey, but what's your son's phone number?"

"Bruce," the old woman called hoarsely. "Bruce."

The paramedics picked her up and took her out the front door. I could see Vinnie and the Picheas still waiting by the gate.

"Bruce isn't her son?" I asked.

"No, honey," Mrs. Hellstrom said. "That's the big dog, the black one."

"Can you take care of the dogs while she's in the hospital? Or at least until we can get her son out here?"

Mrs. Hellstrom looked unhappy. "I don't want to. But I guess I can feed them and let them out as long as they stay over here."

The police stayed a bit longer, asking how we discovered Mrs Frizell, what our relationship to her was, and so on. They didn't pay attention to Todd's annoyed squawks about my breaking

61

and entering. "At least she found the old lady, son. You think she should have been left to die?" an officer who looked close to retirement said.

When they realized Carol was a nurse, they took her to one side for a more detailed set of questions.

"Do you know what's wrong with her?" I asked Carol when the cops finally left.

"I think she broke something, probably her hip, getting out of the tub. She's badly dehydrated, so her mind's wandering a bit. I couldn't get a clear picture of when she might have fallen. She might have been lying there a couple of days. We're lucky we came down, Vic; I don't think she'd've made it through the night."

"So it's a good thing I decided to get involved," Todd put in.

"Involved?" Mr. Contreras huffed. "Involved? Who found her? Who got the medics? You just stood out there keeping your wing tips clean."

That wasn't a fair comment: Pichea was wearing topsiders.

"Look, here, old man," he began, leaning toward Mr. Contreras.

"Don't try to argue with them, Todd. They're not the kind who can understand you." Mrs. Pichea linked her arm through her husband's and looked around the dirty hall, her nose wrinkling in contempt.

Mrs. Hellstrom touched my arm. "You gonna try to find her son, honey? Because I should be going home. I want to change these clothes, anyway.

"Oh, there's a son?" Pichea said. "Maybe it's time he came home and took charge of his mother."

"And maybe she wants to live her own life," I snapped. "Why don't you go to bed now, Pichea? You've done your good deed for the day."

"Nope. I want to talk to the son, get him to understand that his mother's gotten way out of hand."

The dogs, who'd been barking at the ambulance, came roaring back into the house and started jumping up on us. Pichea stuck out one of his topsiders to kick the earmuff. As the little dog went yelping down the hall I clipped Pichea on the shin.

"It's not your house, big guy. If you're scared of dogs, stay at home."

His tight, square face looked ugly. "I could have you brought in for assault, Warshawski."

"You could, but you won't. You're too chicken to take on someone your own size." I muscled my way past him and started a dispiriting search for a piece of paper with Mrs. Frizell's son's name on it. It took me only half an hour to realize I could call directory assistance in San Francisco—how many Frizells could there be? Six, as it turned out, with a couple of different spellings. The fourth one I reached, Byron, was her son. Tepid would be a strong description for his response to the news about his mother.

"You've got her to a hospital? Good, good. Thanks for taking the time to call."

"You want to know what hospital?"

"What? Oh, might as well. Look, I'm in the middle of something right now—Sharansky, did you say your name was? Why don't I call you in the morning."

"Warshawski." I started to spell it but he'd broken the connection.

Todd waited around until Byron cut me off. "So what's he going to do?"

"He's not catching the first plane out. Mrs. Hellstrom will look after the dogs. Why don't the rest of us just go home and give it a rest."

Like Mrs. Hellstrom, I was anxious to change my clothes. Carol had already gone while I was trying the second Frizell. Mr. Contreras had wandered out to the kitchen to put out fresh food and water for the dogs. He was anxious to get back to Peppy, but was too chivalrous to leave me alone here.

"You think they'll be okay, doll?"

"I think they'll be fine," I said firmly. I was damned if he'd saddle me with five more dogs to look after.

As I shut up the house we could hear them whining and scratching at the front door.

7

Signing Up a New Client

The next morning, before leaving for work, I put two hours into cleaning and polishing my apartment. Pichea's remark last night had flicked me on the raw. Not about finding myself alone at eighty-five—I could envision worse fates—but finding myself like Mrs. Frizell: my stacks of newspaper and dustballs crumbling into lung choking dirt; so cantankerous that the neighbors didn't want to call even when they thought I might be ill.

I baled a month's worth of newspapers in twine and set them by the front door to drop at the recycling center. I polished the piano and the coffee table until they would have met even Gabriella's high standard, washed the dishes piled on the sink and kitchen table, threw out all the moldy food in the refrigerator. That left me with a choice of peanut butter or canned minestrone for supper, but maybe I could squeeze in an hour at the grocery on my way home.

I skipped my run and took the el downtown. The work I'd planned for the day would take me to a variety of government offices scattered around the Loop; the car would only get in my way. By four I was able to call Daraugh Graham to report on Clint Moss. He really was anxious for information: his secretary had word to interrupt the meeting he was in to receive my report.

When Daraugh learned Moss had invented his class standing in the University of Chicago's MBA program, he demanded that I go to Pittsburgh to make sure he hadn't manufactured his previous work history. I didn't want to do it, but my payments on the Trans Am meant keeping my good customers happy. I agreed to catch an early flight the next day—not at seven, as Daraugh ordered, but eight, which meant getting out of bed at six. That seemed like enough of a sacrifice to me.

I stopped at Mrs. Hellstrom's on the way home to see how she was making out with Mrs. Frizell's dogs. She seemed a little flustered; she was trying to get dinner for her grandchildren and didn't see how she could manage to look after the dogs at the same time.

"I'm going out of town in the morning, but when I get back on Friday I'll give you a hand," I heard myself saying. "If you take care of them in the morning I'll feed them and walk them in the afternoon."

"Oh, would you? That would be such a relief. Mrs. Frizell is so peculiar, you wouldn't think she'd care, but we could steal everything she has in the house—not that there's anything in there I want, mind you—and she wouldn't notice. But if we didn't feed her precious poochies she'd probably sue us. It just seems like so much work."

She gave me the keys we'd found buried in the living room the night before, confident I planned to start my evening shift at once. "Just put the keys through my mail slot when you're done. I'll get duplicates made while you're away and put them in *your* mailbox. No, maybe I should give them to that nice man that lives downstairs from you. He seems reliable, and I hate to leave someone's house keys lying around."

I asked if she knew which hospital Mrs. Frizell was in.

"They took her to Cook County, dear, on account of her not having any insurance—she'd never even signed up for Medicare—it really makes you think, doesn't it? I don't know what we'll do when my man retires. He was thinking of doing it next year. He'll be fifty-eight, and enough's enough after a while, but when you see what happens to old people—but anyway, maybe I'll try to get over to see her tomorrow. You'd think that son of hers—but of course, he didn't have too easy a time, growing up in that house. Couldn't wait to leave, and small wonder, when you see how she is. His daddy couldn't take it, either: scooted a month before he was born."

I took the keys from her before she could elaborate on the eccentricities that drove both Mr. Frizell and his son from Harriet Frizell's side. Maybe she wouldn't have been so suspicious and inward-turned if her husband had stayed around. And maybe not.

The dogs greeted me with a combination of suspicion and delight. They rushed up to me when I opened the door, then backed down the hall toward the kitchen, growling and making menacing forays. Since the Lab was the ringleader, I concentrated my attention on him, squatting down to let him sniff my hand and remember that we'd met before.

"Only not in nylons and pumps. What a lunatic I am," I addressed the company. "To offer to look after you in the first place and then to do so in my work clothes."

They wagged their tails in agreement. I debated going home to change into my jeans and worn-out Nikes, but I didn't want to have to come back to this squalor tonight. The afternoon sun picked out stains on the wallpaper that hadn't been visible in the dim hall light last night. From the look and the smell, water had been leaking from the roof through the walls. The sun also made the grime covering the floors—and every other surface—more noticeable.

I leashed up the Lab and led the quintet up Racine toward Belmont. He strained against his collar, but I held him in a firm grip: I wasn't going to spend the night hunting for him around the neighborhood. The other four didn't need to be chained—they followed in their ringleader's steps.

When Peppy is in her normal state we do a five-mile run to the harbor together. I didn't feel like investing so much energy in Mrs. Frizell's outfit; I gave them a circuit of the block, saw that they had food and water, and locked them in. They howled dismally when I left. I felt a little guilty, but I didn't want them on my hands past this weekend. When I got back from Pittsburgh I'd see what shape Mrs. Frizell was in and try to make some arrangements for their care until she was fit again. I'd call her enthusiastic son, Byron, to see what kind of financial guardianship he was working out for her, and if we could get some money for a dog-walking service.

Back at my own place I sank thankfully into my spick-and-span bathtub. I wondered if Mrs. Frizell's horrific example would make me change my habits.

"No," Lotty said, when I shared the thought with her later on the phone. "Perhaps for one week you can be immaculate, but then the mess will start to accrete again. . . . Carol says she came over to discuss her plans with you last night. Are you going to join Max in snarling at me?"

"Nooo," I said slowly. "But I'm not going to try arguing with her, either. Maybe you and I are too allergic to family ties, the ties that bind and gag, to see what positive things she gets out of, well, tying herself to her relations."

"Why don't you concentrate on catching criminals, Vic, and leave deep insights to the psychiatrists," Lotty snapped.

We hung up on that brittle note. It sent me to Pittsburgh in a low frame of mind, but I conscientiously devoted two days to Daraugh. His man Moss had been born and raised in one of Pittsburgh's tonier suburbs. His life had followed the usual round of Little League, summer camp, high school sports, drugs, arrests, college drop outs, and finally a steady job at a chemical company. That he had been a stockroom boy instead of a division manager shouldn't have embarrassed him: he'd worked hard for five years and his boss had been sorry to see him leave.

I wrote my report for Daraugh on the plane home. All I had to do was spend an hour in the morning typing it and $1600 was mine. I went from the airport to dancing at the Cotton Club to celebrate my safe return, my virtuous work habits, and my fee.

I took my time getting up on Friday, going for a slow run over to Belmont Harbor and stopping at the Dortmunder Restaurant on my way back for breakfast. Around eleven I packed up my report to take down to the Pulteney to type. I stopped on my way out to let Mr. Contreras know I was home.

He was out back, turning over his eight-foot square of soil. He had put his seedlings in last week and was anxiously ridding them of microscopic weeds.

"Hi, doll. You want to see the princess? You won't believe how much the puppies have grown since you went out of town. Hang on a minute. I'll come open the door. I got something I want to talk to you about before you take off."

He wiped his calloused hands on a giant bandanna and picked up his rake and trowel. After losing all his garden equipment last summer he didn't leave the new ones unattended even for a five-minute break.

While he stowed his tools inside the basement he inquired into my trip, but when he asked for the third time how long the flight took I could tell he had something else on his mind. He has delicate ideas of etiquette, though, and wouldn't bring up his own concerns until I finished petting the dog and admiring her offspring. She didn't object to my picking them up and stroking them, but she washed each one thoroughly when it squirmed back to her side.

Mr. Contreras watched us jealously, talking me through every detail of Peppy's days during my absence—how much she'd eaten, how she didn't mind his picking them up, didn't I think we could keep one or maybe two—the male with one black and one gold ear seemed to have a special liking for him.

"Whatever you say, boss." I stood up and picked up my papers from the couch arm. "Long as I don't have to run them when they're grown, I don't care. Is that what you wanted to discuss?"

"Oh . . ." He broke off in the middle of an expostulation on how he could keep up with three dogs, and anyway, who walked Peppy while I was fooling around in Pittsburgh?

"No. No. It's kinda personal." He sat on the edge of his shabby mustard armchair and looked at his hands. "Thing is, doll, I could use some help. I mean, some of your kind of expertise."

He looked up at that and held up a hand to forestall me, although I hadn't tried speaking. "I ain't expecting charity. I'm prepared to pay the same as those bluenoses downtown, so don't expect I'm asking any favors."

"Uh, what is it you need my expertise for?"

He took a deep breath and got his story out in a rush. Mitch Kruger had disappeared. Mr. Contreras had thrown him out on Monday, exasperated by his drinking and mooching. Then my neighbor's conscience started bothering him. On Wednesday he'd gone over to the rooming house on Archer where Kruger had found a place to sleep.

"Only, he wasn't there."

"Don't you think he might've been out drinking?"

"Oh, yes, that was my idea too. At first I didn't give it a second thought. In fact, I turned around and was heading straight for the bus stop when Mrs. Polter, she's the owner of the place, you know, it's a real boardinghouse—just sleeping space for seven, eight guys and she gives 'em breakfast. Anyway, she hollers at me, thinking I'm looking for a room, and I tell her I'm looking for Mitch."

It took him a good ten minutes to get the whole story out. Boiled down to the bones it seemed Kruger hadn't been back to the boardinghouse since checking in Monday afternoon. He'd promised to pay Mrs. Polter on Tuesday morning, and she wanted her money. Or she wanted Mr. Contreras to take Kruger's belongings away so she could give the bed to someone else. Mr. Contreras shelled out the fifty bucks to hold the bed for a week—retroactive to Monday, he pointed out bitterly—and took the Damen Avenue bus back home.

"So then I called over to Diamond Head and tried to speak to the shop steward, on account of all that smoke Mitch was blowing last week. But the guy didn't answer my message, so yesterday I took the damn bus all the way down again and they tell me Mitch ain't been near the place since we left twelve years ago. So anyway, I'd like you to take it on. Looking for him, I mean."

When I didn't answer right away he said, "I'll pay you, don't you worry about that."

"It's not that." I was about to add that he didn't need to pay me anything, but that's the best way to build grudges between friends and relations—do them professional favors for nothing. "But . . . well, to be brutally frank, you know he's probably sleeping off a hangover in some police cell right now."

"And if he is, you're in a position to find out. I mean, you know all them cops, they'll tell you if he's been picked up drunk somewhere. I just feel kind of responsible."

"Has he got any family?"

Mr. Contreras shook his head. "Not really. His

wife up and left him—oh, way back. Must be going on forty years ago. They had a kid and even then he was drinking the pay. Can't say I blame her. I stole Clara from him back when we was all in high school. Night of our homecoming dance. She used to get all over me when I'd come home with one too many in me, and I'd remind her at least I hadn't let her get stuck with that prize jackass Kruger."

His soft brown eyes clouded over as he dwelt on a sixty-year-old dance. "Well, all that past is dead and gone, and I know Mitch ain't worth much, ain't much to look at, but I'd kinda like to know he's okay."

When he put it like that I didn't have any choice. I drove him down to my office and solemnly filled out one of my standard contracts for him. I wrote down Mrs. Polter's address. I took Diamond Head's location, too—I had a feeling I was going to need all the dead ends I could find to justify my retainer.

Mr. Contreras pulled a roll of bills from his front pocket. Licking his fingers, he separated four twenties and counted them over to me. That would pay for a day of bar-crawling along Archer and Cermak.

8

Extinguish Your Troubles

I dropped my report to Daraugh Graham in the mail on my way to the Stevenson, the expressway that follows the main industrial route through the heart of Chicago's southwest side. Actually, it runs parallel to the Sanitary and Ship Canal, which was built to connect the Illinois and Chicago rivers back in 1900. The thirty-mile stretch of water, crisscrossed by rail beds, houses every variety of industry along its banks. Grain and cement elevators hover over heaps of scrap metal; truck terminals stand alongside the yards where Chicago's mariners dry-dock their boats for the winter.

I got off at Damen, sliding past the little cluster of bungalows perched incongruously next to the exit ramp, and made a sharp left onto Archer. Like the expressway, the street follows the path of the Sanitary Canal; it used to be the main road through the industrial belt, back before the Stevenson was built.

Although this part of the city has pockets of quiet, well-kept streets, Archer isn't one of them. Shabby two-flats and rundown bungalows are built flush with the sidewalk. The only grocery stores are holes in the wall that also sell beer, liquor, and school supplies. With the number of taverns the avenue supports it's hard to know who keeps the grocers in business.

Mrs. Polter's house was about five blocks up from Damen. It was a long, narrow box covered in asphalt shingles, which had fallen off in places to reveal rotting wood underneath. Mrs. Polter was moodily surveying the street from her front porch when I pulled up. "Porch" actually was a grand name for the rickety square of peeling boards. Perched on top of a flight of dilapidated stairs, it was just big enough to hold a green metal chair and leave room for the torn screen door to open.

Mrs. Polter was a massive woman, her neck missing in the circles of fat that rose from her shoulders. Her brown-checked housedress, which looked like a relic from the twenties, had long ago lost the struggle to cover her cleavage. A safety pin tried to make up the deficiency of cotton, but only succeeded in fraying the edges of the fabric.

As far as I could tell she hadn't turned her head while I stumbled up the stairs, and she didn't bother to look at me when I stood looking down at her. "Mrs. Polter?" I said after a long silence.

She gave me a grudging glance, then turned her attention back to the street, where three boys on bikes were trying to rear up and ride on their hind wheels. A piece of asphalt siding flapped behind us.

"I wanted to ask you a few questions about Mitch Kruger."

"Don't you boys think you can get on my property," she shouted when the cyclists jumped their bikes over the curb.

"Sidewalk belongs to everyone, fat bitch," one of them yelled back.

The other two laughed immoderately, dancing their bikes up and down the curb. Mrs. Polter, moving with the speed of a boxer, picked up a fire extinguisher and began spraying over the railing at them. They jumped back onto Archer, out of range, and continued to laugh. Mrs. Polter put the extinguisher on the floor next to her chair. It was clearly a game all parties had played before.

"Too many places get vandalized along here because people don't have the guts to stand up for their own property. Damned little spics. Neighborhood was a hell of a lot different before they moved in, bringing all their dirt and crime with them, breeding like flies." The asphalt shingle behind us flapped in time to her speech.

"Yep. This neighborhood used to be the garden spot of the Midwest. . . . Mitch Kruger?"

"Oh, him." She flicked washed-out blue eyes at me. "Old guy came by and paid his rent. That's good enough for me."

"When did you see him last?"

At this she turned the chair and the mass of her body to face me. "Who wants to know?"

"I'm a detective, Mrs. Polter. I've been asked

77

to find Mr. Kruger. So far as I can tell you're the last person who saw him."

I had called Conrad Rawlings, a police sergeant in my own district, to find out whether Mitch had been picked up drunk and disorderly in the last few days. The police don't have computer capability to check on something like that. Rawlings gave me the name of a sergeant in Area Four, who obligingly called all the stations that reported to him. None of them had picked Mitch up recently, although the guys at the Marquette Station knew who he was.

"What, he dead or something?" Her hoarse voice shredded words like a cheese grater.

"Just gone missing. What did he say to you when he left?"

"I don't know. I wasn't paying attention—those damned spics were out riding around, just like they do every day when school's out. I can't keep my mind both places at once."

"You saw him walk down the stairs, though," I persisted. "And you knew he hadn't paid you. So you must have wondered when he was coming back with his money."

She smacked her forehead with a giant palm. "That's right. You're so right, honey. I hollered at his back as he was on his way down the stairs. 'Don't forget you owe me fifty bucks,' something like that." She smiled, pleased with herself, and rocked so that the metal chair creaked.

"And what did he do?" I prodded in response.

She twisted again in her chair and picked up

her fire extinguisher, menacing it at the three laughing kids down below. When they had retreated to the street she said, "What was that, hon?"

I repeated my question.

"Oh. Oh, sure. He turned and winked at me. 'No need to spray me with that thing,' he says, meaning the extinguisher, of course, 'cause I've got plenty of money. Least, I will have pretty soon. Pretty soon.' "

"Did he turn left or right at the bottom of the stairs?"

She puckered her forehead up to her wispy yellow hair in an effort to remember, but she couldn't call it back; her mind had been on the kids down below, not on one more desiccated lodger.

"I'd like to look at his room before I go."

"You got a warrant for that, hon?"

I pulled out a twenty from my purse. "No warrant. But how about a refill for your gizmo there?"

She eyed me, then the money, then the kids down below. "You cops can't come barging into someone's house without a warrant. That's in the Constitution, in case you didn't know. But just this once, seeing as how you're a female, and dressed neat, I'll let you in, but you come back with any men, they'd better have a warrant. Go up to the second floor. He's two doors down from the bathroom on your left." She turned her head abruptly to the street as I opened the screen door.

Her house had the sharp, sour smell of rank

dishcloths. It was a dark place, built deep and narrow with windows only on the front and back walls. By the smell, they hadn't been opened for some time. The stairs rose steeply in front of me. I mounted them cautiously. Even so, I caught my feet several times on pieces of loose linoleum.

I fumbled my way down the second-floor hall to the bathroom, then found the second door on the left. The room was standing open, the bed made with a careless hand, waiting for Kruger's return. No individual locks or much privacy in Mrs. Polter's domain, but Kruger didn't have much to be private about. I rummaged in his vinyl suitcase, but such papers as he had related to his union membership, his union pension, and a form to send to the Social Security Administration to let them know his change of address. He'd also kept some old newspaper clips, apparently about Diamond Head. Maybe the company stood in for his vanished family as a source of human connection.

His only possession of any possible value was a portable black-and-white TV. Its rabbit ears were bent and one of the knobs was broken off, but when I flipped it on, the picture came with respectable clarity.

Mitch's clothes were sufficiently greasy to make me stop in the bathroom on my way out to wash my hands. A look at the towels convinced me that air-drying was healthier.

A middle-aged man in a frayed undershirt and

shorts was waiting outside the bathroom door. He looked me over hungrily.

" 'Bout time the old bitch brought in someone like you, sugar. Sight for sore eyes. Sight for sore eyes, that's for damned sure."

He rubbed up against me as I passed him. I lost my footing and kicked him on the side of his exposed leg to steady myself. I felt his malevolent gaze on the back of my neck all the way downstairs. A better detective would have taken the opportunity to ask him about Mitch Kruger.

Mrs. Polter didn't say anything when I thanked her for letting me look around, but when I was halfway down the stairs she yelled, "Remember: that room's only paid through Sunday night. After that the old guy better come and collect his stuff."

I stopped and pondered. Mr. Contreras would not want his old pal back on the living room couch. And come to think of it, neither did I. I stomped back up the stairs and gave her fifty dollars. They disappeared behind the safety pin at her bosom, but she didn't say anything. Now I had ten left from Mr. Contreras's advance to get me through the bars of the South Side.

At the bottom of the stairs I stopped the ringleader of the cycling trio. "I'm looking for an old guy who walked out of here Monday afternoon. White man. Lots of gray hair, which he didn't comb, big stomach, probably had on suspenders and an old pair of work pants. You remember which way he went?"

"He some kind of friend of yours, miss?"

"He—uh, he's my uncle." I didn't think this group would respond well to a detective.

"How much is it worth to you to find him?"

I made a face. "Not a whole lot. Maybe ten."

"Here he comes right now!" One of the other youths jumped his bicycle up and down the curb in his excitement. "Right behind you, miss!"

Holding tight to my purse I turned my head. The kid was right. An oldish white man with thick gray hair and a paunch was stumbling up the street toward us. In fact, there was another coming out of Tessie's Tavern just across the way. There were probably a thousand men just like Mitch wandering around the two-mile strip between Ashland and Western. My shoulders sagged at the prospect. I turned to cross the street.

"Hey, miss, what about our money?" The trio suddenly surrounded me with their bikes.

"Well, that wasn't my uncle. But he looks the same, so I suppose that's worth five bucks."

I dug in my handbag and pulled out a five without taking out my billfold. I shouldn't copy Mrs. Polter's suspiciousness, but they had me surrounded.

"You said ten," the ringleader said accusingly.

"Take it or leave it." I stared at him coldly, my arms akimbo.I don't know whether it was the toughness of my expression, or the sudden movement of Mrs. Polter with her fire extinguisher, but the bikes separated. I sauntered across the street, not looking behind me until I got to the door of Tessie's Tavern. They had ridden off toward Ashland, presumably to spend their largess.

9

Diamond in the Rough

Tessie's was a short, narrow room with three pressed-wood tables and a bar long enough to seat eight or nine people. Two men in dusty work shirts were sitting side by side at the counter. One had his sleeves rolled up to show off arms the size of expressway pilings. Neither looked at me when I walked up to the bar, but a middle-aged woman with her back to me turned from the glasses she was rinsing. She had some kind of radar that told her when a customer was arriving.

"What can I do for you, hon?" Her voice was like her face, clear and pleasant.

"I'll have a draw." I slid onto a barstool. Beer is not my favorite drink, but you can't go bar-crawling on whisky and tavern owners aren't too responsive to club soda fiends.

The man in shirtsleeves finished his beer and said, "Same again, Tessie." She pulled two more beers and poured a couple of shots and set them in front of the men. She clattered the empties into the sink and washed them briskly, setting them on a shelf under the bottles in front of her. A trio of men drifted in and greeted her by name.

"Your usual, boys?" she asked, grabbing a set of clean steins. They took their beers over to one of the pressed-wood tables and Tessie picked up the *Sun-Times.*

"You want anything else, honey?" she asked when I forced the last of the thin, bitter brew down.

"Tell you the truth, I'm looking for my uncle. I was wondering if you'd seen him." I started describing Mitch, but she interrupted me.

"I don't run a baby-sitting service, hon. That'll be seventy-five cents for the beer."

I fished in my jeans pocket for a dollar. "I'm not asking you to. But he disappeared on Monday and he has a bad habit of going on benders. I'm trying to see if I can pick up his trail. He just moved in with Mrs. Polter across the street."

She smoothed her hands over her plump hips and gave an exaggerated sigh, but she listened to my description of Mitch closely enough. "Could be any of a dozen guys who drink around here," she said when I'd finished. "But everyone has their regular place; I'd think you'd want to talk to them, not go drinking beer in every bar on Archer. Nice-looking girl like you could get yourself in a lot of trouble in some of them."

She handed me a quarter and waved away my efforts to leave it on the bar top. "Hope you find him, honey. These old drunks eat up a lot of family time."

I stood on the curb trying to figure out my next move. Mrs. Polter had disappeared from her front porch and I didn't see her three tormentors anywhere on the street. A tired woman with two small children in tow was coming up the sidewalk. Another woman was heading into the Excelsior Tap three doors down from Tessie's. Not much street life for a June afternoon.

Tessie was right. If Kruger was going on a bender, he wouldn't do it here. He'd go back to his old neighborhood and drink at his usual tavern. I should have gotten his previous address from Mr. Contreras before I started searching. I could call my neighbor—there was a pay phone at the corner—but I didn't have the stomach for any more landladies or beer this afternoon.

I climbed back into my car. It was only four-fifteen. Someone might still be in the office at Diamond Head. If I didn't go there now it would be Monday before I could check them out.

The plant proved difficult to find. The address, on the 2000 block of Thirty-first Street, was clear enough, but I couldn't seem to get at it. I went up Damen, which crosses the canal at Thirty-first Street, and found a promising road that snaked along the legs of the expressway. Weeds already grew waist-high there, partly concealing discarded mattresses and tires. Semis roared past me, taking the curves at fifty. I realized too late that we were being decanted onto the Stevenson.

By now rush-hour traffic had turned the two miles to Kedzie into a twenty-minute drive.

When I got off, I didn't try to make the return on the expressway. Instead I rode down Thirty-ninth Street and came back up to Damen. This time I parked the Trans Am at the bottom of the bridge and walked up the pedestrian path to the disused drawbridge tower in the middle.

It had been years since anyone had last used the tower. Its windows were boarded shut. The locks on the small iron door were so badly rusted that they couldn't have been opened even if you had a key. Someone had announced the presence of the Insane Spanish Cobras along one wall; a giant swastika filled another.

The parapet had also rusted badly. A number of the rails had come loose. I didn't risk leaning over it—a misstep would land me headfirst on the log pilings tied up underneath. Instead I lay flat on my stomach on the walk and peered below.

Weyerhauser's giant yards stretched away to the east, with some scrap yards alongside them. Directly beneath me were the scruffy trees that grew at the water's edge. They shielded most of the nearby rooftops from my view, but two down on the left I could make out an *A* and an *ND*. It didn't need Sherlock Holmes to deduce that they might be from the word "Diamond."

If I had a boat, I could sail right up to its doors. The trick was getting to it from land. I walked back down the bridge and followed a narrow sidewalk past a row of bungalows built along the road. The houses seemed much older than the bridge, which rose above their tiny dormer windows, blocking their light.

The walk dead-ended at a cyclone fence bordering the canal. I followed the fence, trying to avoid the worst of the refuse that was dropped along it, but tripped a few times on cans hidden in the high prairie grasses. After twenty feet or so of dirty hiking I came to a concrete apron. Right next to it was a loading dock. Trucks were backed into the docks, looking like horses tied up at a giant stable getting their oats.

I squinted up at the lettering that ran around the roof. Gammidge Wire. I followed the apron around the building and finally came to Diamond Head.

Only one truck stood in the open bays at the engine plant. I was afraid that my exploration of the South Side had made me too late to find anyone, but I went over to the truck to inquire.

A man in a coverall stood at the bottom of the loading platform, his back against the truck. He was a huge guy, his head topping my five-eight by a good nine inches. The diesel was running, vibrating the body of the truck and making such a racket that I had a hard time getting his attention. I finally touched his arm. He jumped and swore.

"Who are you and what in hell do you want?" I couldn't hear him over the engine racket, but he mouthed the words pretty distinctly.

He had a big, square face with a scar running down his left jaw. His nose had been broken more than once, judging by the number of twists it took before settling on the right side of his face. I took a step back.

"Anyone inside I can talk to?" I bellowed.

He put his face down close to mine. "I asked who you was, girlie, and what in hell you want here."

The backs of my knees prickled, but I eyeballed him coldly. "I'm V. I. Warshawski. I want the shop steward. That help you any?"

He narrowed his eyes and stuck out his lower lip, ready to be plenty mad. Before he could decide to do anything really violent I ducked behind him and vaulted up onto the platform. He started after me, but his size and his work boots limited his agility.

I looked around for someone to talk to, but the platform was empty. Only a forklift with a crate on it suggested that someone might be loading—or unloading—the truck.

I didn't wait for my friend to join me but sprinted along the lip of the dock until I came to an open door going into a long hallway. Here I did find a small cluster of men, all in shirts and ties, deep in conversation. The bosses. Just what I wanted.

They looked up at me in surprise. One of them, a youngish guy with short brown hair and tortoise-shell glasses, took a step forward.

"You lost?"

"Not exactly." I caught sight of a long tuft of prairie grass stuck in the tongue of my right shoe and wondered how much more debris I was carrying. "I'm looking for someone who might know something about an old Diamond Head employee. Either the shop steward or the plant manager."

Just then my trucking friend came pounding in. "Oh, there you are," he roared, a world of menace in his tone. "She came sneaking around the back of the place just now."

"She did?" The spokesman turned back to me. "Who are you and just what do you want?"

"I'm V. I. Warshawski. And I want to speak either to the shop steward or the plant manager. Despite what Bruno here says, I wasn't sneaking around. But I spent a frustrating forty minutes trying to find you from the road and finally had to come on foot."

No one spoke for a minute, then a second man, older than the first speaker, said, "Who are you working for?"

"I'm not an industrial spy, if that's what you're wondering. I have only the dimmest notion of what you make here. I'm a detective—" That brought a quick outburst from two of the group. I held up a hand. "I'm a private detective, and I've been hired to find an old man who used to work here."

The older man looked at me sharply for a minute. "I think I'd better talk to her in my office, Hank," he said to the brown-haired man. "You go back to the truck, Simon. I'll make sure she's off the premises when she goes."

He jerked his head toward the end of the hall and snapped, "Come on."

He set off down the hall at a good clip. I followed more slowly, stopping to pull the tuft of grass from my shoe. When I stood up he had disappeared. Two thirds of the way down the hall I found a door that led to a short corridor. My guide stood just inside it, his hands on his hips, his dark eyes sharp. When I caught up with him, he whirled without speaking and marched into the utilitarian hole he used as an office.

"Now, just who in hell are you and what are you doing snooping around our plant?" he said as soon as we were seated.

I looked around on his desktop, but didn't see a nameplate. "You got a name?" I asked. "And a position with the firm?"

"I asked you a question, young lady."

"I told you out in the hall there. I haven't got anything to add. But if you want to talk it over, it would be really helpful for me to know your name." I leaned back in my chair and retied my right shoe.

He glared at me. I took off the left shoe and shook some dirt from it onto the floor.

"My name is Chamfers. And I am the plant manager." The words came out as though snapped through a peashooter.

"How do you do?" I took my wallet from my handbag and dug out the laminated copy of my PI license and showed it to him.

He looked it over and threw it contemptuously

onto the desktop. "I don't suppose you'll tell me who's employing you, but I've got dicks of my own. I can check you out fast enough."

I made a disgusted face. "And when you've spent a couple of thousand bucks doing that, you won't be any wiser than you are now. I realize it looks strange, me crawling around your premises, but there's a simple explanation. Your guy Simon was the first person I saw. When I tried talking to him he got kind of ugly, so I scrambled for safety and found you."

He scowled for a minute. "And what's your story on what you want with me?"

"My story, as you put it, is also very simple. I'm looking for an old man who used to work here."

"Did we fire him?"

"Nope. He left the old-fashioned way: he retired."

"So there's no reason for him to be here." He wasn't believing me. His tone and the curl to his upper lip made that clear enough.

"So it would seem. But the last time my client saw him, on Monday, the guy who's missing said he was coming over here to see the bosses—his word. He had something on his mind about Diamond Head. So, since no one who knows him has seen him since Monday, I was hoping he might actually have done it. Come over here, I mean."

"And what is this ex-employee's name?" He gave a little smile to show he appreciated our game.

I smiled back, just as thinly, but with more contempt. "Mitch Kruger. Did he show up?"

"If he did, he never made it past my secretary."

"Then I'd like to talk to him."

"That was crude," he said contemptuously. "Trying to pretend you haven't done your homework on our operation to know my secretary is a woman. I'll ask Angela when she comes in on Monday. And give you a call."

"Chamfers, I'll tell you a little secret. If I were really committing industrial espionage, you wouldn't even know I'd been here. I'd have had you guys staked out and known your comings and goings and made my move after you'd left for the weekend. So relax. Save the strain on your brain and your bankroll. All I want to know is the last time anyone here at Diamond Head saw my boy Mitch. When we know that, we'll shake hands forever."

I picked up my license from his desk and handed him one of my cards. "It'll make it easier for you to call me if you have my number, Chamfers. And I'll take yours.

I leaned over the desk and copied the number stuck at the top of his phone buttons before he could stop me. "Want to give me a safe-conduct past Simon?"

He gave a triumphant smirk. "We're not going through the body of the plant, so don't get your hopes up, missy. We'll go the long way around. And I'll make sure our security forces are on the alert this weekend."

We went back to the hallway and out a door that fronted the canal. In silence we followed a footpath around the side, past the vibrating truck where Simon stood guard, and on to the main entrance. A cracked road led away from it.

"I don't know where you hid your car, but it had better not be on our land. I can't promise to hold on to Simon if he catches sight of you sneaking around here again.

"I'll be sure to bring a bag of raw meat with me next time just in case."

"There won't be a next time. Get that through your head good and solid, missy."

It didn't seem worth it to escalate the conflict further. I blew him a kiss and headed up the drive. Arms akimbo, he glared me out of sight.

10

Going to the Dogs

It was after six when I finally got back to the Trans Am. After hiking down Diamond Head's cracked access road to Bridgeport's side streets, I figured out the route. My mistake had been in trying to get at the plant from Thirty-first Street: you had to go down to Thirty-third and snake up and down a few times.

I laughed a little to myself over my encounter with Chamfers. With all the industrial surveillance I've done over the years it was funny—as well as embarrassing—to make such a clumsy entrance that they took me for a spy. I should have just waited for Monday morning, when I could have spoken to Chamfers's secretary in the accepted fashion. Now I'd have to do it anyway, but I'd have a big hurdle of suspicion to jump over.

I wondered if Chamfers would really get his own detectives to check up on me, or if that had been bravado to make me back away from my supposed espionage. I amused myself during the long drive up the Kennedy with figuring out what steps I would take if I were going to investigate myself. It would be hard for me to prove I *wasn't* spying: by the time they'd checked with some of my corporate references, they'd realize it made up a significant part of my practice. They'd have to start tailing me; that would take a lot of time and money. It wouldn't make me cry to think of Chamfers trying to justify it to his corporate masters, whoever they were.

When I got home, Mr. Contreras jumped out of his front door to greet me. "Got anything on Mitch, doll?"

I put an arm around his shoulder and gently propelled him back into his apartment. "I've started asking people questions, but I've got a long way to go yet. I'm going to tell you the same thing I say to all my clients: I make regular reports, but I work less and less efficiently the more I get hounded for them. So pretend we're neighbors who are both in love with the same dog, and let me handle the investigation as best I can."

Mr. Contreras elected to be hurt. "It's just that I'm worried about him. I ain't trying to hound you or criticize you."

I grinned. "Perish the thought. Can you give me Kruger's old address—the one he had before he came home with you last Friday?"

"Yeah. Yeah, I got it right here."

He pulled the cover from the desk that stood in the middle of his living room. I've never known either why he keeps it there, where he must bump into it a hundred times a week, or why he thinks it's a good idea to drape it. From the jumble of papers stacked on top and spilling from the drawers I figured it wasn't going to be an easy search. I skirted the operation and went over to check on Peppy.

The puppies had grown amazingly in one week. Their soft fur coverings were starting to show distinctive colors. They were still blind, though, and helpless. They squealed and squirmed in terror when Peppy stood up and left them. She sniffed my legs to make sure it was me and indicated that she wanted to go outside.

"Yeah, you take her out, doll. I'm still tracking down Mitch's address," Mr. Contreras called to me.

Peppy didn't want to stay out long. She made a brief circuit of the yard to spot any changes in her domain and headed straight back to the kitchen door. Our quick tour suddenly reminded me of my insane agreement to do evening duty with Mrs. Frizell's dogs.

When we returned to the living room, Mr. Contreras was leafing through a crumbling address book.

"Got it, cookie," he announced. "I'll just write it down for you." A handful of pages dropped to the floor while he hunted for a pencil and paper.

"Just tell me what it is," I suggested. "I can remember it long enough to get upstairs. . . . By the way, did Mrs. Hellstrom up the street drop off keys for Mrs. Frizell's house?"

"Huh?" He was copying Mitch's address onto an old envelope with the slow hand of someone who doesn't write much. "Keys? Oh, yeah, slipped my mind in my worry over Mitch, but I got them here for you. Hang on a second. I thought you wasn't going to get involved with any more dogs. Isn't that what you said?"

"My lips said 'No, no,' but my imbecile conscience said 'Yes, yes.' But I'm not backing down on an addition to our menagerie.

"Okay, doll, okay. Cool your jets." He handed me the envelope with Kruger's old address, Thirty-fifth Street west of Damen, spelled out in caps. Really just walking distance from Diamond Head.

"Is that where you lived too?"

"Huh, doll? Oh, you're thinking about when we was kids. No, no. My folks lived on Twenty-fourth, off Oakley. Part of Little Tuscany. Mitch lived closer to California. We was always on his case about how he was gonna end up at the county jail. It's right there, you know."

"I know." A lot of my life had been spent at Twenty-sixth and California in my days with the Homicide Task Force.

"You gonna go down to his old place tomorrow?" Mr. Contreras asked as I headed up the stairs.

I turned to look at him and bit off a variety of short answers; the concern in his soft brown eyes was too immediate. "Probably. Anyway, I'll do my best."

In my own place I resisted the longing for a bath and a double whisky. I stayed just long enough to dump my handbag and check my messages. Daraugh Graham wanted my report. Lotty hadn't tried to call—maybe we were still pissed off with each other. I didn't have the energy to sort that out tonight.

When I got to Mrs. Frizell's, the house was quiet. The dogs weren't there. I stood in the hallway, foolishly calling to them even though I could tell the house was empty, then made an even more foolish search of the premises. Someone had been through the place, cleaning it—all the bedding was washed and neatly stacked on a freshly polished bureau in the bedroom; the stairs and floors had been vacuumed and the bathroom scrubbed down. Only the living room was still a wreck, with papers strewn all over it. Presumably Mrs. Hellstrom had been continuing her job of good neighbor. She probably had the dogs too.

Relieved, I headed back to my own home. Now I could take a bath and watch the Cubs-Astros game in peace. I was at my front stoop when Mrs. Hellstrom caught up with me. Her round, fair face was flushed and she was out of breath from chasing me down the street.

"Oh, young lady! I'm sorry, I don't remember your name, but I was watching for you only, the phone rang, so I missed you coming up the block. I'm glad I saw you leaving."

I mustered an interested expression.

"It's the dogs, Hattie Frizell's dogs. They've disappeared."

"Into thin air?"

She spread helpless hands. "I'm sure I locked them in the house this morning. I mean, I can't leave them in the yard—that big black dog is always all over the neighborhood, and I don't like it myself. She can't admit they ever do anything wrong, but he dug up all my irises last fall *and* ate the bulbs. Then when I went to talk to her about it . . . well, anyway, I just meant I locked them in the house even if it does seem a little cruel. And I'm sure I did. I don't think I would have been careless and left the door open. But when I came back from the store and went over to let them out they were gone."

I rubbed my eyes with the heels of my hands. "Was the door open when you went over?"

"It was shut but it wasn't locked, that's what

worries me. What do you think could have happened to them?"

"I don't think even Bruce could open the door with his jaws. Have you talked to anyone else on the street? Maybe someone broke in and let the dogs out."

Burglars, like Santa Claus, know when we've been sleeping, or away from our houses. And the living room did look as though someone might have ransacked it. On the surface Mrs. Frizell seemed an unlikely candidate for valuables, but she wouldn't be the first person to live in squalor while sitting on a stack of bearer bonds.

"Burglars?" Mrs. Hellstrom's pale-blue eyes widened in fear. "Oh, dear, I hope not. This block has always been such a *nice* place to live, even if we're not as fancy as that young lawyer across the street or some of the other new people who've moved in. I did ask Maud Rezzori—she lives on the other side, you know—but she was out at the same time I was. I'm going to have to go tell Mr. Hellstrom. He's been annoyed with me, taking on those dogs, but if we have burglars . . ."

She sounded like a housewife distressed over a plague of mice. Despite my fatigue I couldn't help laughing.

"It's not funny, young lady. I mean, it may seem like a joke to you, but you live on the third floor, and it isn't—"

"I don't think burglars are a joke," I cut her off hastily. "But we need to find out if other neighbors saw someone going into Mrs. Frizell's place before we get too hot about it. It's possible you forgot to lock the door and the meter reader came around. It could be anything. You've lived here a long time—you can probably give me the names of the people on the block."

All I wanted was a bath and a drink and a Cubs victory, not a night of interrogation. Why do you do this to yourself? a voice in my head demanded while Mrs. Hellstrom detailed the Tertzes', the Olsens', and the Singers' biographies. I certainly couldn't blame Carol for staying home to look after Cousin Guillermo if I was going to spend my life on the dogs of a disagreeable old woman who didn't have the faintest tie to me.

"Okay. I'll scout around and let you know if anyone can tell me anything."

I walked back up the street with her. Mrs. Hellstrom continued to be worried about burglars, and what her daughters would say, and what Mr. Hellstrom thought, but I wasn't really paying attention.

11

Man Bites Dog

I tried the Olsens first since they lived directly behind Mrs. Frizell and might have noticed someone going in her back door. Unfortunately they'd been watching TV in their living room in the morning. I could see the disappointment in their face—they'd missed a ringside seat on a real drama, maybe burglars going after a neighbor they didn't much care for—but they couldn't tell me anything.

I went to the Tertzes next. Their frame house on the east side of Racine, facing Mrs. Frizell, was sandwiched between the Picheas' and another rehab job. The carefully painted scrollwork on either side made the Tertz house look a trifle shabby, but the lawn was carefully tended, with a few early roses in bud.

Mrs. Tertz must have been about seventy. We carried on the conversation in a shout through her locked front door until she was satisfied that I didn't have assault on my mind. "Oh, yes, I've seen you on the street. You have that big red dog, don't you? I just never saw you close up before, so I didn't recognize your face. You've been helping Marjorie look after Harriet Frizell's dogs for her, haven't you?"

I hadn't heard Mrs. Hellstrom's first name before. I boiled her ten-minute dither down to a few sentences. "So I wondered if you saw anyone go into the house while she was away."

"Yes, yes, I did, but they weren't burglars. What does Marjorie take me for, that I'd let someone break in, even on Hattie Frizell, without calling the police? No, no, they were with the county—I saw it on the side of their van—Cook County Animal Control. I was sure Marjorie knew all about it. They came around eleven o'clock, and that girl next door"—she jerked her head in the direction of the Picheas—"Chrissie, her name is, Chrissie Pichea, was there to let them in."

"Chrissie Pichea?" I echoed stupidly.

"Why, yes. She often comes around to visit." Mrs. Tertz smiled a little. "I think she's doing good works for the elderly. But I don't resent it—it's kindly meant, even if my husband and I are perfectly able to manage our own affairs. It gets him angry, you see, the idea that just because the clock's ticked a little longer for us we've suddenly become incompetent in some people's eyes. So I usually don't let him know if she's stopped by. But I knew she wouldn't have gone into Hattie's without the intention to help, so I just went back to my own work."

I stared at her unseeingly, barely listening to her monologue. Chrissie Pichea let in the animal control unit? How had she gotten keys? That question was immaterial at this point. She and Todd had simply outflanked me. They'd somehow made sure I was away, then gotten the county to come for Mrs. Frizell's dogs.

I left Mrs. Tertz in mid-sentence and tramped down some zinnias as I sprinted across the Picheas' yard. My finger shook as I stabbed their polished brass doorbell. Todd Pichea came to the door.

"Oh, it's you." The trace of a smirk flickered across his mouth, but he looked a little uneasy, his fists tightly bunched inside his linen slacks.

"Yes, it's me. Nine hours too late, but on the trail nonetheless. How did you and your wife get a key to Mrs. Frizell's front door? And who gave you the right to send the county to pick up her dogs?"

"What business is it of yours?"

"You made it my business when you came to my building the other night. How did you get her key?"

"The same way you did: I helped myself to one lying in the living room. And I have a lot more right to what goes on in that house than you do. A *lot* more right." He swayed forward on the balls of his feet, trying to look intimidating.

I moved forward, not back, and planted my nose about an inch from his. "You've got no rights to anything, Pichea. I'm going to call the county and then I'm going to call the cops. You may be a lawyer, but they'll still be glad to arrest you on a B&E."

The smirk became pronounced. "You do that, Warshawski. Go home and do it, or better still, come in here. I'd love to see you with egg all over that self-righteous face of yours. I want to be in the front row watching you when the cops show up."

Chrissie came up behind him, skin-tight jeans showing off her trim thighs. "What is it, Todd? Oh, that busybody up the street. Did you tell her we got appointed guardians?"

"Guardians?" My voice rose half an octave.

"Who was deranged enough to appoint you Mrs. Frizell's guardian?"

"I called the son Tuesday morning. He was glad to turn his mother over to a competent lawyer. She isn't capable of handling her own affairs, and we—"

"There's nothing wrong with her mind. Just because she chooses to live in a different world than Yuppieville—"

He cut me off in turn. "The court doesn't agree. We had an emergency hearing yesterday. And the city emergency services people agreed that those dogs constituted a menace to Mrs. Frizell's health. If she's ever able to live at home again."

The impulse to smash in his face was so strong that I just pulled my fist back before it connected.

"Very smart, Warshawski. I don't know who your police contacts are, but I don't think they'd get you off an assault charge." He was a little pale, breathing hard, but in control.

I turned without speaking. I felt beaten. I wasn't going to add to it by spewing out empty bravado.

"Have a nice night, Warshawski." Todd's mocking voice followed me down the walk.

How could he have done it? I had only the vaguest idea of how probate court and guardianship worked in Cook County. All my legal experience had been on the criminal, not the civil side, although some of my clients had children for whom we'd had to arrange custody. Could you just go to the probate judge and get care of someone else? Mrs. Frizell wasn't deranged or senile, just unpleasant and reclusive. Or maybe it was her son—in my anger I couldn't think of his name—maybe all he had to do was call up someone and turn the rights to his mother over to them? That just couldn't be.

My neck muscles had turned so stiff from rage that when I got to my own front door I was trembling violently. I poured myself a large whisky and started running a bath. While Johnnie Walker worked his magic on my tense shoulders I called the animal control office. The man on the other end was pleasant, even friendly, but after leaving me on hold for ten minutes he told me apologetically that Mrs. Frizell's dogs had already been destroyed.

I pictured Mrs. Frizell, her wispy gray hair scattered on a hospital pillow, turning her face to the wall and dying when she learned her beloved dogs were dead. I could hear that hoarse whisper of "Bruce," and Mrs. Hellstrom's promise that she would look after the dogs. I hadn't felt this helpless since the day Tony told me Gabriella was going to die.

The sound of water splashing on tile brought me back to life with a jolt. The bath had overflowed while I sat in a stupor. I was tempted to let the water find its own way out, especially since that would eventually be through Vinnie Buttone's ceiling, but I made myself fetch a mop and a bucket and clean it up. The bath was tepid by then and the hot water tank empty. I gave a howl of frustration and flung the whisky glass across the room.

"Very smart, V.I.," I said aloud as I knelt to pick up the pieces. "You've shown you can destroy yourself if you get angry enough—now figure out what you can do to Todd Pichea."

When I'd finished picking up glass shards and mopping whisky I turned on the light in the living room and looked Todd Pichea up in the phone book. His home number wasn't given, but he did list his office, at an address on North La Salle that I recognized.

I hunted around the living room for my private address book, which was usually interleaved in the papers on the coffee table. In my cleaning frenzy Tuesday morning I had tidied things so violently that I couldn't find it. After half an hour of going through every drawer in the place I discovered the book inside the piano bench. Really, it was a waste of time to clean.

I dialed Richard Yarborough's unlisted Oak Brook number. He answered the phone himself.

"Dick, hi. How are you? . . . It's me, your good old ex-wife, Vic," I added when it was clear he hadn't recognized my voice.

"Vic! What do you want?" He sounded startled, but not actively hostile.

My normal conversations with him begin with a little brittle banter, but I was too upset tonight for cleverness. "You know a boy named Todd Pichea?"

"Pichea? I might. Why?"

"The one I've met lives across the street from me. About five-ten, thirtyish, brown hair, square face." My voice trailed away—I couldn't think of any way to describe Todd that would distinguish him from ten thousand other young professionals.

"And?"

"His law office seems to have the same address as yours. I thought maybe he was one of your hot young lawyers chomping at the bit."

"Yes, I believe we do have an associate with that name." Dick wasn't going to give me anything willingly.

I hadn't thought this phone call through before making it. Like everything else I'd done tonight, from ringing the Picheas' doorbell to breaking a glass of whisky, it had been impulsive and perhaps stupid. I plunged ahead, feeling as though I were wrestling quicksand.

"He's gotten involved in some extracurricular legal work. Extraterrestrial, really: made himself guardian of an old woman in the neighborhood who's in the hospital, and had her five dogs collected by the county and put to sleep."

"That's not really any of my business, Vic, and I don't see that it's yours either. Now, if you'll excuse me, we're entertaining tonight."

"The thing is, Dick," I said quickly, before he could hang up, "the woman is a client of mine. I'm going to conduct an investigation into the process Pichea went through to become her

107

guardian. And if there's anything, well, unusual about it—I mean, it did happen very, very fast—then it will be in the papers. I just wanted you to know. So that you could be ready for phone calls and TV crews and stuff. And maybe warn your juniors not to let their enthusiasm exceed their legal judgment, or something like that."

"Why do you have to come at me like a tank truck all the time? Why can't you call up just to say hi? Or not call at all?"

"Dick, this *is* friendly," I said reproachfully. "I'm trying to keep you from being blindsided."

I thought I could hear him grinding his teeth, but it might have been wishful thinking. "What's the old woman's name?"

"Frizell. Harriet Frizell."

"Okay, Vic, I've made a note of it. Now I've got to go. Don't phone again unless you want to buy tickets to the next benefit we're sponsoring. And even then I'd rather you spoke to my secretary."

"Good talking to you too. Give my love to Teri."

He snapped the receiver in my ear. I hung up, wondering what I'd done and why. . . . So Mrs. Frizell was a client of mine? Now what? More long hours of wasted time when I needed paying jobs so I could buy running shoes? And what did I really expect Dick to do to Todd Pichea—go tell him what a tiger I was, to watch his step and bring those dead dogs back to life while he was at it?

It was nine o'clock now. I was grubby and tired, and I wanted my dinner. On a Friday night there wasn't much I could do to track down actions at a probate court. I sponged myself off with the tepid bath water and put on clean cotton pants so that I could go foraging for food on Lincoln Avenue.

12

Whom Bruce Has Led— Welcome to Your Gory Bed

I spent six hours in bed, mostly as a way to pass the time until morning, since I couldn't sleep. I hadn't wanted the burden of looking after the dogs, so I'd forestalled Mr. Contreras from suggesting we take them in. I'd even been sharp and a little condescending when I spoke to him about it. And now they were dead. I tried not to imagine their stiff bodies in some dump, or wherever the county sends dogs it's destroyed, but I felt ill, feverish, as if I myself had lined them against a wall and shot them.

On sleepless nights it seems as though the sky will stay black forever, that it's only sleep which makes the day come. I must have finally dozed for an hour or two, because suddenly my room was filled with light. Another splendid June morning, just the weather for telling old women with fractures that their beloved dogs were dead.

I had a friend from college, Steve Logan, who was a psychiatric social worker at Cook County Hospital. We used to work together a lot when I was with the PD—he evaluated some of my less socially acclimated clients. There was even a year when we thought we were in love. We couldn't sustain it, but the memory of our affair warmed our friendship.

Since our work paths stopped crossing we only managed to get together a couple of times a year, but he would probably arrange for me to see Mrs. Frizell. I waited a long two hours until nine o'clock when I could decently try calling him.

Steve sounded pleased to hear from me and clicked his tongue consolingly over my tale of woe. He agreed to locate Mrs. Frizell and take me to see her if I'd meet him in half an hour—it was his day off and he was using it to take his children to the zoo.

I dressed in a hurry and snuck out without Mr. Contreras hearing me. I felt too flayed to tell him what had happened—and to listen to his reproaches.

Cook County Hospital lies on the near west side, just off the Lake Street el, between a VA hospital and Presbyterian-St. Luke's. The latter is an enormous private hospital with the most modern of facilities and an on-going building program that threatens to swallow the surrounding community. Prez, as the locals call it, has no connection to the county hospital, except when their patients run out of money and have to be rolled down the street to be picked up by the taxpayers.

County had been put up around the turn of the century, when public buildings were supposed to look like Babylonian temples. Following its creation the public has declined further acts of generosity. We continue to put money into the county jail and courts, building ever bigger annexes to support ever more law enforcement, but the hospital languishes. Every six months or so the papers spread an alarm that the hospital will lose its accreditation—and its federal money—because the building is so far below code—but then the feds relent and the place continues to hiccup along. The fact that the operating rooms aren't air-conditioned and the hospital has no sprinkler system seems like trivial reasons to deprive the poor of one of their few remaining sources of health care.

In response to Prez and the University of Illinois, which has a campus nearby, a lot of tidy little townhouses have sprung up immediately around the hospitals. Even so, I was reluctant to leave the Trans Am on the street. As I pulled it into one of the private hospital's lots I wished I'd stuck to a car more in keeping with both my income and the kind of neighborhoods I visit. If I'd bought a used Chevy I could have afforded new Nikes.

I'd arranged to meet Steve inside County's

main entrance on Harrison. It was a strange lobby, with a statue of a naked woman and two children in one corner, and a large square of blue light tubes overhead. I wondered if it was a bug zapper or just ultraviolet tubes to kill wandering germs. If that was the case they were fighting a losing battle with the grime on the floors and walls.

People straggled down the hall eating potato chips and drinking coffee. The waiting area, whose chairs filled several alcoves, was practically empty. On weekdays every seat is taken as people wait their turn in the outpatient clinics. On Saturday morning only a couple of drunks were stretched out on the chairs, sleeping off their Friday nights. The hospital is a monster, built like a large *E* with seven stories. Homeless people, kicked out of O'Hare Airport, slide in through the side entrances and curl up in the endless corridors to get through the night.

While I waited for Steve a couple of large policemen brought a man down the hall in handcuffs and leg shackles. He was slender and tremulous, a leaf blowing between two branches, and his face was covered with a surgical mask. The mask was as incongruous as the shackles on his thin legs. Perhaps he was Hiv-positive and had spat on the officers? Tuberculosis was on the rise at County too.

Steve came down the corridor at a run a little after ten, when I'd studied the inlaid pattern in the floor long enough to memorize it. He was in jeans and sneakers; with his lanky blond hair falling in his eyes he looked like a commercial for the great outdoors. I couldn't believe he'd stayed with the county all these years without frying his brains, but he told me once that working here made him feel real.

He put an arm around me and pecked my cheek. "Sorry to be late, Vic. Just thought I'd check on whether we knew anything about your lady. We have a six-month backlog right now, so I wasn't expecting anything, but it turns out there was some kind of emergency hearing on Thursday."

I grimaced. "Yeah, that's why I'm here. I have a damned yuppie neighbor who somehow got himself appointed the lady's guardian, and in an amazing hurry."

Steve's thick brows disappeared under his hair. "That was a superhurry. She only came in on Monday night, right? Seems almost indecent. She leaving him something in her will?"

"Rabies, if she thought about it. The boy got the county to kill her dogs. Her life pretty much revolved around them; I don't know how she's going to react if she learns they're dead."

Steve looked at his watch. "Elaine is giving the kids breakfast and making sure they're dressed. Let me just give her a call to let her know I'm running late—I want to see Mrs. Frizell myself. We can decide then the best way to tell her about the dogs."

We went back up the hall. Steve tops my five-

113

eight by five or six inches. He tried to shorten his stride, but I still had to jog to keep up. He ducked abruptly into a doorway and started up some stairs.

"Elevators," he said briefly. "Only one is working today on this side of the building. I'm afraid we're up five stories, but it's really faster, believe me."

I was panting slightly when we got to his office, but he didn't seem at all winded. He phoned his wife, picked up a clipboard, and relocked the door all in one movement.

"Elaine sends her love. We go back down two flights and over to the orthopedic corridor. I called Nelle McDowell—she's the charge nurse over there. She's cool, she'll let us talk to Mrs. Frizell."

We met Nelle McDowell at the nurses' station, a cubbyhole near the end of the corridor. A tall, squarely built black woman, she acknowledged Steve and me with a nod, but kept up a conversation with two nurses and an orderly. They were reviewing the previous night's newcomers and trying to juggle the workload. We waited in the hall outside until they'd finished—the tiny room barely held the four people already in it.

When the meeting broke up, McDowell beckoned us in. Steve introduced me. "Vic wants to talk to Harriet Frizell. Is she in shape to see anyone?"

McDowell made a face. "She's not the most

coherent person on the ward right now. What do you want to see her about?"

I told my tale once again, about finding Mrs. Frizell Monday night, and then about Todd Pichea, the dogs, and why I cared.

McDowell looked me over like a captain eyeing a dubious new subaltern. "You know who Bruce is, Vic?"

"Bruce is—was—Mrs. Frizell's number-one dog, a big black Lab."

"She keeps moaning his name. I thought maybe he was her husband, maybe a kid. But her dog?" The head nurse pursed her lips and shook her head. "She's not in good shape—she doesn't answer questions and that dog's name is about all she's said since they brought her in. They couldn't get any relative's name out of her on Monday night—the docs finally had to sign her consent form for her. We tried finding a Bruce Frizell in the city and suburbs—if it's a dog, that explains why we didn't have any luck. If he's dead, she's not going to hold up too well. I'd rather not tell her until I'm sure she's strong enough to survive."

"I want to talk to her, Nelle," Steve said. "Try to make an evaluation. One of our babies was there for the attorney hearing on Thursday, but I'd like to make up my own mind."

McDowell threw up her hands. "Be my guest, Steve. And take the detective with you—I've got no problem with that. But don't go doing anything to put her in a frenzy. In case you hadn't noticed, we're shorthanded in this ward."

She pulled out a chart with *Frizell* written along the side. "One thing maybe you can tell me—why the rush to get her a guardian? The times we've needed one appointed in here it's taken us months of rigamarole just to get to court. But Thursday morning there's a guardian *ad litem* as big as life, talking to the lady without a by-your-leave. I got security up, and they pulled him away until we hustled someone from the psych team in, along with that kid from your office"—she nodded at Steve—"but it made me plenty mad."

I shook my head. "I don't understand it myself, except I know Pichea was itching to get rid of those dogs. I talked to her son myself on Monday night. He lives in California and had about as much interest in what was happening to his mother as I do in my cockroaches. I expect when Pichea called him he was ecstatic at being able to make Mrs. Frizell someone else's problem."

McDowell shook her head. "We get people in here with all kinds of problems, but I don't ever remember a patient whose family wanted to dump her off on strangers before. . . . Mrs. Frizell's down in the ward, third partition from the end. Let me know what you think, Steve."

When we left the nurses' station, Steve explained that the ward used to be open, but that they had built partitions around the beds a few years ago. "It's not a great system—the walls are so close in you can't make the beds, and the pa-

116

tients don't have any way to attract someone else's attention if they need help. But the county board decrees and we try to make the best of it."

When I saw Mrs. Frizell my stomach turned cold and I felt faint. Even on Monday night, when she'd been lying half naked on her bathroom floor, she had looked like a person. Now her head was cocked back on the pillow, her eyes staring blankly, her mouth open, and the skin drawn taut across her bones a faint gray. She looked like a corpse. Only her restless, meaningless movements showed she was still alive.

I glanced fearfully at Steve. He shook his head, his lips compressed, but squeezed in between the bed and the partition wall. I moved to the other side of the bed.

I knelt next to the bed. Mrs. Frizell's eyes didn't seem to track either me or Steve. "Mrs. Frizell? I'm V. I.—Victoria. Your neighbor. How are you?"

It seemed like a foolish question and I felt rewarded for my stupidity when she didn't answer. Steve made a sign that I should go on, so I plowed painfully forward.

"I have a dog, you know, that red-old retriever. We run by your house some mornings and you and I sometimes talk." Sometimes she snarled at me, I amended in my head—maybe she'd never really noticed me. "And I found you on Monday night. With Marjorie Hellstrom."

117

I repeated the name a couple of times and made myself keep talking, but I couldn't bring myself to mention her dogs, the one thing that might have caught her attention. My knees were starting to ache from the cold, hard floor and my tongue felt like a furry clapper in a bell. I was starting to push myself standing when she suddenly turned her cloudy eyes to look at me.

"Bruce?" she croaked hoarsely. "Bruce?"

"Yes," I said, forcing a smile. "I know Bruce. He's a wonderful dog."

"Bruce." It looked as though she might be patting the bed, inviting a nonexistent dog to jump up and join her.

"I'm sorry," I said. "They don't let dogs into hospitals. You get well fast, and then you can go home and be with him."

"Bruce," she said again, but she seemed to have a little more color in her face. A few seconds later she'd fallen asleep.

13

Filial Piety

When I got back to the car I stretched the seat out as flat as I could and lay there, limp. I'd thrown up after leaving Mrs. Frizell, a sudden spontaneous retching to purge myself from the lie I'd had to tell. Nelle McDowell had produced a woman with a mop who refused to let me clean up the mess for her.

"Don't worry about it, honey; it's my job. And it's good to see someone care enough about that poor old lady to be sick for her. You just get yourself a glass of water and put your feet up for a minute."

I felt ashamed to lose control in front of Steve and Nelle McDowell, and brushed off their offers of help. "Your kids are going to be furious if you stand them up much longer, Steve. You go on home—I'm okay."

And I was okay, sort of. I'd been out of control since ringing Todd Pichea's doorbell last night. Why worry about losing it further at Cook County Hospital?

It was noon when I finally pulled myself together and started the car. I was on the South Side already, two blocks from Damen; a few more miles south and I could start checking the bars near Mitch Kruger's old home. I just didn't have the stomach for any more broken-down lives today.

Instead I turned toward Lake Michigan and drove north, past the city to the tony suburbs, where private grounds hid the lake from view, and finally to the open land beyond them. Although the day was clear and the water blue and calm, it was still much too cold for swimming. Clumps of picnickers dotted the lakefront, but I was able to find a stretch of deserted beach where I could take off my clothes and go into the water in my underwear. Within a few minutes my feet and my ears were aching with cold, but I kept pushing myself until I felt a roaring in my head and the world turned black around me. I stumbled to the shore and lay panting on the sand.

When I woke up the sun was low in the sky. I'd made a fine spectacle for passing voyeurs all afternoon, but no one had bothered me. I put my jeans and shirt back on and headed back to town.

Depression over my failure with Mrs. Frizell made me sleep heavily that night, too heavily, so that I woke late on Sunday feeling thick and unrefreshed. The air outside had turned unexpectedly thick and heavy, too, not good for jogging. Ninety degrees and muggy in early June? Did this mean that the dread greenhouse effect was kicking in and I should trade in my high performance car for a bicycle? I didn't think I could worry about Mrs. Frizell, Mitch Kruger, and the environment all on the same weekend.

I drank a cup of coffee and drove my high-performance car over to a Y where I sometimes swim. Sunday is family day: the pool was about equal parts chlorine and screaming children. I retreated to the weight room to spend a dull half hour on the machines. Working on machines is monotonous, and people in weight rooms too often seem to share the look of private self-satisfaction you get when you preen in front of a mirror—Gosh, I'm so beautiful, with such fabulous muscle development, I think I've fallen in love.

I stood it as long as I could, then wandered into the gym to find a pickup basketball game. I was in luck. Someone was just leaving to get her kids out of the pool. We could only keep the court for another twenty minutes, but by the time the men arrived to take over I was wet with sweat and the feeling of heaviness had gone from my head.

When I went in to shower I realized I'd left my gym bag in the weight room. Returning to pick it up I was surprised to see Chrissie Pichea on the lat machine I'd been using. Not surprised to see her working on her trapezius, just that she was at the Y. I'd figured her for a high-end Lincoln Park or Loop gym. She turned red when she recognized me.

"Since you and Todd took care of Mrs. Frizell's dogs, I have time to build up my pecs," I said heartily, picking up my bag.

Her face tightened in anger. "Why don't you just mind your own business!"

"I'm like you—I like to help the neighbors. Or when you go barging in on Mrs. Tertz and Mrs. Frizell, is that just your own business you're minding?"

She released the weights so fast, they crashed loudly as they landed. "Just who died and left you God?"

I smiled at her. "Old, tired line, Chrissie. Don't let the weights go so fast—it's a good way to tear a muscle." I sauntered from the room, whistling under my breath. Gosh, Vic, you're so witty, I think I'm falling in love.

Back home I felt alert enough to phone Mrs. Frizell's son in San Francisco. He answered on the eighth ring, when I'd begun to think he must be away for the weekend. I reminded him that we'd spoken last Monday after I found his mother in her bathroom.

"Yes?"

I explained what had happened to the dogs. "I went to see her yesterday. She's not in good shape. It might kill her to learn her dogs have been put to sleep. The nursing staff want to talk to you first—they don't want to run that kind of risk without her family knowing. . . . I gather you're her only family?"

"It's possible my father's still alive, in whatever Shangri-la he fled to before I was born. Since they never got divorced he's technically still her closest family member, but I don't suppose he'd care much more now than he has anytime in the last sixty years. Anyway, I authorized a lawyer who lives near her to serve as her guardian. Why don't you talk it over with him?" His voice was bitter, six decades of grievance giving it an edge.

"There's a bit of a problem with that: he's the one who got the county to put her dogs to sleep. He doesn't much care about the effect that has on your mother—he only wanted to be appointed guardian so he could get rid of the dogs."

"I expect you're exaggerating that," he said. "What's your own interest in my mother?"

Just a concerned neighbor? A busybody who can't keep her nose out of other people's lives? "She's a client of mine. I can't abandon her just because her mind is wandering."

"A client? What kind of—I go over Mother's bills once a quarter, after the bank has paid them. I don't recall your name—Sharansky, did you say?"

"No, I keep saying 'Warshawski.' You wouldn't find a bill—I've been doing *pro bono* work for her."

"Yes, but what are you doing for her? There are plenty of people around preying on the elderly. You'd better spell your name for me. I'd like Pichea to look into this."

"How do you know he isn't one of those people preying on the elderly?" I asked. "Who did you get to investigate him? Are you going to continue examining your mother's bills now that you've given him carte blanche to run her life?"

"He gave me the name of his law firm. I called and they assured me of his credentials and his disinterestedness. Now, if you'll spell your name for me—"

"But he's not disinterested," I squawked. "He wants your mother out of this neighborhood. He wanted the dogs put to sleep; he's probably hoping she'll die in the hospital so he can sell the house to some yuppie like himself—"

Byron interrupted me in turn. "My mother is

a very difficult person. Very difficult. I haven't been to Chicago to see her for four years now, but she was acting senile even then. Of course, she's been acting senile as long as I've known her, but at least she used to keep up the property. Well, four years ago I saw she was letting that house go to rack and ruin." He repeated the phrase as though he'd invented it and liked to hear it rolling around his tongue.

"If it hadn't been for me the whole place would have collapsed around her ears from the water damage. She couldn't be bothered to call roofers. She can't pick up the refuse people dump in the yard. I bet she hasn't used a vacuum cleaner in eighty years. I think it's time she went into a nursing home or some other facility where she'd be looked after."

He was gasping for breath. I didn't think this was the time to tell him most people hadn't owned vacuum cleaners eighty years ago.

"And it doesn't break my heart to hear those damned dogs are dead, either," he went on. "She was always the same. When I was a boy I couldn't bring anyone over to the house because of all the animals she had roaming around the place. It was more like living in a zoo than in a home, just because her dream was to be a vet and she had to work in a box factory instead.

"Well, we all have to give up our dreams—I wanted to be an architect but there wasn't money for that kind of education so I became an accountant instead. I don't go around filling my house with blueprints. I adjusted. Mother never learned that. She always thought rules applied to other people, never herself, and now she's going to have to learn the hard way that it just isn't so."

I'd always wanted to play in the majors but had ended up in law school instead. And I won scholarships and worked nights and summers to make it happen. It was hard for me to snivel over Byron's lost dreams, but I felt sad for Mrs. Frizell.

"Vet schools are hard to get into," I said aloud, "and I bet sixty-five years ago it was nearly impossible for women."

"And I don't need some damned lecture on women's rights either. Until women can look after their children properly, they don't deserve any other rights. I can just imagine what she did to my father to drive *him* away. Who the hell are you, anyway, to come around lecturing me? What kind of work have you been doing for Mother? Bringing her veterinary medicine manuals?" he jeered savagely. "What kind of work do you do?"

"I'm a lawyer. And a private investigator."

"If you're a lawyer, what are you doing for Mother?"

"Trying to protect her assets, mister. She's worried about them."

"I haven't seen—oh, yes. You *claim* to be doing *pro bono* work. Well, I'll talk to Pichea about you and see what he has to say, Ms. Warinski."

"It's Warshawski," I snapped. "And why don't you take my number too. Put it side by side with his so that the next time an attack of filial piety overwhelms you, you can reach me."

He hung up before I'd got the first three digits out.

I sat on the living room floor, looking at the phone. My mother died when I was fifteen; there are still nights I wake up missing her so much that a physical pain sucks at my diaphragm. But I'd rather have that pain every night of the year than get to be sixty and still be swallowing an undigested lump of anger.

My stomach interrupted my morose thoughts. My stomach was probably making me more morose than the situation warranted—I hadn't eaten breakfast and it was long past lunchtime. The kitchen didn't hold anything more appetizing than it had earlier in the week. I changed into lightweight cotton pants and a T-shirt, stopped at the Belmont Diner for a BLT with fries, and drove south.

14

Luther Revisited

Mitch's old address on Thirty-fifth Street proved to be anther rooming house, but it was quite a step up from Mrs. Polter's. The house, a shabby white-painted frame, was scrupulously clean, from the well-scrubbed stoop to the living room where Ms. Coriolano talked to me. A woman of perhaps fifty, she explained that she managed the place for her mother, who had started renting rooms when her husband died falling from a scaffolding twenty years ago.

"It was hard to live on Social Security then—now it's impossible and Mama has arthritis, she can't walk, can't get up the stairs no more."

I clucked sympathetically and brought the conversation around to Mitch. Ms. Coriolano threw up her hands. He had lived with them for three years, brought in by one of the other boarders, Jake Sokolowski. Such a responsible, reliable man, of course they were happy to take in his friend, but Mr. Kruger *never* paid his rent on time. Not once. And stumbling in drunk late at night, waking Mama, who had trouble sleeping—what could she do? She gave him warning on warning, extension on extension, but finally had to throw him out.

"He set fire to the bedding in his sleep when he was drunk. We were lucky it was one of Mama's sleepless nights. She smelled smoke—she screamed—I woke up and put the fire out myself. Otherwise we would all be sleeping on benches in Grant Park right now."

She hadn't seen Mitch since the morning after the fire, when she'd made him leave, but she was happy for me to talk to Sokolowski. He was sitting in the minuscule backyard, sleeping with the Sunday *Herald-Star.* I had met him three years earlier

when he joined Kruger and Mr. Contreras in trying to defend Lotty's clinic. When I woke him
it was clear he didn't recognize me, but like Mitch
he enthusiastically remembered the fight.

Mitch being missing didn't worry Sokolowski
much. "Probably sleeping off a bender someplace. It's not like Sal to worry over a guy like
Mitch. He must be drinking too much of that
swill he calls grappa."

When pressed, he thought back to the last time
he'd seen Mitch. After much internal debate he
decided it had been last Monday afternoon.
Mitch had stopped by to persuade Jake to join
him in a drink. "But I know what those drinks
with Mitch are like. The next thing you know
he's had ten and you either have to carry him
home or pay to repair a window."

As Tessie had suggested, Mitch had a regular
bar near the Coriolano house, Paul's Place at the
corner of 36th and Seely. Jake was sure that's
where Mitch would have gone on Monday. He
resettled himself under the sports pages as I
headed back into the house.

I thanked Ms. Coriolano for her help and
walked over to Paul's Place. It was a sparely furnished storefront, more Spartan than Tessie's,
with a half-dozen men watching the Sox on a
small color set high on the wall behind the bar.
The bartender, a bald man in his sixties with big
forearms and a tidy round potbelly, chewed on
a toothpick. He leaned against the wall at the
end of the bar, watching the game, bringing refills

to his regulars but not paying any attention to me.

I waited respectfully until Ozzie Guillen turned a perfect double play, and then brought out my threadbare inquiries. In a place where people knew Mitch well I didn't try to pass myself off as a niece, but explained that I was a friend of Mr. Contreras. None of them knew him, but they all knew Mitch, as did the bartender.

"I know Tonia finally threw him out," he offered, moving the toothpick to the corner of his mouth. "He was around here trying to cadge a room. None of us would bite: we know the guy too well."

"When did you see him last?"

They debated it, but the Sox came to bat before they reached a conclusion. It wasn't Jack Morris's lucky day: the Sox sent seven men to the plate and scored four runs on a series of errors and Sammy Sosa's double. The half-inning went on so long that the group had forgotten me and Mitch Kruger. I brought them back to the question of when they'd seen him last.

"It had to be Monday," the bartender finally said. "He bought drinks for everyone. Mitch is a generous guy when he's flush, so we ask him did he win big at Hawthorne. He says no, but he's going to be a rich guy before long and he isn't one to forget his friends."

None of them could add to that, although they murmured agreement—Mitch was generous when he had money. After a week had passed they couldn't remember where he'd been heading when he left, or if he'd said anything else about what was going to make him rich. I stayed long enough to see the Tigers go down in order in the sixth before driving northeast to the Loop.

Ever since phoning Dick on Friday night I'd been wondering what I could do about Todd Pichea. After all, I'd told Dick I was on Pichea's case. I could hardly admit it was just bluster. Besides, I really did want to do something about the little flea. But between agitation and humiliation I hadn't been able to think of anything until I saw Jake Sokolowski dozing under the *Herald-Star*.

The South Loop hasn't yet attracted the kind of chichi shops that stay open on Sunday afternoons. I didn't have any trouble parking in front of the Pulteney building. We don't have a doorman or a security guard to keep it open all weekend. The crusty super, Tom Czarnik, locks the front door at noon on Saturday and reopens it at seven on Monday morning. Occasionally he even arranges for someone to run a mop around the lobby floor. I hunted among my keys for the wide brass one that worked the front door dead bolt and wrestled with the stiff lock. Every time I make a Sunday visit I vow to bring a can of graphite with me to loosen the lock, but I do it so seldom that I forget between trips.

Czarnik had shut down the elevator power and locked the fire door at the bottom of the stairs. He doesn't do this because he's safety conscious, but from a bitter enmity against all the tenants. I'd long since managed to make keys for both the elevator and the stairwell, but I took the stairs; the elevator's too chancy and I didn't want to spend the next seventeen hours stuck in it.

Up in my office I tried Murray Ryerson at the *Herald-Star*. He wasn't at work or at home. I left messages at both places and pulled the cover from my mother's old Olivetti, the obsolete machine I use for bills and correspondence. It was one of my few tangible legacies from her; its presence comforted me through my six years at the University of Chicago. Even now I can't bear to turn it in for a computer, let alone an electric typewriter. Besides, using it keeps my gun wrist strong.

I thought carefully before I started to type.

Why was Todd Pichea of Crawford, Mead, Wilton, and Dunwhittie, so anxious to take over the legal affairs of Harriet Frizell that he rushed a probate court representative to her Cook County Hospital bedside? Why was his first action on becoming her legal guardian to put her dogs to sleep? Was his sole aim in making her his ward the power to kill her dogs? Or does he have designs on her property as well? Does the firm of Crawford, Mead support Pichea's action? And if so, why? Enquiring minds want to know.

I signed my name and made five copies—my

concession to modernity is a desktop copier. My own copy I stuck in a folder labeled FRIZELL, which I placed in my client files. I put another in an envelope to Murray. The other four I planned to deliver in person: three at Dick's firm—one to Dick himself, one to Todd, and a third to Leigh Wilton, one of the senior partners whom I knew. The original was addressed to the *Chicago Lawyer.*

I drove over to the new building on LaSalle where Crawford, Mead had moved their offices last year. It was one of my favorites in the West Loop, with a curved amber facade that reflected the profile of the skyline at sunset. I wouldn't have minded an office there. It was second on my list of purchases, after a new pair of Nikes.

The guard in the lobby was watching the last of the Sox game; he motioned me toward the sign-in sheet, but didn't care much what I did as long as I didn't interrupt the final out. Only one elevator was turned on, its interior upholstered in pale orange to match the building's amber glass. It sucked me up to the thirtieth floor, where it decanted me in about twenty seconds.

Crawford, Mead had moved the carved wooden doors from their old headquarters. As soon as you saw those massive doors, inlaid into gray worsted walls, you knew you'd be paying three hundred dollars an hour for the privilege of whispering guilty secrets to the high priests beyond.

The doors were locked. I was tempted to pull

out my picklocks and leave my messages on my targets' desks personally, but I heard muffled voices on the far side of the doors. No doubt juniors hard at work, adding to the firm's blood supply, its billable hours. The door didn't have a mail slot. I moistened the tips of the envelopes and stuck them to the door, with Dick's and Todd's and Leigh Wilton's names typed in black and underlined in red. I felt a bit like Martin Luther taking on the pope at Wittenberg.

The *Chicago Lawyer*'s offices were closed. After dropping the original through their mail slot, I felt I'd earned real food for a change. I stopped at a supermarket and loaded up on fruit and vegetables, new yogurt, staples, and a selection of meat and chicken for the freezer. They had some fresh-looking salmon in their fish case. I bought enough for two and grilled some for Mr. Contreras on my miniature back porch.

Before bringing him up-to-date on my search for Mitch Kruger, I had to tell him about Mrs. Frizell's dogs. He was angry and miserable at the same time.

"I know you don't think I can handle Peppy, but why couldn't you bring the dogs over here? They could've hung out in the back and not gotten in anyone's way."

By the time he finished I was feeling wretched myself. I should have made better arrangements for them; I just didn't expect Todd Pichea to move so fast, or so cruelly.

"I'm sorry," I said inadequately. "You'd think

133

after all these years I've worked with human slime I'd have been prepared for him and Chrissie. Somehow you never expect it to happen in your own neighborhood, though."

He patted my hand. "Yeah, doll, I know. I shouldn't take it out on you. It's just the thought of those poor helpless animals—and then you think, heck, it could be Peppy and her puppies. . . . But I don't mean to pound on you harder than you are on yourself. What are you going to do? About them Picheas, I mean."

I told him what I'd done this afternoon. He was disappointed—he'd hoped for something more direct and violent. In the end he agreed that we had to move cautiously—and with the law. After a few glasses of grappa he left, somber, but not as outraged as I'd feared.

I had planned to make the probate court my first stop Monday morning, but before my alarm rang Dick was on the phone to me. It was only seven-thirty. His light, barking baritone pounded my eardrums before I was awake enough to sort out the harangue.

"Hold on, Dick. You woke me up. Can I call you back in ten minutes?"

"No, you goddamned well cannot. How dare you go pasting envelopes on our office door? Didn't anyone ever tell you about the mail?"

I sat up in bed and rubbed my eyes. "Oh, it's not the content you object to, but the paste on the firm's sacred doors? I'll come over with an S.O.S. pad and scrub them down."

"Yes, I damned well do object to the contents. How dare you make a totally private matter public in this way? Fortunately I got here before Leigh did and took his copy

"Good thing I brought them in person," I interrupted. "You could be facing arrest for tampering with the mail instead of just charges of vulgarity for lifting someone else's correspondence."

He swept past my interruption. "I have a call in to August Dickerson at the *Lawyer*. He's a personal friend; I think I can count on him to quash any mention of Todd's private affairs."

"Why can't you just say 'suppress'?" I asked irritably. "Aren't you past the age where you need to show how many wonderful legal terms you know? You make me think of the Northwestern medical residents who always wear their doctor gowns to the grocery store across the street. . . . Can you really keep the *Chicago Lawyer* from printing my letter? What about the *Herald-Star*? Is Marshall Townley also a personal friend? Or is he just a client of Crawford, Mead?" Townley published the paper.

"You know I can't reveal our client list," he snorted.

I kept my voice humble. "The thing is, I also sent a copy of the letter to a reporter I know. He might not do anything with it as it stands, but you going out of your way to keep it out of the legal rag—well, that *is* news, Dick. You should tell your secretary to stand by for a call from

Murray Ryerson. And I'll mail another copy to Leigh Wilton. Maybe you can bribe the receptionist to bring it to you when it arrives."

His final words to me were not a pledge of everlasting friendship.

15

Step Aside, Sisyphus

The morning went downhill from there. On my way back from my run I stopped to talk to Mrs. Hellstrom. I realized I'd been too upset Friday night to tell her what had happened to the dogs. Distress made her voluble. She grew even more dismayed when I broke in to tell her about Mrs. Frizell's condition.

"I'll have to go over there this morning to visit. Mr. Hellstrom doesn't like me having anything to do with her, she's an unpleasant neighbor in some ways, but we've been through a lot together. I can't leave her rotting there."

"The nurses don't want her told about her dogs until she's stronger," I warned.

"As if I would do such a cruel thing. But that Mr. Pichea—can you be sure *he* won't?"

A new worry. When I stopped at home to shower and have breakfast I called Nelle McDowell, the charge nurse at the women's orthopedic ward. When I explained the situation, and asked her please not to let either of the Picheas see Mrs. Frizell alone, she gave a sardonic crack of laughter.

"It's not that I disagree. I agree a hundred percent. But we're shorthanded here as it is. And he's the lady's legal guardian. I can't stop him if he wants to come visit her."

"I'm going down to the probate court this morning to see what I can do to challenge that guardianship agreement."

"Be my guest, Ms. Warshawski. But I gotta warn you, Mrs. Frizell does not act mentally competent. Even if you arrange a full-blown hearing instead of the shotgun affair we had last week, no one is going to think she can look after herself."

"Yeah, yeah." I hung up disgruntled. The only person with legal standing to complain was Byron Frizell, and he'd approved Pichea's appointment. I drove downtown to the Daley Center, where the civil courts are located, but I wasn't optimistic.

The probate court was less than sympathetic to my inquiries. An assistant state's attorney, who'd been in Little League when I went to law school, greeted me with the hostility typical of bureaucrats whose deeds are challenged. With a lofty tilt to his chin, he informed me that Mrs. Frizell's guardianship hearing had followed "appropriate procedures." The only grounds for challenging Pichea's guardianship—especially in light of Byron Frizell's support—would be incontrovertible proof that he was denuding the estate.

"By which time she'll be dead and it won't matter what he does with her estate," I said savagely.

The attorney raised supercilious eyebrows. "If you find any grounds for questioning Mr. Pichea's probity, you can come back to see me. But I'm going to have to report your inquiries to him; as the guardian, he needs to know who shows an interest in his ward's affairs."

I felt my eyeballs bulging with frustration, but forced an affable smile to my lips. "I'd be glad for Pichea to know I'm interested. In fact, you can tell him I'll be sticking to him like his underwear. There's always the faint chance that will keep him honest."

To make my morning as useless as possible I stopped across the street at the city's Department of Human Services to find out why they'd labeled Mrs. Frizell's dogs a menace to her health. The bureaucrats there weren't as hostile as the ones at the probate court; they were merely lethargic. When I identified myself as a lawyer with an interest in Mrs. Frizell's affairs, they dug up the report that had been filed with Emergency Services when the paramedics picked her up last Monday. Apparently Mr. Contreras hadn't scrubbed down the front hall well enough: one of the paramedics had trod in "fecal matter," as the report identified it, on her way out the door.

"That was just because Mrs. Frizell had been lying unconscious for twenty-four hours. She couldn't let the dogs out. The rest of the house was clean."

"The rest of the house was filthy, according to our report," the woman behind the counter said.

I flushed. "So she hadn't vacuumed lately. The dogs hadn't relieved themselves except by the door. She was very conscientious about letting them out."

"Our report says otherwise."

We batted it back and forth for a while, but I couldn't budge her. Helplessness was making me feel savage, but screaming obscenities would only hurt my cause. I finally got the woman to give me the name of the public servant who'd made up the report, but by now there wasn't any point in seeking him out.

As I hiked across the Loop to my office I wondered whether I could file a multimillion-dollar suit against Pichea and the city on Mrs. Frizell's behalf. The problem was, I didn't have standing. My best bet would be to find out something really disgusting about Todd and Chrissie. Other than their personalities, that is—something that would disgust a judge and jury.

Tom Czarnik was waiting for me in the lobby of the Pulteney Building. He hadn't shaved today. With his bristly chin and angry red eyes he looked like an extra from *Mutiny on the Bounty.*

"Was you in here on Sunday?" he demanded.

I smiled. "I pay my rent. I can come and go when I please without your permission."

"Someone left the stairwell door unlocked. I knew it had to be you."

"You track my footsteps through the layers of dust? Maybe I'll take you on; I could use a sharp-eyed assistant." I turned toward the elevator. "Machine working today? Or do I use the stairs again?"

"I'm warning you, Warshawski. You interfere with the safety of the building and I'll report you to the owners."

I pushed the elevator call button. "You get rid of a paying tenant and they're more likely to lynch you." Half the offices in the Pulteney were empty these days—people who could afford the rents were moving north to newer buildings.

The elevator creaked to the ground floor and I climbed in. The squeak of the shutting doors drowned Czarnik's farewell curse. When we clanked to a halt on the fourth floor I discovered his rather childish revenge: he'd used his master key to open my door, and propped it wide with an iron weight.

When I checked with my answering service I found Murray had returned my call. Max Loewenthal had also phoned, asking if I'd stop at his house for drinks tonight. His son and Or' Nivitsky were leaving for Europe in the morning. And I had a message from a company in Schaumburg wanting to know who was slipping their production secrets to a competitor.

I called Max to accept with pleasure. The serenity of his Evanston home would make a welcome relief from the places and people I'd been seeing lately. I phoned the Schaumburg outfit and arranged to see their operations vice president at two. And I caught Murray at his desk. He agreed to meet me for a sandwich at a place near the paper, but he wasn't enthusiastic about my story.

Lucy Moynihan, who owns and runs Carl's, plucked us from the line at the door and ushered us to one of the tables she saves for her regulars. She grew up in Detroit and is an unregenerate Tiger fan, so I had to wait for her and Murray to finish dissecting yesterday's game before I could tell him about Mrs. Frizell and her dogs.

"It's sad, Vic, but it's not a story," Murray said through a mouthful of hamburger. "I can't bring this to my editor. The first thing he'll want to know is how much you're motivated by your hatred of Yarborough."

"Dick hasn't got anything to do with this. Except that he and Pichea are at the same law firm. Don't you think it's interesting that he's getting the *Chicago Lawyer* to suppress my letter?"

"Frankly, no. I think he's protecting Crawford, Mead's fair name. Anyone would under the circumstances. Bring me some real dirt and I'll go to bat for you. This just doesn't cut it. You're on a crusade for the old lady and it's distorting your perspective."

"This *is* a story. It's happening all over the Lincoln Park perimeter as the yuppies muscle into old neighborhoods. People forced out of bunga-

141

lows they've spent a lifetime in to make way for the sacred gentrifiers. Only in this case Pichea's added a personal vendetta against an old woman because he hates her dogs."

Murray shook his head. "You're not selling me, V.I."

I pulled a five from my billfold and slapped it on the table, too angry to eat. "Don't come around asking me for favors in the future, Ryerson, because there won't be any."

As I stormed to the door I saw him pick up my turkey sandwich and start eating it. Great. Perfect conclusion to a bad morning.

On my way to Schaumburg I stopped at a fast foodery for a milkshake. I couldn't go indefinitely on anger and I wanted to present a professional front to my prospective clients. Fortunately I'd dressed for success today in a taupe trouser suit with a black cotton top. And since I drank the shake through a straw I didn't even spill any on myself.

The meeting took all afternoon. At five-thirty I left them with a proposal and joined the parking lot on Interstate 290 crawling back to Chicago. There wasn't any good way to get from the northwest suburbs to Evanston. There wasn't any good way to move in the northwest suburbs at this time of day, period. I got off at Golf Road to drive directly east. It wouldn't be any slower than staying on the expressway.

The Cubs were playing in Philadelphia. I

turned on the radio to see if the game had started, but got the inane blather Harry Carey called his pregame show. I switched to WBBM and the news. Nothing was going on in the world that I cared much about, from the baking of the Southwest to the news that the savings and loan bailout was now estimated at five hundred billion.

"Surprise, surprise," I muttered, trying NBC. Traffic was backed up on all the expressways as people like me returned to the city after frolicking in the suburbs. On Golf Road, too, although the man in the helicopter didn't mention it. I braked hard as a maroon Honda pulled into traffic from one of the five thousand strip malls lining the street. Stupid jerk. He pulled in behind me, close enough to ram me if I had to stop suddenly.

No one had identified the body of an elderly man pulled from the Chicago Sanitary and Ship Canal near Stickney earlier today. We got an agitated live report from Ellen Coleman, who had found the body when she and her husband, Fred, were walking along the side of the canal, scavenging for coins.

"And I said to Fred, I don't think I can face meatloaf tonight after seeing all that ground-up flesh," I mimicked savagely, turning back to Harry Carey.

It was six before I reached the outskirts of Evanston. My linen jacket was limp from sweat. When I checked my face in the rearview mirror I saw a black smudge across my cheek. My dark curls were lying wet on my forehead. I found a

Kleenex in my purse and scrubbed my face clean with spit. I couldn't do anything about the rest of my appearance.

Max's house was part of a small block that shared a private park and beach at the south end of Evanston. When I pulled into the driveway Max leaned over the side of the second-story porch.

"The front door is open, Vic; you can come on up."

A shallow step led to the porticoed front entrance. The air inside was still and cool. I couldn't imagine heat or sweat among the Chinese porcelains that filled niches and stands along the hall and stairwell. I felt sloppy and out of place in the midst of Max's immaculate tidiness. My black pumps had a film of dust on them that didn't belong on the red Persian runner lining the stairs.

The red carpeting continued in the upper hall, leading to the porch door. The porch had been enclosed with sliding screens, which were open now so that Max and Michael and Or' could watch the lake stained orange and pink in the reflection of the setting sun. Michael and Or' were sitting in one corner drinking iced tea. Max came forward to greet me, leading me by the hand to a nearby chair, and pressing a drink on me. I took a gin and tonic and felt some of the stress leave my shoulders.

Like the rest of the house, the porch was immaculate and beautifully furnished. The deck chairs were made of dark, polished wood covered in thick, flowered cushions. The occasional tables, unlike the glass or cast iron of most porch furniture, were constructed of the same wood with bright tile inlays. Blooming plants in Chinese pots stood on ledges around the perimeter.

A brake of dawn redwoods screened the porch from the house to the south; the front of the other house lay further back. Although shrieks from neighborhood children drifted up, we couldn't see anyone.

Lotty arrived a few minutes later and the conversation turned to music, and Or's and Michael's summer schedules. Or' was conducting at Tanglewood, he touring in the Far East. They would join up again in the fall for a tour in Eastern Europe, although both were worried by the anti-Semitic violence in that part of the world. Lotty seemed to have put her anger over Carol to one side, greeting me with a kiss and taking enthusiastic part in the conversation.

At seven-thirty I got up to go. They were moving on to a restaurant for dinner, but I'd had too long a day. I just wanted to get to bed.

Michael stood up with me. "We're flying back to London tomorrow. I'll go downstairs with you to say good-bye, Vic."

I thanked Max for his hospitality. "Good-bye, Or'. Good to meet you—and to hear your music."

The composer swung her arm in a farewell, as if signaling an orchestra. She didn't move from her chair. As Michael shut the screen door to the hall behind him I heard her commenting on the Cellini Quintet, which Max and Lotty knew well.

Michael held the door to the Trans Am for me. I shook his hand through the open window.

"Have a safe journey to London. I hope you didn't mind playing for those musical cretins last week?"

He flashed a grin. "At the time, I was ready to break my cello over their heads. The only thing that stopped me was its age. Now I can shrug them off with good grace. Or' and I will play her concerto at the Albert Hall this winter. She should get the response she deserves then. We raised a good-sized amount for Chicago Settlement; I keep reminding myself that that's the only reason we did it anyway."

"If I'd known my ex-husband was going to be filling the place with lawyers and tycoons, I could have warned you what the audience would be like. At least I can promise you he won't be in London."

He laughed and waited by the edge of the drive until I'd backed into the street. He didn't look much like Max, but he'd inherited his father's beautiful manners.

I honked at a maroon Honda that had suddenly decided to turn into traffic from a driveway. I turned the radio back on in time to hear Ellen Coleman's nausea again over finding the bloated body in the sanitary canal. I suddenly remembered Mitch Kruger. With the emotion I'd packed into worrying about Harriet Frizell I hadn't had a thought to spare today for the missing machinist.

Stickney. That was miles west of Kruger's hangouts around Damen. It couldn't possibly be he. But the old man could have fallen into the water, wandering around drunk and disoriented. I didn't know if the canal had a current. How far could a body travel in it in the course of the week since Kruger had last been seen?

I made the turn from Sheridan onto Lake Shore Drive. The traffic around me quickly speeded up to sixty, a good fifteen miles over the limit, but I dawdled along in the right-hand lane, trying to calculate how far away Stickney was and how fast the water would be moving to get a body down there. It wasn't a straight run, though. A corpse might get caught in the pilings going round a bend and be hung up for a few days.

I realized I didn't have the data to make any kind of analysis. Checking the traffic I moved the Trans Am into a higher gear. A Honda hovered a sedate two lengths behind me on the left; everyone else was zooming past at a good clip. I watched the Honda for a second to make sure it wasn't gaining on me, flashed my signal, and gave the car some gas.

It's stupid to buy a car whose cruising speed is one-twenty when the limit in your area is fifty-five or under. Stupider still to nose it toward its maximum without checking for blue-and-whites. One of them brought me down a few blocks north of Belmont. I pulled over to the verge and got out my license and bond card.

I squinted at his name badge. Officer Karwal, not a name I knew. He was in his fifties, with deep lines around his eyes and the usual slow moves of the traffic detail. He frowned over my license, then looked at me intently.

"Warshawski? Any relation to Tony Warshawski?"

"He was my father. Did you know him?" Tony had been dead thirteen years now, but there were still plenty of men on the force who'd worked with him.

It turned out Officer Karwal was one of the many rookies who'd trained with Tony during the four years my dad spent at the police academy. Karwal spent a good ten minutes reminiscing about my dad with me, patting my arm as he told me how sorry he was Tony had died.

"And you're all alone, huh? I never knew your ma, but everyone who did was crazy about her. Now, you know what Tony would say if he heard you'd been hot-rodding in that sports car of yours."

I did indeed. I'd been grounded for speeding when I was eighteen. Tony had pulled too many bodies from mangled cars to tolerate stupid driving.

"So you be careful. I'm not going to write you up this time, but I will if I have to stop you again."

Promising to be good I meekly put the Trans Am back into gear and drove to the Belmont exit at a placid forty-five. It was when I was stopped at the light on Broadway that I saw the Honda again, two cars behind me. Under the streetlamps I couldn't be sure it was maroon, but it looked that way.

Of course, Hondas are a dime a dozen and maroon is one of their more popular colors. Could be coincidence. I flashed my right-turn signal and dawdled up Broadway to Addison, then made a quick unsignaled turn onto Sheffield, where I parked next to Wrigley Field.

I walked briskly to the ticket booth, made a show of examining the hours it was open, then swung around to my left. The Honda had pulled over on the far side of Clark. I didn't stare at it, didn't want to let the guy know I'd spotted him, but walked briskly back to the Trans Am. He was in trouble, anyway; I could just head up Sheffield into the night and there wasn't much he could do about it.

I made a quick right onto Waveland, then took Halsted down to Diversey, where I headed for home. With an effort I remembered the name of the man I'd met at Diamond Head on Friday. Chamfers. He'd said he was going to investigate me—it looked like he was doing it.

16

Showdown at the OK Morgue

I needed to talk to Mr. Contreras, but first I wanted to bathe. Just a short bath and a short nap and I'd get back to my appointed rounds, I promised the conscience gods. The whisky I drank while I soaked was a mistake: it was after nine-thirty when the phone woke me again.

I stuck out an arm for it, but when I picked up the receiver the line went dead. I rolled over again on my side, but without fatigue and Johnnie Walker to numb me I remembered Mitch Kruger and the unknown body pulled out of the Sanitary Canal. I sat up in bed and began massaging my neck, stiffened from the anger I'd carried around most of the day.

I moved sluggishly to the kitchen and made coffee. Drinking it in quick, burning gulps I whipped together a frittata out of onions and chopped spinach. I ate it while I dressed, in cotton slacks and a cotton shirt since the evening was still muggy, and left the plate by the front door on my way downstairs. Mr. Contreras was still up; I could hear the faint blare of the TV from the other side of the door when I rang the bell.

"Oh, it's you, doll." He was wearing a sleeveless

undershirt over old workpants. "Let me just put something on. If I'd known you was coming I never would have got undressed."

I wanted to tell him I could stand the sight of his armpits, but knew he wouldn't feel comfortable talking to me without a shirt on. I waited in the doorway until he had covered himself.

"You got some word on Mitch, doll?"

"Can I come in? I don't. At least, I hope I don't. I got sidetracked today." I told him about my abortive efforts to go on the offensive with Todd Pichea.

Mr. Contreras spent several minutes on a highly colored description of both Todd and my ex-husband, ending with a predictable chant that he didn't know what I'd ever seen in Dick. "And it don't surprise me to hear Ryerson wouldn't help you. Guy's only interested in himself, if I've told you that once I've told you a hunnert times. I can see why you haven't had time to worry about Mitch, and anyway, you was down there yesterday, down at his old place. I guess I was jumping off the deep end, worrying about him. He'll just turn up again one of these days, like the bad penny he is."

"This is the hard part," I said awkwardly. "When I was listening to the radio on the way home, they had a report about pulling a man out of the canal. That was over in Stickney, so I don't see how it could be your friend. But I couldn't help wondering."

"In Stickney?" Mr. Contreras repeated.

"What would Mitch've been doing down in Stickney?"

"I agree. I'm sure I'm wrong. But I thought maybe we should take a look at the guy's body anyway."

"Now, you mean?"

"We can wait until morning. If it isn't Kruger I can't do anything tonight to find him. And if it is, well, he'll still be at the morgue in the morning."

Mr. Contreras rubbed the side of his face. "Well, if you're up to it, doll, I guess I'd just as soon go now and get it over with."

I nodded. "I brought my car keys with me just in case. You ready to leave?"

"Yeah, I guess. Maybe I'll just let the princess out first."

While I waited for Mr. Contreras to go through the laborious business of securing his front door, I suddenly thought of the phone call that woke me up. If I'd lost someone I was following that's what I might do: phone her home base to see if she answered. If my companions were back in business, did it matter if they followed me to the morgue? If they belonged to Diamond Head it couldn't possibly be of interest to them.

"What did they say that made you think it might be Mitch?" Mr. Contreras asked when we were buckled into the Trans Am.

I shook my head. "I don't know. It just sounded possible. I'd been down Friday looking at the Sanitary Canal. Diamond Head fronts it; Mrs.

Polter's boardinghouse isn't that far away. I could just see it happening somehow, his being drunk and going over the side while trying to make his way around the Diamond Head property."

"I ain't saying you're wrong, but Mitch and me worked there forty years, just about. He knows that place."

"You're right. I'm sure you're right." I forbore reminding him that it had been over a decade since they'd quit. I couldn't have found my way around the public defender's office drunk and in the dark after all these years. Probably not sober, either.

I turned right onto Diversey without signaling and looked in the rearview mirror. A couple of seconds later another set of lights followed me around the corner. It wasn't a Honda. Maybe someone else going down Racine to Diversey, or maybe they realized I'd spotted the Honda and had changed cars. At Ashland the second car let a few people turn onto the street in front of him, but it was still with me four blocks later when I started south on Damen.

Mr. Contreras was rambling on about some of his drunken adventures at Diamond Head, which were meant to prove you wouldn't fall in the soup even if you were stewed. I debated whether to tell him about the tail; it would take his mind off his worries and get him prepared for battle, if it came to that. Although my friends were following carelessly enough to invite con-frontation, I didn't want to push it. Giving into my angry impulses over the last four days had brought me nothing but misery. I wasn't going to compound my problems by confronting thugs when I wasn't at my best physically or mentally. I let Mr. Contreras ramble on, checking periodically to make sure they weren't going to ram us or start shooting.

The morgue was uncomfortably close to Cook County Hospital, just on the other side of Damen from it. An easy progression from surgery to autopsy. As I pulled into the lot outside the concrete cube housing the dead I glanced up the street, wondering what Mrs. Frizell was doing. Was she still lying like a corpse on her bed? Or was she trying to get well enough to go home to Bruce?

I turned off the ignition, but didn't get out until the car that had been tailing us continued east on Harrison. In the dark it was impossible to tell what model it was: anything relatively small and modern, from a Toyota to a Dodge.

An ambulance had pulled up outside the big metal doors marked DELIVERIES. Really, it was just like the loading bays at Diamond Head and the neighboring plants I'd seen on Friday. Here it was bodies instead of motors, but the attendants handled their load with the same casual familiarity.

I waited with Mr. Contreras for someone to buzz us in through the main door. The place was kept locked even during the day. I don't know if the pathologists needed protection from the demented bereaved, or if the county was afraid

154

someone would run off with evidence in a murder case. Finally one of the guards deigned to listen to the doorbell and release the lock.

We went to the high counter immediately inside the entrance. Despite having watched us through the reinforced glass for five minutes, the attendant on duty continued his conversation with two women in lab smocks lounging in a nearby doorway.

I cleared my throat loudly. "I'm here to try to identify a body."

The attendant finally looked up at us. "Name?"

"I'm V. I. Warshawski. This is Salvatore Contreras."

"Not yours," the man said impatiently. "The person you've come to ID."

Mr. Contreras started to say "Mitch Kruger," but I cut him off.

"The man who was pulled out of the Sanitary Canal this morning. We may know who he is."

The attendant eyed me suspiciously. Finally he picked up the phone in front of him and carried on a low-key conversation, his palm cupping the mouthpiece.

When he'd finished he gestured to some vinyl chairs chained together against the wall. "Have a seat. Someone will be with you in a minute."

The minute stretched into twenty while Mr. Contreras fretted at my side. "What's going on, doll? How come we can't just go and look? This waiting is getting on my nerves. Reminds me of when Clara was in the hospital having Ruthie, they kept me waiting in a place that looked like a morgue"—he gave a bark of self-conscious laughter—"matter of fact, it did. Looked just like this place here. Waiting to see if it's good news or bad. You got her pregnant and she doesn't make it through, you carry that load around the rest of your life."

He rambled on nervously until the attendant unlocked the door again and a couple of sheriff's deputies came in. My stomach knotted. Chicago's finest can be a pain to deal with, but for the most part they're professional police. Too much of the county law enforcement payroll is double-dipping for the mob to make them easy companions in the search for truth and justice.

The attendant jerked his head at us and the deputies came over. They were both white, young, and had the squared-off, mean faces you get when you have too much unrestrained power. I read their badges: Hendricks and Jaworski. I'd never remember which was which.

"So you two think you know something." It was the one labeled "Hendricks." His ugly tone set the scene.

"We don't know if we know anything or not," Mr. Contreras said, exasperated. "All we want is a chance to look at a body, 'stead of sitting around here all night waiting for someone to be good enough to pay attention to us. My old pal, Mitch Kruger, he's been missing for a week and my neighbor here's been trying to find him for

156

me. When she heard the story on the radio she thought maybe it was him."

It was a whole lot more story than I would have given under the circumstances, but I didn't stop him: The last thing I wanted was to make it look like Mr. Contreras and I had something to hide. I kept my face solemn and earnest: just a good-hearted neighbor helping out the elderly when they misplaced their pals.

The deputies stared at us unblinkingly. "You file a missing persons report on him?"

"We notified the nineteenth district," I said, before Mr. Contreras could blurt out that we hadn't.

"When was the last time you saw your friend?" Jaworski asked.

"I just finished telling you, it's been a week. What do we have to go through to see this body you got here?"

Both deputies' faces tightened into the same ugly expression. "Don't try to make trouble for us, old man. We ask the questions. You answer them. If you're a good enough boy we'll let you look at the body. That'll be a real treat for you."

The morgue attendants were leaning against the walls, waiting to see which way the fight developed. "Mr. Contreras is seventy-seven," I said. "He's old, he's tired, and the guy who's missing is his last friend from his neighborhood. He doesn't want trouble, and he's not trying to make it; he just wants to put his mind at rest. I'm sure

157

you wouldn't like to see your fathers or grand-fathers in this situation."

"What's your interest in this, babe?"

Hendricks again. As long as they kept their badges facing us I'd know who was talking. I resisted an impulse to crack his shinbone against my right toe.

"Just helping out my neighbor, sugar. Shall I call Dr. Vishnikov and get his permission to view the body?" Vishnikov was one of the assistant ME's, whom I knew from my PD days.

"Keep your pants on. We'll get into the morgue as soon as you answer our questions."

The outer door opened again. I looked past Jaworski's left shoulder and relaxed fractionally. It was Terry Finchley, a violent crimes detective from Area One.

"Terry," I called.

He'd gone to the counter to check something with the intake man, but he turned at my voice. "Vic!"

He came over. "What are you doing here?"

"Trying to ID a body. These deputies apparently pulled an old man out of the canal near Stickney today. My friend and I want to make sure it's not someone we know. Deputies Jaworski and Hendricks, this is Detective Finchley with the Chicago police."

They didn't like it, not one bit, me being on first-names with a Chicago cop and a black one to boot. They exchanged glares and jutted their chins out some more.

"We need to ask the girl and the old man a few questions, detective, so why don't you just butt out." The two had turned to look at Finchley, so I couldn't make out which was speaking.

"Can't do that," Finchley said easily. "Not if it's the guy they pulled out at Stickney. I just got asked to come in and take a look at him—seems they think he may belong to Chicago, not the county."

The deputies started looking meaner. I wondered if they were going to slug me or Finchley first. The hostility in their bodies radiated throughout the room; the man at the counter felt it and came around to the front. The attendants leaning on the wall behind us stopped their light conversation and moved closer to us too.

Hendricks and Jaworski saw them coming and looked angrily at each other. Since all three attendants were black, it was a good guess that they would side with Finchley if it came to a fight.

"Take him, then," Hendricks spat out. "We got better things to do than look after some dead alkie anyway."

He and Jaworski turned on their heels in unison and marched to the exit. I thought I heard one of them mutter "jigaboo" on his way out, but I didn't want to make a federal case of it.

17

Another Chicago Float Fish

"Thanks, Terry," I said gratefully. "I don't know if they were throwing their muscle around just to have a good time or if there's some real problem with the dead man."

"Both," Finchley said. "They like sticking out their chests and looking like storm troopers. And the guy they pulled out was dead before he went in the water. You think you know him?"

"We didn't get that far. We'd like to be able to look at the body." I tried to keep from sounding acerbic—Finchley had saved us from grief that might have taken the form of a blow to the jaw or an arrest.

"Who's your friend?"

"Salvatore Contreras. The closest thing to family the guy we're looking for has."

Mr. Contreras held out a hand to Finchley automatically, but said, "Strictly speaking, you know that ain't so, doll. He's got a wife and a kid out in Arizona, at least they was last I heard about them. She walked out on him thirty-five years ago, same as any sensible woman would do if her husband was drinking away his paycheck every Friday and leaving her and the kid in rags. But Mitch and I go way back, and he really doesn't have anyone else, officer, detective, I mean."

Finchley blinked under the barrage. "I don't think we need to send to Arizona for a next of kin. Let's just take a look at him."

He headed toward the dissecting room that lay to the right of the entrance. I put a hand on his arm.

"Maybe Mr. Contreras would rather look at the video screen. He's not as case-hardened as you are."

If you're too squeamish for a direct look at a body, the county will run a video camera over it; you can watch a screen in a small viewing room outside the cooler. That way it can seem like one more show where the dead all rise to walk again.

"Don't worry about me, cookie," Mr. Contreras assured me when I explained the procedure. "I was at Anzio, in case you forgot."

One of the attendants wheeled the body out of the cooler for us. A black plastic bag covered it up to the throat, but we got a good look at the head.

It had been in the Sanitary Canal for some days and the last week had been warm. The face was swollen and purple. I wouldn't have sworn to my own father in that shape, let alone a man I'd only met three or four times. The hair looked like Kruger's and the general shape of the head, beneath its bruised distension, seemed the same.

I felt a little queasy. I'm not as used to looking at dead bodies as I got to be in my days on the county defender's homicide task force. Mr. Contreras, by the greenish cast to his face, had likewise lost the immunity he'd acquired on the battlefields of Italy fifty years ago.

He cleared his throat and spoke in a husky voice. "It kinda looks like Mitch. I just can't be sure. The face—the face . . ." He waved a hand and his legs buckled.

The attendant caught him before he fell. I found a chair against one wall and pushed it over. The attendant sat him down and pushed his head into his lap. In the bustle of looking after him, finding a glass of water, and getting him to drink it, my own nausea passed.

After a few minutes Mr. Contreras sat up. "I'm sorry. Can't think what came over me. I don't know if that's Mitch or not. It's kind of hard to tell. Could you look at his left hand, cookie? He sliced off the top of his middle finger maybe thirty years ago, working drunk like he did too many afternoons. I was there and I shoulda seen what was coming, got him off the mill, but I just didn't think it was dangerous." Tears that had nothing to do with the old injury were flowing down his cheeks.

I forced myself back to the distended body. The attendant pulled the plastic down so that the left hand was visible. The fingers, too, were swollen and discolored, but it was clear that the middle one was missing most of its first joint.

Finchley nodded at me across the gurney. "That's good enough for me to go on. I need

162

to ask the two of you some questions. Think your friend can keep going for another few minutes?"

Mr. Contreras joined in my assurances about his toughness. Finchley led the way to a barren lounge around the corner from the cooler. Mr. Contreras didn't move with his usual bounce, but he'd recovered some of his color by the time we sat down.

"Not my lucky day," Finchley said, "finding you on top of a stiff I'm sent to look at."

"You mean it is your lucky day," I corrected. "For one thing, you wouldn't have an ID without me. For another, you'll be glad to have my help. I can work full-time on this, and you have dozens of other cases on your plate. . . . That is, was he killed? Or did he hit his head on something and fall in?"

Finchley pulled a scribbled note from his jacket pocket. "He had a pretty hefty blow to the back of the head, Vishnikov says. If he fell and hurt himself, he fell backward. And since he was dead before he went into the water, it would have had to've happened on the way in. It's possible some lowlife found him dead and rolled him in—lots of drugs get done along the water there. The punks wouldn't want to be burdened with calling the cops on a dead body. It wouldn't surprise me if it happened that way."

I agreed. "Or Mitch was lurching around down there and interrupted a buy and some guy knocked him cold for his pains. And then panicked when he realized he was dead. I can see that."

"But why was he at the canal?" Finchley asked. "It's all industry down there—not the kind of place you go for a midnight stroll, no matter how drunk you are."

I looked over at Mr. Contreras. He didn't seem to be listening to our conversation.

"He used to work for Diamond Head Motors, down at Thirty-first and Damen. He might have been over there to see about work—he was pretty hard up by all reports."

Finchley jotted Diamond Head on the crumpled paper on his knee. "And what are you doing down here, Warshawski? You know that's the first question the lieutenant's going to ask me." The lieutenant being Bobby Mallory, less hostile to me than he used to be, but still not a big fan of my life's work. "Just pure dumb luck, detective. Mr. Contreras and I are neighbors. He hired me to find his friend. This is not my favorite way of meeting my professional obligations. . . . How long does Vishnikov think he was in the water?"

"About a week. When did either of you see him last?"

I shook my neighbor's arm gently and repeated the question to him. That jerked him back to the present, and he gave a stumbling account of his final weekend with Mitch, filled with self-reproach for kicking his friend out. Finchley asked him a few gentle questions and let us go.

164

"Just don't go charging around the South Side on this without talking to me first, okay, Vic?"

"If Mitch interrupted some druggies, they're all yours. I don't have the resources to go hunting out dopeheads, even if I had the desire. But something tells me that a dead old man without much family or connections isn't going to demand round-the-clock resources at Area One, either."

Finchley's shoulders sagged. "Don't lecture me on police and the community, Warshawski. I don't need it."

"Just talking about real life, Terry. It wasn't meant as an insult." I got up. "Thanks for saving Mr. Contreras and me from a rubber hose at the sheriff's office."

Finchley flashed one of his rare smiles. "We serve and protect, Vic; you know that."

Mr. Contreras didn't speak during the slow drive home. I was exhausted, so tired I could barely focus on the changing lights as we drifted north. If someone wanted to trail us back again, they were welcome to the job.

The day had begun with Dick's bellowing and ended with a decomposed corpse, with a trip to Schaumburg thrown in for light relief. I longed for some remote mountainside, for snow and a sense of perfect peace, but tomorrow I would have to rise and be ready to do battle again.

I waited with Mr. Contreras until he managed to undo his front door. "I'm coming in with you. You need hot tea with lots of milk and sugar."

He put up a half-hearted protest. "I'm going

165

to have some too," I told him. "Not a night for grappa or whisky."

The hands on his kitchen clock stood at midnight. It wasn't that late, not really. Surely it wasn't age that made my hands shake as I hunted in drawers and cupboards for tea. I finally found an old box of Lipton buried under some greasy potholders. It smelled stale, but tea never really goes bad. I used two bags to make a black potful. Mixed with sugar and milk it was a good restorative.

I watched Mr. Contreras while he drank his; his face lost some of its blankness and he wanted to talk. I listened while he went over stories from his and Mitch's boyhood, the time they'd put a frog in the collection bag at church, how they'd signed their apprenticeship papers the same morning—a detour about Ted Balbini, who sponsored them—and then how Mr. Contreras got drafted but Mitch was 4-F.

"He was already drinking too much, even then, but it was his flat feet that did him in. Broke his heart. Wouldn't come see me off when I left for Fort Hood, silly old goat. But we hooked up again after the war. Diamond Head took me back soon as I got home. That was when it was still owned by the family, not like nowadays when it's all a bunch of bosses out in the suburbs who don't care if you live or die." He paused to finish his tea. "You gotta do something about it, doll, go find who killed him."

I sat up, startled. "I don't think the police are

treating it like a murder case. You heard what Finchley said. He stumbled and fell while he was drunk and someone rolled him into the canal. I suppose some punk might have killed him after rolling him." I tried to imagine canvassing Pilsen for teenage drug lords and shuddered.

"Damn you, no!" Mr. Contreras shouted. "What would he've been walking around the river there for? That ain't sense. There's no place for anyone to walk—it's all company docks and barbed wire and dumps. You going to join the cops in pinning accident or suicide on him, you can just take your butt to hell as fast as possible."

I looked at him, astonished by the violence of his language, and saw the tears coursing down his leathery face again. I knelt by his chair and put an arm around his shoulders. "Hey, hey, don't carry on like that. I'll talk to Vishnikov in the morning and see what he thinks."

He grabbed my hand in a fierce hold, his jaw working as he tried to control his face. "Sorry, doll," he said huskily. "Sorry to break down and take it out on you. I know he was a pain in the tail, all that drink, but when it's your oldest friend you kinda overlook it."

He took his hand from mine and collapsed his face into his palms, sobbing. "I should never have made him leave. Why did I have to make such a goddam fuss over the puppies? Peppy don't notice that kind of stuff, people snoring, it's all one to her. Why didn't I just let him camp out here a few days?"

167

18

Not the Jewel in the Crown

When I went for my run the next morning, I slipped out the back gate. Instead of my normal route to the harbor and back I ran west along side streets as far as the river. I kept my pace slow, not so much to check on my tail as to protect myself from shin splints on the rough roadway—it's hard to follow someone who's on foot when you're driving. I didn't think I was in physical danger from any tracking Chamfers might choose to do; I just hate for anyone to nose into my whereabouts.

I stopped to see Mr. Contreras before going up to shower. He'd recovered some of his normal vitality—his color was better and he was moving at a more natural gait than he had last night. I told him I was going down to Diamond Head and asked if he knew anyone who still worked there.

"It's all new people since my time, cookie. It might be there's one or two guys on the line who I'd recognize if I saw 'em, but the bosses are all new; the foreman and the shop steward, I don't even know their names. You want me to come along with you?"

I grinned at the eagerness in his voice. "Not

this trip. Maybe later if I don't make any head-way." I was planning a surreptitious approach to the plant; I figured I'd have better luck doing it solo.

I'd have even better success if whoever had tailed me yesterday didn't follow me there. And that meant shedding my wheels. My Trans Am, like Magnum's Ferrari, is about as easy to track as the linseed oil Sherlock Holmes laid down for Toby.

Lotty is the only person I know well enough to trade cars with. Since hers always show dents within the first month she owns them, I didn't want to turn my baby over to her. But the client must come first, I admonished myself sternly. After all, what was I paying two-fifty a month in insurance for?

While I finished dressing, I phoned Lotty at the clinic and explained my problem. She was happy to let me have the Cressida.

"I haven't driven a sports car since I had the use of a Morgan in 1948."

"That's what I'm afraid of," I said.

Lotty elected to be hurt. "I've been driving since before you were born, Victoria."

I bit back the obvious retorts—after all, she was doing me a favor. I told her where she'd find my car—Carol would drop her off at my place on her way home. I kissed the Trans Am good-bye as I passed it on my way to Belmont. "It's only for one day. Be brave and don't let her strip your gears."

When I got to the clinic, after a couple of bus changes, I was pretty sure I hadn't been followed. Even so, I made a few loops around the north side in Lotty's Cressida. When I decided I was clean I went over to the Kennedy and turned south.

In addition to the inevitable dents on the fenders, the gears were hard to find and the bearings seemed to be going on the clutch. I hoped I didn't have to get away from any place in a hurry. At least the car fit into Pilsen well.

Diamond Head was at the bottom of a cul-de-sac. I didn't want to drive up to the front door, where I'd not only be spotted easily but could also be trapped. I parked on Thirty-second Street and walked the few blocks north to the plant.

Semis were rocking the side streets, bringing materials in and out of the nearby factories, deepening the holes in the pockmarked asphalt. I stayed off the roadway and hiked along the weedy verge, tripping occasionally on the hillocks hidden in the high grasses. By the time I got to Diamond Head's entrance I was sweating freely and cursing myself for wearing loafers instead of my beat-up Nikes.

A few cars were parked on an asphalt square near the entrance. One was a late-model green Nissan, the others more pedestrian—Fords, Chevys, and a maroon Honda. I went over to look at it, but couldn't tell if it was the one that had been on my tail yesterday or not.

Inside the old brick building the air was cool

and quiet. I stood in the small foyer for a few minutes to recover from the heat. A hall opened in front of me, leading straight ahead to some old iron stairs and to metal double doors.

The doors and interior walls must have been built quite thick—I had to strain to hear any sounds of activity from the other side. Diamond Head made small motors for highly specialized use, primarily for controlling aircraft flaps. Maybe that didn't involve the kind of screaming tools I associate with industrial plants.

I tried to place the entrance in relation to where Chamfers had brought me last week. I was at the south end of the building and the loading bays were on the east. When I'd come in I'd been at the north end. Chamfers's office must lie somewhere on the other side of the iron staircase directly in front of me. I'd have to make a circuit of the place.

The heavy metal doors were locked shut. I tried both sets for several minutes, straining my shoulder muscles with the effort, but I had to give it up. I could go back out and retrace my ignominious entry through the loading bay, or I could see if the iron staircase led anywhere promising.

I started up the stairs when I noticed a normal-size door behind them. It was unpainted and in the dim hall light I hadn't seen it earlier. I came back down and tried it. It opened fairly easily and took me to the hall where Chamfers's office lay.

Six or seven office doors topped with chicken-wire glass were cut into the hall wall on the left side. On the right, just beyond the entrance I'd used, was another set of metal double doors. I tried these out of curiosity and found myself looking at a long, open assembly room. A dozen or so women were standing at high tables putting screws or something into the machines in front of them. A lone man was going over a piece of equipment with one of them. The room could easily have handled five times that number. It looked as though Diamond Head might have fallen on hard times.

I shut the doors and went on down the hall to try to find Chamfers. Or actually his secretary. I was hoping not to see the plant manager at all. I raked my fingers through my hair, hoping to make myself look a bit more professional, and poked my nose into the first door I came to.

Like most offices carved out of industrial space the room was a tiny cube, just big enough to hold some filing cabinets and a battered desk. A middle-aged man was hunched over a stack of papers, grasping the phone in his left hand as if it might float away otherwise. A few brown strands were combed over the receding hairline in front, but he'd given up the struggle to fit into his seersucker trousers. I didn't think he'd been part of the team I'd seen with Chamfers on Friday.

He didn't look up when I opened the door, but continued frowning over his papers. Finally he said, "Of course you haven't been paid. That's because you're not paying attention to our new payables policy. Everything has to be routed through Garfield in Bolingbroke." He listened some more, then said, "No, it wouldn't make sense for them to handle the orders as well. How can they possibly know out there what our requirements are? I can talk to the federal prosecutor if you won't deliver the copper by Friday."

They went back and forth some more on whether the feds needed to be involved. I eavesdropped unashamedly. My man apparently won, because he dusted his hands triumphantly when he hung up the phone. It was only then that he noticed me.

"I'm looking for your benefits manager," I said.

"What for?" His victory over the copper supplier made him truculent.

"Because I have a question about some benefits. For my father, who was laid off seven weeks ago. He's had to go into the hospital." That seemed like a safe bet, given the empty benches in the assembly room.

He frowned, not wanting to give away anything to anyone, but finally directed me to the third door up the hall from him.

My luck didn't hold when I found the proper door. The man in the tiny office had been in the cluster that saw my undignified entrance into the plant four days ago. At first he didn't recognize me, but as soon as I mentioned Mitch Kruger's name, Friday's episode came back to him. He frowned ferociously and picked up the phone.

"Milt? Dexter here. Did you know that female dick was back? The one who came around last week? You didn't? Well, she's with me right now."

He slammed the receiver down and folded his arms. "You just don't learn, do you, girlie?"

"Learn what, pork chop?" I saw a folding chair next to his filing cabinet and pulled it out flat to sit on.

"To mind your own business."

"I'm here doing just that. Answer a few simple questions about Mitch Kruger and you won't see me again."

He didn't say anything. Apparently we were waiting for Milt Chamfers. The plant manager arrived a few seconds later, his tie knotted up to his throat and his jacket on. This was going to be a formal meeting, and I was wearing socks instead of pantyhose.

"What are you doing here?" Chamfers demanded. "I thought I told you to get lost."

"Same thing that I was here for last week—to see who saw Mitch Kruger and when and where and all those other *w* questions they teach you in journalism and detecting schools."

"I don't know *who* this Kruger was, let alone when and where," Chamfers mimicked in a savage falsetto.

"Then I'll have to talk to everyone here at the plant until I find out who does, won't I."

"No you won't," he snapped, tightening his

thin lips until they disappeared into his chin. "This is private property and I can have you thrown out if you don't leave at once."

I tilted back in the folding chair until it touched the filing cabinet, and smiled a little. "It's a murder investigation now, sonny. I'm going to give you to the cops and you can explain to them why Mitch Kruger's name makes you so angry and agitated."

"I don't let *anyone* come into my plant snooping around, pretending they're looking for missing persons when they're really engaged in industrial espionage. If the cops want to talk to me about some old man who worked here twenty years ago, I'll talk to them. But not you."

"Then I'll just have to come at it from a different direction. You got a pretty small work crew here for such a big management staff, don't you?"

Chamfers and the benefits guy exchanged a look—guarded, wary—I couldn't quite make it out. Then Chamfers said, "And you keep wanting me to believe you're not scoping us out for someone. Who you really working for, Nancy Drew?"

I stood up and looked at him solemnly. "Lockheed, sonny, but keep it to yourself."

Chamfers once again stayed at my elbow while we made the long hike around to the front. Before we parted I said, "You want me to tell the guy tailing me where I left my car?"

His face shifted momentarily beneath its frown. He was surprised. At the news I had spotted my

175

tail? Or at the news I had one? Pondering that little conundrum I forgot to wave goodbye.

I walked down the road to where the tall grass cut off his view from the side of the building. Once there I hunkered down to wait. It was just about twelve. Maybe Chamfers brought a sandwich, but I was willing to bet he headed over to the little block of Italian restaurants four streets over. I pegged him for the later Nissan as well.

The grass hid me from the road, but it didn't protect me from the sun. It was also a favorite hangout for flies and bees. I was so hot and sweaty after a while that I stopped trying to brush them away when they landed on my arms. At one point I got a rather nasty fly bite. Finally, a few minutes before one, the Nissan drove past me with the flare of gravel I expected from Chamfers.

Staying in the grass along the verge I walked back to the plant. Another car was heading my way from the asphalt square; the maroon Honda, with the benefits manager at the wheel. I waited a few more minutes, but that seemed to be their output from the first shift.

I went back inside, to the door behind the stairwell, and reentered the machine assembly room. By now I figured I looked like someone who'd been doing roadwork on a chain gang all morning. The tops of the high windows had been pulled out on their hinges to let in some air, but it was still cooler in here than it was outside. The women in their tank tops or T-shirts and work pants didn't look particularly ruffled.

A half dozen were sitting near the door, eating sandwiches and talking softly in Spanish. The others stood alone or in pairs under the windows, looking vacantly at nothing, or talking desultorily. A couple in a far corner were having an intense interchange. This time they all saw me, all but the pair in the far corner, and conversation stopped.

"I'm looking for the foreman," I said.

"He's at lunch," one of the Spanish speakers said in heavily accented English. "You are looking for work?"

"No. Just the foreman. Is he in the building?"

One of the women pointed silently at a door at the far end of the room. It had a chicken-wire glass top; neon shone dimly through it. I made my way past the assembly tables toward it, but then stopped.

"Really, I'm looking for someone who might have seen my uncle last week. He used to work here, and he came back around a week ago yesterday." They stared at me blankly. "After that he fell into the canal and drowned. They only found his body yesterday."

A little buzz started behind me in Spanish. The group near the windows coalesced as though drawn by gravity. After a few minutes one of them asked what I wanted.

"I'm hoping someone might have seen him." I spread my hands in embarrassment. "He was an old man, a drunk, but my mother's brother. She wants to know if he talked to anyone, or if anyone saw him. The police don't care about him, but she needs to know—she'd like to know just when he died. He'd been in the water too long for the doctors to be able to tell her."

The buzz sounded approving. "What did he look like, this uncle of yours?" a heavyset woman about my own age asked.

I described Mitch as best I could. "He used to be a machinist here. For many years."

"Oh, a machinist. They work on the other side, you know." It was one of the women by the window speaking, a person of about fifty with a matted yellow perm. When she saw my blank look she added, "You have to go around all the offices and turn left, and then you come to the machine shop, honey."

I was turning back to the door when she said thoughtfully, "Maybe I seen your uncle, honey. Last Monday, you say? But I don't think it was then. It was before that he was around here. We were just getting off shift, see, and we could hear some hollering coming from the other end of the hall, and then this old guy came around the corner, kind of shuffling, and laughing a little to himself, and one of the bosses showed up behind him, still yelling."

"Do you know who it was? Which one of the bosses?" I tried not to speak too quickly.

She shook her head. "I wasn't really paying that much attention. You know, my mind was on dinner, what I felt up to cooking, what I might be able to find in the store, you know how that goes, honey."

"You don't remember what he was saying, do you?"

She chewed on her lower lip a minute, trying to remember. "It was more than a week ago, and I wasn't paying that much attention."

A younger woman standing near her spoke up. "I remember, because he looked just like my uncle Roy." She looked at me apologetically, as if not wanting to imply I had an uncle as bad as Roy. "I don't know who it was yelling, because the light was behind him, I could only see his shape, but he was just yelling at him to get the hell away from Diamond Head."

The far door opened and the foreman came out. "Time to get back to work, girls. Who you talking to here?"

"Just a girl."

He looked at me suspiciously.

"She thought maybe you were hiring, but we told her we were all lucky to still have the jobs we got." It was Roy's niece, protecting me the way she probably had to protect him, and her own mother, and perhaps herself as well.

"You shouldn't be on the work floor, girlie," he said to me. "You looking for a job, you should go to the office. It's marked real clear and this door ain't. So scoot."

I didn't say any of the things I was thinking of. He was the kind of guy who'd take it out on the other women as soon as I'd shut the door.

I moved down the hall at a good clip, not wanting to run into Dexter or any of the others on their way from the can or the lunchroom or whatever they did this time of day. Following the directions the woman in the assembly room had given me, I made it to the far side of the building and another set of high double metal doors. Beyond these clearly lay a machining room: it was filled with gigantic machines.

Their size was so monstrous that I somehow couldn't imagine a function associated with them. Large curls of steel lay on the floor near me, like the curls of wood that used to fall when my uncle Bernard was planing boards for shelves. Perhaps the monster above it was some kind of metal plane.

Lost in the scale of the machines were a dozen or so men in overalls or work clothes. The ones actively engaged with the tools wore goggles. As I saw sparks fly near me I stepped back nervously. I needed to find someone who wouldn't torch me or lose an arm himself if startled by a stranger. Finally I spied a man sitting at a drafting table in a corner and went over to him.

"I'm looking for the foreman."

He stared at me briefly, then pointed to the opposite corner without speaking. I threaded my way back past the machines, stopping to watch a giant drill move in and out of a thick metal bar on one side. On the other someone was raking more metal curls onto the floor. The men operating the equipment were totally oblivious of me.

Finally I moved to the far end of the floor, where I found yet another minuscle office. A man of about fifty sat behind a desk inside talking on the phone. His shirtsleeves were rolled up to reveal massive forearms. I'd be careful not to make him mad enough to want to pick up one of the presses and hit me over the head.

When he finally finished his conversation—which consisted mostly of a series of grunts and the statement that the fifteenth wasn't possible—he looked up at me and grunted again. I went through my wornout spiel about Uncle Mitch.

"Did you know him when he worked here?"

The foreman shook his head slowly, not blinking his flat, rather lizardlike eyes.

"I'd like to talk to some of the guys. A couple of them look old enough that maybe they overlapped a few years. He was around here a week or ten days ago. One of them was bound to have talked to him."

He shook his head again.

"You know they *didn't* talk to him?"

"I know you don't belong on this shop floor, girlie. So why don't you get your cute ass out of here before I move it for you."

I looked from his flat, lizard eyes back to his massive forearms and left with as much grace as I could muster.

19

The Prodigal Son

I sat in Lotty's car, drumming my fingers on the hot steering wheel, trying to decide what to do next. I felt as though everyone in Chicago had been bullying me the last few days, from Todd Pichea through the sheriff's deputies and now the crew at Diamond Head. It was time to fight back, or at least to prove that I wasn't just lying down in my sweaty clothes and dying because they'd frowned at me.

I couldn't decide what to do about Pichea after the failure of my letter to the *Chicago Lawyer* but the easiest way to take on Diamond Head would be to lie in wait for the end of the shift and tackle the guys as they came up the road for their cars or the bus. It would be a good two hours until then; I could fill in the time by getting a photo of Mitch Kruger to show them. Anyway, a photo would be essential if I was going to do door-to-door canvassing at the row of bungalows tucked beneath the Damen Avenue bridge. I didn't think Terry Finchley really had the enthusiasm necessary to add those inquiries to his investigation.

I didn't want to drive back north to see what Mr. Contreras might have. He might dredge up some old group picture from the local, but I doubted he had anything that would make a good identity aid. The real stumbling block, though, would be his desire to come down and take on the bosses in person. Not that I was doing such a great job on my own, but the old man saw himself as Mike Hammer and I wasn't ready yet for confrontation on that scale.

I thought I remembered a photo ID among the documents I'd found in Kruger's room at Mrs. Polter's house. Her place was almost close enough to walk to, but my hours in the hot sun had taken their toll; I moved Lotty's Cressida over to Archer.

Mrs. Polter was alone at her battle station—her tormentors must have found some cooler entertainment for the afternoon. A couple of men were coming out of Tessie's, but the rest of the street was quiet.

When I mounted the rickety steps I saw Mrs. Polter drinking something murky-brown out of a corrugated glass. It might have been instant iced tea, but it looked as though it had been mixed with transmission fluid. She was still wearing the brown gingham housedress. The fabric had frayed further on both sides of the safety pin, so her décolletage was better covered, but ominous holes were starting to open on the sides.

"That old man you was looking for—he's dead," she said abruptly.

"Oh, yeah? How'd you find out?"

"His son came. His boy. He told me when he come to collect the old man's stuff."

"All the way from Arizona, huh?" Mr. Contreras would have told me if he'd gotten in touch with Kruger's family. Had Terry Finchley done it? If so, young Kruger got here mighty fast—it was only fifteen hours since we'd identified the body.

"He didn't say nothing about Arizona. Just that he wanted his father's things. Not that he took all of them, but I figured since you'd paid for the room through the end of the week I might just as well leave them lay."

"I guess I could pick up the rest of his stuff. Take it off your hands."

She finished the brown murk and pulled a pitcher from the left side of the chair. "I'd offer you some, but I've only got the one glass. You look kinda thirsty."

I made a hasty gesture of refusal. I wasn't that hot.

"I was kinda thinking of his clothes for the Goodwill," she added.

Meaning she thought she could sell them, perhaps to her other lodgers. "If you think they want his clothes, be my guest. Let me just make sure this—son—didn't overlook something valuable."

Of course, anything valuable would be long gone, but Mitch Kruger hadn't had stocks or bearer bonds to worry about. There was no reason to be gratuitously offensive to the lady by suggesting as much. Mrs. Polter gave gracious consent to my searching Mitch's room once again.

184

After the glare of the street I couldn't see in the unlit stairwell. I felt my way cautiously up the stairs, not wanting to stumble on any loose pieces of linoleum. None of the other inhabitants was roaming the halls, but a fresh smell of bacon overlay the stale grease and cabbage in the air. Someone was having a late lunch, or a very late breakfast. My stomach rumbled sympathetically. I wondered if I could get a cheese sandwich at Tessie's when I finished here.

By the time I reached the top my eyes had adjusted enough to the dim light to find Mitch's room. Between Mrs. Polter and the son not much remained. Certainly not Kruger's union card or his pension paper—not even the newspaper clippings. I hadn't paid much attention to his clothes, so I couldn't tell if the landlady had already skimmed off anything, but the portable black-and-white set was gone. If I poked around until I found Mrs. Polter's room I'd probably discover it there. The temptation was strong, but I didn't have any real desire to confront her over it.

As I made my way back down I thought gloomily about my own old age, if I lived that long, and probable end. Would it be like this, in a derelict boardinghouse, with nothing but an old TV and some threadbare jeans for an ungrieving landlady to pick through? I wouldn't even have Mr. Contreras to mourn me. Just as my fantasies were reaching a peak of dreary loneliness, I caught my foot in a loose piece of linoleum and reached the bottom on my hands and knees. I swore and dusted myself off—nothing injured but my pride. If I went around daydreaming instead of keeping my wits about me, Mr. Contreras would at least survive to mourn me.

"That you falling in there?" Mrs. Polter asked when I regained the porch. "Thought I heard kind of a thud."

"But not worth your while to come investigate. You should get that linoleum tacked down. It'd be kind of hard for you to haul away your boarders' bodies if they tripped and croaked. . . . When did Mitch Kruger die?"

She shrugged majestic shoulders. "Couldn't tell you that, honey. But his son was by here first thing this morning. Matter of fact, I wasn't even up. He caught me still in my curlers."

That must have been an awe-inspiring sight. "What did he look like, this son?"

She moved her shoulders again. "I didn't take his picture. He was a youngish fella, maybe your age, maybe a little older."

"Did he leave a phone number in case you needed to reach him?"

"I don't have any call to reach him, honey. I told him the same I'm telling you: take what you want while the room's still paid for, 'cause at the end of the week I'm turning the rest over to the Goodwill."

It made me uneasy to give up the room, give up Mitch's last connection to life. I thought about shelling out another fifty to hang on to the room through next week. And yet, what could I possibly find in there?

Still uneasy, I crossed the street to Tessie's. She remembered me at once, even what I'd been drinking.

"You look kind of hot today, honey. Want another draw?"

I slid onto the stool. The thin brew soothed my raw throat. Her bar wasn't air-conditioned, but it was out of the glare of the sun. A fan blowing down the counter dried my sweat, giving me the illusion of coolness.

"I didn't have time for lunch. Do you sell sandwiches or anything?"

She shook her head regretfully. "The best I can do for you is a bag of chips or pretzels, honey."

I ate the pretzels with my second beer. We had the bar to ourselves. She was watching *Donahue* on a small black-and-white set tucked under the whisky bottles. The TV was too clean to have been Mitch's.

At a commercial break Tessie spoke without looking at me. "I hear they found that old man you were hunting last week, drowned in the San. They picked up his body yesterday, what I hear. Your uncle, did you say?"

I grunted noncommittally.

"Lily Polter said you were a detective. So was he an uncle or a skipper?"

"Neither. He grew up with an old friend of mine. My friend got upset when the guy went missing."

187

She flicked a fly with her bar towel. "I don't like being lied to. Most especially not in my own bar."

My cheeks reddened under my sunburn. "I figured if I came in here and announced I was a detective, someone might break a bottle of Old Overholt on my head."

Her eyes crinkled with unexpected laughter. "I might still do that. Especially if I find out you're lying to me this time around. What happened to the old boy?"

I shook my head. "You know as much as I do. He fell into the Sanitary Canal, but he was dead before he went in. I was over at Mrs. Polter's trying to find a photo, but some guy came by this morning, said he was my man's son, and took his union card and all his stuff that might have had a picture on it."

"Said he was his son?" she repeated. "You think he wasn't?"

"I don't think. All I do is ask questions. I didn't know anyone here in Chicago had an address for the son, and even if they did, he got here mighty fast. Still, maybe he had a nightmare warning him his father was dead and flew into town on the chance. You didn't see the guy, did you? Mrs. Polter couldn't give me a description."

"I'm not open that early, hon. But if I hear anything I'll let you know. Could be my old man saw something. He's had a stroke, but he likes to sit outside in the evenings and mornings, watch the street, same as he has for seventy years now."

I gave her my card and two dollars for the beers and the pretzels. As I headed for the door Tessie spoke again.

"You just somehow don't look like the kind of girl who would let a drunk old uncle drag around in circles. Something about the way you hold yourself, honey. I figure you're telling the truth when you say you're a detective."

That sounded like enough of a compliment to take some of the drag out of my step. I sketched a wave and went back into the heat.

It was getting to be time to go back to the plant and try to intercept some of the machinists on their way home, but my heart didn't leap at the idea. Two beers on any empty stomach after a day in the sun made me long for any alternative to physical action. Like a nap. Anyway, how effective could I be in my current shape? If someone looked at me cross-eyed I'd fall over. My wits weren't nimble enough to phrase questions that would be irresistible to answer.

I coaxed the Cressida into third and headed north on Halsted. At this hour it was faster to stay away from the expressways. Even Halsted was dense; I kept having to shift up and down at the lights. Tomorrow I'd return the Cressida and rent a car that worked right.

What I needed was a different approach to Diamond Head. I'd been butting my own head against a rock-hard wall there. I needed someone who might open the doors for me. I do a lot of work for industrial outfits in Chicago. It was possible that a grateful former client sat on the Diamond Head board. It was even possible that the owners, whoever they were, overlapped with some other company I'd worked for. Mr. Contreras kept saying Diamond Head had new owners; all I had to do was locate them. And that was something my trusty lawyer could do for me. He had a computer and access to the Lexus system—I didn't.

I got off Halsted at Jackson, where the remnants of Chicago's Greek community lie. I'd only turned there because Jackson was the direct route to my office, but the smell coming from the restaurants on the corners was too much for me. It was almost five, anyway, too late to ask Freeman Carter to start a search. I settled down with *taramasalata* and a plate of grilled squid and put the heat and frustrations of the day behind me.

20

Legal Enterprise

I had a hard time getting through to Freeman's office the next morning. The first three times I dialed I counted twenty rings before hanging up. What on earth had happened to their phone system? The call should have gone to a message center. The fourth time I rang someone picked up the phone without knowing where Freeman was.

His reluctance to take a message made me decide to go down in person.

I hadn't been inside Crawford, Mead's offices since they'd moved to their new crib near Wacker, but the walnut paneling, the russet Ferraghan hanging to the right of the entrance, and the two outsize Tang urns were all the same as they'd been on South LaSalle. Why move at all if you were just going to replicate your old surroundings at treble the cost?

Leah Caudwell had been the firm's receptionist since before Dick joined the firm. She had always liked me, and had seen me as an aggrieved party when Dick and I split up. Without exactly encouraging her to believe it, I'd never directly contradicted the idea; the wear and tear on Dick were my substitute for alimony.

I walked over to the reception counter with a cheery greeting on my lips, but found myself looking at a strange young woman easily thirty years Leah's junior. She was pencil thin, wearing a green knit sheath and a lavish amount of lipstick.

"Leah sick today?" I asked.

The young woman shook her head. "She quit when we moved last November. Can I help you?"

I felt unreasonably hurt that Leah had left without notifying me. With a little brusqueness I gave the young woman my name and told her I'd come to see Freeman.

"Oh, my. Did you have an appointment with him?"

"Nope. I spent the morning trying to get through on the phone and thought it would be easier to come in person. I'll talk to his secretary, though; what I need doesn't require his personal attention."

"Oh, my," she repeated helplessly, shaking her feathered curls. "Well, maybe you'd better talk to Catherine. If you'll have a seat I'll page her for you. What did you say your name was?"

Catherine Gentry was Freeman's secretary. Since she hadn't been answering his phone I didn't know that she would answer a page. The receptionist's manner made it clear that something was wrong with Freeman, but it seemed hopeless to get her to tell me anything. I handed her one of my cards and went over to the russet armchairs underneath the Ferraghan. When Dick started at the firm fourteen years ago he'd told me, awed, that the rug was insured for fifty thousand dollars. I suppose it was now worth three or four times that, but Dick's awe had probably diminished commensurately.

After I'd waited ten minutes, thumbing through the *Wall Street Journal* and back copies of *Newsweek*, a thickset young woman came out, whispered something to the receptionist, and came over to me.

"Are you Ms. Warshawski?" She made a credible stab at my last name. "I'm Vivian Copley. I'm one of the paralegals—I've done a lot of work for Mr. Carter recently. What did you need to see him about?"

"It's certainly something you could help me with, but is something wrong with Freeman? I haven't talked to him for a few weeks."

She put a hand over her mouth and giggled nervously. "Oh, dear. I hate . . . I don't know if we're supposed . . . but it'll probably be in the papers anyway."

"What?" I demanded sharply. I was getting tired of the helpless fluttering of the office staff.

"He announced his resignation from the firm on Friday. They asked him to pack up on the spot. Catherine's here today taking care of his files, but she'll be gone tomorrow. We're redirecting his clients to other partners, so if you tell me what you needed to see him about we can figure out who the best person to help you would be."

I studied my nails for a moment, wondering whether to ask for Dick or Todd Pichea. The effect would be electric, but what would I gain from it?

I got up. "Freeman's been handling my affairs for so many years I wouldn't feel comfortable working with anyone else. Why don't you just take me back to Catherine?"

She twisted a strand of hair around a finger. "We're really not supposed to—"

I smiled firmly. "Why don't you just take me to Catherine?"

"I think I need to talk to my boss about it first." She whisked back inside the doors that led to the firm's offices.

I waited about thirty seconds and followed her. Since I'd never been here before I didn't know where Freeman's office might lie. I picked the right-hand corridor at random and walked through the ankle-deep carpet, poking my head into offices and conference rooms. I passed lots of myrmidons laden down with files and computer printouts, but none who knew anything about Freeman Carter.

Crawford, Mead was renting four floors of the building. I came at one point to a private stairwell connecting the floors on the inside. Like the rest of the place it was heavily coated in wood and plush. It seemed weird to me—you buy space in the most modern of glass towers, and then cover it with wood and velvet to make it seem like an ancient courthouse.

When I got to the second floor I finally found an assistant somebody who could direct me to Freeman's office. The general interdict on giving information to clients apparently had only been issued to the frontline troops. Freeman was—had been—at the far end of the floor we were on. I followed the woman's directions with only a few missteps and finally found Catherine Gentry stuffing files into packing boxes.

"Vic!" She dropped what she was holding and wiped her hands on her jeans. I'd never seen her out of the severely tailored clothes she thought necessary for her job, or with her hair falling in wisps around her face. I wouldn't have recognized her on the street.

"Catherine! What's going on here? They act like Freeman ran off with the company pension fund."

"They're acting like the scumbags I always knew they were. I can't tell you how *happy* I am that we're out of this cockroach pit. I don't even mind having to do all this packing on my own. Well, hardly mind, anyway. Were you on Freeman's calendar? I thought I caught everyone." Catherine had grown up in Jackson, Mississippi, and she'd never made any effort to accommodate her accent to the Yankees around her.

"No. I was trying to call this morning and couldn't get through, so I came down in person. You need some help?"

She grinned. "I need it, honey, but these are all confidential files. I've got to look after them myself. What can we do for you? Freeman's spending the day at home, but if you've been arrested or something he'll be glad to leap into action."

"Nothing that interesting. I just wanted to look something up on Lexus; it can wait until you're in your new quarters." Or I could drive to Springfield and look up the records manually. Not my favorite activity, but maybe better than sitting on the problem another few weeks.

Catherine grunted. "Why don't you write down what you need for me? I've still got a couple of friends in this rathole. If they're not too jealous of me getting to jump ship, one of 'em might do the work for me."

I wrote down Diamond Head's address and line of business. "I just want the owners and the board of directors. I don't need any financial reports, at least not right now. Where will you be setting up shop?"

"Oh, Freeman found us a sweet little place down on South Clark. Nine hundred square feet. All we have to do is move in the desks and plug in the machine—not like here, where they were painting and papering and God knows what under our feet the first six months we were here. We're taking a week off first, and I can't wait."

"What's Leah Caudwell doing now?" I asked, handing her the piece of paper.

She made an unhappy face. " 'Bout eighteen months, two years ago, we just started handling so much business—I won't say she couldn't stay on top of it—but it wasn't like the old days, where she knew all the clients personally and they remembered her at Christmas and stuff. Some of the new people coming through here were just purely rude and she didn't like the atmosphere. So when we moved, they suggested that she not come along. I felt real sorry for her, but what could I do? . . . You gotta excuse me, Vic—I've got movers coming in three hours and I need to get all this stuff boxed up. Here's our new address you be sure 'n' come see us."

She handed me a business card with Freeman's name neatly embossed on it. He'd waited to leave until his new quarters were ready—the card listed both a phone and a fax. I was going to have to break down and get a fax myself—it was too hard to do business, at least my kind of business, without one. Even my favorite Loop deli wouldn't accept phone orders for lunch anymore—you had to fax ahead during the noon rush.

I was so deep in contemplation of the gap between me and modern technology that I didn't notice the people around me until someone grabbed my arm.

"That's her!" a voice shrieked.

It was the young receptionist. The person holding my arm was a member of the building's security force. When I tried to twist free his hold tightened.

"Sorry, ma'am. They tell me you went busting into their offices without permission, and they've asked me to see you off the premises."

"I'm a client," I protested. "At least, I was until you grabbed my arm."

We were blocking the stairs. A crowd was gathering below us when a man behind me demanded to know what the trouble was. I turned and smiled thankfully: it was Leigh Wilton, one of the senior partners. While we'd never been friends, he didn't share the active disdain toward me of many of his peers.

"Leigh—it's me—Vic Warshawski. I went back to try to talk to Freeman—didn't know you and he had parted company—and your receptionist here thought I was a mugger."

"Vic! How are you? Looking great." He patted the guard's shoulder. "You can let her go. And

Cindy, check with me before you turn the dogs loose on our clients, okay?"

The receptionist flushed. "Mr. Pichea came through. When I explained it to him, he called the guard. I just came along to identify her. I didn't mean—"

"I know you didn't, honey. But Mr. Pichea doesn't make the decisions around here. So why don't you go back to your desk. And you"—to the guard—"do you need me to clear anything up with your superiors?"

The guard shook his head and followed Cindy on a fast track to the door. Leigh thought it was such a good joke, my almost being arrested, that he insisted I come to his office for a cup of coffee. He called Pichea and made him join us. My neighbor's chagrin made up for a little of the humiliation I'd experienced the last few days.

"I'm going to have to put together a photo album of our clients so you young eager beavers don't send them all to jail," Leigh added.

"Todd and I know each other," I said. "We met over dogs. Fact is, he's got such an active social conscience, he's just about looking after our whole block right now."

Todd flushed a dull mahogany. "Mr. Yarborough knows about it, sir. He can explain it to you. If you'll excuse me, I was with a client when you called."

"Ah, these young guys, just can't take a joke. What's this about dogs, Vic?"

I gave him a short summary, in between a series

of phone calls. His attention was wandering long before I finished. "I'll look into it for you, Vic, let you know if I learn anything. Good to see you. Just give me advance notice the next time you come, so I can have the cops ready."

I forced a smile and left for my own office. I spent the afternoon on odd jobs—typing invoices, preparing a presentation for the Schaumburg company I'd seen on Monday, catching up on correspondence.

By the end of the day no word had come from Catherine on my Lexus search. I didn't have any way to get back in touch with her until she and Freeman started work next week. I left a message on their new office's answering machine just in case, but it looked as though I would have to drive to Springfield tomorrow.

At six I called Lotty to see if we could swap cars back tonight; with the Trans Am I could probably make the round trip in under five hours. She agreed, but without enthusiasm.

"What's wrong? You busy?"

She laughed self-consciously. "No. Just feeling sorry for myself. Today was Carol's last day. I feel—personally bereft. And Max keeps trying to make me be reasonable, which only makes me want to be as unreasonable as I possibly can."

"Well, I still love you, Lotty. Want me to take you out for dinner? You can scream and shout to your heart's content."

At that she gave a more natural laugh. "That's what the doctor ordered. Yes. Great idea. I'm running behind here. How about seven-thirty at I Popoli?"

I agreed readily and started going through the motions of tidying my office for the night. I was just heading out the door when the phone rang again. Thinking it might be Freeman, I went back to my desk. A smooth-voiced woman asked if I was indeed Ms. Warshawski, then commanded me to hold for Mr. Yarborough.

"Vic, what in hell were you doing poking through our offices this morning?" he demanded without preamble.

"Dick, that question is just loaded with negative pregnants. How on earth do you handle the affairs of your impressive clients when you express yourself so loosely?" I picked up a pen and sketched a row of jagged teeth on an envelope in front of me. Then I added a ball of fire erupting from them.

"You can't deny you were there. I heard about it from two people."

"You boys ever do any work in between bouts of gossip? I would like to remind you that my lawyer was a member of your firm until Friday. And if, not knowing either of his resignation or his dramatic expulsion from Paradise, one of his clients happened onto the premises, a judge would probably consider that an honest mistake. Especially since Leigh Wilton thought it was such a big joke."

"But if that judge learned you'd been told about it and then gone snooping through our private premises against our express orders he might think it was something else, even with Leigh on the stand for you."

Dick's voice had tightened to a hiss. I added a snake to the other side of my sketch and drew a couple of arms ending in boxing mitts. "What kind of creepy stuff are you doing that you're scared I'll come across?"

"We don't have anything to hide." Dick recovered his voice and reverted to petulance. "But knowing that you've got a vendetta against one of our associates, I would just as soon you didn't have a chance to damage any of his files."

"I know the boy's scared I'll break his kneecap, but his wife looks pretty fit and she's ten years younger than me—tell him I'd be afraid of the revenge she'd take."

"Vic, I know you like to turn everything I say into a joke just to make me mad. And it works. Every time, or damned near. But I'm calling to warn you to mind your own business. Regard it as a favor, okay?"

I stared at the phone in amazement. "Dick, what on earth are you talking about? I wanted some help from Freeman. I'm entitled to get it without your permission."

"Not when he's no longer a member of the firm, you're not. We tracked you down, unfortunately after you'd gone. Catherine Gentry was keeping her lip buttoned—I won't miss her smart mouth one minute—but the girl she gave your search request to wasn't afraid to do her duty."

"Meaning she was afraid of being fired. And unless you're breaking the child labor laws I expect it was a woman, not a girl."

Dick laughed tolerantly. "Woman, if it'll make you feel better. Be that as it may, you may not use Crawford, Mead's resources. Period."

"Aye, aye, captain. Just out of curiosity, why did Freeman have to leave so suddenly?"

"An internal matter of the firm, Vic. None of your damned business. Just keep to the affairs that are your concern. You do a good job with them. Why do you have to mess with mine?"

"Oh, you know those vows we swore—till death parted us—those old feelings die hard."

"If you'd cared about my affairs fourteen years ago, we'd still be married. Keep that in mind while you're scrambling for your rent.

He hung up without giving me a chance at the last word. So it still rankled, my lack of doelike devotion. Old feelings do indeed die hard.

21

Throwing a Friend to the Wolves

I got to the restaurant ahead of Lotty. A light, bright seafood place on Lincoln, I Popoli has a small garden where I like to sit in summer. During the afternoon, though, heavy storm clouds had moved into the city. It looked as though the unnaturally hot weather might be going to break. I took a table inside.

When I'd waited half an hour I figured Lotty'd been held up by a late-breaking emergency. I ordered a rum-and-tonic to tide me over and settled at the end of the bar, next to the window, where I could watch the street. Rain had started to fall, fat heavy drops that spattered on the pavement like broken eggs. By the time I finished my rum, the drops had built to a heavy curtain of water.

I started wondering if Lotty had crashed the Trans Am and was too chicken to tell me about it. Of course, that wasn't in Lotty's character: she had no fear of confrontation. Besides, she saw herself as a constant victim of other reckless maniacs. When I tried to ask her why my cars never suffered the damage hers did, she would pierce me with a stare and change the subject.

I went to the phone in the back of the restaurant to try calling her. I didn't get an answer, either at the clinic or her apartment, but when I left the booth she was standing in the middle of the room, water dripping around her, looking for me. It was only when I came up to her that I saw she was hurt. She had a graze and a purple lump on her forehead and I could see a stream of blood mixing with the rainwater on her left arm.

"Lotty!" I pulled her to me. "What happened to you?"

"Someone hit me." Her voice was dull and she held herself stiffly in my embrace.

"Hit you? Hit the car, you mean?"

"You know, Victoria, I think I would like to lie down."

The precision of her speech and her frozen posture frightened me as much as her wounds. I wondered if I should get her to a hospital, but decided to take her home and try to find someone to come look at her there. Maybe she needed her head x-rayed, but hospital emergency rooms are cold comfort for someone in shock; I'd rather get her warm before a doctor decided on the next move. I fumbled in my purse for the bills to pay my tab, couldn't find any and ended up just tossing a twenty on the bar.

I got an arm around Lotty and half lifted her to get her outside. She'd left the Trans Am parked rakishly against the curb. Despite the rain, which had darkened the sky, I could tell that the windshield was cracked. I couldn't help inspecting the left fender as I ushered Lotty into her own car. The headlamp had sprung, and the grille and the body had inverted their normal positions. I suppressed a twinge of anger: Lotty was badly hurt. The car was only a chunk of glass and metal, repairable after all.

My place is just around the corner from the restaurant, but Lotty would be more comfortable in her own home. Cursing the Cressida's slippery gears I made my way through the downpour to her building on Sheffield. She didn't say anything during the fifteen-minute drive, just stared in front of her, occasionally pressing her left arm, the arm that had been bleeding.

As soon as I got her undressed and tucked into bed with a cup of hot milk I called Max. When I described her injuries he demanded to know why I hadn't taken her to a hospital.

"Because—I don't know—I don't like hospitals. I've sat in emergency rooms with bruises and cuts like hers and they only make me feel worse. Can you find someone to look at her here? Let them decide whether she needs to be fed into the machine?"

Max didn't like it. As a hospital administrator he sees the places differently than I do. But he agreed that since she was home it would be a mistake to move her again right now. He was coming over himself, but said he would first roust out Arthur Gioia, an internist at Beth Israel.

"You don't know what happened?"

"She hasn't been talking. I wanted to get her into bed first."

When he finally hung up I went back to Lotty. I brought in a sponge and a bowl of warm water to clean the blood from her forehead and left arm. She had finished drinking the milk and was lying with her eyes closed, but I didn't think she was asleep.

I sat down next to her and started bathing her wounds. "Max is going to come over—he's pretty worried. And he's hunting up a doctor to take a look at you."

"I don't need a doctor. I am a doctor. I can tell there's nothing serious the matter with me."

It was a relief to hear her speak. "Do you remember how the accident happened?"

She frowned impatiently. "It wasn't an accident. I told you at the restaurant, someone hit me. Could you bring me some ice for my head, please?"

I sighed to myself as I went back to the kitchen. The accident was going to go into Lotty's annals of traffic mishaps—someone had hit her. Just more forcefully than usual.

I wrapped the ice in a kitchen towel and placed it gently on the purple bump. "Did you report it to the police?"

"The police came. They tried to make me go to a hospital, but I knew I was late to meet you, and I had to see you, Victoria."

I gently squeezed the fingers of her injured arm. She lay silent for a few minutes.

"I think they wanted you, you see."

"The police want me?" I asked cautiously.

"No, Vic. The people who hit me."

The ground shifted underfoot. "Lotty, darling Lotty, I know you're in pain and maybe concussed besides, but can you please tell me what happened? I thought you were in a car accident. I know the Trans Am is bashed in."

She nodded, then winced. The towel with the ice fell off her head onto the pillow with her movements. When I'd retrieved the cubes from the bed she marshaled her wits and told me her story. She'd come home from the clinic to shower and change. On her way out, just before she turned from Sheffield onto Addison, another car had come out of nowhere—as they always did with her—and ploughed into the front of the Trans Am.

She frowned. "I must have hit my head on the windshield then, but I don't think that cracked it—I think they did that when they started hitting the car with their bats. Anyway, I was furious. I can't stand these reckless drivers. They were never like that in London, and London traffic makes Chicago look like a cow town. So I got out of the car to tell them what I thought of them and to get their insurance information. That's when they climbed out and started hitting me. I was too stunned to react. Besides, I'm not like you, I didn't train under Muhammad Ali.

"I was yelling for help, but the rain was starting; no one was on the street. Any passing drivers were keeping strictly to themselves. The men were pounding on me and telling me to learn the hard way to mind my own business when a police car came by. As soon as they saw the police the men ran down the street. One of the police-men got out and tried chasing them, but of course they had a head start. They just abandoned their car right there. But as we were driving home I thought, they must have been confusing me with you. Because I was driving your car."

She was right. I knew she was as soon as she told me the men leaped out of their car to attack her. How many men, and what did they look like, I wanted to ask, but she wasn't in the mood for

207

interrogation. And it explained why she'd been in such a peculiar state: not from shock, but anger with me for putting her at risk.

"I'm sorry," I said. I couldn't think of anything else to say.

She kept her eyes shut, but her mouth twisted in the parody of a smile. "I am too. More than you, no doubt."

"Is that why you came to the restaurant? To twist a knife into my side?"

She opened her eyes at that and looked at me from under the ice pack. "No, Victoria. I came to you because I've never been so scared in my life, at least not since coming to America. And it seemed like your business. Something you might perhaps fix, make right for me, so I'm not frightened every time I step outside my house into my car."

I got down on my knees and put my arms around her. "I'll do my best, chief."

She shut her eyes again and lay there, breathing lightly, holding my hand, while we waited for Max and Art. I shivered to myself, picturing her under the assault, wishing I could remake the last few days and have it turn out that I'd kept the Trans Am, that I was the one they stopped. How far would they have gone if the police hadn't shown up? Left her with some broken bones? Maybe lying unconscious in the street, brain-damaged, or dead?

I couldn't keep my mind from its feverish circling. It was a relief when Max rang the bell, even though it was the prelude to a tough encounter with him. He hadn't found Art Gioia, but he'd brought Audrey Jameson. She was one of Beth Israel's more promising young house physicians; I knew her because she spent fifteen hours a week helping Lotty at the clinic.

Max went straight to Lotty, but Audrey stopped to talk to me before going to look at the patient. When I told her what had happened she clicked her tongue impatiently and followed Max into Lotty's bedroom. I sat under the fire-red painting in Lotty's living room and thumbed through a back issue of *National Geographic*. Max joined me a few minutes later.

"I can't believe you would do that to Lotty. Put her life at risk in that way."

I leaned back in the couch and squeezed my forehead with my left hand. "I don't want to hear about it, Max, at least not in that angry way. You must know I wouldn't have traded cars with Lotty if I thought there was a physical risk attached. And if you think I *would* do such a thing, then there's no point in talking."

"Why'd you do it, then?"

"I was being tailed. I wanted to move around with some freedom. Lotty agreed to trade cars with me. I see now I shouldn't have done it—but I couldn't have known it then."

Whoever had been following me didn't know me by sight or they wouldn't have jumped Lotty. Would Chamfers have used his own men instead of a detective agency? I thought of the guy I'd met on the loading dock last week. Bruno, I'd called him. What name had Chamfers used? I couldn't remember—my brain was scraping at the edges, like a needle on a record that wouldn't lift itself clear.

"I've known Lotty since she was fifteen," Max said abruptly. "She's sometimes the most infuriating person in the world. But I can't imagine the world without her."

"I've only known her since she was forty, but I can't imagine it without her either. Anyway, you can't blame me more than I blame myself."

Max finally moved his head, an almost-nod of not-quite assent. He went to the cupboard where Lotty keeps her brandy and poured some out. I took a glass from him, but set it down beside me untasted. We sat without speaking until Audrey came back out.

"She'll do. I'd like to send her in for X rays—I think her arm is cracked and should be in a cast, and just to be on the safe side she should have a CAT scan of her brain. But it'll keep till morning. I wrapped the arm up and gave her something to make her sleep. The only thing is, she wouldn't take it unless I promised her that Vic would stay here tonight. Okay with you, War-shawski?"

I nodded. Max, hurt that Lotty hadn't chosen him, offered to stay with me.

"Fine with me. You can have the spare bed—I'm going to pull the mattress off the daybed here and sleep on her bedroom floor in case she needs me."

Audrey's teeth showed momentarily, white against her mahogany skin, as she gave a snort of laughter. "No need to be a Victorian damsel, Vic. She's really going to be all right. You don't need to sponge her with lavender water or what-ever they used to do for fever victims."

"It's not that—it's just that she was badly frightened. If she wakes up disoriented I want to be there for her." It was the least I could do, after all.

"Whatever you want. . . . How about a snifter of that brandy before I head back into the rain?"

22

Bedside Watch

Before Audrey left she reminded me that she needed to report the assault to the police. She spoke belligerently, as though expecting me to try to conceal it.

"No, I agree," I said. "In fact, I want to call the local station and see what they know about it. You want to wait while I do that? They might send someone around."

Audrey went to the kitchen to make coffee. Like Lotty, she's an abstemious drinker—one glass of brandy would tide her over for the rest of the month. Max was on his second snifter, but then Lotty only buys Cordon Bleu for him.

211

I was in luck when I called the district station. Conrad Rawlings, a sergeant I know and like, was working the four-to-midnight shift. He promised to look up what they had on the assault and send someone over to talk to Audrey and me. Half an hour later, as Audrey, Max, and I were making laborious conversation, Conrad showed up in person. He had another officer, a young woman whose head barely cleared his armpits, in tow in case Lotty was up to making a statement.

"Absolutely not," Audrey said firmly. "She's sleeping now and I hope she'll keep on doing it until morning."

"Skolnik and Wirtz—the officers who interrupted the attack—got a sketchy statement from her," Rawlings said. "So I guess it can wait until tomorrow. But she wouldn't let them take her to a hospital—kept telling them she was a doctor and she would make decisions about her health care. They thought she was in a pretty good state of shock, maybe concussed besides, but her car was drivable and she could drive it, so they couldn't force her."

He waved an arm at the young woman. "This is Officer Galway. She'll be keeping some notes as we talk. Since we can't ask the doc, you tell us what happened, Warshawski, and why."

Audrey brought the coffee she'd made from the kitchen. Everyone took a cup except for me. I just couldn't feel like eating or drinking while

Lotty slept off the blows that had been meant for me.

I told Rawlings everything I knew—my visit to Chamfers five days before, Bruno the dockman, the tail, switching cars with Lotty. "I think the attack was meant for me. Especially because they kept telling her that maybe this would teach her to mind her own business. She said they abandoned the car—whose was it?"

Rawlings made a disgusted face. "That's one thing we *do* know. It belonged to an Eddie Mohr, who reported it stolen this morning. He lives south, near Kedzie.

"Anyone can report their car stolen," I said.

Before Rawlings could answer, Max asked how.

I shrugged. "You just call up and say it was stolen. It could be anywhere—at the bottom of a gravel pit where you pushed it, or being used by your pals—even by yourself—to attack people."

Max smiled sadly, depressed by this view of human nature, and slipped away to take a look at Lotty.

"Give me a break, Ms. W," Rawlings protested. "First thought on my mind. But the guy is seventy-two, retired, looking after his begonias or whatever they do down there, and the car had definitely been hot-wired. No, they must have realized you were wise to the tail. They wanted a car you couldn't ID when they managed to pick you up again. But they didn't know you personally. So that lets out this Bruno you talked about."

213

I hunched a shoulder impatiently. "He doesn't know me—I was just another dumb broad to him. And it's true I'm eight inches taller than Lotty, but compared to him we both look like shrimp. I wouldn't discount him."

Audrey gave a sharp nod of agreement; Officer Galway, who'd been mute through the interchange, suppressed a smile and made a note. All women have known guys who treat us like so many interchangeable parts.

"Anyone else on your case these days?" Rawlings asked.

I gave a bark of laughter. "Yeah, my ex. He's peeved at me, but then that's a chronic state with him."

After all, Dick had been laying down the law with an iron fist this afternoon. He'd even told me to mind my own business, the same words the thugs used to Lotty. For an evil minute I was tempted to present a damning case against him to Rawlings, just for the inconvenience of having the cops rooting around his life for a few days. But really, I didn't hate him—it wasn't worth the energy to be so spiteful.

"You know what they teach us at the academy, Ms. W—stay out of domestic quarrels unless you absolutely can't avoid 'em. You never told me what you were doing to get this Chamfers so agitated."

"Oh—that was Mr. Contreras." I explained about him and Mitch. "Terry Finchley's handling the case for Area One. I haven't talked to him

214

for a few days. Maybe he's found someone who saw Mitch go into the canal."

"If the Finch is on it, don't you think you could leave it in his hands?" Rawlings asked dryly. "He's quite capable, you know."

Finchley and Rawlings were active together in an African-American police fraternity. Each took a D'Artagnan-Athos view of slights toward the other.

"Your turn to give me a break, Sergeant. I know Finchley's a good detective, but I do wonder how much time he has to investigate a drunk rolling. And that seems to be how the department has tabbed it."

"And you don't?" Rawlings asked sharply.

"I don't have any evidence, Sergeant, of any kind, about anything."

But I had a lot of nagging questions, with the attack on Lotty heading the list. I was desperate to find some lever for prying Chamfers's mouth open. Someone down there had seen Mitch, someone knew what he was mumbling on about. Something they didn't want me to find out bad enough that they'd hire thugs to beat me up? Something so potent they knocked Mitch on the head and rolled him into the canal?

I looked up to see Rawlings staring at me narrowly. "You'd better not be concealing something I want to know."

"I know you well enough to like you, Sergeant, but not nearly well enough to figure out what kinds of things you want to know."

"Yeah, bat your baby blues at me. I think I'll just check in with the Finch, see what he's dug up on Kruger."

He busied himself with his lapel mike; a couple of minutes later Lotty's phone rang. Max, on his way back from the bedroom, reached to answer it. His face registered annoyance when Rawlings snatched the receiver from him, but he moved over to Audrey without saying anything.

Max and Audrey kept up a low-pitched conversation while Rawlings told Finchley about the attack on Lotty. Officer Galway got up to look at Lotty's books. With Rawlings's attention on his phone conversation much of her stiffness left her; she seemed young and rather frail for the weight of her equipment belt.

I moved restlessly to the bedroom to look at Lotty myself. She was breathing evenly, if deeply; her skin felt a little hot to my touch. When I came back to the living room Rawlings was still on the phone.

"So you want to check on this guy, this Simon, whose last name Warshawski doesn't know? What've you dug up down there?"

The next few minutes were a series of grunts. Before he hung up I tapped him on the arm.

"Mind if I ask a question, Rawlings?"

He covered the receiver with one large palm. "I'll be glad to pass it along, Ms. W."

Even good cops like to play power games. I curled my nose and turned away. "It'll keep until morning. Tell him I said 'hi.' "

216

Rawlings tapped my arm. "Don't get on your high horse, Ms. W. Enough bad will around here tonight already. . . . Terry? Vic Warshawski wants a word with you."

"Hi, Terry. How's it going? Did you locate Mitch Kruger's son?"

"You feeling good tonight, Vic? I did ask— beg—you to leave the investigation to me. Now that Dr. Herschel's been hurt, can't you understand why?"

I stiffened, but kept the anger out of my voice. "I didn't authorize the attack on her, Terry. You change your mind about Mitch? He didn't fall drunk into the canal after all?"

"I told Rawlings what progress we'd made on our investigation. If he wants to pass it along to you that's his decision."

"A citizen gets attacked and you guys turn ugly on me. I guess there's a connection, but it's not especially attractive. Before you hang up all hot and bothered, did you ever locate Kruger's son?"

Finchley breathed heavily. "He's been gone thirty-five years. I didn't think we needed to invest resources into tracking him down. Are you working on a theory that he came back to Chicago and killed his old man in a fit of rage over some hurt that happened all those years ago?"

I couldn't help laughing a little at the idea. "Gosh, I don't know. It's neat—I like it. If it was Ross Macdonald I'd even believe it. Just wondering. You want to talk to your buddy again before I hang up?"

217

Rawlings snatched the phone back from me. After a few more grunts he finished with, "You're the boss, Finch," and hung up.

"So what have the police found out about Mitch Kruger?" I asked.

"They're following some leads, Ms. W. Give them time."

"Oh, for God's sake, Rawlings. I'm not the local news. They haven't done anything, for the simple reason that his death doesn't seem important. Why can't you spit it out for a change? Have they even canvassed the neighborhood?"

His brown eyes narrowed, but he didn't say anything.

I smiled. "A week of my pay against a week of yours that they haven't talked to the neighbors."

His face loosened into a reluctant smile. "Don't tempt me. Terry talked to your boy Chamfers. Chamfers acknowledges that Mitch had been around trying to cadge some odd jobs, but said he'd never seen him himself—just heard from the foreman. Even if they were hiring, he says he wouldn't take on a guy as old as Kruger and a drunk in the bargain. The Finch is going to follow up on this dockhand who got so pissed at you, but he doesn't see a tie-in between the attack on the doc here and the plant."

"So why did he chew me out over it?" I demanded.

"Maybe he doesn't like you riding his tail. None of us enjoys it too much."

"Well, there's just one of me and ten thousand of you, so I think you guys can hold your own."

A quiet snort behind us from Officer Galway made Rawlings turn around. "You want something, Officer?"

She shook her head, her small oval face so devoid of expression that I thought I'd imagined the snicker.

Audrey patted Max's hand and came over to me. "And I think all of you can look after yourselves too. Vic, will you bring Lotty over to Beth Israel in the morning for X rays and stuff?"

"She okay? She felt feverish to me."

"She probably is a little. If she seems to get really hot or terribly restless in the night, give me a call. Otherwise I'll see you in the morning. Say around ten?"

I agreed and saw her to the door. Max decided to escort her to her car—Lotty's street isn't the most savory place to be alone in the dark.

I watched from the window with unseeing eyes, wondering who had gone to Mrs. Polter's posing as Mitch Kruger's son. Even if Finchley hadn't tried locating him the son might still have heard about Mitch's death some other way. Maybe through Jake Sokolowski. Since Jake and Mitch had lived together recently, Jake might have known how to get in touch with Mitch's old family. Even so, the son would have had to work some travel miracles to get to Mrs. Polter's so fast.

"What's on your mind, Ms. W.?" Rawlings said sharply.

I shook my head. "Not much. I'd like to get some sleep, tell you the truth."

He snorted. "Tell it for a change. I've been around you long enough to tell when you've suddenly felt a rabbit wriggling around in your hat. You can't wait to be by yourself so's you can pull it out and take a look at it. If you decide to share your little magic trick, call me in the morning. Galway—let's pack it in."

After he and the officer left I felt suddenly exhausted. Max helped me drag the mattress from the daybed into Lotty's room.

"You'll wake me if something goes wrong?" he demanded.

"Of course, Max," I said gently. It was only worry driving him, after all.

He smoothed her forehead with one square hand and went to the spare room.

23

Stiffed by Technology

Lotty made it safely through the night. She woke up around eight in a lot of pain, prepared to be grumpy. I moved the mattress back to the living room and helped her get dressed. Max brought her coffee and toast. She rejected the first for being too weak and the latter as too black.

Max kissed her on the side of the neck. "I didn't sleep last night, *Lottchen*, too worried about you. But if you're this rude I know you must be all right."

She gave a twisted smile and put out a hand. I didn't think I was necessary, either for the rest of that scene or for transporting Lotty to the hospital—that was clearly a duty Max was longing to take over. Telling Lotty I'd check in with her later I retrieved my car keys from her handbag and left.

I didn't have the patience today to save money by riding the CTA—I flagged a cab on Irving Park and headed for home. I hadn't had much sleep—every hour or two I'd imagine that Lotty had cried out and would sit up on my mattress, wide awake. After brushing my teeth and showering I was tempted to climb into my own bed for a real nap, but there was just too much to do.

I called Luke Edwards, who looks after my car for me. He's a terrific mechanic who has the outlook of a mortician. I cut off his gloomy prognostication on my Trans Am before he could turn it into a funeral oration and told him I'd have the car over in an hour. "I'll need a loaner. Can you give me one?"

"I don't know. Not if you drove the Trans Am into a tree, I can't."

"Yeah, well, someone else was driving and the

person who smashed into it did it on purpose. Do you have something I can borrow?"

"I suppose. Got an old Impala. It'll seem like a boat to you after driving that little Pontiac, but I'll bet you anything the engine runs better."

"I'm sure it will," I agreed hastily. "See you in an hour."

Next I explained my tale of woe to my insurance agent. She told me that before they could authorize any repairs their own inspector would have to look at the car. Not wanting to waste time arguing the point I gave her Luke's address and hung up.

Lack of sleep and the number of things I needed to do were making me frenzied. I kept buzzing from task to task, starting things that I couldn't finish. I looked up Eddie Mohr, the guy whose stolen car had rammed the Trans Am. Before calling him I remembered I wanted to get in touch with Freeman, and dropped the city directory to hunt for my address book. In the midst of my search I wondered if I should go see Mr. Contreras, get him to check on whether Jake Sokolowski had rousted out Mitch Kruger's son in Arizona.

And what about my gun? If someone was peeved enough with me to go ramming my car and assaulting the driver, I ought not go out unarmed. I went to the safe I'd built into my bedroom closet and took out the Smith & Wesson. It's the one thing in the house I always keep clean: an automatic that jams causes a lot more grief to the shooter than the shootee. Just to be sure I took it apart and started working a rag through the barrel. The methodical work helped steady my frenzied brain.

I was reassembling the gun when my phone rang. I carefully slipped the magazine in and reached across the bed for the phone.

"Vic! Freeman here. I left a message with your answering service. Didn't you get it?"

"Sorry, Freeman. I haven't checked with them." Before he could expostulate on my untidy business habits I explained about the accident to Lotty. "You must be a mind reader—calling you was my next to-do. Where are you?"

"Minding my own business in Northbrook. What the hell do you want with Diamond Head's directors?"

I'd been sprawled across the bed since reaching the phone, but at the vehemence in his voice I sat up straight. "Material to an investigation I'm undertaking. Why do you care?"

"You wouldn't be trying to spin me around without telling me the rules of the game you're playing, would you?"

"No games here, but it sounds pretty playful at your end. I went to your office without knowing your pals had locked the door after you. When I saw Catherine, she offered to do a search for me. Tell me how that spins you around."

"It's time you got your own computer, Warshawski. I'm not going to do that kind of errand for you. We may not have parted in the way I'd like best, but I'm not going to sign onto a vendetta against my partners. Former partners."

I clutched my hair, trying to steady the wobble in my head. "Why is it a vendetta for me to look something up on Lexus—to ask you to look it up, I mean."

"I wish I could see your face, V.I. I just can't be sure. . . ."

"About what?"

"About the purity of your heart. You're not always as frank with your own counsel as a lawyer could wish. Get your own computer," he repeated. "That's my best advice for you today."

He hung up while I was still fishing around for a response. I stared at the phone, too astounded even to feel angry. Dick must have called him to read him the riot act, but why would that make him treat me to such a tirade? Nothing Dick had ever said or done in the past had had that kind of effect on him. The parting from Crawford, Mead must have been exceedingly painful.

I wondered what would take longer—driving the four hundred miles to Springfield and back to look at the paper copy of the corporation files, or buying my own machine and figuring out how to dial up Lexus. I phoned Murray at the *Herald-Star.*

"You know Lotty Herschel got beat up last night?" I said without preamble.

"Christ, Vic. I'm fine, thank—how are you? Glad to see you're not bearing a grudge from the other day."

224

"I should be—you ate my sandwich, trough-hound. You care about Lotty?"

"Lots. How is she? How did she get beaten up? Where did it happen?" He sounded as though he was choking down a doughnut as he spoke.

"I'll tell you the whole story when you're through with your current snack. Only I need to come down and look at something on Lexus."

"You never call just to say hi, Warshawski. It's always because you want something."

The buzzing in my brain was starting to concentrate into a throb over my right temple. "Maybe if you hadn't been drooling at my bedside every time I had a close call the last few years I'd feel more like a friend and less like a piece of meat at a barbecue when we talk."

He paused a second, trying to decide whether that was a justifiable complaint. "Tell me what you want to know and I'll dial it up for you.

"N-o, no. You wouldn't give me the time of day over Pichea and Mrs. Frizell. I'll tell you what happened to Lotty, but the rest of my business is my business."

"I can get one of my gofers to find the story on Lotty."

"True," I said, "but they wouldn't have any of the inside details. Like how she happened to be driving my car. Stuff like that."

"Oh, screw you, Warshawski. Lotty's important to you, but she's not big news in this town. And I know neither of you will let me in with a camera. But come on down here. Let's get it over with."

"Thank you, Murray," I said meekly. "See you in two hours, okay?"

He grunted. "I won't be here, which maybe is just as well. But I'll fix you up with Lydia Cooper. Just ask for her when you get to the second floor."

It's hard to have a professional relationship that turns personal, although maybe the other way round is worse. When Murray and I first met a decade or so ago we'd felt a mutual attraction and had become lovers for a time. But our competition over the financial crime we both cover soured our private life. And now the memory of our love life gave a sour tinge to our professional dealings. Maybe I needed to invite him out for dinner and talk it through. That would certainly be the mature thing to do, but I was still a year from forty; I didn't have to be mature yet.

I stuck the gun in my shoulder holster and went down to Mr. Contreras's place. He was dismayed by the news about Lotty. I went through the details with him several times; on the third recital he suddenly realized I might be in danger.

"And you're just going to romp around the streets with no one looking after you."

"No one can look after me," I said. "Even a bodyguard can't protect you if someone is determined to get you. Look at whats-is name—the mobster who was gunned down in Lincolnwood."

"Alan Dortman," he supplied. "But even so, doll—"

"Even so, I don't see the point of you coming along and getting hurt too. You've taken a bad hit on the head and a bullet in the shoulder from getting too close to my problems. The next time someone assaults you I'm going to have to hand in my license and find a new career."

"I just hate sitting on the sidelines," he muttered.

I put a sympathetic arm around him—I sure knew that feeling. "There is something you could do." I told him about the guy who'd come by Mrs. Polter's claiming to be Mitch's son. "Can you talk to Jake about that?"

He brightened somewhat. It wasn't as good as the possibility of slugging someone with a pipe wrench, but at least it was action. I told him I'd be out all day, but I'd check in around five.

"Mind you do, doll. Maybe you could call me around one or something—I don't want to spend the whole day wondering if someone took after you with a bulldozer."

Normally his protectiveness makes me prickly, but the attack on Lotty had shaken me. I could see how you could sit around worrying about someone you loved. I promised, kissed him on the cheek, and took off.

It was past noon by the time Luke finished his funeral oration on the damage to the Trans Am. Since he wouldn't hand over the keys to the Impala until he'd had a chance to say everything he wanted on the subject of the state of modern car manufacture in general, Pontiac more specifically, and my car as a particular example, I had to listen with what grace I could muster.

He was right about the Impala: it rode like a bus after the Trans Am. But its engine felt like spun silk to handle. I maneuvered it cautiously into traffic, getting a feel for its sidelines, and keeping an eye out for uninvited company. I didn't think anyone had followed me to the garage, but I didn't want to be foolhardy.

Remembering my promise to Mr. Contreras, I phoned from the lobby of the *Herald-Star.* When he didn't answer I figured he was out with Peppy and went on up to the news floor to talk to the young reporter Murray had assigned me to.

Lydia Cooper, Murray's gofer, looked as though she was fresh from journalism school. In fact, with her red, round cheeks and fluffy black bangs she looked as though she were on her way to a high school class. She had a thick Midwestern twang; when I asked, she grinned and said she came from Kansas.

"And please don't ask about Toto or whether everything there's in black and white. Believe me, I've heard it a million times already and I've only been in Chicago eleven months."

Murray had apparently passed along my request without any baggage—she cheerfully offered to fix me up with the Lexus system as soon as we finished talking.

I gave her the details of the attack on Lotty.

With Lydia dutifully taking notes at my shoulder, I called Max to see how Lotty's tests had gone. As Audrey thought, Lotty had a hairline fracture of her left arm, but the CAT scan didn't show clots or other head problems. Carol, shocked by the attack, was coming into the clinic for a few hours a day, but Lotty was fretting to get back to work herself.

Lydia went through a conscientious list of questions, but she had a lot to learn about probing behind partial answers. When she finished, she led me to a computer with a modem and called up Lexus for me.

"Murray said I should warn you that we might not use the story," she drawled. "But thanks for talking to me. Just exit the system when you're done—you don't need to see me before you go."

When I got the Diamond Head file I felt a stab of frustration, and a sweep of irrational anger. The only name given was their registered agent, Jonas Carver, at an address on South Dearborn. Perfectly aboveboard, since they weren't a publicly held company, but I'd been expecting great things from the computer. I'd imagined finding some close associate of Daraugh Graham, who would quickly put pressure on Chamfers to talk to me.

Technology had failed me. I was going to have to do my detecting the old-fashioned way, by breaking and entering.

24

The Labors of Hercules

I phoned Mr. Contreras again from Murray's desk before leaving the paper. He still didn't answer. I tried not to worry about it—what could be wrong with him, after all? But he'd made such a point of my calling him at one, and anyway, he wouldn't leave Peppy alone for so long. Maybe he forgot he had a doctor's appointment when he was talking to me. Maybe Peppy had had some kind of veterinary emergency. He wouldn't have slipped and fallen, be lying helpless on the bathroom floor like Mrs. Frizell. Certainly not. I took the stairs from Michigan to the service road beneath it two at a time.

I'd parked the car illegally on underground Wacker, hoping the location was too remote for the traffic detail. Pulling one of the city's new orange missives from the Impala's wipers, I realized I should have known better: when the dice are rolling against you, the traffic cops will always find you. I'd have to pay it too—Luke's histrionics if the Impala got booted didn't bear imagining.

I pushed my falling luck on the Drive going home, but managed to make it to Belmont without a blue-and-white pulling me over—the Impala didn't attract the same kind of attention the Trans Am got. Once on Belmont I had to take it easy because of the traffic. I drummed impatiently on the wheel at lights and took stupid risks around double-parked delivery trucks.

It wasn't until I got to Racine that I remembered to look for tails. At this point I couldn't be sure I didn't have one, although I didn't think anyone had followed me to Luke's to begin with. I certainly didn't want to make their job easy by parking near the building where they could see what car I was driving. I found a space on Barry and sprinted the two blocks home.

When I rang Mr. Contreras's bell, Peppy barked sharply from behind the door, but the old man didn't appear. I bit my lip in momentary indecision. He had the same right to his privacy that I demanded for myself. Unfortunately the attack on Lotty had made me too jumpy about the welfare of my friends to leave room for Ninth Amendment debates. I ran upstairs to my own place, dug my state-of-the-art picklocks from the jumble in the basket by my front door, and made my first illegal entry of the day.

Peppy kept up a steady, extremely fierce barking while I worked on the locks. I hoped she would frighten off a genuine housebreaker—even though Mr. Contreras had two locks, they were woefully easy to undo. As soon as she realized it was me, she wagged her tail perfunctorily and returned to her squealing offspring.

The old man wasn't in the building. I checked

the back in case I'd made a fool of myself while he was nurturing his tomatoes, but he wasn't outside, either. Peppy came to the back door with me while I looked.

"Where'd he go, huh? I know he told you."

She gave an impatient bark and I let her out briefly. He hadn't been attacked and dragged from the building by force—there were no signs of battle. I gave it up. Something had come up and I'd hear all about it in due course. I checked Peppy's water bowl, then left a note on top of his phone telling him I'd been by and would see him tonight.

After relocking his door I stopped in my own place for a glass of water and a sandwich. I also left the Smith & Wesson—I didn't think anyone was going to take potshots at me on Racine.

Marjorie Hellstrom was in her backyard doing something to a rose bush. Except for Mrs. Frizell and me, the block was infested with fanatical gardeners. I couldn't grow parsley in a window box, while Mrs. Frizell's yard was returning to native prairie—native prairie replete with hub caps and beer cans, just the way it was when the Indians lived here.

Mrs. Hellstrom came over to the fence separating her handclipped turf from the dump. "Are you going into Hattie's place, Miss . . . uh? I washed some of her clothes yesterday and took them over to the hospital, but she didn't know who I was. I don't think they'd been laundered since she bought them. Mr. Hellstrom didn't like me washing them, he was afraid I'd catch some-thing from touching them, but you can't leave your neighbors in the lurch, and we've lived next door for thirty years."

"How did Mrs. Frizell seem?" I interrupted.

"I don't think she even knew I was there, to tell you the truth. She just lay there with her eyes half shut, kind of snorting but not saying any-thing, except calling for the dog every now and then. So if you were thinking of taking her some of her things, I wouldn't bother, Miss . . . uh."

"Warshawski. But you can call me Vic. No, I just wanted to make sure her papers were in order."

Mrs. Hellstrom frowned. "Isn't that what Chrissie Pichea is supposed to do, with her and her husband taking over Mrs. Frizell's affairs for her? It's awfully generous of them to take it on, when they have their own work to do, although I don't think they should have been in such a hurry to put the dogs to sleep. At least they should have talked to me first, they must have known I'd been looking after them."

"Yes, I agree. I have some financial expertise that Todd and Chrissie lack. And I feel some responsibility to Mrs. Frizell—I should have done something to protect the dogs."

"I know how you feel, dear—Vic, did you say? —because I feel just the same. You go on in, but you may want to open a window. Even though I tried cleaning the floors a bit, the place, well, to be frank, dear, it *smells.*" She lowered her voice on the last phrase as if using a word too dreadful for polite conversation.

I nodded portentously and let myself in the back. I'd half expected Todd and Chrissie to have changed the locks, so I'd brought my picks with me, but they must not have felt there was anything in the place that needed guarding. So technically I wasn't breaking, just entering.

Mrs. Hellstrom was right about the smell. Years' accretion of dog, unwashed dishes, and unswept floors produced a thick, cloying atmosphere that made me feel faint.

I pushed open windows in the kitchen and the living room, in itself quite a task since the ropes and pulleys were stiff with disuse, and made a quick survey of the house. Mrs. Frizell seemed to do fine without the trappings of modern technology: she had a small radio, but no television, no CD, not even a turntable. She did own a camera, an ancient Kodak that wouldn't have brought a nickel bag on the street.

Back in the living room I pulled a wobbly chair in front of the secretary. It was an old, dark piece of furniture with a rolltop-covered writing shelf in the middle, book shelves above, and drawers below. The rolltop had been wedged shut years before by the papers stuffed into its edges. Papers were crammed against the diamond-glass doors of the book shelves and were stuffed into the drawers. Everything was covered with a fine layer of grime.

If I hadn't been fed up to the gills with Todd,

Dick, Murray, and even Freeman, I would have shut the windows and gone home. It was ludicrous to think anything of value, let alone of interest, might be in that landfill. But I needed something, a crowbar to pry Todd Pichea loose from Mrs. Frizell, and I was out of ideas. All I wanted was some kind of document that would give me, if not a crowbar, at least a wedge.

As I surveyed the horrors in front of me I couldn't help wondering how much of my determination was due to concern for Mrs. Frizell, and how much was due to my own feelings of humiliation. I'm a sore loser and so far Todd—and Dick—had beaten me in every encounter.

"You're not driven by revenge—you fight for truth, justice, and the American Way," I grinned to myself.

Presumably Mrs. Frizell had filed her papers on the LIFO system—last in, first out. The trick would be to remove the top layer—from the book shelves as well as the writing shelf—without disturbing the Paleozoic regions underneath.

Despite Mrs. Hellstrom's work the living room carpet—a threadbare gray mat that might once have been maroon—was still too thick with dust to sit on. I went upstairs and found one of the sheets she'd laundered. Spreading it on the floor, I carefully began lifting documents from the secretary and putting them on the sheet.

In the midst of the kitchen squalor I'd noticed a huge pile of paper bags—Mrs. Frizell never threw anything away. I brought those in and stood a row of them next to the secretary. I was making an arbitrary decision to examine everything dated after 1987 and to put earlier stuff in bags by year.

By five o'clock I'd filled two dozen bags. The sheet below me had turned black from the grime I'd shaken from the papers. Mrs. Frizell was on the mailing list of every animal-care products company in North America and she'd saved all their catalogs. She'd also kept her vet bills going back to 1935—the earliest year that had floated to the top so far—and newspaper clippings detailing cruelty to animals. I hadn't found anything that concerned her son, but most of the stuff I'd handled only dated to the late seventies.

Her own financial papers were wedged in pell-mell with the vet bills and newspaper clippings. There wasn't much to them. She drew a monthly Social Security check, but apparently the box factory she'd worked in hadn't been union. Or at least there didn't seem to be any pension plan beyond the U.S. government. The Bank of Lake View had paid her real estate taxes for her and looked after her modest savings. They apparently had also paid her utility bills. I found a couple of copies of the quarterly statements they sent Byron Frizell in San Francisco detailing their transactions on her behalf.

Social Security doesn't have an electronic transfer system. They had to send their checks to Mrs. Frizell herself, and she had to be responsible enough to remember to take them to the bank. She apparently was collected enough mentally to do this, since her passbook, which I found under a 1972 Jewel flyer advertising Purina at ten cents a pound, had regular monthly entries.

That was a feeble straw to catch at, that my self-appointed client was mentally alert enough to take her money to the bank. And it didn't help deal with the painful condition she was in right now. Obviously no one could say she was competent to handle her own affairs today.

On closer inspection the passbook didn't look like much of an ally, either. Mrs. Frizell had brought her check to the Lake View bank on the tenth of every month for eighteen years, but she'd stopped abruptly in February, when the balance stood at just over ten thousand. What had she done with them since? Was I going to find four checks floating in this paper sea someplace?

I rubbed the back of my neck and my shoulders with my filthy fingers. I felt hollow and depressed. I wasn't finding evidence of Mrs. Frizell's vibrant mental state. And certainly not of a cache of assets worth inveigling her estate for.

I went to the kitchen to rinse myself off under the tap. Even though the weather had broken with last night's storm, I was stiff and sweaty from my work in the landfill. The sink was dirty enough that I didn't want to drink from the tap, and I was pretty thirsty. I should have thought to bring a Thermos from home. One half hour more and I'd pack it in.

When I got to the living room and surveyed the mess with fresher eyes, I was tempted to quit on the spot, but a nagging sense that I'd invested too much time to go away empty-handed pushed me forward. Of course, that's the classic mistake that drives businesses into bankruptcy: "We've put five years and fifty billion into this worthless product, we can't abandon it now." But the impulse pushes you deeper into the quag.

The room faced west. The setting sun gave a lot more light than the forty-watt bulb in the lone lamp Mrs. Frizell kept there. I opened the curtains and continued the search. So far I'd only looked at the middle section and the glassed-in bookshelves. For my last surge I pried the three bottom drawers open. Squatting on my heels, I started removing envelopes. It must have been close to seven when I found the letter from the Bank of Lake View.

15 March

Dear Mrs. Frizell,

Acting on your instructions we have sold your Certificates of Deposit and closed your account, sending the balance to your new account at the U.S. Metropolitan Bank and Trust. It has been our pleasure to serve your financial needs for the last sixty years and we are sorry you no longer find the relationship desirable. Should you change your mind in the future please do not hesitate to call. We will be happy to reopen your account at no charge to you.

The letter had been personally signed by one of the bank officers.

The Bank of Lake View is a small, neighborhood institution—they handle my mortgage with the concern and attention most banks reserve for big corporate customers. They must be about the only place in the city that still handles small passbook accounts. It was typical of their character to write a personal note to Mrs. Frizell.

What was strange was her transferring her money to U.S. Metropolitan. I hadn't found a passbook or any other documents from them. Either those had slipped down to the Jurassic stratum or she'd kept them someplace else. But that was a detail compared to the bigger question: Why had she moved accounts to a downtown bank? And not just any old bank, but one that was in the news every other week because of the political ties its directors had in the area. The Du Page County Board was only the most recent group to raise journalistic eyebrows for keeping demand deposits in U.S. Met's noninterest-bearing accounts.

I was grasping at straws and I knew it. Probably U.S. Met had had some marketing campaign that Mrs. Frizell had found irresistible. I got to my feet, my hamstrings stiff from sitting so long. I didn't know what to do with the mess I'd created on the floor. The secretary was still overflowing with papers—I couldn't imagine stuffing all these back inside. At the same time I could scarcely leave them lying around as evidence of my labor.

Although maybe Chrissie would assume it had been Mrs. Hellstrom's work; presumably the Picheas knew she'd done some laundry.

A key turning in the front door solved the problem for me. I folded the letter from the bank into my back pocket a second before Chrissie and Todd bounced in. They looked radiant with health, Chrissie in a mattress-ticking romper suit, Todd in tan shorts and a Polo T-shirt. I didn't even want to imagine how I appeared—the smell coming from my armpits was discomforting enough.

"What are you doing here, Warshawski?"

"Cleaning the Augean stables, Todd. You can call me Hercules. Although I think he had help. In a way I've outperformed him."

"Don't try to turn this into a joke, because it isn't funny. When Mrs. Hellstrom told us you were in here looking at financial records, my first impulse was to call the cops. I could have you arrested, you know. This place is private property."

I rubbed the back of my neck. "But not, I think, belonging to you. Unless you've used your guardianship powers to sign over the title?"

It dawned on me suddenly that that was the one valuable document Mrs. Frizell had. Maybe it was at the bottom of one of the drawers. Or maybe Todd and Chrissie had already absconded with it. I didn't feel up to burglarizing their house to see, at least not tonight.

"Why don't you just get out of here," Todd

snapped. "Since we found the old lady you've been determined to undermine my care of her, even calling her son—"

"What care?" I interrupted. "The first thing you two beacons of light did was kill her dogs, the only thing in the world Mrs. Frizell loved. Everything you've done since last Friday may be legal, but I wouldn't touch it with a barge pole. You stink, Pichea, worse than any heap of dogshit Mrs. Frizell may have left lying around."

"That's enough!" he shouted. "You think your moral superiority gives you the right to break the law? I have papers that prove my right to control who enters this place, and any judge in the city will agree."

I laughed. "You have papers? You sound like a pedigreed dog. Speaking of documents, though, where's Mrs. Frizell's title? And where's her passbook at U.S. Met?"

"How do you know—" Chrissie began, but Todd cut her off.

"You have two minutes to leave, Warshawski. Two minutes before I call the cops."

"So you do have her bank book," I said, trying to infuse my voice with a wealth of meaning. Privately wondering what possible difference it could make, I sauntered out the front door.

25

Sticking to the Ribs

Mr. Contreras had evidently been on the lookout for me: he was outside his apartment by the time I had the lobby door open.

"Where you been, doll? You look like the short end of a mudwrestling match."

I patted my sweaty curls self-consciously. "I could ask you the same thing. I thought we were supposed to talk at one to make sure no one had attacked me."

"Yeah, I thought it wouldn't hurt you to get a dose of your own medicine. Not at the time, I mean, but later, when it occurred to me to go see him in person. I thought, well, Vic'll be worried when she calls—*if* she calls—and don't get an answer. But I didn't have any way of reaching you and I thought, all the times you've kept me hanging without word one, it won't hurt you none to be in a bit of a stew."

"Well, I'm glad you had a good time." I was too tired to fight. "By the way, how long were you gone? Peppy seemed pretty eager to get outside when I stopped by at one."

That was a low blow; I was sorry as soon as the words left my mouth. One of Mr. Contreras's jealously guarded prerogatives is having the dog live with him on the grounds that I'm gone too much of the time to be a fit owner.

His brown eyes clouded with hurt. "That ain't fair, doll, when you know I'm here day and night for the princess. I wouldn't go off for days at a time without a thought for her needs the way— well, anyway, I wouldn't leave her in the lurch."

He, too, was pulling his punches—cutting himself short instead of launching a full-scale attack on my periodic absences. I patted him on the shoulder and turned to go upstairs.

"Don't you even want to know what I found out?" he demanded.

"Yeah. Yeah, sure I do. Just let me wash up first."

"I'm barbecuing some ribs," he called after me. "Want me to save some for you?"

News about cholesterol and colon cancer had no effect on Mr. Contreras's diet. In fact, maybe years of spare ribs had made him the hale, fit man he was today. They certainly sounded more comforting after my dreary afternoon than the low-cal, high-nutrition dinner I'd been planning. I thanked him, but warned him it would be a good hour before I'd be ready.

The bath turned black as soon as I stepped into the tub. I couldn't soak in such filth. Submerging for a few seconds to rinse the sweat from my hair, I climbed out and emptied the tub, wiping the grimy ring away as the water receded. I turned on the shower, but I'd drained the heater filling the tub and cleaning it.

Snarling under my breath, I wrapped myself in a towel and went to phone Lotty while I waited for the hot water heater to fill again. When I didn't get an answer I tried Max's number. It turned out she had gone up to Evanston to stay with him for a few days. She was doing well, or as well as could be expected, but there was a strain between us—guilt on my part, fear on hers. I tried to patch it as best I could, but we didn't part in our usual harmony.

I was shivering by the time we hung up, and was glad to find the water hot again. I stood under it until the shower began running cool, long after the final traces of Mrs. Frizell's dirt had gone from my hair. Had Todd and Chrissie bested me in yet another encounter, or was I on to something? It's true U.S. Met wasn't a great bank, but Mrs. Frizell had moved her account four months ago, long before Todd and Chrissie entered her life.

Maybe Chrissie worked there—I pictured her going around to all the old people in the neighborhood, getting them to transfer their money to the Met's noninterest-bearing accounts. I realized I didn't know if Chrissie worked outside the home. As to the missing title to Mrs. Frizell's house, maybe that was in a safe deposit box someplace. Or up by her bed. Since she'd slept with the dogs, maybe she figured her bedroom was the safest place to keep valuables.

I toweled my hair dry and lay down for a short rest. I still had a third stop to make on my day of burglary, and I wouldn't be able to manage it in my present shape. The phone woke me at nine-thirty: Mr. Contreras, wanting to know if I was angry and punishing him by hiding out upstairs.

I sat up groggily. "I fell asleep." I cut off his apologies. "I'm glad you called—I need to get up. Be down in five minutes."

I pulled on jeans and a white cotton shirt with long sleeves—I was still feeling chilly despite the warm summer evening. I looked at the clock again and decided to leave straight from Mr. Contreras's. Strapping my shoulder holster on, I pushed driver's license, money, and keys into various pockets. The picklocks dug into my thigh; I took them out and stuck them in the pocket of a denim jacket, which I put on to conceal the shoulder holster. Now I felt hot, but that couldn't be helped.

When I got downstairs Mr. Contreras had his door open for me. "You didn't eat, did you, doll? I'm heating your ribs in my toaster oven right now."

He waved a bottle of Valpolicella at me, but I declined. I couldn't afford to drink anything this late at night if I wanted to be able to move fast. He bustled off to the kitchen.

I went over to the maternity ward—I hadn't taken time to coo over the puppies earlier. Their eyes had opened and they were making tentative sorties from Peppy's side. She watched me closely when I picked them up to stroke them, but it didn't upset her the way it had when they were first born.

Mr. Contreras came back with a plate of ribs, some garlic bread, and—in deference to my eating habits—a plate of iceberg lettuce. He unfolded a TV table for me and sat down with the wine. As soon as I saw the ribs I realized how hungry I was.

"Tell me about your day. You went to see Jake Sokolowski?" I asked through a mouthful of food.

"No. I just phoned him at Tonia Coriolano's place. I didn't figure he'd know anything about Mitch's kid—none of us did. Mitch didn't care enough to keep up with the boy and Rosie when they up and left thirty-five years ago." He swallowed some wine reflectively. "Or maybe he was just too ashamed at not being able to look after them the way a man ought to do and don't go telling me women can look after themselves. You marry a woman and get her a baby, you're obligated to look after them."

After glaring at me a minute to see if I would respond to the challenge in his voice, he went on. "No, who I went to see was Eddie Mohr."

"Eddie Mohr?" I echoed.

"The guy whose car was stolen. The one that the guys used for beating up the doc."

"I didn't know you knew him."

"Well, I wasn't sure I did, until after I checked with Jake. I mean, it's not a common name, but there could be more than one."

I put down my ribs, controlling an impulse to shout at him. When Mr. Contreras has hot news, he tells it in pieces and usually backward.

"I'll bite: Who is Eddie Mohr? Besides owning the death car, of course."

"Guy used to be president of our local. He's a few years younger'n Jake and me, maybe only just turned seventy, so he started after us and wasn't in our particular crowd. But of course I knew him, so I went to see him. Got a nice little house on Fortieth, east of Kedzie, lives with his wife, keeps a nice Buick. Besides the Olds that got stolen, I mean. The Buick is his wife's car, see—the other one, the Olds, that's his." Mr. Contreras beamed in satisfaction at being able to report important news.

"I think I understand. What did he have to say?"

"Oh, he was real shocked. I just wanted to make sure, you know, that he really didn't have anything to do with following your car, beating up the doc, that kind of stuff."

I had wanted to know those things too. I would have liked to ask Eddie Mohr those questions myself. One reason for doing my own legwork is that the people's reactions tell you more than their actual words. Of course, I could go see him myself tomorrow. I'd only be the third person to interrogate him, behind the cops and Mr. Contreras. He should have his answers totally memorized by then.

I started to ask about where Mohr parked the

cars—street or garage? And did it make logistical sense that it was the Olds the hot-wirers took? And didn't it seem like a strange coincidence that the president of the Diamond Head local was involved, however tangentially, in trying to run Lotty over when I was trying to investigate the death of an old Diamond Head employee? But Mr. Contreras wouldn't be able to answer these questions, and it would only puncture his balloon if I asked them.

"Was he surprised to see you?" I said instead.

"Well, naturally, me turning up out of the blue after twelve years, of course he was surprised."

"Disconcerted, do you think?"

He snorted. "I'm not sure what you're driving at. You mean, did he act like he had a guilty conscience, yes he did—he felt guilty as all get-out when I told him who the doc was and how bad she'd been hurt. But of course he couldn't know his car would be stolen, let alone it would be stolen to attack her with."

"How come he owns two cars and you take the bus?"

He opened his eyes in astonishment. "You trying to suggest he's got more money than he should? I could own a car if I wanted to—I sure don't need two—but what do I need it for? Waste of money, the taxes, the gas, the insurance, worrying about parking it, whether hot-rodders'll steal it. You think just because a guy gives his life to the union he can't afford to own a car?"

I shook my head, abashed. "Of course not. Just grabbing at straws."

I picked at the iceberg lettuce. "You know, Terry Finchley didn't try to find Mitch's son. And Jake didn't. But someone claiming to be young Kruger did go to Mrs. Polter's and ransack Mitch's room only a day after his body was found. Either the guy did come to town unbeknownst to anyone but Mitch, or someone wanted something out of Mitch's things bad enough to pretend to be him. I mean, either way, the person knew where he lived. Which meant Mitch had to tell them, because you and he—and Jake—were the only ones who knew."

Mr. Contreras cocked an intelligent eye. "You want me to ask Jake did someone call trying to find Mitch's new address?"

I hunched a shoulder impatiently. "I suppose. I'd like to come up with some photos, show 'em on the street. You know, we don't know whether Mitch's son stayed in Arizona. Hell, he'd be my age—older. He could be anywhere. You remember his name?"

"Mitch, junior," Mr. Contreras said promptly. "I always remember resenting the fact that he had a junior and I only had Ruthie. Stupid kind of thing. It doesn't mean nothing, I can see that now, but at the time . . . oh, well, you don't want to hear about that."

I wiped my fingers on the wet paper towel he had provided. Mounting a search for a person who could be anywhere was way outside my resources—it meant going into state motor-vehicle departments, writing the Pentagon, all kinds of activities I didn't have time or money to undertake. Still, a picture of Mitch, Jr. would be very helpful.

"You want to bankroll some ads, since you don't waste your money on a car? We could run some in all the Arizona papers, and ones around here. You know, if Mitch Kruger, once of Chicago, writes a certain address, he'll hear something to his advantage."

Mr. Contreras rubbed his hands together. "Just like out of Sherlock Holmes. Good idea, doll. Good idea. Want me to take care of it?"

I graciously gave my consent and stood up. "I'm going downtown and I'd like to go out the back way. In case the boys who took your pal's car are waiting with another one out front. Can you let me out through your kitchen?"

"Downtown?" His eyes flicked to my left armpit. "What're you doing downtown?"

I smiled. "A little office work."

"That why you need the gun? To shoot holes in a letter and hope it'll go away?"

I laughed. "Cross my heart and hope to die, I am not going off for a violent confrontation. I'm hoping I won't see a single soul. But you know my methods, Watson: guys start taking shots at me, or my friends, I don't walk the mean streets without a little protection."

He wasn't happy; he wasn't even sure he believed me. But he undid the dead bolts on his back door and walked me to the alley. "I'm gonna fix you up with one of those things the cops carry, so if you get in trouble you can give me a signal."

The thought of a twenty-four-hour umbilical cord to the old man made me gulp. I went down the alley as fast as I could, as if to get away from the very air that had carried the suggestion.

26

Bad Girls Stay Out Late

The South Loop is a ghost town at night. Its bars close with the evening rush hour. Although the Auditorium and a movie theater are on its eastern edge and Dearborn Park has sprung up on the south, little night life has spread north of the Congress Expressway. A lot of that is of such dubious quality that you'd rather encounter an actual ghost.

The address for Jonas Carver—the man Lexus showed as Diamond Head's registered agent—proved to be just north of Van Buren. I parked the Impala a discreet distance away, waited for a drunk—or perhaps dopehead—to drift across the street, and went into the lobby.

It was an old building that had been given a superficial rehab—just enough paint to justify a rent increase commensurate with the new construction in Dearborn Park. One of the cosmetic features was a heavy glass door with a double lock: you had to have working keys in both of them at the same time for the door to open. This would be a good test of the range of my picklocks. They had set me back seven hundred dollars, but were supposed to be up to this kind of job.

I also noted bitterly that the tenant addresses —listed next to a phone outside the outer door— were coded. Doubtless useful for private residents, but if you wanted to see a business, like Jonas Carver's, how were you supposed to know what floor to go to? Fortunately the building was only eleven stories high—that would cut my exploration time down significantly.

Just to be on the safe side I dialed Carver's code number. No one answered. Why would anyone be here at midnight, anyway?

Looking around to make sure no one was watching me, I set to work on the locks. After half an hour I began to wonder if I should bunk down in the Impala and go in on the coattails of the first person to arrive in the morning. I was also tempted just to pull out the Smith & Wesson and blow the door down. I didn't think the noise would rouse anyone.

It was almost one when my delicate probers finally released the spring in the upper lock, enabling me to work the bottom one fairly quickly. The small of my back ached from bending so long. I rubbed it and stretched against the wall, trying to ease out the cramping.

A small night-light gave just enough of a glow

to see the elevator buttons. The lobby was minuscule, about big enough for four people to wait together. I pulled out a quarter and flipped it: heads I would ride to the top and make my way down to Carver; tails I'd start on two and go up. In the dim light I could just make out Washington's profile. I summoned the elevator.

The door opened at once. This meant the last person to use it had been heading down, a good sign even though I didn't seriously expect to encounter anyone. As the door closed on me I saw an address board on the facing wall. I stuck a foot out, got the door open, and leaned out to get Jonas Carver's suite number. He was on the sixth floor. Whether I had started at the bottom or the top it would have made no difference. Maybe my luck was turning a bit.

The lock on Carver's office was much easier to negotiate than the lobby had been. A good thing, since my back protested when I leaned over to play with it. I knelt, trying to find a comfortable working angle, and managed to slide the dead bolt back in about five minutes.

Carver's office faced the air-shaft side of the building. No streetlamps bent their rays up here. The only light in the room came from a cursor blinking importunately in the middle distance. I groped my way toward it, found the desk it was sitting on, and fumbled around until I found a lamp switch. I don't know why I hadn't brought a flashlight with me.

The room, which had seemed immense in the

dark, showed up small and austere under the lamplight. Besides the metal desk with the computer, it held two filing cabinets and a small table with an electric coffeemaker. A door at the far end led to a second room, presumably Mr. Carver's personal headquarters. The desk here was veneered in fake wood; an imitation Chinese rug covered part of the floor. Carver, too, had a computer ready for action.

Information on the companies Carver managed was no doubt waiting behind the blinking cursor and would be revealed at the right command. My computer skills were not my strong suit; figuring out the right command would be a chore. I tried instead to find some hard copy in the filing cabinets, but they seemed devoted to tax laws and government guidelines on how to run closely held corporations. I also found manuals for using the computer. Gritting my teeth I opened the binder and began to read.

Around half an hour later I figured I knew enough at least to get started. I bowed politely to the computer and asked it for a directory. The machine obliged with a speed and thoroughness that left me thoroughly confused. A line at the bottom asked what I wanted to do—browse, create, edit, save, exit—and blinked impertinently when I hesitated.

I finally figured out which function key allowed me to browse. The machine, impatient with my retardation, barely allowed me to hit it before demanding a file name. I gave it "Diamond

Head." It spat it back, "File not found." I tried a variety of permutations on the name, but the machine didn't like any of them.

Finally I found my way back to the directory and studied it carefully. Something called "Client.Exec" sounded promising. I fiddled around with different letters and managed—after numerous false starts—a combination the computer liked. A few blinking lights and the client files lay in front of me. Not, of course, in ledger form—just another set of menu options.

I looked at my watch. It was close to three. It had taken longer to figure out how to use the damned computer than it had to get in through the front door. After another period of trial and error I found the Diamond Head records.

As soon as I came to the list of directors and officers, I realized why Freeman had been so upset this morning. Jason Felitti was the chairman, Peter Felitti the vice chair, and Richard Yarborough the secretary. I let my jaw drop. I didn't know who Jason was, but I'd met Peter at the benefit Michael and Or' had given. He was Dick's father-in-law and the chairman of Amalgamated Portage.

I laughed out loud, a little hysterically. Yeah, I knew one of the directors who could put pressure on Chamfers for me, all right. Jeez, Louise. No wonder Freeman thought I was trying to pull him into a private war with Dick! That still didn't excuse his rudeness, but at least I could see his point of view.

I scanned the rest of the file perfunctorily. It was past four now and my eyes were having trouble focusing on the shimmery green letters. I wished I knew how to print the file, but I was too tired to figure out any more computer shenanigans, and I didn't want an early arrival to find me on the job.

If Carver kept Diamond Head's books, they were in a separate set of ledger files, which I also couldn't figure out how to hunt down. The summary data presented here showed that Diamond Head was heavily leveraged. In fact, debt seemed to exceed retained earnings by about a 1:2 ratio. And the company had a relationship with Amalgamated Portage, which held a big chunk of the debt. That was cozy—just keep it all in the family.

In addition, Diamond Head had a connection to Paragon Steel. Carver's files didn't spell out how, but Paragon seemed responsible for a lot of Diamond Head's cash flow. Paragon Steel. For such a huge conglomerate to be involved with a tiny outfit like Diamond Head made no sense to me. I rubbed my eyes a few times to make sure I was reading it correctly.

Paragon was one of the few companies that had seen the writing on the U.S. steel industry wall fifteen years ago. They had restructured themselves so that they could produce relatively small lots of different specialty grades of steel on very tight turnaround; they had gone into plastics in a big way; and they were also one of the few

Illinois companies to make out like bandits during the Reagan defense buildup.

The *Wall Street Journal* had done a major story on them only a month or so ago—that's why the details were fresh in my mind. I could see Paragon owning Diamond Head—the small engines the latter made would fit right into their defense operations. But Paragon providing a stream of cash to the smaller firm? I shook my head over it, but time was rushing past. I'd have to worry about it tomorrow.

I rummaged in Carver's desk and found a legal pad. I tore off a piece so that my writing wouldn't leave telltale dents underneath, and jotted down the key points. There wasn't anything else I could do right now. Anyway, I was longing for sleep.

Fortunately the keyboard offered me the choice of exiting. I did so, and more by luck than skill found myself back at the blank screen with the blinking cursor. I looked carefully around the two rooms to make sure I hadn't left anything of myself there.

On the way downstairs I felt a faint twinge of conscience. What had Jonas Carver ever done to me that I should invade his office? If he came into my place rummaging through my files I'd break his kneecaps; he'd have every right to do the same to me.

Gabriella certainly would have disapproved. Her face set in stern lines, telling me I had been a very bad girl, followed me into my dreams.

27

Down the Street
and Through the Diner

Before going to bed I took the precaution of slipping a note under Mr. Contreras's door. I didn't want to be awakened at the crack of dawn by his frantic leaning on my bell. I also unplugged my phone. As a result I managed almost six hours sleep, enough to get me going, although not with any real enthusiasm.

I hadn't been running for several days and badly needed the exercise, more for my mental than my physical well-being. The small of my back no longer ached, but I could feel the stiffness in the muscles when I did my warm-up routine. I'd have to take a chance on the guys who beat up Lotty hunting for me.

I left my gun at home. It's too hard to run with a shoulder holster under your sweatshirt—the gun digs into your breast in an unpleasant way. I kept to side streets instead of the more pleasant route over to the lake, and made it home again without incident. After a shower and a late breakfast—fruit, yogurt, and a toasted cheese sandwich to make it do for lunch as well—I tried to figure out what to do next.

I had to talk to Chamfers about the attack on

Lotty. The cops claimed they'd covered it and that he was clean as hand-laundered money, but I wanted to hear it from him in person. I also needed to go to the public library and do a computer search on Jason Felitti. Presumably he was a brother to Dick's father-in-law, or maybe an uncle, but I'd like more information than that. I wondered if anyone at the Bank of Lake View would talk to me about Mrs. Frizell. Probably not, but it was worth a try.

I looked at my watch. All that would have to wait. The first thing I needed to do was see whether anyone at Paragon Steel would talk to me.

The decision on what to wear was complex. I needed to look professional for a conversation with Paragon managers. I wanted to be cool. I needed to be able to carry my gun. And I needed to be able to run if necessary. In the end I decided on jeans with a silk houndstooth jacket. It would look professional in California. That would have to be close enough.

Before I left I dug out my address book and dialed Freeman Carter's home number. I was pleased to find him in—he could easily have spent his week off in the country.

"V. I. Warshawski, Freeman. I hope I'm not interrupting your lunch."

"I'm on my way out the door, Vic. Can it wait?"

"No, it can't, but I'll be brief. Until four this morning I had no idea that Dick or his father-in-law were involved with Diamond Head Motors. I think you owe me an apology."

"Four this morning?" Freeman picked on the least significant part of my remark. "What were you doing at four this morning?"

"Back-breaking labor to find out what you could have told me with no loss of sweat. Did you think I was trying to lasso you into a fight with Dick? It would have been gracious of you to ask first."

"Back-breaking labor, huh? Well, I never thought it would hurt you to work for a living."

"But did you think I was trying to rope you into a standoff with Dick?" I persisted.

"The thought did cross my mind," Freeman said after a pause. "And it hasn't quite left it. It's an incredible coincidence, your being interested in Diamond Head."

"Oh, I don't know. Crawford, Mead must be involved with a lot of mid-sized firms around Chicago. Those are the ones I typically work with too. We simply have . . . overlapping spheres of interest, that's it." The phrase, pulled from an old course on political history, pleased me more than it did Freeman, who didn't say anything.

After a long silence I plowed ahead. "You know, I've been thinking. About you and Crawford, Mead, I mean. I can't help wondering if they started working on mergers and acquisitions during the Drexel glory days. I remembered at the concert you said the firm was doing business you didn't like—I don't think you would have stayed on board if it was something downright immoral, like fronting for money launderers. But mergers—a lot of firms have found the tail starts wagging the dog when they take that on, so it did seem like that was what you might have had in mind. Since Peter Felitti is Dick's father-in-law, maybe you thought there was a conflict of interest handling that particular transaction."

Freeman gave a sharp bark that might have been laughter. "I should know better by now than to say anything in front of you that I don't want used in court against me later. You come up with this theory on your own? Or you been talking to people?"

"I've been thinking. It's what I do for a living, you know. A lot of my work is figuring out why people do what they do. Diamond Head is carrying a huge debt load—that sounds like junk financing. Dick's name is on their board. That sounds like he handled the business. You were angry. That sounds like you knew about this and felt I was cutting too close to the bone."

"Well, I'm still not going to discuss the firm's business with you, Vic. You could be right—or you could be blowing smoke. That's all I can tell you about this—except I'm sorry I misjudged you the other day—but I sure as hell wish you would work on something besides Diamond Head. Now I've got to go: I'm standing up a friend."

"There is one other thing," I said quickly before he could hang up. "I really need someone who will get the plant manager at Diamond Head to talk to me. He's been stonewalling me for two weeks. That's why I wanted the names of the directors—I thought I might know one of them."

"You do, Vic. You know Richard Yarborough. I keep telling you that you misjudge Dick. He might respond to you if you could bring yourself to ask him in a nice way." The phone clicked in my ear.

It had been an outside chance that Freeman would feel dismayed enough at misjudging me to help me see Chamfers. It would have required his pretending he was still with Crawford, Mead, and he was too scrupulous for that kind of shenanigan.

"Besides, hard work builds character," I said out loud.

Before leaving for the day I called Lotty. She was still at Max's but thought she would be well enough to go to the clinic for half a day in the morning. I asked her if she'd talked to the police.

"Yes. Sergeant Rawlings drove out here yesterday afternoon. They don't know anything, but he seemed to think you were obstructing their investigation—I think that was his phrase. Vic . . ." She paused and fished for words. "If there's something you're keeping from the police, tell them, please. I'm not going to be able to drive without looking over my shoulder every five seconds until the men who beat me up are caught."

My shoulders slumped. "I told the police about the guy who threatened to put a tail on me, but they think he's clean. I don't know what else I can do, except try to conduct my own investigation."

"There's telling and telling. I've watched you operate for years and I know you often hold back the—the key emphasis, maybe, or some little thing that will make them able to make the same connections you do."

Her voice, which lacked its usual crisp vitality, was more depressing than her words. I tried to remember my conversations with Conrad Rawlings and Terry Finchley. I hadn't told them about the person masquerading as Mitch Kruger's son who'd lifted his papers from Mrs. Polter's. Maybe I should do that. I couldn't bear the thought of Lotty suddenly aging out of fear, especially a fear I'd helped foster.

I was silent so long she said sharply, "There is something, isn't there?"

"I don't know if there is or not. It didn't seem relevant to me, but I'll call Detective Finchley and tell him before I leave."

"Do that, Vic," she said, her voice cracking. "Pretend I matter, that I'm not just a little piece of your game plan that didn't work the way you hoped."

"Lotty! That's not fair—" I began, but she hung up before I could hear her crying.

Was I really that lacking in feeling? I loved Lotty. More than any living person I could think of. Was I treating her like a pawn? I didn't have a game plan; that was half my trouble. I was floundering from action to action, not knowing in what direction I was going. Nonetheless, the distaste I'd felt for myself after breaking into Carver's office last night came back to me. A knot of self-disgust twisted my stomach.

I suddenly felt an overwhelming urge to go back to bed. My lids were so leaden I could scarcely open my eyes. I leaned back in the couch and let the wave of depression wash over me. After a time, not feeling better but knowing I had to get moving, I called over to Area One to talk to Finchley. He wasn't in; I left my name and number and asked him to phone me this evening. At least no one hung up on me mid-sentence. That was a distinct improvement over my first two calls.

I moved drearily down the stairs. Before heading for the street I knocked on Mr. Contreras's door. It was a sign of my desperate state that I even accepted a cup of his overboiled coffee before setting out. This afternoon the old man had enough zip for two, maybe even four. He'd spent the morning drafting our ad and calling around Arizona to get the names and rates of their biggest dailies; he was eager to show me his handiwork. I tried to drum up an appropriate level of enthusiasm, but he suddenly noticed my spirits didn't match his.

"What's eating you, doll? Rough night?"

I gave a self-conscious laugh. "Oh, I just feel like I let Lotty in for a bad time and haven't done anything to help her."

Mr. Contreras patted my knee with one horny palm. "Your way of helping people ain't the same as most people's, Vic. Just because you're not rushing around with flowers and a tub of soup don't mean you're not helping her."

"Yeah, but she feels I should cooperate more with the police, and she's right," I muttered.

"Yeah, cooperate with them," the old man jeered. "Ninety percent of the time they don't listen to you. I was there when you talked to that black detective, what's his name, Finchley, and I saw how he listened to you. Far as the cops are concerned, Mitch hit his head and fell in the canal. Mitch, who knew every inch of that waterfront! They sure don't care that you was tailed for a week before those goons attacked your car and beat up the doc. I don't see you've got any cause to go around blaming yourself, not for one minute, doll. You just pull yourself together and go do the work God made you fit for."

He slapped my knee again for emphasis. I patted his hand and thanked him for the pep talk. The odd thing was, I really did feel better. I scribbled a few changes onto the ad copy, but left the gist of the message unchanged. I agreed with my neighbor that we would ask young Mitch to contact him, not me, in case he was involved in his father's death—if he was, he might have heard my name from someone at Diamond Head.

"You want to do something else?" I asked, getting up to go. "Talk to some of the people on the block—Mrs. Hellstrom or Mrs. Tertz, maybe.

See if you can find out whether Chrissie Pichea works for a living."

Mr. Contreras assented eagerly, thrilled that I was finally considering him a full-fledged partner. He saw me to the door, talking enthusiastically until I was out of earshot.

My conversation with Lotty had made me uneasy about who might be dogging my steps. Or her steps. I wondered if we were all barking up the wrong tree—maybe she'd been attacked by relatives of a patient whom they thought she'd mistreated. I'd have to talk to Rawlings, see if he was pursuing that possibility. I certainly couldn't mention it to Lotty, not unless I wanted the other side of the Trans Am stove in.

By the time I got to the end of the block I changed my mind. A couple of guys had been sitting in a late-model Subaru across from my building when I left. One of them climbed out of the car and started trailing me up the street. I looked around. The Subaru pulled away from the curb and dawdled behind us. I continued up Racine to Belmont; my friend stayed with me. The Subaru tagged along about half a block back. I considered taking a bus over to the el and doubling back again through the Loop, but that seemed unnecessarily time-consuming. I walked into the Belmont Diner.

It was well past the lunch hour. The place was nearly empty. The waitresses, who were relaxing with cigarettes and newspapers, greeted me with the easy camaraderie they gave their regulars.

"BLT with fries, Vic? Tammy just pulled a hot batch from the grease." That was Barbara, who usually waited on me and knew my weaknesses.

"I'll have to take a pass today. I got a couple of guys a little too interested in me. Can I leave through your back entrance?" I looked around and saw my trailer opening the door. "In fact, here comes one of them now."

"No problem, Vic."

Barbara bustled me toward the back. My pal started to follow when Helen dropped a pitcher of iced tea right in front of him. I just heard her say, "Oh, honey, I'm so sorry. . . . No, don't move, I'll clean that right off those nice trousers of yours . . ." before Barbara opened the back door and pushed me into the alley.

"Thanks a bunch," I said gratefully. "I'll remember you guys in my will."

"Get a move on, Warshawski," Barbara said, pushing me smartly between the shoulder blades. "And save the soap: we all know you've got nothing to leave."

28

Paragon of Virtue?

I ran flat out through the alley to Seminary, then made a mile loop around Racine so that I came to the Impala from the west. By the time I flopped into the driver's seat I was gasping for air and had a painful stitch under my right ribs. My legs wobbling slightly on the pedals I drove west along Barry until the street-dead ended at the river. After that I meandered around the side streets toward the Kennedy.

Barbara and her friends had clearly derailed my attackers. I was dawdling just to catch my breath while I figured out my next steps. I needed to do a library search on Jason Felitti, whose name had popped up as the owner of Diamond Head in my late-night research. I also wanted to visit the people flowing cash to Diamond Head—Paragon Steel. I flipped a mental coin: I could always use the library on Saturday. I turned north onto the expressway.

Paragon used to have their own skyscraper downtown, but they'd sold it during their cost-cutting days fifteen years ago. Their headquarters now occupied five floors of one of a nest of modest towers in Lincolnwood. The outdoor lot at the complex was packed so densely that I had to park over a block from the entrance to the first building.

From my space at the edge of the lot I could see the purple Hyatt where Alan Dorfman had breathed his last. As I locked the Impala's door the thought of the gunmen who'd blasted the gangster—on a nod from his driver—reminded me of my own frailty. I patted my own gun for reassurance and strolled into the lobby.

No guards or receptionists waited to direct the

ignorant. I wandered around, looking for a sign-board. Apparently I'd come in a back way—I had to go through a couple of corridors before I found a directory. It pointed me to the building next in line, where Paragon held floors four through eight.

The whole complex seemed oddly empty, as though all those cars in the lot had decanted their owners into outer space. No one passed me in the halls and I waited alone beside the elevators. When I got to the fourth floor I faced a bare aqua wall with a minute sign directing me to reception. Presumably in Paragon's days of penury they'd decided not to waste money on big letters.

The place was so empty I was beginning to wonder if a blinking computer screen would greet me at the reception area. I was relieved to see an actual person, a woman about my own age with shoulder-length curls and a brownish jacket dress that was limp and faded from years of wear. I began to feel more confident about my blue jeans.

I gave a smile intended to convey both empathy and self-assurance and asked for the controller. She obligingly dialed a number, then put her palm over the mouthpiece.

"Who can I say is calling?"

"My name's V. I. Warshawski." I handed her a card. "I'm a financial investigator."

She transmitted the information, stumbling a little over my name, as receptionists so often do, then turned back to me. "They're not hiring any-one."

"And I'm not looking for work. This will be so much easier to explain directly to the controller, instead of through you to her secretary."

"It's a him. Mr. Loring. What do you have to say to him?"

I counted on my fingers. "Six words. Diamond Head Motors and debt financing."

She repeated my words dubiously. When I nodded she said them again into the phone. This time she seemed to be on hold. She answered incoming calls and routed them through, checked back with her own blinking light and waited again. About five minutes later she told me I could have a seat: Sukey would be down for me.

The wait stretched to twenty minutes before Sukey showed up. She was a tall, thin woman whose skin-tight skirt emphasized the painful boniness of her pelvis and hips. Her pale face was pitted with acne scars, but her voice, when she asked me to follow her, was deep and sweet.

"What did you say your name was?" she asked as we got on the elevator. "Charlene wasn't very clear over the phone."

"Warshawski," I repeated, handing her a card.

She studied the little rectangle gravely, until the doors opened for the eighth floor. As soon as we stepped off the elevators I realized I'd found the secret cache of Paragon employees. The place was a maze of cubicles, each holding two or three computer stations and the people to staff them.

As we moved toward the end of the floor the cubes gave way to offices, still filled with computers and their minders.

We finally reached a small open area. Sukey's desk stood outside an open corner office. It was labeled as Ben Loring's lair, but he wasn't home. Sukey directed me to one of the foam-core seats and knocked on a nearby door. I couldn't hear what she said when she stuck her head around the jamb. She disappeared briefly, then came back to escort me in.

The conference room was filled with men, mostly in shirtsleeves and all of them looking at me with a mix of suspicion and contempt. No one spoke, but two or three of them were darting glances at the second guy from my left, a burly fiftyish man with a thick bush of gray hair.

"Mr. Loring?" I held out a hand to him. "I'm V. I. Warshawski."

He ignored my hand. "Who are you working for, Warshawski?"

I sat uninvited at my end of the oval table. "Salvatore Contreras."

This time all seven of them exchanged glances. Normally, of course, I keep my clients' identities secret, but I wanted to watch them all try to figure out what big financial interest Mr. Contreras represented. Maybe they'd even think he was with the Mob.

"And why does he care about Diamond Head?" Loring asked at last.

"How about this, Mr. Loring: you explain to

me what Paragon's connection to Diamond Head is and I'll tell you what my client's is."

There was a little rumble through the room at that. I heard the man on Loring's right mutter, "I told you this was a waste of time, Ben. She's just going to dick us around."

Loring shook him off like a bad pitch. "I can't talk to you unless I know who you represent. There's an enormous amount at stake here. If you work for—well, certain people—then you already know all about it and our legal staff will be filing papers to deal with what looks like a rather naive attempt at espionage. And if your client—Contreras, did you say? —has his own ax to grind, then I'm not going to make you a present of very explosive information."

"I see." I studied my fingernails while I thought it over. "I'll ask you a different question. Two questions. How many people in this room know that Paragon is bankrolling Diamond Head? And how many of you know why?"

This time the rumble became a roar. Loring let it go for a minute, then brought the meeting back under control.

"Any of you boys know anything about Diamond Head? Or bankrolling?" His voice was light with sarcasm.

The room responded to his tone. People forced out guffaws as they gave their negatives, punching each other on the arms and stealing secret glances at me to see how the show was going over.

I waited for them to finish enjoying themselves.

"Okay, you've convinced me: you're all too naive to manage a multinational. I do find it curious, though, that you agreed to see me cold just because I mentioned Diamond Head's name in connection with debt financing. And not just you, Loring—all these guys came along to protect your ass."

"I agreed to see you cold because I thought you might have a business proposition for us, not an accusation."

"Really!" It was my turn for light sarcasm. "That must be why the *Journal* raved about you guys a few weeks ago—because you interrupt your workdays every time some stranger walks through the door without an introduction or advance material or anything. Just in the hope she may have a business proposition."

The man on Loring's right started to speak, but the controller waved him into silence. "What is it you want, Warshawski?"

"We could dance this tango all afternoon. I want information. About you and Diamond Head."

"I think we made it clear that we don't have anything to tell you." The man on Loring's right ignored the controller's silencing hand.

"Come on, guys. I *know* you're bankrolling Diamond Head. I've seen their cash statements."

"Then you've seen something I'm not privy to. I can't comment on it," Loring said.

"Who could I talk to who might be able to? Your CEO or COO?"

"Neither of them would be able to tell you anything. And unlike me, they wouldn't even grant you an interview."

"So should I ask the feds about it?"

A buzz went around the table again at that. The man to my own right, lean with a shock of white hair, slapped his palm on the table. "Ben, we've got to check on her bona fides. And find out what she really wants."

I nodded approvingly at him. "Good idea. You can easily find out about me by calling Daraugh Graham at Continental Lakeside. He's the chairman; I do a lot of work for him."

Loring and the man who'd just spoken exchanged long glances, then Loring, fractionally, shook his head. "I may do that, Warshawski. *If* I do, I may get back to you. But you'd still have to sell me on why you're asking questions."

"I guess I want to know how deep you are in Diamond Head's decision-making. Because if you *are* privy to their inner workings—well, then there are a lot more questions I'd like to ask."

Loring shook his head. "You're not selling me. You're anti-selling. And as you were so quick to point out, we're busy men. We need to get back to acting that way."

I got to my feet. "Then I'll just have to keep digging. And I never make advance guarantees on what I do if my shovel hits a rotting compost pile."

No one said anything to me, but as I left the room a major uproar started. I wanted to lean my ear against the jamb, but Sukey was looking at me from behind her desk. I went over to her.

"Thanks for your help. . . . You have a beautiful voice, you know. Do you sing?"

"Only in church choirs. With this—" she gestured at her acne scars, flushing miserably— "No one wants to audition me for the stage."

The intercom on her desk buzzed loudly; Ben Loring needed her in the conference room. I wondered if I could take the chance on her absence to try to look in her file cabinets, but it would be impossible to explain away if she came bouncing out and caught me at it. Besides, it was close to three now. I'd just have time to get downtown to check up on Jason Felitti before the library closed.

After two decades of dickering, Chicago is actually building a new public library. Named for the late, great Harold Washington, the memorial—under construction—has the unfortunate look of a Victorian mausoleum. Until it opens the city keeps what collections it possesses in a series of out-of-the-way locations. They had moved recently from an old barracks just off Michigan Avenue to an even more desolate dump on the west edge of the Loop.

Unfortunately that corner is also the edge of the hottest new gallery and retail part of the city. I had to go to the underground streets to find a vacant meter. Even though I was confident I'd lost my tail, I still felt uneasy in the labyrinth of truck routes and loading docks. Someone could jump me here and no one would ever notice. These macabre fantasies made my heels tingle with nervousness. I ran up Kinzie toward daylight with more speed than I thought my legs had left in them.

An hour with the library's computer specialist reinforced my need to buy my own machine. Not that the specialist wasn't helpful—she was, very. But the amount of information available at the end of a phone line was so great, and my need for it so strong, that it didn't make sense to be dependent on the hours the library was open.

I carried the sheaf of printouts to a crowded table in the periodicals room, one of the few places in the building where one could actually sit and read. My immediate seatmates included a small gray man with a thin mustache who was poring over *Scientific American* and keeping up an anxious commentary under his breath. It wasn't clear whether he was reacting to the article or life in general. On my other side a bigger man was reading the *Herald-Star* one word at a time, running a finger under the sentences as he moved his lips. I hoped the new library would include showers in the rest rooms. It would be a big help, if not for my seatmate at least for anyone who had to sit near him in the future.

Blotting out the smell as best I could, I began reading about Jason Felitti, owner of Diamond Head Motors. He was Peter's brother, younger by three years (born in 1931), educated at Northwestern (business), dabbling in politics and entrepreneurship. Peter, one clip mentioned, had also attended Northwestern, taking an engineering degree. Jason, who'd never married, lived in the family home in Naperville, while Peter had moved to Oak Brook with his wife and two daughters in '68. A portentous year in lives around the world—why not for Dick's father-in-law as well?

Amalgamated Portage, the family business, had been founded by Tiepolo Felitti in 1888. It had started as a simple operation—a single pushcart for hauling away scrap. By Tiepolo's death in the 1919 flu epidemic Amalgamated had become one of the region's largest cartage firms.

The First World War had helped their rail line enormously. In the thirties they saw the future and it looked like long-distance trucking. They were one of the earliest carriers to build a fleet. Since the Second World War they had diversified into mining and smelting, at first with great success and then with what sounded like equally great disaster.

Peter had sold the mining operations at a loss when his father died in 1975. The business now tried to stay closer to its original mission: cartage. In 1985 Peter had bought one of the fledgling overnight delivery services; that seemed to be doing modestly well. Amalgamated remained a closely held family company, so information on it was sketchy.

Jason had inherited shares in Amalgamated when his father died, but it was Peter who took over the firm. In fact, Peter had been on the management committee for years while Jason just seemed to sit on the board. I wondered if Jason had been tagged early as incompetent, or if the family was so rigidly structured that only the oldest son was allowed to manage. In which case, what would happen to it when Peter died, since Jason had no children and Peter only had daughters? Was Dick the shining knight or did the other son-in-law have to fight him for the spoils?

For years Jason's main energy had gone into Du Page County politics. He had been a water commissioner, had worked on the Deep Tunnel project, and finally had spent twelve years on the county board itself. At the last election he'd decided not to seek a fourth term.

According to a speech that got a few lines in the *Herald-Star's* metro edition, Jason announced he wanted to devote himself full-time to business. Ray Gibson at the *Trib* thought Jason had been worried about some stories his political challenger was digging up, conflict of interest between his role as a county commissioner and his position as a director of U.S. Metropolitan Bank and Trust. But Gib was always expecting the worst of Illinois elected officials—not that they often disappointed him.

Last year Jason had acquired Diamond Head. The story hadn't merited more than a paragraph in the business pages. The meager coverage didn't reveal anything about the financing, although the *Sun-Times* hinted Peter might have provided some backing through Amalgamated. No one seemed to know how much ready cash Amalgamated had, or whether they, too, had acquired a heavy debt-load during their mining fiasco. It didn't sound as though Dick had married into the colossal financial empire I'd always imagined.

"U.S. Met," I said aloud, forgetting I was in a library.

I startled the little gray man into dropping his magazine. He stared at me briefly, muttering to himself, then scuttled to a distant table, leaving the *Scientific American* on the floor. I picked it up and laid it on the table, patting it in what was intended as a reassuring manner. He had picked up a paper and was staring at me over its edge. When he realized I was looking at him, he raised the paper to cover his face. It was upside down.

I folded my clips into a tidy square, stuck them in my shoulder bag, and left. I couldn't resist glancing back to see if he'd returned to his magazine, but he was still hiding behind the *Sun-Times*. I wished I had that much effect on Dick, or even on the goons staking out my apartment.

It was past five by the time I jogged back down Kinzie to the Impala. Too late to tackle Chamfers again. I sat in the car massaging the small of my back; it had kinked up during my research. Jason Felitti sat on the board of U.S. Met and— probably—had steered Du Page County funds there.

Now, three years later, Mrs. Frizell had closed her account at the Bank of Lake View and opened one at U.S. Met.

"You only want there to be a connection," I said sharply to the dashboard. "But it's a pretty thin thread from Jason Felitti to Todd Pichea." Although it did run through Richard Yarborough. Maybe Freeman was right—that I did harbor a grudge against Dick—for being a supersuccess while I still struggled to make ends meet. Or for preferring a younger, prettier woman to me?

I didn't think I minded Teri: she was so much more suited to Dick's combination of ambition and weakness than I was. But perhaps it did rankle that I had been the promising graduate, third in our class, with a dozen job offers, and now I couldn't afford a new pair of running shoes. I'd made my own choices, but one's resentments are seldom rationally grounded. At any rate, I didn't want to risk proving Freeman right by starting a vendetta against Dick over the kind of business he did.

On that moral high note I started the car and joined the congealing traffic leaving the Loop. It wasn't until I found myself driving past west side exits on the Stevenson that I figured out where I was going: Naperville, to the Felitti family home.

29

Drinking with the Idle Rich

Naperville, about thirty miles west of the Loop, is one of Chicago's fastest-growing suburbs. It's ringed by genteel tract houses on sizable lots—home to the middle managers of Chicago, and to a depressing amount of concrete. Mighty tollways crisscross the southwest suburbs, eating up farmland and leaving steep, jagged cols in their wake.

Inside the concrete stilts and the endless succession of malls, fast-food places, and car dealers sit the remains of the town. A hundred years ago it was a quiet farm community, without much connection to Chicago, beyond a river that carried freight between the city and the Mississippi. A number of people, rich either from the land or the water, built themselves solid Victorian homes there. One of those had belonged to Tiepolo Felitti.

I found the house on Madison Street easily enough, by stopping at the library and asking. Tiepolo was one of Naperville's illustrious fathers; his home was a local landmark. It was a pale dove-blue, with a small plaque in front explaining its historical interest. Other than that it had no remarkable features. The small front porch held a bench swing, but the house lacked the leaded windows or stained glass that make some Victorian homes interesting. The front door itself was a slab of unadorned wood, painted white to match the rest of the trim.

The house stood on a minute lot typical of the inner town. I could see why Peter had moved to Oak Brook: It gave far more scope for opulence. Would Dick ever have fallen in love with Teri if her father had stayed in this unpretentious place?

"But if it hadn't been Teri there would have been someone much like her," I muttered aloud, moving to the doorbell.

"Did you say something?"

I jumped slightly at the voice. I hadn't heard the man come up the walk behind me. His well-fed, close-shaved face seemed the embodiment of the Chicago politician. I'd somehow always thought of it as a Democratic look, but realized that was because I lacked suburban experience.

"Mr. Felitti?" I smiled in what I hoped was a pleasant way.

"In the flesh. And you're a welcome surprise to find on my doorstep after a long, hard day." He looked at his watch. "Been waiting long?"

"Nope. I was hoping to talk to you."

"Well, come in, come in and tell me what you're drinking. I'll fix you up while I check on Mother."

I hadn't expected such exuberance. It made my job both harder and easier.

He held the door for me. Naperville apparently hadn't yet grown to the point that he had to lock it. I felt a twinge of envy, mixed with anger that someone could live the happy, blissful life of not needing two or three dead bolts between himself and the rest of the world.

Jason led me down a long, unfurnished hall. The walls were papered in a faded gold print, apparently unchanged since the house was built. The room he brought me to showed the first signs of the family's money. It was a study overlooking the small back garden, with a Persian rug in bold reds on the polished wood floor, another in pale gold silk hanging on the wall, and what looked like a museum trove of small statues strewn among the books.

"Now, you're not one of those modern girls who only drinks white wine, are you?"

My smile became a little fixed. "No. I'm a modern woman, and I drink neat whisky. Black Label, if you have it."

He laughed as though I'd said something really delightful and pulled a bottle from a cabinet underneath the silk hanging. "Black Label it is. Now, you fix yourself what you'd like and I'll go check on Mother."

"Is she ill, Mr. Felitti?"

"Oh, she had a stroke a few years ago and can't walk anymore. But her mind is still working, oh yes, still sharp as a tack. Still can tell Peter and me a thing or two, yes indeed. And the ladies from the church are good about coming by, so don't imagine she's lonely."

He laughed again and went back down the hall. I amused myself by idly inspecting the statuary. Some of the pieces, miniature bronzes with perfectly sculpted muscles, looked as though they might date to the Renaissance. Others were contemporary, but very fine modern work. I wondered what I would invest in if I had millions of dollars to strew around.

After Jason had been gone five minutes it dawned on me that I might find Chamfers's home number in the room. A large leather desk had a tempting array of drawers. I was just opening the middle one when Jason returned. I pretended to be studying a miniature globe, an intricate model with the stars carved out above and fanciful sea-monsters peeping from the oceans.

"Pietro D'Alessandro," Jason said cheerfully, going to the bar. "The old man was mad for anything from the Italian Renaissance—proved he'd made it in the New World and was a worthy successor to the old. I think that sounds nice, don't you?"

I nodded dumbly.

"Then why not write it down?" He poured himself a martini, drank it rather fast, and poured a second.

"It's a catchy line—I think I've memorized it." I wondered if his exuberant good cheer to strangers was a sign of mental illness or alcoholism.

"I bet a good memory comes in real handy in your line of work. If I don't write everything down in triplicate I forget it five minutes later. Now, take a pew and tell me what you want to know."

Bemused, I sat in the green leather armchair he gestured to. "It's about Diamond Head Motors, Mr. Felitti. Or specifically, Milton Chamfers. I've been trying to see him for two weeks and he won't talk to me."

"Chamfers?" His pale-blue eyes seemed to pop slightly. "You want to talk about Chamfers? I thought the story was supposed to focus on me. Or did you want me to talk about the acquisition of the company? Can't really do that, because it's family, and we don't discuss our business with the public. Of course, we had a public bond issue, but you'd have to talk to the bankers about that. Not that I want to disappoint a pretty girl like yourself."

So he wasn't crazy—he was expecting a reporter. I was about to disabuse him when the last sentence came out. I'm as vain as the next person, but I prefer compliments on my appearance in the right context, and more aptly phrased.

"I like to get as many sides to a story as I can," I murmured. "And Diamond Head is your first personal business venture, isn't it? You can tell me that, can't you, without violating the family *omertà?*"

He laughed again, a loud, merry peal. I was

beginning to see why no one had ever married him.

"Good girl! Do you speak Italian, or did you dig that up for the occasion?"

"My mother was Italian; I'm reasonably fluent, at least through an adolescent vocabulary."

"I never learned. My grandmother spoke Italian to us when we were kiddies, but after she passed on we lost it. Of course, Dad didn't marry an Italian—Granny Felitti was beside herself, you know how people were in those days—but the long and the short of it was that Mother refused to learn the language. Did it to spite the old lady."

He laughed again and I winced involuntarily.

"What made you want to buy Diamond Head, Mr. Felitti?"

"Oh, you know how these things go," he said vaguely, looking into his glass. "I wanted to own my own business—do my own thing, your generation would say."

I braced myself for the merry peal, but he held back this time. I didn't really care why he'd bought the company; I was fishing around for ways to get to Chamfers and not having many ideas for bait.

"You were lucky to get Paragon Steel interested in your company," I finally offered.

He studied my face over the brim of his glass. "Paragon Steel? I guess they're one of our accounts. Not too many people know about them, though. You must have been doing your homework, young lady."

I flashed a big grin. "I like to have enough background to make things interesting when I finally talk to a . . . uh . . . subject."

His laugh came again, but this time it seemed a little forced. "I admire thoroughness. The old man was forever telling me I didn't have it, though. So I have to confess that I leave the thorough details about the business to other people."

"Does that mean you won't talk about Paragon?" I kept the grin plastered to my face.

" 'Fraid so. I expected this interview to be about personal matters and I'm all set to talk about those." He made an ostentatious business of looking at his watch.

"Okay. If we have to talk about people and not about money, how about the guy who got killed down by Diamond Head last week? Can't get much more personal than death, can you?"

"What?" He'd been tilting his head back to drain the last few drops from the glass. His hand shook and the gin splashed his shirt front. "Nobody told me anyone died down there. What are you talking about?"

"Mitch Kruger, Mr. Felitti. Name ring a bell?"

He stared at me aggressively. "Should it?"

"I don't know. You keep telling me you don't take much part in the business side down there. But what about the personal, since that's your forte? Do you direct them to hire investigators? Beat up doctors? Dump old men into the San?" I guess I was too tired for finesse.

"Who are you, anyway?" he demanded.

287

"You're not with *Chicago Life,* that's for damn sure."

"What about the attack on Dr. Herschel. Did Chamfers organize that? Did you know about it in advance?"

"I never heard of Dr. whoever, and I'm getting damned sure I never heard of you. What's your name?"

"V. I. Warshawski. Does *that* ring any bells?"

His face reddened. "I thought you were the girl from the magazine, Maggie. She was coming out this afternoon. I'd sure as hell never let you in my house if I'd known who you were."

"It's a help, Mr. Felitti, that you know who I am. Because that means that Chamfers has discussed me with you. And that means you are just a bit involved with what your company does. All I want is to talk to Chamfers—about Mitch Kruger. Since you're a director, you could make it so easy for me."

"But I don't want to make it easy for you. Get the hell out of my house—before I call the cops and make you leave."

At least he had stopped laughing, an enormous relief. I finished the whisky.

"I'm going," I said, getting up. "Oh, there was one last question. About U.S. Met. What did you have to offer an old lady that would make her close her account in her neighborhood bank and move it to Met? You guys are notorious for not paying interest on your accounts, but you must have told her something."

"You're off your rocker. I'm not going to call the cops—I'm going to get the boys from Elgin to come with a straitjacket. I don't know anything about U.S. Met and I don't know why you come busting into my house asking about it."

"You're a director, Mr. Felitti," I said reproachfully. "I'm sure their insurance company would like to think you knew what the bank was up to. You know, for directors' and officers' liability claims."

The red in his face had subsided. "You're talking to the wrong person. I'm not clever enough to think of bank marketing plans. Ask anyone. But not on my premises."

I didn't think I was going to make any progress by staying. I put my empty glass on the desk.

"But you know who I am," I repeated. "And that means that Chamfers was concerned enough to call you. And that means my suspicions that Mitch Kruger knew something about Diamond Head are correct. At least I know now where to focus my energies. Thanks for the whisky, Mr. Felitti."

"I don't know who you are; I never heard your name before," he made a last-ditch attempt at bluster. "I just know it was supposed to be a girl named Maggie here, and your name isn't Maggie."

"Nice try, Mr. Felitti. But you and I both know you're lying."

As I sashayed down the hall in front of him the doorbell rang. A petite young woman with a mound of frizzy black hair was standing on the step.

"Maggie from *Chicago Life?*" I asked.

"Yeah." She grinned. "Mr. Felitti here? I think he's expecting me."

"Right behind me." I fished a card from the side of my handbag and handed it to her. "I'm a private investigator. If he says something interesting about Diamond Head, give me a call. And watch out for his laugh—it's a killer."

Getting the last word brings a certain emotional satisfaction, but it doesn't help an investigation. I drove aimlessly around Naperville, looking for a place to have a soft drink before going back to Chicago. I didn't see anything that looked like a coffee shop. At last I pulled off at the park that borders the river. I walked past parties of women with small children, necking teenagers, and the assorted homeward-bound commuter until I found an empty rustic bridge.

Peering over the wood railing at the Du Page River I tried to interpret Felitti's and my conversation without too many shades of wishful thinking. I believed what I'd said to him at the end: he did know who I was. Chamfers had been in touch. That meant I really had to focus on Diamond Head.

On the other hand, I believed what he'd said about U.S. Met. He was the wrong person to ask about marketing plans. The way he phrased it made me think it was his brother Peter I should be talking to: I'm not clever enough, ask anyone. Even though his tone wasn't especially bitter, it was the expression of someone who was used to being told about his own stupidity. Peter, after all, was the one who'd been trusted with the family business. Jason had never been invited to participate.

I should have done a search on Peter at the same time that I looked up Jason. I didn't know much about him, but I was willing to bet he was on the U.S. Met board.

30

Boardinghouse Reach

I got off the Stevenson at Damen and drove up to County Hospital. My bones were aching with exhaustion. I negotiated the distance from my car to the building, and then down its endless corridors, by sheer willpower. Although it was past seven, Nelle McDowell was still at the nursing station.

"When do you go off duty, anyway?" I demanded.

She made a wry face. "We're so shorthanded here I could work a hundred-and-sixty-hour week and it wouldn't make a dent. You here to see the old lady? It's good some of you neighborhood folks care enough to keep in touch. I see she's got a son out in California and he hasn't even bothered to send her a card."

"Is she talking yet?"

McDowell shook her head regretfully. "She keeps calling for that dog, Bruce, I guess. I don't know how much she understands of what anyone says to her, but we've given strict orders to all the shifts not to say anything about it."

"Has either Todd or Chrissie Pichea been by? They're the couple who got themselves named her guardians." I was afraid their native cruelty might lead them to tell Mrs. Frizell the bad news in the hopes it would hasten her death.

"Hotshot young couple? They came by last night, kind of late, maybe ten. I was gone by then, but the night charge nurse, Sandra Milo, told me about it. Seems they were desperate for her financial papers. Title to her house or something. I guess they figured they needed it to put up as security for her medical bills or something, but they were much too rough for her in the state she's in—shaking her shoulder, trying to make her sit up and talk to them. Sandra threw them out in pretty short order. Other than that no one's been by but one of the neighbor ladies. I couldn't tell you her name."

"Hellstrom," I supplied mechanically. "Marjorie Hellstrom."

So Todd and Chrissie didn't have her critical papers. I'd just assumed they were down in the Jurassic layer of the old secretary, but the Picheas could have searched the house at their leisure. If they hadn't found the title, where was it?

"How long are you going to keep Mrs. Frizell here?" I finally asked.

"She's not fit to be moved right now. The hip isn't healing very fast. Ultimately she has to go to a nursing home, you know, if the guardians can find one she can afford, but that's a ways in the future."

She sent me down the hall to Mrs. Frizell's cramped cubicle. The death mask of the old woman's face was more pronounced than before, the hollows under her cheeks sunk so deep that her face looked like gray putty lightly patted over a skull. A thin stream of drool ran along the right side of her mouth. She snorted heavily as she breathed and kept tossing restlessly on the bed.

My stomach gave a convulsive twist. I was glad I hadn't eaten since my toasted cheese sandwich six hours ago. I forced myself to kneel next to her and take her hand. Her fingers felt like a collection of brittle twigs.

"Mrs. Frizell!" I called loudly. "It's Vic. Your neighbor, Vic. I have a dog, remember?"

Her agitated movements seemed to slow a bit. I thought she might be trying to focus on my voice. I repeated my message, placing special emphasis on "dog." At that her eyelids did flutter slightly and she muttered, "Bruce?"

"Yes, Bruce is a wonderful dog, Mrs. Frizell. I know Bruce."

Her parched lips curved infinitesimally up-ward. "Bruce," she repeated.

I massaged her frail fingers gently between my own. It seemed a hopeless prospect, to move her from Bruce to banking, but I tried anyway. Hating myself for lying I suggested that Bruce needed to eat, and that for that he would need money. But she couldn't respond enough to talk about something as complicated as her decision to change banks last spring.

She did finally say, "Feed Bruce." That was hopeful in terms of her mental state—it showed she was connecting what I was saying to the right synapses—but it didn't help me investigate her finances. I patted her fingers one last time and stood up. To my surprise Carol Alvarado was standing behind me.

We exclaimed at each other in unison. I asked what she was doing on the orthopedic floor.

She grinned a little. "Probably the same thing you are, Vic. Since I helped find her I feel responsible for her. I come over every now and then to check on her."

"But in uniform?" I asked. "Did you come straight from Lotty's?"

"Actually, I took a job in the night trauma unit." She laughed self-consciously. "I was spending all this time over on the AIDS ward with Guillermo, and of course exchanging shop talk with the nurses on duty. They're always shorthanded here and it just sounded like a great opportunity. When

Guillermo goes home I can still look after him during the day."

"And when do you sleep?" I demanded. "Isn't this going from the frying pan to the fire?"

"Oh, I suppose, in a way. I'm only spending afternoons at Lotty's for a few days until her new nurse feels up to taking over full-time. But . . . I don't know. You can do real nursing here. It's not like most hospitals, where all you do is fill out forms and act like a grunt for the doctors. Here you're working with patients, and I see so many different kinds of cases. At Lotty's it's mostly babies and old women except when you come in with your body rearranged. Anyway, it's only been two nights now but I'm loving it."

She checked Mrs. Frizell's bedding. "It's good that you got her to say something else, another word. You should come more often: it might help her recovery."

I rubbed the back of my neck. That sounded like one of those good deeds that make the angels in heaven cheer but prove a burden to the doer.

"Yeah, I could try to get over more."

I explained the information I was after and why. "I don't suppose you could think of a way to get her to talk about her bank."

Carol looked cautiously down the hall to make sure no one was in earshot. "I might, Vic. Don't get your hopes up, but I might come up with something. Now I've got to get back to the trauma unit. Walk you to the stairs?"

Once again the elevators were out of service.

It was too much like my own office for me to complain. On the way downstairs I asked Carol whether she had a concrete plan in mind. "I'd like to find out about her money while she still has some."

"What—you think those neighbors of yours are defrauding her? You got proof of it? Or you just don't like them?" Carol's tone was derisive.

I forgot that Carol had seen me showing my hackles at Todd Pichea and Vinnie. I flushed and stammered a bit as I tried to explain myself. "Maybe I am mounting a vendetta. It's because of the dogs—it seemed to me the Picheas raced around to get guardianship rights just to put the dogs to sleep so that they could safeguard their property values. Maybe they were being altruistic. But I still don't understand why they had to muscle in like that, kill the dogs before she'd even been away from home a week."

My voice trailed away uncertainly. I should be spending my energies on Jason Felitti and Diamond Head; it looked as though I might have stumbled onto something hot there. I should stop being a pest in the neighborhood and just let Todd and Chrissie work things out however they chose. After all, Mrs. Frizell wasn't the most wonderful specimen to be spending time on. But all my hectoring myself on the subject could not stop the nagging in my brain that I should have done something more to protect the old woman and that I should be looking after her now.

Carol squeezed my arm. "You're too intense,

Vic. You take everything too hard. The world won't stop spinning its way around the sun if you don't rescue every wounded animal in your path."

I grinned at her. "You're a fine one to lecture me, Carol, after leaving the intensity of Lotty for the laid-back leisure of the Cook County trauma unit."

She laughed, her teeth gleaming white in the dim stairwell. "And on those words I'd better get back there. It was quiet when I left, but now the sun is setting the bodies will start streaming in."

We hugged each other and went our separate directions. I'd parked the Impala on the street, a few blocks west of the hospital. One thing about driving an old car with a rusty body, you don't worry so much about strangers helping themselves to it. As I started the engine I could hear sirens in the distance. Ambulances bringing in their first loads of the night.

It was dinnertime and naptime, but I didn't want to go home just now. I figured I could get one more free pass into the building through the alley before the guys in the Subaru realized how I was coming and going. I didn't want to waste it on supper.

I parked the car on a side street near Belmont and Sheridan and climbed into the backseat for a brief rest. My late-night visit to Jonas Carver's Loop office had left me tired and gritty all day. And onto that I'd added treks to the north and west suburbs. Not to mention fleeing flat out from some ugly muscle.

Another good thing about the Impala, I thought as I squirmed around to find a comfortable position—my Trans Am would never accommodate my five-eight frame across its minute backseat.

I actually slept for an hour. Bright lights shone in my eyes and woke me with heart-jolting speed. I reached for my gun and sat up, fearing my pursuers had found me. It turned out just to be a car trying to parallel park across the narrow street from me; it had managed to get turned at right angles to the roadway. Its headlights pointed directly into the backseat.

Feeling rather foolish I put the gun back inside my armpit. I dug in my bag for a comb and did the best I could to style my hair in the dark. The people across from me were still having trouble maneuvering their car when I climbed from the Impala. Proving that Carol was wrong, that I could overlook someone in trouble, I left them to it.

The Dortmunder restaurant, one of Lotty's and my favorite hangouts, was only a few blocks away. In the basement of the Chesterton Hotel, it serves sandwiches and hearty dinners surrounded by a fabulous wine cellar. Normally I like to get a bottle of something rich, a Saint-Emilion or the like, but this was strictly a refueling stop before getting back to work.

I stopped in the hotel lobby's rest room to wash up. I was wearing jeans and a cotton knit top, not elegant dining apparel, but also not ruined by sleeping in a car. They were smelling a little ripe.

The staff at the Dortmunder greeted me enthusiastically, wanting to know if the doctor was joining me. When I explained that the doctor had been injured in a car accident the other day, they were appropriately concerned: How had it happened? How was she? My conscience rubbed me as I explained the bare outlines of the situation.

Lisa Vetec, granddaughter of the owner, ushered me to a table in a corner and took my order. While they made me a sandwich from their famed Hungarian salami I called Mr. Contreras. He was relieved to hear from me.

"Someone came around looking for you an hour or so ago. I told him you wasn't in, but I didn't like his looks."

I asked Mr. Contreras what the visitor looked like. His description was sketchy, but I thought it might have been the man who followed me into the Belmont Diner this morning. If he wanted to see me urgently, our confrontation was only a matter of time. But if possible I'd be the one to choose both the time and the place.

I tapped my front teeth with a knuckle while I considered the situation. "I think I'm going to move out for a day or two. I'll be over in about an hour to pick up a few things. I want to come in through the alley. I'll call right before I get there—if you let me in maybe they won't know I've come."

"But where can you go, doll? I know you usually hang out with the doc, but . . ." He broke off with unusual delicacy.

"Yeah, I can't involve Lotty in this anymore, even if she'd let me. It just dawned on me that I might be able to get a room down where Jake Sokolowski lives."

He didn't like it, not for any special reason, just because he didn't like me moving so far from his orbit. It's not so much that he wants to control me, I've realized recently, but because he needs the reassurance of being able to touch me. He finally agreed to my program, on the grounds that I call him—"Regularly, doll, not just once a week when the spirit moves you"—and only hung up when I promised.

My sandwich and coffee were waiting for me, but I looked up Tonia Coriolano in the directory. While my coffee cooled she apologized profusely, but she had no vacancy. Normally to oblige a friend of a lodger she might allow them to sleep a night on the living room couch, but even that was occupied right now.

Lisa waved an arm at me and gestured at my table. I nodded. Desperate times call for desperate measures. I looked up Mrs. Polter and didn't know if I was relieved or disappointed to find her listed.

She answered on the ninth ring. "Yes? What do you want?"

"A room, Mrs. Polter. I'm V. I. Warshawski, the detective who's been around lately. I need a place to sleep for a few nights."

She gave a rasping laugh. "Men only in my house, honey. Except for me, of course, but I can take care of myself."

"I can take care of myself, too, Mrs. Polter. I'd bring my own towels. It'd be for three nights at the most. And believe me, none of your lodgers will bother me."

"Yeah, but what about—ah, what the hell. You paid for the old guy's room and he never used it. I guess you can sleep there if you want. No more than two nights, though, you hear? I got my reputation to think about."

"Yes, ma'am," I said smartly. "I'll be by around ten-thirty to leave my things and get a key."

"Ten-thirty? What do you think this is, the Ritz? I close up shop—" Again she cut herself off. "Oh, what difference does it make? I usually stay up until one in the morning looking at the damned tube, anyway. Come on by."

When I got back to my table, Lisa brought me fresh coffee. It pays to be a regular.

31

Creeping Up on a Plant

I walked up the dark, narrow staircase behind Mrs. Polter, my feet tripping on the torn linoleum. In deference to the remembered smell I'd brought my own sheets as well as towels, but memory couldn't compete with the reality of grease and stale sweat. A cheap motel would have been ten times cleaner and more private.

Mrs. Polter's arms brushed the walls of the stairwell. She stopped frequently to catch her breath. After bumping into her bulk on her first rest I kept a good three steps between us.

"Okay, honey, this is it. Like I said, no cooking in the rooms; the wiring won't stand it. No smoking in the rooms either. No loud radios or TVs. None of that kind of stuff. You can help yourself to breakfast any time between seven A.M. and noon. You'll find the kitchen easy enough—it's at the end of the hall downstairs. Try not to hog the bathroom in the morning—guys gotta shave before they go to work. Here's a key to the front door—you go and lose it, you pay to put in a new lock."

I nodded solemnly and made an ostentatious show of tying it to one of my belt loops. She had put up quite a fight about letting me have a key. When I told her the choice was between that and my rousing her in the middle of the night, she started to demand that I stay elsewhere. In mid-fight she'd broken off and glared at me, then abruptly agreed to the key. It was the third time she'd voluntarily overridden a major objection to my presence. I was here against both our better judgments—that certainly gave us a common ground for conversation.

She turned on the naked forty-watt bulb with obvious reluctance. To save money on electricity she moved as much as possible in the dark. She hovered in the doorway, eyeing my suitcase, which had a number lock.

"You want me to tell you the combination?" I asked brightly. "Or would you like to figure it out for yourself?"

At that she muttered darkly and heaved her bulk out of the entrance. When I heard her slow tread back down the stairs, I undid the lock and surveyed the contents. Except for refill cartridges for my gun there was nothing in there she couldn't see, nothing that revealed my address or my income. My change of underwear was sober white cotton, not my prized silks. I'd also brought a can of bathroom cleanser and a rag so I could scrub down the sink enough to stand to brush my teeth in it. Let her make of that what she would.

I scooped up the cartridges and stuffed them in my jacket pockets. They could stay in the Impala's glove compartment for the time being.

Whipping the rank sheets from the thin mattress, I stuffed them under the bed and put my own on in their place. It seemed faintly amusing to me that someone of my slovenly habits should have invested so much energy lately in cleaning other women's houses.

The room sported an ancient plywood bureau lined with papers that dated to 1966. Fascinated, I read part of an article on Martin Luther King's speech at Soldier Field. I remembered that speech: I'd been one of the one hundred thousand people who came to hear him.

Tonight wasn't the right time for nostalgia. I pulled my eyes from the grimy page and slid a hand around the drawers to see if Mitch might have left some revealing document behind. All I came away with was a black smudge from the accumulated grit. I decided to leave my clothes—really just a clean T-shirt to go with the underwear—in the suitcase.

I scrutinized the room for possible hiding places, pulling back pieces of loose linoleum, peering in the hems of the frail window shades. None of them seemed suitable for concealing anything bigger than a Kleenex. The small stack of papers Mitch had considered important enough to take around with him must have been the limit of his sacred possessions. And those were gone. To his son, or a facsimile thereof.

When I finished my survey I left the suitcase unlocked. I knew Mrs. Polter would be up here pawing through it as soon as I was gone; I didn't want her to spring the lock to get at the inside. The can of Comet and the rag I left on the floor.

There were four guest rooms on the floor. Pale light poked feebly underneath one door and a radio, tuned to a Spanish station, played softly. Someone was snoring loudly behind the door of a second, but the third seemed empty. Maybe it was just desperation for cash that prompted Mrs. Polter to let me stay—she'd demanded another twenty on top of what I'd paid her for Mitch as soon as I came up the front steps.

My landlady was watching television in the living room when I came down the stairs. The big color console was tuned to pro wrestling. The light coming from the screen far outdid the miserable efforts of the only lamp in the room.

Mrs. Polter sensed my approach over the screaming fans on the screen and turned to look at me. "You taking off, honey?" She didn't bother to lower the volume.

"Yup."

"Where you going?"

I brought out the first thing that came to mind. "To a wake."

She eyed me narrowly. "Kind of strange hour for it, isn't it, honey?"

"He was kind of a strange guy. Expect me when you see me." I turned to go.

She tried heaving herself from the armchair. "If someone comes looking for you, what am I supposed to tell them?"

I felt a prickle down my scalp and turned back

to the living room. "Now, just why would anyone come around looking for me, Mrs. Polter?"

"I . . . your friends, I mean. Young girl like you must have lots of friends."

I leaned against the wall and crossed my arms. "My friends know better than to bother me when I'm working. Who might come around?"

"Anyone. How should I know who you know?"

"Why did you decide to let me come here, when it's against your rules?" I'd been shouting to be heard over the television; now my voice rose another decibel.

Her snuff-colored cheeks quivered—with anger? fear? It was impossible to tell. "I have a good heart. Maybe you're not used to seeing someone with a good heart in your line of work, so you don't know it when you see it."

"But I do hear an awful lot of lies, Mrs. Polter, and I sure know them when I hear them."

A door opened somewhere beyond the television and a man yelled quaveringly, "You okay out there, Lily?"

"Yeah, I'm fine. But I could use a beer." She flicked her eyes in the direction of the voice and back to me. "Sam. He's my oldest lodger and kind of takes an interest. You're going to be late for your friend's wake if you hang around here talking all night. And don't go banging the front door when you come in; I'm a light sleeper."

She turned determinedly back to the television, using the remote device to crank up the volume. I looked at the heavy folds of her shoulders, trying to think of something to say that might force her to tell the truth.

Before anything occurred to me Sam came shuffling in with the beer. He was wearing pajama bottoms and a faded, patched bathrobe. His face was totally incurious; he gave me a brief glance, handed Lily her beer, and shuffled back to whatever netherland he inhabited. Mrs. Polter swallowed the can in one long mouthful, then crushed it in her palm. I know they're making them out of flimsier stuff these days, but I felt I was being given a message.

I'd left the Impala at the end of the street. Before getting into it I turned and walked back to the house. The curtain in the tiny front window moved suddenly. Mrs. Polter was watching me. For whom, though?

Maybe Mitch's son really had come back to town. I pictured someone growing to resentful adulthood, not forgiving the insult of abandonment, obsessed with a desire for revenge. Trying to talk to Mitch, becoming furious with his drunken self-absorbtion. Hitting Mitch on the head and flinging him into the canal.

I turned onto Damen. If that was true, why was Chamfers so unwilling to talk to me? Who had beaten up Lotty, and why? And who was on my ass this morning? An obsessed son didn't seem to fit that profile.

The streets were almost empty this time of night, although traffic continued to roar on the Stevenson Expressway overhead. Once I turned off Damen I had the roads to myself. Thirty-first Place had enough room to park even a big old Impala without power steering.

After maneuvering it to the curb I pulled an equipment belt from the trunk. I double-checked the flashlight, made sure the picklocks were secure on the belt, then stuffed a Cubs cap low on my forehead to keep light from reflecting off my face.

My heart pounding, I slipped from the glare of the streetlamps beating down on Damen to the weed-infested ground lining the canal. The rank grass and black water made my hackles rise with a greater nervousness than the errand itself called for—although the moment of entering, when you're moving from contemplation of the deed to the deed itself, always makes my stomach turn over.

Using the flash as little as possible, I picked my way along the broken fence separating me from the canal. Really, Diamond Head was so close to Mrs. Polter's I could have walked. That might have been in Mitch's mind as well when he'd landed on her doorstep.

The Stevenson stood behind me. The concrete stilts seemed to amplify the noise of the trucks, making the air thick with their roaring, masking the sound of my heart crashing in my chest and my feet, clumsy from nerves, kicking cans or bottles. I kept the Smith & Wesson in my hand. I hadn't forgotten Detective Finchley's words, that this area was thick with drug users.

I didn't stumble on any dopers. The only signs of life beyond the expressway traffic were the frogs I disturbed in the rank grass and the occasional glow from a passing barge. I slipped behind Gammidge Wire, Diamond Head Motor's nearest neighbor, to where a narrow lip of cement abutted the canal.

Gammidge had a single night-light shining on their back entrance. I shrank back against their heavily padlocked door to keep from casting a shadow. The noise from the expressway and the canal would drown any sound I made on the ledge, but I found myself tiptoeing, clinging to the corrugated metal of the Gammidge walls. On my right a barge suddenly hooted. I jumped and stumbled. I could see the guys in the pilothouse laughing and waving. If anyone was waiting around the corner, I hoped they assumed the signal was directed at them.

My cheeks burning, I continued my stealthy approach along the lip of the canal. When I got to the clearing between Gammidge and Diamond Head I dropped low into a thick clump of prairie grass to look around the corner.

Trucks were backed up to three of Diamond Head's loading bays. Their engines were running, but the bays behind them were shut. No lights were on. Cautiously lying on the damp ground, I squinted through the grass. From this distance, in bad light, I couldn't make out any legs or other human appendages.

I hadn't seen trucks at the place since my first

visit there last week. Since I didn't know anything about Diamond Head's business flow, I couldn't speculate on whether that meant orders were slow. And I couldn't guess why the diesels were running—whether preparatory to picking up a morning load, or waiting for someone to empty them.

I was tempted to hoist myself onto the loading platform in hopes of finding a way in through the bays. The thought of Mrs. Polter made me cautious. It seemed pretty clear that she was watching me for someone. If it was Chamfers maybe he'd promised her a fire engine all her own if she called him when I showed up again. He could have the Hulk who'd chased me last Friday waiting in the back of one of the trucks to jump me. The Hulk didn't strike me as patient enough to put on an indefinite stakeout, though. I imagined one of the managers sitting in the truck with the Hulk, holding him on a leash: "Down, sir! Down, I say!" The picture didn't make me laugh quite as loudly as I'd expected.

My knees and arms were getting wet from the muddy grass. I looked around at the canal—I didn't want someone startling me into falling over the side. The concrete lining the canal would make it hard to climb out. Crouching low, I moved from the clump of grass to the back of Diamond Head. No one shot at me or even called out.

The rear doors, which slid open to allow access to barge traffic, were bolted shut with some fairly sophisticated locks. I didn't want to spend the time it would take to undo them: it was a pretty exposed place to stand for an hour or more. And the expressway wasn't loud enough to mask the sounds of burglary from anyone waiting on the inside.

I padded quickly along the walkway to the side of the building and peered around the edge. The windows of the assembly room still stood open, their panes gleaming black in the dark. The bottom sills stood about five feet above my head.

Using my pencil flash I checked out the terrain underneath. This side of the factory faced west, away from the canal, where the sun could bake the ground to a firmer clay. The tall grasses that covered the area were thinner and browner here. I carefully culled a lane about a yard wide below the nearest window, pulling away empty cans and bottles and stowing them around the corner of the building.

When I thought I had an obstacle-free zone, I rehooked my flashlight to my belt. I studied the window, trying to make my leg muscles absorb the height I'd have to jump. It was about the distance of a lay-up, and I'd proved only last week I could still play basketball.

My fingers were tingling and my palms damp. I wiped them on the sides of my jeans. "Okay," I whispered to myself. "This is your lane, Vic. On 'three.' "

I counted to three under my breath and charged up the path I'd cleared to the window.

About four feet shy of it I started my jump, arms extended, pulling myself through the air. My fingers caught on the bottom of the sill. Sharp metal ledges cut my palms. I grunted in pain, scrabbled for a handhold, and hoisted myself up. Move over, Michael Jordan. This here is Air Warshawski.

32

Swinging Evening

Perching on the metal runners lining the window, I used the flash briefly to make sure I wasn't going to fall onto a spindle or some other death-dealing machine. Except for the radiators lining the walls, the floor beneath was clear. I turned, grabbed the sill as comfortably as I could, lowered my legs into the room, and let go.

I landed with a soft thud that jolted my knees. Rubbing my sore palms I crouched behind one of the high work tables, waiting until I was sure the noise of my arrival hadn't roused anyone.

The assembly room door had a simple latch lock, open on the inside. I pushed back the catch on my way out: if I needed a quick escape route I didn't want to have to pick even a simple lock. No one was in the hall. I stood by the door for a long moment, straining to pick up breathing or some restless twitch on the cement floor. The width of the factory lay between me and the trucks. In the stillness of the building I could hear their engines faintly vibrating. Other than that all was calm.

Fire lights placed at wide intervals gave the place a faint green glow, as though it were under water. The murkiness upset my sense of place; I couldn't remember how the assembly room connected to the plant manager's office. I took a wrong turn down a connecting hall. Suddenly the diesels sounded very loud: I was coming to the corridor that led to the loading bay.

I pulled up abruptly and tiptoed to the corner. I was looking at the cement cavern that opened directly onto the bays. Again the only light came from two green fire blocks. I couldn't see clearly but I didn't think anyone was there.

Although the corrugated doors still covered the bays, diesel fumes were seeping around them. My nose wrinkled as I tried to fight back a sneeze. It came out as a muffled explosion.

Just at that moment another explosion sounded above my head. My heart hammered against my ribs and my calves felt wobbly. I forced myself to stand still, not to give away my presence by jumping or fleeing back up the hall. And in another second I felt like a fool: the motor operating a huge gantry had sprung to life, its gears clanging like a foundry under full steam.

The gantry's tracks crisscrossed the room's high ceiling. They ran parallel between a wide concrete shelf built about two-thirds of the way up the wall and the doors to the bays. Two perpendicular tracks, each with a gigantic crane hanging from it, connected the two. Presumably the concrete shelf led to a storage area.

When I'd been here before I'd noticed iron stairs at the main entrance leading to a second story, probably the same area fed by the gantry. It didn't seem very efficient to me, keeping heavy materiel on the second floor when your work was all down below. Still, that might be the best they could do with the constraints on their space; the construction around the canal was so tightly packed that they couldn't expand sideways.

Al I squinted in the dim light to follow the crane's route I noticed movement above me. Someone had emerged from the gloom of the upper deck and was climbing down a steel ladder built into the wall. He didn't look around but headed straight for the bays and began unlocking the doors.

I began to feel uncomfortably exposed and started a backward retreat up the hall. Just as I moved from the doorway the loading cavern was flooded with light.

I looked nervously over my shoulder. No one was behind me. I turned and sprinted up the corridor, hugging the south wall to stay as far from the sightlines in there as possible.

When I got back to the main hall I stopped to catch my breath and reorient myself. A right turn would lead me to a T crossing; a couple of turns there and I'd find myself back in the administrative offices. Or I could go left, which would bring me to the front entrance with the iron stairs leading upward.

The trouble was that I wanted to see both places. People loading trucks in the middle of the night at what appeared to be a deserted factory deserved a closer scrutiny. If I chose the office first they might finish whatever they were doing with the trucks before I got back to them. On the other hand, if someone saw me watching the trucks I'd have to flee without seeing Chamfers's files. Choices, choices. I turned left.

The floors were so thick that not much noise came through them. I couldn't hear voices above me, but every few minutes there'd be a dull thud as someone dropped a heavy object. I moved quickly, not worrying that anyone above me would notice my sounds. I even sneezed again without trying to choke it back.

I grew cautious at the door separating me from the main entrance. Solid metal, fitting flush to the floor, it didn't even have a keyhole I could peer through. Its dead bolt locked from the outside but could be pushed back by hand on my side. Moving with infinite care, I slid the bolt open . . . waited a count of ten. No one hollered or came charging at me.

I pulled slowly on the heavy metal handle, opening the door by a crack just wide enough to see around. It was constructed awkwardly for sneaking, since the handle was at chest height and obstructed the view. I looked around it as best I could. The coast seemed clear. Such noises as I heard seemed to be coming only from the floor above.

I pulled the door open wider and slipped through it, putting my hand on it to slide it gently shut. The lock clicked in with a faint snap. I froze. I thought I'd slid the bolt free, but apparently it sprang back as soon as I removed my thumb. Now I was locked on the far side with whoever was waiting above me. Since this exposed entrance was a terrible place to work on a complex lock, I'd have to make the best of it. The worst thing to do at times like these is upbraid yourself. You make a mistake, you should tie a knot and go on, not fuddle your wits with recriminations.

Since the door opened behind the staircase, I couldn't tell if anyone was on the stairs or not. I could hear voices now, just grunts and faint cries of "Hold it!" or "Shit!" followed by a loud thump.

I crept out from my sanctuary. The front door stood ajar. Through it I could make out two or three cars, but the angle was too poor and the light too dim to tell whether I'd seen any of them before.

The door at the top of the stairs, which had been shut on my previous visit, stood open wide. From the bottom I could just make out the first yard or so beyond it. No one seemed to be in the immediate entrance. Hugging the side of the stairs, I went up as quietly as I could.

I climbed the last few steps on my hands and

knees and lay flat at the top to peer ahead. An unlit walkway led from the door to a brightly lit, open area beyond. The grunts and thumps were coming from there. I could also hear the cranes clanking away. A handful of men were slowly moving past the entrance, maneuvering a giant hoop.

The walkway itself was dug from a small storage area. On either side of me loomed giant shapes about the size of cows. They were probably old machines, but the light from the room beyond cast ungainly shadows behind them; not of cows, but of monsters from the primordial swamp that spawned Chicago. The fancy made me shiver.

I waited for the four pairs of legs in front of me to finish moving their hoop, then hoisted myself upright and skittered for a nearby shadow. The bulk in front of me was definitely metal, not flesh, and had a thick coating of dust on it. I held my nose firmly to pinch back another sneeze.

My eyes were accustomed enough to the dim that I could make out the major shapes, but not the small bits of debris that cluttered the floor. The area seemed to have been Diamond Head's dumping ground for years. As I moved cautiously across the floor I kept running into pipes and bits of wire and other things I could only guess at. I finally got myself into a position where I could see a good chunk of the lighted area.

I was looking at the big shelf built above the loading dock. This led to a major storage area, which was out of my sightline. There seemed to be four men using hand operated lifts to move giant spools over to the edge. That, too, was out of my range, but I presumed the gantry was taking them to the dock below, where they could be loaded onto the trucks.

From the size of the one spool they shoved past while I was watching, I couldn't believe they could put more than one on a truck. In fact, it was the kind of load usually moved on a flatbed. I didn't know how they proposed getting them into the trailers, nor yet how to strap them down. I also didn't know what was on them. What was packed that way? Some kind of coiled metal.

I craned my neck, trying to see if anything was written on the side. "Paragon" was stamped in such large letters that I didn't notice them at first. Paragon. The steel company whose controller didn't want to discuss Diamond Head. Maybe because he knew the motor company was taking Paragon products and selling them on the black market?

Without warning, the sneeze I'd been suppressing came bursting forth with the intensity of a machine gun blast. I hoped the noise of the belt would drown me, but two of the men were apparently just on the other side of the entrance. They called to the others, their voices all too audible. A brief argument: had they heard something or were they just imagining it?

I crouched low behind a giant metal plane. The

ostrich approach. If I couldn't see them, they wouldn't notice me.

"Oh, for Chrissake, Gleason. Who's gonna be here?"

"I told you the boss called, warned me that there's been a detective snooping around. And he got wind she's in the neighborhood tonight."

The first speaker gave a crack of laughter. "A girl detective. I don't know who's a bigger fool—you or Chamfers. If it'll make you happy we can take a look around—want to hold onto my hand?" The last words came out in an ugly jeer.

"I don't give a fuck. You call the boss and tell him you were too chicken to look for snoopers."

I slid my hand inside my jacket for the Smith & Wesson. A flashlight beam, industrial strength, pierced the gloom of the storage room. Footsteps approached, retreated, stirring the dust, making my nose tingle unbearably. I held my breath, my eyes tearing. I kept back the sneeze, but the movement rocked me back on my heels; my hand with the gun grazed the side of the metal plane.

The flashlight beam poked a long finger at me. The skin on my cheeks tingled and the hair stood on my arms. I watched the floor, waiting for the feet to declare the line of attack. They came from the left. I darted out to the right, into the loading area.

I was blinded at first by the brightness of the light and couldn't make out anything. The sound was loud enough out here to drown the shouts of the men behind me. I skidded around the Paragon spool and almost bumped into two more men. They were steadying a second reel at the edge of the platform and didn't look up, intent on fitting a sling around it. As I danced about the deck, figuring the layout, I noticed the label on the reel: COPPER WIRE. INDUSTRIAL GRADe.

"Stop her, damn you!"

The men who'd flushed me were bearing down on me. The two in front finished strapping their load and gave a signal to a crane operator on the other side of the room. They turned slowly, surprised, not believing anyone had really been in the back room.

"Now, just a minute there," one of them said calmly.

A hand grabbed at my jacket from behind. I kicked reflexively, gaining a second to wrench myself free, and brandished the Smith & Wesson at the two in front of me. One of them reached out an arm as a man behind me grabbed me again. "Now, honey, let's have that gun and stop playing games."

I fired in front of me and the two men jumped aside. A half turn and another hard kick backed off the one snatching at my jacket.

The spool was about four feet from the edge of the platform. I jammed the gun into my jacket pocket and leapt. My hands, wet with sweat, slipped on the steel-and-canvas strips of the sling. I scissor-kicked violently, too much so. My legs swung back behind me, arcing my back into a bow. I made myself relax; let my legs sweep forward, waiting for gravity to draw them up. At the height of the swing I hooked a knee over the rod threading the spool.

My thighs were shaking. I ignored their weak complaining and pulled myself upright, my wet hands trembling as I gripped the slings. I couldn't see behind me, couldn't tell what my four pals were doing. I didn't think they had guns, at least not up on the platform with them.

I couldn't jump down—the floor was thirty feet below me. I looked at the gantry above me. If I could climb the crane cable faster than they could wind it up, I might shinny up and crawl along the tracks to the wall. I was trembling so violently right now I didn't think I could manage the gymnastics.

The control booth was on the ground, on the far end of the room from the docks. When I got down I'd have to outrun the man in the booth. And the two men gaping at me from one of the open bays. They both looked big enough to be the Hulk who'd chased me on my first trip here.

The spool was swaying slightly from my jump. Suddenly it began swinging violently. The crane operator was grinning dementedly. I clutched the canvas stripping. As the arc grew wider nausea rose up in my gut. We were moving toward the side of the building. It was an old gantry system and could only manage about five miles an hour, slow enough for me to figure out their plan: they were going to swing the load around and smash me into the wall.

The two hulks from the loading bays were looking up. The sound didn't carry, but from their body language I guessed they were laughing pretty hard.

When we got to the wall the crane operator gave one tentative tap to set the load in motion sideways. We swung out from the wall and started back with greater force. Just before we hit I wrenched one hand free from the canvas sling and scrabbled at the wall behind me. I clutched at metal and jumped free from the load. For a terrifying second my left hand closed on air. Dark spots swam in front of me and I grabbed blindly at the wall. An instant after my feet connected with a girder, the copper spool slammed against the building.

The blow jarred the girder. I was holding on with a death grip. The metal edges cut into my palms. I shut my eyes and made myself unhook one hand . . . flex it. . . . Move it down, move my right foot down, fumble for a new toehold. . . . Unhook my left hand, lower it. My triceps were trembling, but my weight workouts stood me in good stead. As long as I kept my eyes shut and didn't think about what was waiting for me below, I could keep up the rhythm of clutching and releasing the metal cross-strips.

Every twenty seconds or so the girder jarred as the operator slammed the spool against it, following me down the track. The cables have built-in brakes to keep their loads from slipping down too fast. Even knowing that, I jumped the last six feet, landing in a rolling heap as far from the crane and the hulks as I could manage.

I pulled my gun free as the men came for me. They were brandishing giant wrenches, but when they saw the gun they backed off a bit. From the corner of my eye I could see the other men climbing down the ladder from the upper platform. Seven men, eight bullets. I wouldn't have time to reload. I couldn't possibly shoot them all.

The hulks were between me and the loading dock. One of them suddenly slid his wrench across the floor to the reinforcements and disappeared outside. The other charged at me, brandishing his wrench like a torch. I fired and missed, fired again. He stumbled as he came up to me. I jumped clear of his flailing wrench and ran past him without stopping to see if I'd winged him.

I got outside before my pursuers realized what had happened. Jumped off the platform, and sprinted toward the front of the building and the road. Rounded the corner when headlights came up, blinding me.

The Hulk had gone to get one of the cars. The engine roared as he floored it. My legs knew what to do almost before my brain registered the car. I found myself hugging the foundation of the plant.

The Smith & Wesson had landed a good eight feet from me. Panting, wet with sweat, I started crawling for it as the car backed up. I reached the gun as the Hulk went into drive again. I could just sense the rest of my pals behind me, when I saw another pair of headlights join the first. I couldn't run behind the trucks: the rest of the gang would pin me like a trapped rat.

My arms were quivering so badly, I could hardly lift the gun. I waited for the cars as long as I dared, shot once at each windshield, stuck the gun back in the holster and ran all out toward the canal. With the last strength I could muster I dove clear of the pylons into the middle of the foul water.

33

Recollections of a Midnight Swim

"You were lucky, Warshawski, fucking lucky. What would you have done if that barge hadn't happened along?" Conrad Rawlings was shouting loudly enough to keep me awake.

"I wouldn't have drowned, if that's what you're thinking. I had enough left in my shoulders to climb up the side."

"You were just goddamn lucky," he repeated. "That side is solid concrete. It isn't meant for shinnying."

"Out of curiosity, what were you doing along the canal at three in the morning?" That was Terry Finchley, his tone conversational.

I blinked at him from under the protective shroud of my police-issue blanket. When the *Santa Lucia* saw me floundering around under the Damen Avenue bridge, they'd fished me out and called the police department's water patrol. I was blacking out by then and couldn't see far enough to tell whether my Diamond Head pals were on the far bank dancing up and down in frustration.

The tugboat crew wrapped me in a blanket and gave me hot soup while we waited for the cops. When the river patrol came, the crew took their blanket back and the police issued me a nice blue-and-white job. It looked like the kind the mounted patrol put on their well-tended horses.

The river cops were pleasant, so pleasant that I suddenly realized through the mists of fatigue that they thought I'd been trying to kill myself. They took the Smith & Wesson from me and kept trying to find out who they should call.

"Terry Finchley at Area One," I muttered, waking with a start every time they asked. "He can tell you about it."

It wasn't until the third or fourth iteration that I figured out they wanted a husband or sister or someone that they could turn me over to. I was exhausted, but I hadn't lost my wits. I knew I wasn't in shape to take on anyone who might be waiting for me, either at home or at Mrs. Polter's. Normally at such a crisis I'd call Lotty, but I couldn't do that tonight either. Anyway, she was staying with Max. I just kept mumbling Finchley's name and dozing off.

It must have been close to four when one of the patrolmen shook my arm. "Up you get, honey. We found Terry Finchley for you."

"She doesn't have any shoes," I heard one of the patrol crew say.

"She's tough." Finchley's voice came from several miles away. "Her feet'll take a few splinters without breaking."

I stumbled behind the patrolman who'd awakened me. When we got to the gangway he turned and lifted me over the side and propped me up next to Finchley's driver. I'm not used to being handled like a negligible load. It added a dimension of helplessness to my fatigue.

"She was carrying this; I don't know if she has a license." The sergeant handed my gun to Finchley.

"It needs cleaning," I heard myself saying. "Cleaning and oiling. It's been underwater, you see."

"She needs a doctor and a hot bath, but she wouldn't tell us who to call." The sergeant was talking about me as if I were lying dead in the next room.

I patted myself under the blanket. They'd left the holster. My belt with its seven-hundred-dollar picklocks was gone though. I could just remember struggling free of it underwater, when I shed my jacket and kicked off my shoes, trying to lighten my load. My wallet was still in my back pocket. The cops could have picked it and found my address easily enough, but they were mostly concerned that I not throw myself back into the steamy waters of the Sanitary Canal.

"Want to talk about it, Warshawski? Klimczak from the water patrol says you insisted on seeing me. I got out of bed to meet you—I'm not going to be a happy cop if you clam up on me now."

Finchley's sharp tone brought me back to the bare Area One interrogation room. In his starched shirt and knife-point trouser creases he didn't appear to have just tumbled out of bed. Rawlings, whom he'd called at some point in the proceedings, looked more the part in a rumpled T-shirt and jeans. His eyes were red and he seemed angry, or jumpy, or some combination of the two. I was having too much trouble staying awake to sort out the nuances behind their speech.

"I'm afraid I'm going to get cholera. From the canal, I mean. But I didn't have any choice. They would have run me over if I hadn't gone in." Under the blanket my hair felt matted with sewage.

Finchley nodded as if my words had made perfect sense.

"Who?" Rawlings exploded. "Who would have run you over? And what the hell were you doing there? Klimczak was worried you were suicidal, but I told him not a hope of that."

"Figure it out, guys." My words came out slowly, from a great distance. I couldn't make myself talk faster. "You know what's going on at Diamond Head, right? I mean, to you, nothing. Nothing's happening there. To me, it's where a man got killed. And the head of the plant won't talk to me. And Jason Felitti, who owns it, throws me out of his house. So I went down to have a look for myself. And voilà!"

I waved a hand like a comic-book drunk. I couldn't seem to control such extravagant gestures.

"And voilà what?" Finchley prodded.

I jerked my head upright—I'd started to drop off again. "They were loading Paragon copper onto trucks in the middle of the night."

"You want me to arrest them, Warshawski?" Rawlings demanded.

I looked at him owlishly. "It's a thought. A definite thought. Why do they have spools of Paragon copper to begin with? No, that's an easy question. They bought it to make their little engine gizmos with, I guess. Why are they shipping it out? Secretly in the dark? That's the hard question."

"How do you know they're doing it secretly? An active business might ship supplies at any time." Finchley crossed his legs and adjusted the crease.

"They were loading it onto closed trucks. Spools go on flatbeds. Anyway, when they saw me watching them, why didn't they call you guys? Why'd they chase me into the canal instead?"

A ghost of a smile flitted across Finchley's

ebony face. "If you caught someone on your premises, I doubt your first act would be to call me, Vic. I expect you'd get up a load of steam and drive them off yourself if you could."

I couldn't prod my brain into making cogent arguments. "I shot at them. I think I hit one guy. Has anyone reported that? Maybe come around wanting to file charges?"

Finchley's brows went up at that. He gestured at a corner and I saw a uniformed woman get up and slip out the door. I hadn't noticed her until then.

"Mary Louise Neely," I said out loud.

"Yes, that's Officer Neely," Finchley said. "She'll check on your wounded man. So what's the point, Warshawski? You're trying to build a case against Diamond Head, but it's not holding water—forgive the expression. A drunken old man hits his head and dies and falls or is rolled into the canal. It's too bad, but it doesn't mean every corporation in Chicago has to roll over and do tricks because you're steamed about it."

The edge to his words whipped blood to my cheeks and momentarily cleared my brain. "Right, Finchley. I tried calling you tonight because you—no, it was Rawlings here, but I expect you knew about it—called Dr. Herschel to complain I was holding out. You get my message?"

He nodded frantically.

"What I wanted to tell you, someone came around the boardinghouse where the old guy was living and scooped up all his papers. Guy claiming to be his son. Why'd he do that? The papers a derelict carries around are useless. Then when I come back to the boardinghouse the landlady calls the Diamond Head plant manager to tell him I'm back in the neighborhood. I heard the guys at the plant *say* that when I was there tonight. I know that a big steel company is funneling cash their way and I see copper spools disappearing in the middle of the night with this steel company's name printed on the side."

I shoved the blanket out of my eyes and turned to Rawlings. "And meanwhile, Eddie Mohr, the old local president, his car is stolen by creeps who bash Lotty Herschel three ways from Sunday. That was on *your* turf, Rawlings, remember? So you guys tell *me* what the point is!"

"How do you know it wasn't his son?" Rawlings skipped all the stuff about Paragon Steel and went for the inessential.

"I don't. But the son grew up in Arizona. He hadn't heard from his old man for thirty-five years. Finchley here didn't try to get in touch with him. How'd he know to show up out of the blue? And on top of that, how'd he find the flophouse Kruger'd picked to crash in only eight days earlier?"

I stopped for a minute, fishing in the depths of my weary mind for an essential piece of information. It surfaced just as Officer Neely came back into the room to lean over Finchley's shoulder.

I turned to Rawlings. "We ID'd Mitch Kruger

330

on Monday. The stalled son came to Mrs. Polter's on Tuesday. Even if someone called the son in Arizona, how'd he get here so fast?" Unless, of course, he'd been here all along after murdering his father.

"Take it easy, Ms. W., take it easy." Rawlings went over to join Finchley and Neely in the huddle.

While they talked, my sudden spurt of energy died. I shrank back inside the blanket, the skin on my arms trembling from fatigue. Finchley's slender, muscled frame was as still as a statue, like one of the Buddhas at the Art Institute.

I'd first seen the Buddhas when I was six and my mother took me downtown to look at masterpieces of the Italian Renaissance. They sat outside the main exhibit hall. Their faces were so calm, so unblinkingly benign, I wanted to stroke them. Gabriella couldn't understand my fascination with them; we were there for me to experience the glory of her ancestry, not gawk at lower art forms.

The Buddha grew large and beckoned me. I let go of Gabriella's hand and climbed onto his lap. One cool stone hand clasped me lightly while his soothing voice uttered great truths.

"When you wake up you will remember everything, my daughter, everything of importance." He kept stroking me with his cool hand and repeating the mantra, until I became aware of Rawlings's arm around me and his deep voice adjuring me to wake up.

"You gotta get to bed, Warshawski. You're no use to anyone like this. Want me to run you home?"

"Take me to a motel," I mumbled. "You don't believe anyone's after me, but they chased me this morning. Yesterday morning. Ask Barbara at the Belmont Diner—she'll tell you it's the truth."

"You know a motel that's gonna let you in looking like this? You don't even have any shoes on. You better let me take you home, Nancy Drew. If you're seriously worried I'll get someone to drive by your place every twenty minutes."

I felt weak and helpless, abandoned by the Buddha. I fought back the impulse to collapse on the floor in tears. "You better see me up into my apartment. I can't deal with anyone jumping me tonight."

"Okay, girl, okay. Personal police escort. Round-the-clock protection, at least until you leave the crib again. Now, come on home. Detective Finchley has to do some thinking. It's ugly work and he doesn't like an audience."

I looked at Finchley. "So do you believe me? What did Neely tell you?"

He permitted himself a small smile. "A man at Christ Hospital came in around two-thirty with a bullet in the left thigh. Claims his gun went off accidentally when he was cleaning it. Could be your guy, or—it could be what he says.

"As for the rest of your story—it's not a story, Vic. It's just another way of looking at a company and a death. But I will take a second look at it. Now, let Conrad take you home. He's been jumping out of his skin ever since he heard we pulled you from the drink."

Yet another way of looking at the same story. Rawlings wasn't mad at me, just worried. Maybe the Buddha was looking out for me after all.

"I want my gun back, Terry. I've got a license for it." I let the horse blanket drop and dug in my back pocket for my wallet. It was gummy with mud and water. I pried it open and tried separating the different bits of identification and credit cards from its sodden slots.

Finchley watched me fumble with it for a minute or two, then relented and handed me the Smith & Wesson. "I ought to get ballistics to check you against the slug Christ Hospital dug out. And then I ought to arrest you for assaulting the guy."

"And then I'd have to have a big trial proving self-defense, and his six buddies would be the only witnesses."

"It's tempting, Vic, very tempting. I bet the lieutenant would get me promoted on the basis of it. You be careful how you fire that thing in the future."

"Yes, Detective," I agreed meekly. I took the clip out and stuck it in my jeans pocket before putting the gun back in the holster. A rusty gun could misbehave in some ugly ways.

Rawlings picked up the blanket and draped it

across my shoulders. I leaned gratefully into the strength of his arm on my way out the door.

34

The Strong Arm of the Law

I was so exhausted, it wasn't until I had fumbled uselessly with my keys for several minutes that I realized something was wrong. "Someone's been trying to break in, but all they did was smash up the lock."

My lips were swollen with fatigue; the words came out in an incomprehensible mumble. Rawlings took one look at the door frame and saw the damage at once. He was starting to bark commands into his lapel mike before I realized it.

I put a hand over the speaker. "Not now, Sergeant, please. I need to sleep—I just can't face any more servants or protectors tonight. We can go around the back way, see if we can get in through there. And if not . . . I'll sleep on Mr. Contreras's couch." Sharing my rest with Mitch Kruger's ghost. The thought made me shudder.

Rawlings looked at me dubiously. "Let's see what we find when we get around back," he temporized.

My legs seemed to have come unhinged from my torso. They moved with heavy, robotlike strides, but showed a distressing tendency to buckle without warning. Rawlings, his gun in his right hand, kept an arm around me after my first collapse. When he saw how feeble I was he drove around the block to the alley.

Before going into the yard he shone a brilliant spot up and down the stairs and into all the corners. I heard Peppy's faint bark from behind Mr. Contreras's door. A curtain twitched in the north corner bedroom of Vinnie's place.

I've had so many work-related break-ins over the years that I've encased my apartment in stainless steel. The front door, in addition to its treble locks, is reinforced with steel plate. The back has conventional grates on the door and windows. These were intact, but by now I was past being able to negotiate the locks. I handed my key ring to Rawlings and slumped against the window bars while he figured out the keys he needed.

All I wanted was to be left alone so I could fall into a hole of sleep. I almost screamed from exhaustion when Rawlings insisted on searching the place.

"No one's here, Conrad. They tried the front, couldn't do it, and decided the back was too exposed to mess with. Please . . . I just need to sleep."

"Yeah, I know you do, Ms. W. But I won't sleep myself if I don't just make a quick runthrough."

I slumped at the kitchen table, knocking yesterday's papers to the floor with my elbows.

I dropped off at once; it took Rawlings's lifting my head forcibly from my forearms to wake me again.

"I hate to do this to you, Vic, but unless your housekeeping's reached new lows someone sure has been in here."

My brain had jelled; I couldn't even think of a response, let alone force my swollen lips to say anything. I followed him dumbly into the living room.

Someone had broken one of my north-facing windows, climbed in, and torn the place to shreds. They hadn't been very subtle about it. Broken glass lay on the floor under the sill. One piece had migrated as far as the piano bench. The bench itself stood open. All the music lay on the floor or the piano, spines broken, sheets hanging by a single thread. Every book and paper in the room looked as though it had been similarly treated.

"I've got to call this in," Rawlings said sharply.

"It'll keep until morning," I said as forcefully as I could. "I'm not tampering with the evidence tonight. But you're going to have to pack me off to Elgin if I don't get to bed. I just can't cope with this right now."

"But that window—"

"I've got a hammer and nails. There must be some boards in the basement."

"You can't! There might be fingerprints."

"And then what? I've never known *yet* when you guys had the resources to spare to track

336

down a residential B&E. Give me a break, Raw-lings."

He rubbed his eyes. "Oh, nuts, Vic. I could sleep in here on your couch, but there'd be hell to pay at the station for why I didn't call in a team as soon as I saw it. Let alone why I spent the night here. I've *got* to call it in. Didn't you say you'd crash at your neighbor's?"

"I said it, but I don't want to do it. Look, call the boys in blue if you have to, but let me go to bed."

He agreed after an examination of the bedroom. My clothes had been turned out of their drawers, but no furniture was broken. I looked in the closet. They'd rifled the clothes, but had missed the little wall safe at the back. Amateurs. And angry, at that.

"You know anything about this, Ms. W.? Why someone would go to all the trouble? You know, if they were just street punks they would've given up after they found they couldn't trash the front door."

"My brain isn't working, Sergeant. Call your pals if you want, but leave me alone." My voice was cracking now, but I was past minding.

Rawlings gave me a long look, seemed to decide he wouldn't get anything more out of me even if he beat me, and walked back down the hall to the living room. I could hear his mike crackling as he went.

Even so, I couldn't go to bed until I'd stood under the shower for twenty minutes, washing the grime from the canal out of my pores. The troops were arriving as I returned to my bedroom. I ostentatiously slammed my door, then fell deeply and heavily asleep, into dreams of climbing walls, trying to reach a Buddha who sat always just out of my reach while giant men chased me in trucks. At one point I slipped and fell from a high scaffolding. Just before smashing into the concrete I woke with a jolt. It was twelve-thirty.

I made a half-hearted effort to get up, but my legs and arms seemed too thick to move. I sank back against the mattress and watched sun motes dancing between the top of the curtains and the ceiling.

If someone asked me to recommend a good private eye about now, I'd have to send them to one of the big suburban firms. I was trying to be an advocate for a woman sunk deep in senility whose life when sane had been pretty dreadful. After a week of prodding Diamond Head Motors to give me information on Mitch Kruger, the only thing I had to show for my pains was sore muscles, a rusty gun, and a busted-up apartment. Oh, no. Also a two-thousand dollar repair bill for the Trans Am. And Lotty Herschel hurt, scared, and angry up in Evanston.

"What a tiger," I said aloud in bitter mockery. "What a fucking useless waste of time you are. You ought to go back to serving subpoenas. At least that's something you know how to do. Although you'd probably trip over your feet and break your neck going upstairs."

"You always talk that loud to yourself, Warshawski? No wonder the neighbors complain about you." Conrad Rawlings appeared in the doorway.

I had jumped out of bed when I first heard a voice, looking wildly around my bedroom for a defensive weapon. When I saw who it was, my cheeks burned. I grabbed a sweatshirt and a pair of shorts at random from the floor and pulled them on.

"You always walk unannounced into people's bedrooms? If my gun didn't need cleaning, you might be dead. I should haul your ass into court."

Rawlings laughed and handed me a cup of coffee. "Officer of the law serving and protecting, Ms. W. Although after the way you failed to cooperate last night, I shouldn't bother."

"Failed to cooperate? I give you guys a story on a platter and all you do is harass me over a stupid broken window. . . . You spend the night here, or just let yourself in first thing in the morning?"

He sat on the end of the bed. "We finished up here around seven. I saw you had a set of spare keys; I was going to borrow them so I could lock up behind me. Then your old boy downstairs intercepted me on my way out. He cross-examined me pretty hard, and when he made up his mind I wasn't a punk he gave me his version of the facts. We decided I should come back in. I slept on the couch. Wasn't too uncomfortable, really. Besides, I already got four or five hours before the Finch woke me up. You can thank me later for picking up the papers and washing your dishes."

I curled my legs up under me on the bed. "I'll put an extra five in your pay envelope. I take it your boys didn't find much of anything?"

He pulled a wry face. "Whoever came in was wearing gloves and size ten Reeboks—they found a print in the dust by the window. Maybe there's something to be said for bad housekeeping."

I gave a tight smile. "I don't need the commentary, Sergeant. What about the neighbors? They must have seen someone on a ladder."

He shook his head. "Whoever did it took a risk, but not too big a one. You left here when? Ten last night? So, after ten and before four. This is a quiet block. Anyway, that side isn't very visible from the street—there're trees that screen you from the north, and the fake front shields you if someone's walking right by. What were they looking for, Vic?"

"I wish I knew," I said slowly. "I haven't got a clue. I've been looking for some papers—Mitch Kruger had them at the boardinghouse he lived in. But Mrs. Polter says his son turned up the next day and took them. Anyone who's talked to her knows I don't have them."

Of course, I'd also been looking for papers at Mrs. Frizell's, and Todd and Chrissie didn't know whether I'd found them or not. It would be easy for them to know I was gone—but would they have had the enterprise to break in?

"Any ideas about the ladder?" I asked.

"New, probably. Its safety feet left a good impression and they still had the little grooves on them—hadn't been used enough to wear them out." He finished his coffee and put the cup on the floor. "I'm asking a squad car to drive by here every now and then. Just to make sure your visitors don't come back."

"Thanks." I hesitated, trying to pick my words. "I appreciate that—I really do. And you staying the night—I was dead to the world. But, well, I didn't ask for a bodyguard, and I don't think I need one. The day comes I can't look after myself, I'm retiring to Michigan."

Light glinted on his gold front tooth. "That's probably why I like you, Ms. W. Because you're so ornery. I just love to watch you get on other people's nerves."

"You didn't seem to be liking it too much over at Lotty's last week."

"I said *other* people's, Warshawski, not my own."

I couldn't help laughing. "That your hobby?"

"Yeah, but I haven't had too much chance to practice it lately."

I put my own coffee cup on the bedside table and stretched an arm out to him. My muscles suddenly didn't feel as heavy as they had ten minutes ago.

"Thought you'd never ask, Ms. W." He leaned

across the bed and slid strong fingers under my sweatshirt. "I've been wanting to do this for three years."

"I never figured you for a shy guy, Sergeant." I traced the long line of a scar across his torso up his back. "You don't have a wife or girlfriend or someone I should know about, do you? I thought you were seeing a lot of Tessa Reynolds."

Tessa was a sculptor we both knew.

Conrad made a face. "It's been a while. She needed a shoulder to lean on after Malcolm's death and mine was handy. I don't know—maybe a cop isn't classy enough for a lady artist. How about you? What's with you and that newspaper boy I see you with every now and then?"

"Murray Ryerson? He and I barely speak these days. Nope. There're a couple of guys I see—but no one special."

"Okay, Ms. W. Sounds okay to me."

We moved closer and kissed. We didn't talk about much of anything for a while. I reached out an arm and fumbled in my nightstand for my diaphragm. Afterward I dozed off in Rawlings's arms. My dreams must still have been haunting me, because I suddenly blurted out, "You're not the Buddha, you know."

"Yeah, Ms. W. Someone already told me that."

His hand stroking my hair was the last thing I remembered for a while. When I woke up again it was close to two. Rawlings had left, but he'd propped a note by the coffeepot explaining that he'd gone to work. "I gave your spare keys back to the old man, so don't be afraid I'll come breaking in again uninvited. I've got a squad car coming around every so often looking for that Subaru you mentioned. Don't go facing down any gangs without calling me first. P.S.: How about dinner tomorrow?"

I found myself whistling Mozart under my breath as I got dressed. The Scarlett O'Hara syndrome. Rhett comes and spends the night and suddenly you're singing and happy again. I pulled a face at myself in the mirror, but the thought didn't dampen my spirits the way maybe it should have. Of course, on principle a private investigator should discourage close entanglements with the cops. On the other hand, where would I be if my mother hadn't climbed in bed with a police sergeant? If it was good enough for her, it ought to do for me.

I continued with "Mi tradi quell'alma ingrata" as I cleaned the Smith & Wesson. The melody is so buoyant that the aria often comes to me at happy moments, despite its despairing words. Later, though, as I scrubbed the oil from my fingers, I wondered who the ungrateful wretch might be. Certainly not Conrad Rawlings or Mr. Contreras. But that left a wide-open field including Jason Felitti, Milt Chamfers, and my good old ex-husband, Dick. Unlike Mozart's heroine I didn't feel too much pity for the crew at Diamond Head, but some spark of sentimentality made me hope Dick wasn't up to his eyeballs in their muck.

35

Hangover from a
Hard Day's Night

By the time the gun was clean and I was dressed, it was after four. I called Larry, the guy who puts my apartment back together when it's been ransacked, and explained my problem. He wouldn't be able to make it over until next Wednesday, but he referred me to an emergency glazier who agreed to take care of the window in the morning.

After debating the matter I decided to call an alarm company to wire my doors and windows. I got their machine with instructions to call back Monday morning. I hate living in the middle of a fortress. It's bad enough to seal the place up every night—although an alarm system might let me cut back on the hardware—but I just couldn't afford to have people climbing in through the windows after me.

I spent the rest of the afternoon nailing boards across the broken window and installing crude braces on the others. After that I felt restless, and to my dismay, forlorn. Solitude usually brings me a sense of peace, but right now I felt under siege. I didn't think I could stand to spend a night in here with the boarded-over windows.

I could call Conrad, but it would be a mistake

to start a relationship in a state of dependency. After a few minutes hesitation I tracked Lotty down at Max's.

"I think I've found the people who attacked you," I greeted her abruptly. "Or they found me."

"Oh?" Her tone was cautious.

I explained what had happened last night, stressing that I'd given Finchley and Rawlings everything I knew about Mitch Kruger and Diamond Head. "But I don't think they're taking it very seriously. They think being chased into the San was my just deserts for breaking into the plant."

I took a deep breath. "Lotty, I know you've been upset with me because you were attacked in my stead. I don't blame you. But . . . I just can't be by myself tonight. There's been too much—there are too many people trying . . ." To my dismay I found tears were choking me; I couldn't go on.

"Vic, don't!" I flinched from the sharpness in her voice. "I just can't help you right now. I'm sorry. I'm truly sorry you had a rough night last night. I wish I could help you put your pieces back together—but I'm in too many pieces myself to be able to help you."

"I . . . Lotty . . ." but she had handed the phone back to Max.

When he came on the line he was unexpectedly gentle, even apologizing for his harshness the night Lotty had been attacked. "You each expect the other to be invincible; when you aren't you both suffer," he added. "Lotty . . . well, she's not in good shape right now. She's not angry with you, but she needs to feel angry to keep herself in a semblance of functioning. Can you understand that? Give her some distance, some time?"

"I guess I have to," I said bitterly.

When we'd hung up I stood in the middle of the room with my hands pressed against my head, trying to keep the boiling inside from spilling out through my temples. I could *not* stay in this apartment one more minute, that much was certain. Randomly stuffing clothes into an overnight bag, along with an extra clip, I headed downstairs. I'd take the el out to O'Hare and get on the first plane I came to with a spare seat.

I thought about sneaking past Mr. Contreras's place on the way out, but decided that would really be unfair to the old man. I needn't have worried about it: he had the door open before I reached the bottom of the stairs.

He surveyed me with his hands on his hips. "So you went and got yourself pushed into the San, huh? After letting me think you was just going off to lay low for a few days. I can't take too many more nights like last one, and that's a fact. Don't think I'm gonna apologize for getting that Sergeant Rawlings to go back into your place, because I'm not. If you can't share your plans with anyone, least I can do is get the cops to look after you."

"Thank you. I appreciate your care. Although I slept until noon without knowing there was a cop on my couch, I'm sure the subliminal knowledge was what enabled me to rest."

He grunted in exasperation. "Oh, don't go using your tony vocabulary on me. I know you only do it when you're pissed, but you got no call to be. I'm the one suddenly finding out at five in the morning you almost got yourself killed."

"Don't!" I cried more sharply than I'd meant. "I just can't take any harassment right now."

He started to expostulate—that I'd have to learn to take it until I could pay attention to how he felt, left alone to worry—but my distress must have been writ large in my face. After a minute he broke off and asked me what the problem was.

I tried to summon a smile. "Rough night last night and too many people on my ass right now."

"It'd be easier for me not to be one of those people if I knew what you was up to."

I closed my eyes a minute, as if that could make the world disappear. But the sooner I started my tale, the sooner I could get it over. "I broke into Diamond Head. To do that I had to take a flying leap through a window a good ten feet off the ground. Then I hung around on a spool of copper dangling from a crane, crawled down the gantry supports so I wouldn't be crushed into the wall, and dove into the San to avoid being run over by a car. I know you're a hell of a guy—you're certainly wonderful to me—but if I'd told you my plans you would have insisted on coming

347

along. And you're just not up to the action. I'm sorry, but you're not."

His eyes flooded unexpectedly. He turned his head so I couldn't watch him dashing the tears away. Great. Now everyone I knew was crying in unison. Including me.

"Ah, you don't understand, doll. I care about you—ah, what the heck, you know I love you. I know I got Ruthie and my grandsons, but they ain't part of my everyday life like you are." He spoke with his head turned from me; I had to strain to catch the words.

"I grew up in a different time than you. I know you like to look after yourself, but it hurts me to know I can't take care of you, go along jumping through windows with you. Twenty years ago— oh, what's the use of complaining, though. It'll happen to you someday, too, and you'll know what I mean. Least, it will if you don't let someone knock you off first."

I shepherded him gently into the living room and sat him on the mustard-covered armchair. I knelt next to him, keeping a hand on his shoulder. Peppy, sensing his distress, briefly left her nurslings to come sniff at his knees. He stroked her absently. After a few quiet minutes he smiled with a heart-wrenching gallantry.

"So, you was swinging from the gantry, huh? Wish I could've seen it. Who was there? What made you do it?"

I gave him a thumbnail sketch of my evening. "Why would they be shipping so much copper

348

out? Finchley says 'normal business,' but I can't figure it; they're not running a graveyard shift. And what they ought to be unloading are beautiful little motors, not big spools of copper."

"Yeah, they should. They don't use that much copper, anyway. Sounds like someone's warehousing it there. You know, that big old upper shelf where they cornered you, they haven't used that for manufacturing since the war—the Second World War, I mean—when they was running three shifts trying to keep up. Anyone who knew the plant would know that upper deck would be available for storage. You know, if they was stealing something and wanting to keep it quiet for a while."

I chewed on a knuckle. It made as much sense as anything I'd thought of. "The spools were all labeled 'Paragon.' Where would those have come from?"

"Paragon?" His bushy gray brows shot up. "Paragon used to own Diamond Head. They bought it just about the time I retired. Then they sold it a year or so ago to some guy. I remember reading about it in the *Sun-Times,* but none of it means anything to me anymore, so I didn't keep track of the names."

"Jason Felitti," I said mechanically, but my eyes were blazing with rage. They used to *own* the damned company, but Ben Loring couldn't tell me jackshit about Paragon's relations with Diamond Head? I pounded the chair arm in fury.

Mr. Contreras eyed me with concern, so I explained my abortive conversation with the steel company controller. "Do you know about any scams people at Diamond Head would've taken part in? I'm sure guys talk on the floor—you might have heard something."

He shook his head regretfully. "You know, doll, it's been a while. And like I said, Paragon came in when I was on my way out."

We both sat quietly for a few minutes. Peppy went back to her puppies. They were exactly two weeks old now and starting to explore. She had to collect a couple who'd strayed into the dining room, carrying them back to the nest in her soft, strong jaws.

"Oh, doll, I forgot to tell you. I did ask some of the ladies about Chrissie Pichea. About whether she had a job, you know."

I pulled my mind away from Ben Loring's iniquities and tried to think about Todd and Chrissie Pichea. "And does she?"

"Not as far as they knew. But Mrs. Tertz and Mrs. Olsen said she was supernice, wanting to help them with their investments, so they wondered if she'd done that kind of work before she got married."

I stared up at him. "Really! Help with their investments? I hope none of them gave into the impulse."

He shrugged. "As to that I couldn't say. But what I did think was interesting was who came around with her talking to them. Guess."

I shook my head. "From your tone of voice

I know it wasn't her husband, but—not the first Mr. Warshawski, surely."

"The first? Oh, I get you, your ex, you mean. Nope. It was the kid lives across the hall from me. Vinnie Buttone, who's always giving you such a hard time."

I sat back on my heels. Vinnie the Banker. That's how I always thought of him. I just never bothered to wonder which bank. It had to be U.S. Metropolitan Bank and Trust. I whistled through my teeth. Vinnie was tied to Todd and Chrissie. So that connected them to the bank.

I'd have to call to confirm it, of course. But say I was right—U.S. Met was connected to Diamond Head, owned by Jason Felitti, who also sat on the Met board. I could feel the two halves of my brain trying to come together, trying to juggle Chrissie, Vinnie, and Mrs. Frizell with Diamond Head Motors. I couldn't do it.

I pushed myself upright.

"Where're you off to, doll? Want to talk to Vinnie? You think maybe he's a con artist trying to steal their money?"

I laughed. Vinnie was such an uptight, tight-assed little goober, it was hard to see him as a criminal mastermind. Anyway, I wasn't going to face him until I had some unassailable facts to dangle in front of him. I was sick of getting burned from charging in on people without the ammunition to make them talk.

I explained this to Mr. Contreras. "I'm heading up to O'Hare. I've got to get out of town."

"Where're you going? Back to Pittsburgh?"

"I don't know. The Cubs are in Atlanta this weekend. Maybe I'll just head south and see if I can get a ticket."

He didn't like it. He hated letting me out of his sight. But if I stayed in town there'd be at least one more dead body on the police records and maybe more.

36

Last Will and Testament

Fulton County Stadium was a big place compared with Wrigley Field, and not nearly as many fans came out to cheer on the Braves. I had no trouble getting a ticket on Sunday. The Cubs won—in itself a miracle. The boys were having trouble figuring out what game they were suiting up for this summer.

I made a dutiful pilgrimage to Martin Luther King's birthplace and drank a Ramos gin fizz at Brennan's. Just separating myself from Chicago for two nights was a help, but I couldn't get over the dull ache from Lotty's misery: being estranged from her is like missing a piece of my own body.

I caught a noon flight back to Chicago on Monday. During the el ride back into town I tried to marshal my thoughts back to the work that lay ahead.

I knocked on Mr. Contreras's door to let him know I was home, but he was out—with his tomatoes, I saw from my kitchen window. I'd forgotten the emergency glazier, but my generous neighbor had swallowed his hurt feelings and let the man in, as a note taped to the new window informed me.

I fiddled with a leftover piece of putty. The only way I know to keep depression at bay is by working. I needed to visit the Bank of Lake View, to try to discover why Mrs. Frizell had moved her account from them. I also wanted to put a little pressure on Ben Loring at Paragon Steel. First, though, I tried the alarm people. I got them just before they closed, but was able to schedule an installation for the next morning.

It was far too late now to go to the bank, but Ben Loring would doubtless still be wrestling away with Paragon Steel's controls in Lincolnwood. I dialed their number and got put through to Sukey's deep, sweet voice. I realized I hadn't learned her last name.

"This is V. I. Warshawski. I was by Friday afternoon to talk to Ben Loring and his pals."

"Oh, yes, Ms. Warshawski. I remember clearly."

"I had another question for him. Something I learned after I left."

"I'm sorry, but he specifically said he didn't

want to talk to you if you called." Her rich voice conveyed personal regret. Someone ought to be auditioning her for the stage.

"Well, I won't try to muscle my way past you. But could you tell him I now know that someone at Diamond Head is shipping out spools of Paragon copper wire in the middle of the night? Ask him if he thinks that's curious, or just a normal part of their business."

She put me on hold. Five minutes later Ben Loring was rasping at me, demanding to know what the fuck I was talking about, who was I working for, what the hell did I want.

"To share information with you. Are you surprised to hear it?"

He brushed that aside. "How do you know? You got pictures? Proof of any kind?"

"I saw them with my own eyes. I was clinging to one of your spools while it hung from a gantry. In fact, it probably saved my life. So really, I'm calling out of gratitude."

"Don't play the cute fool with me, Warshawski—you don't strike me as the type. Give me some details. And tell me why you're calling."

I gave him a succinct picture of what I'd seen. "I am getting so tired of being jacked around by people connected to Diamond Head. If someone doesn't start talking to me soon, I'm going to be sharing my bits of information with the feds. Maybe even the newspapers."

I heard him whisper "Oh, fuck" under his breath, but he didn't say anything else. "We need to talk, Warshawski. But I have to speak to my management group first. When can you come back out here? Tomorrow morning?"

I thought of the alarm installation. "I'm pretty busy. Unless you want to come down here?"

"Just can't get away tomorrow morning. I'll call you. But don't go talking to anyone until you hear from me."

"Ah, nuts, Loring. I'm not going to dangle on a spool for you forever."

"I'm not asking you to, Warshawski. Just a couple of days. I may even get back to you tonight. Give me your number."

"Aye, aye, skipper." I saluted the phone smartly as we hung up, but of course he couldn't see that.

So now what? Was he involved and trying to gain a few hours either to frame a cover-up or blow my brains out? At least Rawlings's squad car might make the latter less likely.

I didn't have enough information to worry about it any more this afternoon. I needed to retrieve the Impala, collect my belongings from Mrs. Polter before she sold them for fire extinguishers, and return home.

On my way out I knocked at Mr. Contreras's door. He was inside again and much relieved to see me. I let his waves of information about the glazier wash over me, thanking him when there was a break in the surf, then explaining my going back out. "I'm returning here. Probably by eight."

"I could make us dinner," he offered tentatively.

I hugged him briefly. "I've got some chicken upstairs that I ought to cook tonight. Why don't you let me make you something for a change?"

He walked me to the door. "Stay out of the San this time, doll. I know you drink a lot of water, but that stuff ain't good for you."

Vinnie was coming in as I left. Mr. Contreras and I both stared at him, trying to picture him as a con artist. In his pale-gray summer suit and tightly knotted tie he looked so stodgily corporate that I had to give it up.

"Evening, Vinnie," I said brightly. "Got any investment advice for us?"

He looked at me stonily. "Sell your share in the co-op, Warshawski. Neighborhood's coming up and you won't be able to afford your tax bill."

I laughed, but I could feel Mr. Contreras start to bristle. As I went out the door I heard a diatribe that began with "young man" and might end anywhere.

I walked over to Belmont and Halsted to catch the el. No one seemed to be following me. My legs ached as I climbed the stairs to the platform. Mr. Contreras was right: the day was coming when I wouldn't be able to swing from the chandeliers any longer—I could already feel its shadow in my muscles.

The air-conditioning wasn't working on the train I caught and its windows didn't open. The

Sox were playing a night game at home. Happy fans in cutoffs had joined the overflow of commuters to make the ride one of suffocating misery.

When I got off at Thirty-first, I was so glad to be outside again I decided to walk to the Impala. I sketched a wave to the Number 31 bus as it left the station, relieved not to be one of the standing sardines packed on such a muggy night.

My Nikes were at the bottom of the San. The loafers I'd put on didn't offer much support. My feet began to hurt about halfway to the car, but I plodded on past bus stops. The evening sky was starting to thicken with rain clouds again. The first drops began to fall as I got to Damen. I sprinted the half block to Thirty-first Place, where I'd left the car. No one seemed to have vandalized it. I'd been worrying about that on the ride south, wondering whether Luke would even bother to fix the Trans Am if his own precious baby were damaged.

The keys had been in my jeans pocket when I went into the drink. The ring looked rusted out, but the ignition turned without faltering. I'd also salvaged Mrs. Polter's front-door key. The knot I'd tied through my belt loop had held through my gyrations Friday night.

When I got to her house on Archer, the rain was falling in a thick sheet. I ran full-tilt up the rickety stairs, slipping on the worn wood in my loafers. I was soaked before I got to the top. My fingers, thick with cold from my drenching, fumbled with her front-door lock.

By the time I got it open Mrs. Polter was waiting on the other side. The hall was so dark it was hard to see, but the twilight behind me glinted from the fire extinguisher she was pointing at me. I hunched my head down under my forearms to protect my eyes, and lunged under her outstretched arms into her abdomen. It was like butting my head into a mattress. We both grunted. I turned underneath her armpits and wrestled the extinguisher from her grip.

"Mrs. Polter," I panted. "How kind of you to welcome me in person."

"You're wet," she announced. "You're dripping all over the linoleum."

"It's the canal. Your pals pushed me in, but I managed to climb out. Want to talk about it?"

"You got no call to break in here and attack me. I oughtta call the cops."

"Do, Mrs. Polter. Be my guest. There's nothing I'd like better than for you and me to talk to the cops. In fact, I'm kind of expecting one of them to call you. You hear from a Detective Finchley over at Area One?"

"He the nigger cop? Yeah, he was by. I got nothing to say to any of 'em."

"Niggers or cops?" I tried to get the words out lightly, but a picture of Conrad Rawlings's copper torso against my own flashed through my head and made me choke. I tried to push

358

my anger back—she wouldn't share information more readily for a lecture on the evils of racism.

"Either of 'em. I told him he wants to talk to me he oughtta get himself a search warrant. I know my rights, I says to him, and he can't come pushing me around."

"So which is it? You don't want to call the local station to complain about my being here? Or you want me to get Finchley back here with a warrant?" My teeth were starting to chatter from cold. This made it harder to focus on the conversation, which didn't seem to be going anywhere anyway.

With one of her abrupt turnarounds Mrs. Polter said, "Why don't you go upstairs and change, honey. You got something dry up there you can put on. Then you and me can have a bit of a talk. Without dragging the cops into it."

I was still holding the fire extinguisher. Before going into the dark stairwell I handed it to her. I didn't think she was going to attack me at this point.

Under the forty-watt bulb in Mitch's old room I took off my wet clothes and rubbed myself warm with a towel out of my suitcase. From the disarray in the case it was apparent my landlady had indeed gone rummaging.

I pulled on the clean T-shirt and sweatpants and wondered what to do with my gun. The jacket that had concealed my shoulder holster was too wet to put back on. In the end I strapped the gun next to my bare skin, where it rubbed uncomfortably.

The floor creaked outside my door. I whirled and opened it. One of my fellow boarders had been drooling at me through the keyhole.

"Yes, I've got breasts. Now you've had a chance to look at them, go someplace else and play."

He blinked at me nervously and scuttled backward up the hall. I shut the door, but didn't bother to try to block the view—what I really didn't want people staring at was the gun, but it was too late now to try to hide that.

I had a change of socks, but no shoes. My loafers were too wet to put back on. I decided to keep my clean pair of socks for the drive home. I padded back downstairs in my bare feet, going slowly so as not to cut myself on nails or loose edges of linoleum.

My landlady was watching a high-speed chase scene involving Clint Eastwood and a chimpanzee. Her oldest lodger, Sam, was sitting on the couch, drinking a Miller and laughing at the chimp. When Mrs. Polter saw me behind her, she jerked her head at Sam. He stood up obediently, disentangling a couch spring from his threadbare suit.

She waved a hand from me to the couch. It was the only other seat in the room besides her outsize vinyl armchair. I looked at it dubiously. The places where fabric still covered the springs were littered with cracker crumbs. I perched on one of the arms, which wobbled dangerously beneath me.

Mrs. Polter regretfully muted the sound just as Clint and the chimp pushed a second car off the road. I'd certainly rather watch that than talk to me too.

"So you went into the canal, huh?"

"Didn't your pals tell you? We had quite an evening together. When they tried to use my body as part of the roadway, I decided that she who fights and runs away would live to fight another day."

"Who tried to run you over?" she muttered, her eyes on the screen.

"Milton Chamfers, Mrs. Polter. You know him: you phoned him as soon as you heard from me, to tell him I was returning to the neighborhood."

"I don't know what you're talking about."

"Yes, you do, Mrs. Polter." I got off the couch arm and snatched the remote device out of her hand. "Why don't we get back to Clint later? My adventures Friday night were every bit as exciting as his. I promise to describe them in vivid Technicolor if you'll just listen to me."

I clicked the power switch and the giant Mitsubishi went blank.

"Hey, you got no call—" she yelled.

"Lily, you okay?" Sam hovered nervously in the doorway. He must have just moved a few steps into the dark hall, ready to leap to her defense.

"Oh, go eat your dinner, Sam. I can take care of her."

He tried beckoning to her. When she didn't budge, he sidled into the room and leaned over her chair. "Ron says she's got a gun. He seen it when she was dressing."

Mrs. Polter gave a crack of laughter. "So, she's got a gun. She'd have to have a cannon to cut through my flesh. Don't worry about it, Sam."

When he'd disappeared into the gloom again, she eyed me narrowly. "You come here to shoot me?"

"If I'd wanted to do that I'd have pulled my gun when you were waving that damned fire extinguisher at me—the cops would have bought self-defense then."

"I didn't know it was you," she said indignantly. "I heard someone at my door. I got a right to defend myself, too, same as you, and in this neighborhood you can't be too careful. Then you come barreling at me like a mad bull, what do you expect? The mayor and a welcoming party?"

I grinned at her last comment, but continued my attack. "Did Chamfers call you Saturday? Tell you I was dead?"

"I don't know anyone named Chamfers," she shouted. "Get that through your head."

I slammed the television with the palm of my hand. "Don't give me that shit, Mrs. Polter. I *know* you called him; they told me Friday night at the plant."

"I don't know anyone named that," she repeated stubbornly. "And don't you go banging on that TV. I spent a lot of money on it. You break it you buy me a new one, if I have to take you to court for it."

"Well, you called someone. Who was it?" Light suddenly dawned. "No, don't tell me—you phoned Mitch Kruger's son. He gave you a phone number when he came by for Mitch's stuff and asked you to tell him as soon as anyone came round asking about his dad. You must have warned him I'd been here and he made it real clear that he wanted to know right away if I came back."

Her jaw dropped. "How did you know? He said no one was to know he'd been here."

"You told me. Remember? Last Tuesday when I came by looking for Mitch's papers?"

"Oh." It was hard to read her expression in the dim light, but I thought she looked chagrined. "I promised I wouldn't say anything. I forgot. . . ."

I squatted on the dusty floor under the lamp so that we could see each other's faces more clearly. "The guy who came by, told you he was Mitch's son—he about my height? Clean-shaven, short brown hair brushed straight back from his forehead?"

She eyed me warily. "Could be. But that could be a whole lot of guys."

I agreed. It's hard to think of something about a corporate manager's appearance that makes him really stand out in a crowd. "Tell you what, Mrs. Polter. I'd be willing to bet a good sum, say a hundred bucks, that the person who said he was Mitch's son is really Milt Chamfers, the plant manager over at Diamond Head. You know—the engine factory over at Thirty-first by the canal. Would you be willing to drive over with me in the morning and take a look at him? Prove me right or wrong?"

Her black button eyes gleamed greedily for a minute, but as she thought it over the glint died away. "Say you're right. Not that I'm believing you, but just say you are. Why'd he do it?"

I took a deep breath and picked my words carefully. "You didn't know Mitch Kruger, Mrs. Polter, but I'm sure you've met lots of guys like him over the years. Always looking for an easy buck, never willing to work to get ahead."

"Yeah, I've met me a few like that," she said grudgingly.

"He thought he was onto something at Diamond Head. Don't ask me what, because I don't know. All I can say is, he hung out over there, hinted to folks that he was onto a scam, and died. Chamfers probably thought Mitch really had some proof about something illegal. So as soon as his body was discovered, Chamfers came over here pretending to be Mitch's son so he could go through his papers."

It didn't seem likely that Mitch would have come on any written proof of a theft ring involving the copper. Although who knows—maybe he went pawing through dumpsters looking for documents that might give him blackmail material.

It sounded like more work than I could picture him doing, but I'd only met the guy a few times.

"So say I did phone him Friday." Mrs. Polter interrupted my thoughts. "Not that I did—just supposing. What of it?"

"I've been trying to talk to the boy about Mitch Kruger for two weeks and he won't see me. I went over to the plant Friday night, hoping to find some way of making him talk to me. He had seven people lying in wait for me. We fought, but they were too much for me, and as I said, when they tried to run me over I dove into the canal."

I didn't think I had to tell Mrs. Polter about the copper spools. After all, if she started blackmailing Chamfers about the theft ring hers might be the next body to go floating down to Stickney.

"Seven guys against you, huh? You have your gun with you?"

I smiled to myself. She really did want the Technicolor version. I gave her a graphic description, including the sneeze that led to my uncovering. And including the comments about "the boss" having warned them that I was coming around. I glossed over the part about the trucks and the copper, just let her believe they started the crane when I jumped out on it.

She sighed noisily. "You really climb down that crane scaffolding? Wish there'd been someone there with a camera. 'Course, I was young once. But I don't think I ever could have jumped off a ledge onto a crane. It's my head—I'm scared of heights."

She brooded in silence for a few minutes. "He sure had me fooled, that guy, claiming to be Mitch Kruger's son. I should've known when he offered me so much money. . . ." She eyed me uncertainly, but relaxed when I didn't shriek at her.

"It's my one weakness," she said with dignity. "We were too poor growing up. Used to carry lard sandwiches to school. The good days were when we had two slices of bread to put around it. But I'm good at sizing up men and I should've known he was too slick, that he had my number."

She pondered some more, then abruptly began heaving herself from the chair. "You stay here. I'll be right back."

I got to my feet. My knees ached from kneeling on the linoleum so long. While she held a whispered colloquy in the hall with Sam, I sat on her footstool and did quad raises. I'd managed fifty with each leg before she came back.

"I took these out of Mitch's room when his son or whoever he is came by. You might as well know the worst about me. I could see he was itzing to get his fingers on his old man's papers, and I thought maybe they were worth something. But I've been through them a million times and I don't for the life of me see what was so important about them that he wanted to lug them all over the South Side with him. You can have 'em." She thrust a packet wrapped in newspaper into my hands.

37

A Chicken for Mr. Contreras

It was close to eight-thirty when I turned off the Kennedy at Belmont. Mrs. Polter had wanted to share a beer or two before I left, to show there were no hard feelings over my dip in the canal. Although I'm not much of a beer-drinker I thought it politic to keep up the better feeling she had for me.

Sam had brought a six-pack and two glasses and hovered anxiously in the doorway to make sure I wasn't going to attack her. By the time I extricated myself from her highly colored flood of reminiscence she was slapping me on the thigh and telling me I wasn't nearly as stuck-up as I'd seemed at first.

I stopped at a pay phone near Ashland to call Mr. Contreras, partly to let him know I was still alive even though late. I also wanted some assurance that the building wasn't under siege. He was voluble with relief at hearing from me; I cut him short with a promise to tell him all about it over dinner.

I figured there wasn't any point trying to hide the Impala. By now anyone who wanted to know where I was must have a pretty clear fix on every move I was making. I certainly wasn't convinced that Mrs. Polter wouldn't call Milt Chamfers the minute I left her house. I sat across from my apartment for several minutes, scanning the street for anyone who looked out of place.

Finally I slid across the seat and out the passenger door, my gun in my hand. As I got to the front door a squad car cruised slowly by, its spot ostentatiously playing on the entrance. I put down my suitcase and waved with my left hand, hoping the shadows concealed the Smith & Wesson. Sergeant Rawlings on the case. I didn't know if I liked the little flicker of warmth the idea gave me: it's a mistake to get too dependent on someone else for your own well-being.

Mr. Contreras surged out to meet me in the lobby. He insisted on taking the suitcase from me and carrying it upstairs. I offered him a choice between wine and whisky, but he'd brought a bottle of his own grappa. He settled down at the kitchen table with a glass while I changed into dry shoes and a clean pair of jeans.

I hadn't looked at Mrs. Polter's newsprint package—just stuck it into the band of my sweatpants when she handed it to me. I didn't want to seem too eager in front of her. Besides, I was afraid to unwrap it—afraid that the collection of papers would mean as little to me as to her. I'd put the bundle on my dresser while I changed, but I kept eyeing it. When I went back to the kitchen I took a deep breath and carried it with me.

I dumped it casually in front of Mr. Contreras. "These are Mitch's private papers. Mrs. Polter had filched them from his room after he died, but she decided to turn them over to me. Want to see if there's anything hot in them while I start dinner?"

I bustled around with a skillet and olive oil, chopping mushrooms and olives as if the little bundle held no interest for me. Behind me I could hear the newspaper rattle as Mr. Contreras peeled it off, and then his laborious picking apart of the contents. I dusted the chicken with flour and dropped it in the pan. The sound of frying drowned the noise of the paper.

Finally, after flaming some brandy over the chicken and covering the pan, washing my hands with the deliberation of a surgeon, and pouring a large whisky to cover the thin beer that kept making me burp, I sat down next to Mr. Contreras.

He looked at me doubtfully. "I sure hope this isn't what you almost got yourself killed for, doll. It looks like a whole bunch of nothing. 'Course, it meant something to Mitch, and some of it's got sentimental value, his union card and stuff, but the rest . . . It's not much, and it don't mean sh— Well, anyway, see for yourself."

I felt a sinking in my diaphragm. I'd been expecting too much. I picked up the stack of documents, grimy from the intense handling they'd had lately, and went through them one at a time.

Mitch's union card. His social security card. A form to send the feds showing his change of address, so he could continue to collect social security. Another for the local. The *Sun-Times* story on Diamond Head's change of ownership, so worn it was barely legible. A newspaper photo of a white-haired man, smiling widely enough to show his back molars, shaking hands with a well-fed man of perhaps fifty. The inscription to this had been thumbed over to the point it was also illegible. Picking it up by one of its top corners, I showed it to Mr. Contreras.

"Any idea who either of these gents is?"

"Oh, the guy on the left is the old president of our local, Eddie Mohr."

"Eddie Mohr?" A prickle ran up the back of my neck. "The man whose car was used to attack Lotty?"

"Yeah . . . What're you getting at, doll?" He stirred uneasily in his chair.

"Why did Mitch carry his picture around with his most cherished possessions?"

Mr. Contreras shrugged. "Probably he wasn't used to seeing people he knew in the paper. Sentimentality, you know."

"Mitch didn't strike me as sentimental. He lost track of his son and his wife. He didn't have one scrap of paper that showed he cared about a soul anywhere on earth. And here, along with the article about Jason Felitti buying Diamond Head, is a photo of Diamond Head's old local president. But if Mohr was photographed for a newspaper, he couldn't possibly be doing something he didn't want known," I added, more to myself than to the old man.

"That's just it, doll. You want it to mean something. Heck, I do too. We've been scratching around for the better part of two weeks without finding anything—I know how bad you *want* this to be important."

I swallowed my whisky and pushed myself away from the table. "Let's have dinner. Then I'm going to take this down to my office. If I make a copy, the text may show up more clearly: it does sometimes."

He patted me awkwardly on the shoulder, trying to show sympathy for my desire to chase after wild geese. He helped me serve up the chicken and carry it to the dining room. I brought Mitch's little stash to the table and laid the papers out in a circle between Mr. Contreras and me.

"He needed his social security card. I guess he needed his union card, too, for his pension. Or maybe it was the one thing he'd achieved in life that he felt he could cling to. Why keep track of who owned Diamond Head?"

I wasn't expecting an answer, but Mr. Contreras popped up with one unexpectedly. "When did that Felitti fellow buy the company? A year ago? Two years? By then Mitch knew he couldn't make ends meet on his pension. Maybe he thought he could go to him for work."

I nodded to myself. That made sense. "And Eddie Mohr? He could help Mitch too?"

"Doubt it." Mr. Contreras wiped his mouth with his napkin. "Wonderful chicken, doll. You put olives in it? Never would have occurred to me. No, being as how Eddie's retired, he wouldn't have any input into who the firm hired. Of course, he could make his recommendations—they'd carry more weight than just someone walking in cold off the street—but him and Mitch wasn't especially friendly. I can't see him going out on a limb for a fellow who didn't have too much going for him to begin with."

"Who's that shaking hands with Eddie?"

Mr. Contreras took his glasses out of his shirt pocket and scrutinized the picture again. "Search me. Doesn't look like anyone I ever saw before. . . . I can see you're chomping at the bit to get out of here, go see what you can make of this sucker. We can wait to have coffee when we get back."

I grinned at him. "Didn't know I was *so* transparent. You coming?"

"Oh, sure. You going on wild goose chases, I want to see how they come out. Even if I can't jump off a ledge onto a moving crane anymore. Bet I could, though," he muttered under his breath as I carefully did up all three locks. "Bet I've got more left in me than you imagine."

I decided our friendship would last longer if I pretended I hadn't heard.

We had a quick run downtown. Now that the

office workers were gone for the day I found a place big enough for the Impala only a few doors from the Pulteney.

I wondered if the people who'd ransacked my place last night had gone tearing through my office as well, but the door was intact. Amateurs. Despite what Rawlings said, these were people who didn't know me. If they were really looking for something they thought only I had, they would have tried my office too.

My desktop Xerox sprang smartly into life. By enlarging the photo and increasing its contrast I was able in a few minutes to get enough of the inscription back to see what Eddie Mohr had been up to. The South Side retiree, as the paper labeled him, was accepting an award from a blurry name that I thought was probably Hector Beauregard. Hector, the blurry secretary of Chicago Settlement, was thrilled at the contribution Eddie had made to his favorite charity.

Mr. Contreras, following along with a horny finger as I deciphered, whistled under his breath. "I never figured Eddie for the charity type. Knights of Columbus, maybe, but not some downtown outfit, which I guess Chicago Settlement is."

I sat on the end of my desk, hard. "It's not just a downtown charity, it's a pet of my good old ex-husband, Dick Yarborough. Max Loewenthal's son, Michael, played at a benefit for them two weeks ago and I saw Dick there, leading the charge at a feeding frenzy. This is not just curious, it's downright creepy. I think I need to talk to Mr. Mohr. Can you bring me along? Make the introductions?"

Mr. Contreras removed his glasses again and rubbed the bridge of his nose. "Why do you want to talk to him? You don't think he's doing something, well, underhanded with this Chicago Settlement outfit, do you? They wouldn't put it in the papers if there was something fishy to it."

"I don't know what I think. That's why I want to talk to him. It's just too—too much of a coincidence. Mitch carries his picture around along with a story about Diamond Head. My old husband Dick is really pimping Chicago Settlement. Meanwhile Dick's father-in-law has a brother who owns Diamond Head. Eddie and Dick and Jason Felitti all know each other. I've got to find out why Mitch thought that was valuable."

"I don't like it, doll."

"I don't like it either." I spread my hands in appeal. "But it's all I've got, so it's what I have to use."

"It makes me feel, I don't know, like a sneak. A scab."

My mouth twisted in unhappiness. "Detective work is like that; it isn't usually glamor and excitement. It's often drudgery, and sometimes it feels like betrayal. I won't ask you to come along if it really makes you feel like a scab. But I'm going to have to talk to Eddie Mohr, whether you're there or not."

"Oh, I'll come if you're set on it," he said slowly. "I can see I kind of don't have a choice."

38

An Old Husband Surfaces

Rawlings called shortly after I got home. "Just wanted to hear your sweet voice, Ms. W. Make sure you hadn't fallen under a semi or something. I tried reaching you yesterday, but didn't put out an APB—figured if you were dead your corpse would keep another day."

"I went out of town," I said, annoyed to find myself offering an explanation. "It's been almost three days since anyone tried to kill me. Life is getting dull. I kind of like the squad cars, though. I never thought the sight of a blue-and-white would cheer me so much."

"I figure a classy dame like you expects presents, Ms. W., and since I can't afford diamonds I gotta offer you what I have. How about dinner tomorrow?"

I laughed a little. "How about Wednesday? I'm going to be working late tomorrow."

He was busy Wednesday. We settled on Friday, at Costa del Sol, a Mexican place on Belmont just west of the yuppie fringe. "If your work tomorrow involves taking on armed punks and you're not telling me about it, I'm going to be just a little peeved," he added before hanging up.

I felt an unexpected spurt of anger, but tried to speak temperately. "I appreciate the squad cars and the concern, Sergeant, but I'm not turning my life over to you. If that's the exchange, I'd rather take my chances on the street." Temperateness and I apparently don't mix too well.

"Is that how it looks to you, Vic?" He sounded surprised. "I'm a cop. And however much I like you, I don't want civilians in the line of fire—it makes police work ten times harder. I also get cold chills when I think about someone climbing a ladder to your window and breaking in as cool as ice."

"It gives me cold chills, too, but I'm taking care of the situation. Anyway, I'm a civilian—I don't like cops telling me how to do my job. Besides, for a week you guys wouldn't believe there *was* a line of fire out there. Now I've proved it to you, you want me to pack up and go home. Maybe cops and PI's shouldn't get so friendly together." I regretted the last sentence as soon as it left my mouth.

"Unh. Low blow, Ms. W. Low blow. I don't see that our work has to be in conflict, but maybe you do."

"Conrad, I know there are good cops; my dad was one. But cops are like any other group of people—when they get together they act clannish. They like to show their collective muscle to people outside their clique. And society gives you guys a lot of power to bulk up your muscle. Sometimes I think my whole job consists of standing outside different cliques—of cops or businessmen or whoever—with a yellow flag to remind you that your outlook isn't the only one."

He was quiet a minute. "You still want to have dinner with me Friday?"

I felt my cheeks redden. "Sure. Yes, unless you've changed your mind."

"Well, let's just leave things here before we say so much we don't want to get together again. I can't think fast enough to do a discussion like this on the phone." He hesitated, then said, "Will you promise to call me if someone tries to hurt you? Run you over, climb through your window, whatever? Would that be a violation of your principles?"

I agreed amiably enough, but my fists were still clenched when I hung up the phone. I should have known better than to get in bed with a policeman. Every day for the last two weeks I'd been acting before I thought. And every day it had gotten me into trouble.

The phone rang again as I was heading into the bathroom to get ready for bed. I was tempted to let it go—it was after eleven, after all. But maybe it was Rawlings wanting to smooth things out. I picked up the bedroom extension on the fifth ring. It was Murray Ryerson. By the noise in the background, he was calling from a party in full swing.

"You drunk, Murray? It's way past a respect-able time to call anyone."

"You getting old, Warshawski? I thought your night just got going about now."

I made a face into the phone. "Yes, I'm getting old. Now that you know that, is your investigative reporter's mind at ease?"

"Not really, Vic." He was shouting to be heard over the music. I held the receiver a few inches from my ear.

"How come you go falling into the Sanitary Canal without telling me about it? One of my gofers just came sidling up to me with the news at the bar here. Of course, he thought I must already know, since everybody believes you and I are pals. You made me look bad."

"Come on, Murray, you told me the last time I saw you that what I was doing wasn't news. Don't you come playing that 'all pals together' tune on your violin. I won't stand for it." I was so angry, I snapped a pencil I'd been fiddling with in two.

"You can't pick and choose what's news, Warshawski. An old lady losing her dogs because she's senile and they're a nuisance—that just isn't interesting. And neither is a drunk deadbeat fall-ing into the canal. But when *you* go in, people want to know about it."

"Fuck you and the horse you rode in on, Ryer-son." I slammed the phone down as hard as I could.

I was panting with rage, my fragile calm from

378

my trip to Atlanta completely shattered. What was with these guys, trying to run me around? I dug a basketball from the back of my hall closet and started bouncing it up and down, with an evil disregard for the family trying to sleep below, hoping to pound away some of my fury.

I'd been dribbling for about five minutes when the phone rang again. It was either Murray, hoping to bludgeon me into giving him a story, or my downstairs neighbor, Mrs. Lee. I hastily stuffed the ball back in the closet before picking up the receiver.

"Vic?" It was Dick's light baritone. "I know it's late, but I've been trying to get through for two hours."

I sat down hard on the piano bench, surprise knocking the rage out of me. "And that gives you the right to call at eleven-fifteen?" Just because I'd stopped feeling angry didn't mean Dick got a free ride.

"You and I need to talk. I left two messages with your answering service today."

I realized I hadn't checked with my service since returning from Atlanta. "This is really sudden, Dick, so I don't have a response ready. Does Teri know?"

"Please don't clown around right now, Vic. I'm not in the humor for it."

"Well, that's kind of why we split up to begin with, wasn't it," I said reasonably. "Because I didn't care enough about the stuff you were in the humor for."

"Look. You've been sticking your nose into my business for the last two weeks. I think I've been pretty tolerant about it on the whole, but you're really asking for trouble now. And strange as it may seem to you, I don't want to see you in major trouble."

I made a face at the mouthpiece. "Funny you should say that, Richard. I just had that identical thought about you recently. I'll trade you—you tell me what major trouble you think I'm headed for and then I'll tell you about yours."

He sighed ostentatiously. "I might have known better than to try to do you a good turn."

"You should have known better than to think calling up to lay down the law would sound like a good turn to me," I corrected.

"I'd like you to come to my office tomorrow. I'm free around ten."

"Which means I'd kick my heels in your waiting room until eleven or twelve. No, thanks. I've got a very tight day scheduled. Why don't you stop here on your way into the Loop? It's just a hop, skip, and jump off the Eisenhower to Belmont."

He didn't like it, mostly because he wasn't controlling the program. He tried to make me come downtown to the Enterprise Club, the favorite embalming center for Chicago's top lawyers and bankers. I wanted to start my day in the neighborhood, at the Bank of Lake View. He finally consented to meet me at the Belmont Diner, but it had to be seven o'clock: his important meetings started at eight-thirty. Since Dick knows early mornings and I aren't on speaking terms, it enabled him to salvage a small triumph from the conversation.

Before going to bed I checked in with my answering service. Sure enough, there were two messages from Dick, both stressing the urgency of my calling him *immediately*. Detective Finchley had phoned, as had Luke Edwards and Sergeant Rawlings. I was glad I'd missed Luke. I wasn't in the humor for a long, lugubrious account of the Trans Am's woes. I unplugged the phone and went to bed.

39

Postmarital Upset

My dreams were tormented by images of my mother. She appeared at the gym where I was playing basketball. I dropped the ball and ran from the court to her side, but just as I held out a hand to her, she turned her back on me and walked away. I felt myself crying in my sleep as I followed her down Halsted, begging her to turn and look at me. Behind me the Buddha was saying in Gabriella's heavily accented English, "You're on your own now, Victoria."

When the alarm woke me at six, it was a welcome release from the trap of dreams. My eyes were gummy with the tears I'd shed in the night.

I felt so sorry for myself that I hiccuped back another crying bout as I brushed my teeth.

"What's wrong with you?" I said derisively to the face in the mirror. "Feel deprived over losing Dick Yarborough's love?"

I turned the cold water on in the shower and held my head under it. The shock cleaned my eyelids and cleared my head. I did a complete workout in the living room, including a full set of weight exercises. At the end my arms and legs were trembling, but I felt purged of my nightmare.

I dressed with a care that made me feel a little annoyed with myself, in a soft gold top with a charcoal pantsuit. I didn't think I wanted to show off for Dick, at least not in a sexual way. I just wanted to seem cool and prosperous. Big earrings and a chunky necklace added a touch of modernity. The jacket was cut full enough to hide my shoulder holster.

It had been almost four days since I'd gone into the drink. I was beginning to feel nervous about the peace my pals were leaving me in. No threatening calls, no firebombs through the window. That wasn't all due to the watchful eye of Conrad's minions. I couldn't help thinking they were saving up for some huge, ugly surprise.

I studied the street carefully from my living room window before leaving. It was hard to tell from this angle whether anyone was staking me out from the cars out front, but the Subaru that had dogged me last week wasn't there. No one shot at me when I came out. Always a welcome beginning to the day.

I took a long way around to the Belmont Diner, in keeping with the first rule for terrorist targets: vary your route. Although it was a few minutes after seven when I got to the diner, Dick hadn't arrived yet. In my eagerness to remember the rules for terrorism I'd forgotten those for power breakfasting: make the other person wait.

Barbara and Helen greeted me enthusiastically. Business was heavy, but they managed to give me the details of what had happened to my tail after I left Friday.

"Honey, you should have been here," Barbara called over her shoulder, depositing a short stack and fried eggs at the table behind me. "Helen here practically undressed the poor slob, sobbing all over his trouser legs how sorry she was about the tea. And then—well, I'll tell you in a minute. . . . You want your usual, don't you, Jack? And how 'bout you, Chuck—two over easy, hon? And hash browns?" She whisked back to the kitchen.

Helen, who'd been unloading an armful of food in the corner, called over, "The high point was Marge. She came out from the kitchen to see what the commotion was and dropped a can of hot grease along the hallway. The poor slob's backup had come tearing in. When the first guy yelled you'd gone out the rear, the second one went ass-over-teacup through the grease." She roared with laughter.

Barbara reappeared with a fresh pot of coffee and poured out a cup for me. "It was great, Vic. God, I wish I'd brought my camera. It took 'em about an hour to get out of here and all the time we're boo-hoo-hooing like we're the Three Stooges and can't help ourselves. . . . What are you having today, hon?"

"I'm waiting for someone before I order. You guys are great. I wish I'd stayed for the show. If I had a fortune, I'd split it among the lot of you."

Most of the crowd this time of day were regulars, people from the neighborhood who'd been coming in for years on their way to work. They obviously had heard the story already—they kept cutting in with embellishments. At my comment a couple of them gave catcalls. "Easy to promise when you know you'll die broke, Vic." "You oughtta give it up and turn your business over to these girls here—they're the pros."

The uproar suddenly trailed off. I looked over my shoulder and saw Dick come in. His pearl-gray summer worsted had the glow of wealth to it. The faint hauteur with which he viewed the chipped formica tables stirred a ripple of resentment. The men in work clothes and shabby jackets busied themselves with their food. When Dick saw me and sketched a wave, a low murmur went through the crowd.

"Who's the talent?" Barbara whispered, refilling my coffee cup. "You land him and you've

384

got that fortune all right. And don't think I'll forget your sweet talk."

When Dick sat down she flicked her rag in front of him. "Okay if he joins you, Vic?"

I felt a bit embarrassed—I hadn't asked Dick here in the hopes he'd be actively insulted. "He's my guest, Barbara. Dick Yarborough, Barbara Flannery. Dick used to be married to me, but that was in another country."

Barbara pursed her mouth in a wise "O," which indicated understanding that we had confidential business. "Need a menu, Dick?"

Dick lifted frosty eyebrows. The Enterprise Club waiters murmured "Mr. Yarborough" at him deferentially.

"Do you have fresh fruit?"

Barbara rolled her eyes, but held back her favorite retort. "Honeydew, cantaloupe, and strawberries."

"Strawberries. With yogurt. And granola. Skim milk with the granola."

"Fruit, nuts and flakes, lean," Barbara muttered. "Yours, Vic?"

Dick's ostentatious good health made me feel as perverse as everything else about him did. "Corned beef hash and a poached egg. And fries."

Barbara winked at me and took off.

"You ever hear of cholesterol, Vic?" Dick inspected his plastic waterglass as if it were an unknown life form.

"That what you wanted to talk to me about

385

so urgently? You know you've seen plastic before—it's what we used to drink out of when we lived together down on Ellis."

He had the grace to look a little ashamed. He drank some water, fiddled with his cuff links, and looked around.

"It's probably good for me to come to a place like this now and then."

"Yeah. Kind of like going to the zoo. You can feel superior to the creatures in cages even while you're sorry for them."

Barbara swept out with his food before he could snap anything really clever back at me. He poked cautiously through the strawberries, picked out four or five that apparently didn't meet his standards, and spooned some yogurt onto the rest. It was because of guys like him moving into the neighborhood that the diner had started carrying things like yogurt and granola. When I first arrived four years ago, you couldn't get such arty food.

"So what'd you want to talk about, Dick? I know your time's valuable."

He swallowed a mouthful of berries. "You went out to see Jason Felitti on Friday."

"Thank you for sharing that information with me."

He frowned, but plowed ahead. "I'd like to know why you felt you had to bother him."

Barbara brought my food. I cut into the egg and stirred the yolk up with the hash. The fries were golden-brown and crisp; I ate a few and then turned to the hash. I thought Dick was eyeing the fries a little enviously.

"I know you're on the Diamond Head board, Dick. I have a feeling that you handled the legal work involved when Jason bought the company. After all, he's your father-in-law's brother, and even in Oak Brook I expect families stick together." I was studying his face as I spoke, but he'd been through too many high-stakes poker games to show any surprise at my knowledge.

I sketched out the story of Mitch Kruger and of Milt Chamfers's refusal to talk to me. "So I just hoped I could persuade Jason to get Chamfers to meet with me. Your daddy-in-law been complaining to you?"

Dick gave a tight little smile. "Vic, believe it or not, despite all the ragging you do every time you see me, I don't wish you ill. I even wish you well, as long as you don't start disrupting my family or my professional life."

He swallowed some coffee and made a face. "But Peter Felitti is connected to some very powerful people in this city. He's annoyed that you've been harassing Jason. I gather you even tried breaking into the plant the other night. Peter could put pressure on the cops to hound you every time you try to conduct an investigation. He could even see that you lost your license. I'm just talking to you as a friend. Believe it or not, I'd hate to see you go through that kind of misery."

"Of course, if you really cared about my happiness you could persuade Peter not to do all those mean things—he is your father-in-law, after all." I finished the hash, savoring the richness of the egg yolk. "But I've got a few worries about you, Dick. Something ugly's going on over at Diamond Head. Something involving Paragon Steel and some of the retired machinists and who knows what-all else."

I waved a hand to show the scope of ugliness I had in mind. "I don't want to see you up before the SEC or the bar's disciplinary committee or something for signing onto unethical activities. Maybe coercing people into giving money to your favorite charities in exchange for special legal favors."

Off and on since leaving my office last night I'd been wondering about Eddie Mohr and Chicago Settlement. It had occurred to me that the Felittis might have Dick's firm muscle people for contributions in exchange for high-priced legal work. That seemed like a relatively flimsy idea, but I watched Dick's face expectantly to see if I was closing in on anything.

He put his spoon back into the granola and gave me a grim little smile. "Those are very heavy accusations, Vic. I can see why you didn't want to meet at my office. It would be hard for you to retract those remarks if I had a witness to them."

"You've been practicing law in a mighty strange place lately if you bring in witnesses to this kind of conversation. By the way, you notice I'm not asking you how you know I was down at Diamond Head last week. That's because your daddy-in-law Peter must have told you. I already know the manager is working hand-in-glove with the goons who are using the plant as a front for stolen goods. So that must mean Peter knows about that stuff too."

Dick's face turned pale with anger, so much that his eyes blazed like sapphires against his skin. "There are slander laws in this state, and they're specifically designed to stop people like you from uttering garbage like that. A front for stolen goods? You can't offer me one shred of proof of that. You're flailing around because you got caught with your pants down the other night."

"Dick, I saw seven men loading spools of Paragon wire onto trucks in the middle of the night."

He snorted. "And so it must be theft."

"They tried to kill me."

"They'd caught you breaking and entering."

By now I really was flailing around. "Chamfers told them who I was. They were tipped off, and they were waiting for me. Anyway, they get tons more wire from Paragon than they use in production. What do you think they're doing with it when the plant is shut down? Sending it to the Salvation Army?"

"If—and I mean *if*—some employees are stealing from the company, do you think Peter would condone it?" He gave a pitying smile. "Despite all your bravado, I can't help thinking you're a teeny bit jealous of Teri. Her life must look pretty good to you sometimes. So you're trying to get at her through her father."

"Me? Jealous of Teri? Jealous of someone who has to go to Neiman-Marcus just to have something to do with her day?" My voice rose a register to a falsetto. "Jesus, Dick! Get a grip on yourself. What do you think I've been doing for the last decade: lying in wait until our paths crossed by total accident so I could take a bead on your wife?"

He flushed and frowned. "Be that as it may, I'm warning you for your own good to back away from Diamond Head. Certainly to stop throwing around outrageous accusations like theft. Words like that won't let you down any more lightly if this thing comes to a major confrontation. Peter was most upset when he heard it was you who'd gone into the canal. In fact, it was a major embarrassment to him, given your connection to me. Thank God he was able to persuade the papers not to print anything about it—"

"You weren't born stupid, Dick." I cut him off, my own eyes blazing. "Use your goddamn head. I just finished telling you I can link goons at Diamond Head to the plant manager. And you've just connected Peter Felitti to the plant manager and the goons. Which side do you want to be on when all this comes out? Not even Peter Felitti can suppress it forever. Besides, I know a guy at the *Herald-Star* who's itching to run a piece on what I was doing at Diamond Head Friday night."

Dick curled a lip. "Oh, yes, you and the guys you *know.* Being divorced has certainly been an asset to your women's lib lifestyle, hasn't it?"

My hand swept up reflexively; I flung coffee down the front of his charcoal-striped shirt. Barbara was hovering nearby in case I needed protection. I pulled a twenty from my purse and thrust it into her apron pocket.

"Maybe you and Marge can reenact your Good Samaritan routine for the talent here. Boy can't go to all his high-priced meetings with coffee on his shirt." I was on my feet, panting.

"You'll be sorry for this, Vic. Very sorry you ever chose to have this conversation with me." Dick was white with humiliation and fury.

"You called the meeting, Richard. But by all means, send me the dry cleaning bill." My legs were trembling as I left the diner.

40

No Longer Missing

I found a bench at a bus stop across the street and sat there, taking in great gulps of air. I was still shaking with fury, pounding my right fist against my thigh. People waiting for the bus backed away from me: another crazy on the loose.

When I realized the public impression I was creating, I brought myself under control. The end of active rage left me exhausted. Listlessly I watched Dick emerge from the diner, shut off the alarm to his Mercedes convertible, and spin down the road with a great roar from his exhaust. I didn't even care enough to hope a blue-and-white stopped him. At least, not enough to hope very hard.

By and by I crossed the street again and returned to the diner. The place had emptied out; the waitresses were clustered at a table, drinking coffee and smoking.

Barbara sprang up when she saw me. "You okay, hon?"

"Oh, yeah. I just need to wash my face and pull myself together. Sorry to treat you to a nursery-school display."

She grinned wickedly. "Oh, I don't know, Vic. You've given us more action in five days than we usually see all year. Livens up the place and gives us something besides our bad backs to talk about."

I patted her shoulder and went to the tiny bathroom in the rear, along the corridor where Marge had dropped the grease on Friday. That was another good turn I'd done them: the hall was cleaner than I'd ever seen it.

I bathed my face in cold water for several minutes. It was no substitute for a nap, but it would have to get me through the day. I put on lipstick under the flickering neon light. Its pallid glow emphasized the planes of my face, digging harsh grooves into it. It was a foreshadowing of what

I might look like in great age. I grimaced at my reflection, emphasizing its grotesque lines.

"You look dressed for success to me, my girl." I saluted my image.

I suddenly remembered the arrangements I'd made to have a security system installed this morning. I used the restaurant pay phone to call Mr. Contreras; he would be home all morning and would be glad to let the workmen in. He sounded subdued, though.

"Are you sure you don't mind? I'll come back home and wait if it's going to be a hassle for you."

"Oh, no, doll, nothing like that," he assured me hastily. "I guess I'm worrying about going to see Eddie."

"I see." I rubbed my eyes. "I'm not going to push it down your throat. You should stay home if the idea makes you that unhappy."

"But you're going anyway?"

"Yeah. I really need to talk to him."

He didn't say anything after that, except that he'd be on the lookout for the workmen, and hung up.

Barbara brought me a cup of fresh coffee to take with me. "Drinking something hot will calm you down, hon."

I sipped it as I walked along Belmont. The reflexive swallowing did indeed make me feel more myself. By the time I reached the Bank of Lake View on the corner of Belmont and Sheffield, I felt able at least to undertake a conversation.

In a squat stone building with iron bars on the windows, the bank looked sleepy and remote from the financial gyrations of its big downtown brothers. The barred windows allowed little light to penetrate; the lobby was a dingy, musty place that probably hadn't been washed since it opened in 1923. The bank took its commitment to the neighborhood seriously, though, investing in the community and serving its residents with care. They'd eschewed the high-stakes projects that had ruined many small institutions in the eighties; as far as I knew they were in good financial shape.

Most bank functions took place in a high-ceilinged room beyond the lobby. The three loan officers sat behind a low wooden rail across the floor from the tellers. I could see Alma Waters, the woman who'd helped me with my cap mortgage, but I followed protocol and presented my card to the receptionist.

Alma bustled out to meet me. She was a plump woman somewhere between fifty and sixty who wore bright, tight-fitting dresses draped in scarves and gaudy jewelry. Today she sported a combination of red with shocking pink and a series of black and silver bead necklaces. Sailing toward me on spiky black patent-leather pumps, she shook my hand as warmly as though I'd borrowed a million dollars instead of fifty thousand.

"Come on back, Vic. How are you? How's your apartment? That was a good investment you made. I think I told you at the time you could expect that stretch of Racine to start coming up, and it has. I just renegotiated a mortgage for someone on Barry, and you know, the value of her little two-flat had gone up eight-fold. Is that why you're in today?" She had whisked my folder from a drawer while she spoke.

It was a stretch for me sometimes just to come up with the seven hundred a month on my place on top of my rent downtown. That's what I needed, all right—to treble my mortgage.

I smiled. "Partly. The part about that piece of Racine coming up. I need some help—help that you may not feel able to give me."

"Try me, Vic." She gave a rich laugh, showing a mouthful of bright, even teeth. "You know our motto: 'Growing with the community we serve.'"

"You know I'm a private investigator, Alma." She should: my uncertain income had made me a tough sell to her managers. "I'm working for an old woman who lives up the street from me, Harriet Frizell. Mrs. Frizell . . . well, she belongs to old Racine. The part that hasn't come up yet. And now she's fallen on hard times."

I gave a brief but—I hoped—moving picture of Mrs. Frizell's plight. "She used to be a customer here, but sometime in February she moved her account to U.S. Metropolitan. I can't believe she's got much. But I also can't believe the pair who leaped in to act as her guardians are neighborhood angels. I'm not asking you to tell me what her assets were—I know you can't do that.

But could you tell me if she gave any reason for making the move?"

Alma fixed bright, merry eyes on me for a minute. "What's your interest in this, Vic?"

I spread my hands. "Call it neighborly. Her world rotated around her dogs. I agreed to help look after them when she went into the hospital, but came home from a trip out of town to find they'd been put to sleep. It keeps me suspicious of the people who did it."

She pursed her lips, debating the matter with herself. Finally she turned to the computer on the far side of her desk and played around with the keys. I would have given a week's pay—from a good week—to read the screen. After a few minutes of tinkering she got up with a brief "I'll be right back," and headed for the rear of the bank.

When Alma had disappeared into an office built into the back of the lobby, my baser instincts overcame me: I got up and looked at the screen. The only thing visible was an opening menu. Untrusting woman.

Alma spent quite a while pitching my case to her boss. After ten minutes or so the phone rang on one of the other loan officers' desks. The woman spoke briefly, then got up and disappeared into the back office as well. I finished the coffee Barbara had given me, memorized an upbeat pamphlet on auto financing, found an ornate ladies' room in the basement of the bank, and still had time to study a home mortgage brochure before the two women emerged.

They stopped at the second officer's desk long enough for her to pull a file from her cabinet. Alma brought her over to me, introducing her as Sylvia Wolfe. Ms. Wolfe, a tall, spare woman of about sixty, wore a tidy gray cardigan suit more in keeping with a bank than Alma's flamboyance. She shook hands briskly, but let Alma do the talking.

"We had a long talk with Mr. Struthers about what we could tell you. Sylvia came along because she actually worked with Mrs. Frizell. Your neighbor had been a customer here since 1926 and it was a blow to lose her. Mr. Struthers decided we could show you the letter Mrs. Frizell sent us, but of course, Sylvia can't let you look at any of her financial records."

Ms. Wolfe thumbed through a fat file with expert fingers and wordlessly handed me Mrs. Frizell's letter asking that her account be closed. The old woman had written on a piece of yellowing lined paper, torn from a pad she might have had since first opening her account. Her writing was disconnected, as though she'd written the letter over a period of several days without bothering to check what she'd said on the previous occasion, but the content was clear enough.

I have had an account at your bank for many years and never would believe you would cheat an old customer, but people take advantage of old women in terrible ways. My money with you is all I have, yet you are paying me only

8 percent, but at another bank I can earn 17 percent, and of course I have my dogs to think about. I want you to sell my seedees [sic] and close my savings account and send my money to U.S. Meterpoltan [sic], I have a form for you to use.

"Seventeen percent? What on earth could she be talking about?" I asked.

Sylvia Wolfe shook her head. "I called her and tried to discuss it with her, but she refused to talk to me. I even tried stopping by to see her, tried to tell her only someone who *really* is preying on old people would promise her seventeen percent, but she said of course I'd take that line now that it was too late. We wrote and told her we'd reopen her account without any fees if she ever decided she wanted to come back to us. We had to leave it at that."

"How much did she have in certificates of deposit?" I asked.

Ms. Wolfe shook her head. "You know I can't tell you that."

I turned the letter over in my hand, studying it, but it didn't tell me anything. No one else had written those words, and they didn't sound as though she'd been under duress, although there was no real way of telling.

"Did she keep a safe-deposit box here?" I asked abruptly.

The loan officers exchanged guarded glances. "No," Ms. Wolfe said. "I talked to her about it a few times over the years, but she preferred to keep any important documents at home. I didn't like it, but she wasn't the kind of person you could tell things to: she pretty much had her mind made up before a conversation started."

I handed the letter back to Ms. Wolfe. As I thanked her for her help, I wondered where Mrs. Frizell's private records were. Todd and Chrissie wouldn't have been trying to pry the information from her if they had them.

"You get what you need, Vic?" Alma interrupted me.

I hunched a shoulder. "It's something, but I'm baffled. What I'd like to see is her account with U.S. Met, find out what on earth they were offering her that paid that kind of money. And I'd like to know where the title to her house is if she didn't keep a safe deposit box."

"That's disappeared?" Ms. Wolfe asked, alarm flickering in her pale-brown eyes.

"The kids who've taken over her affairs don't have it: they showed up at the hospital on Thursday with a song and dance about not being able to raise the money to pay Mrs. Frizell's bill. Of course, she's at Cook County—they're not going to throw her out—but since she owns a house they do expect her to pay for her care."

Ms. Wolfe shook her head. "I don't know where she'd have it, have the title. But it must be in the house someplace."

I thought of the great heap of papers still untouched in the secretary. But surely Todd and

Chrissie had searched the place thoroughly by now. If the title was there they must have found it. I wondered if Mrs. Hellstrom might know. I thanked the bankers again, and went back into the muggy June day.

Mrs. Hellstrom was in her garden, doing something industrious with a huge bag of peat moss and a hoe. A straw hat shaded her face from the sun while gloves and a smock protected her hands and clothes. She expressed herself as happy to see me, inviting me into the kitchen for iced tea, although she looked wistfully at the yard on her way in.

She laid her gloves and hat carefully on a small shelf just inside the back door. "I was at the hospital last night. They told me you'd been around, that you got Hattie to talk a little more than usual."

My ministering angel routine apparently was what had earned me this tête-à-tête. I didn't spoil it by saying that I'd wanted to get Mrs. Frizell to talk about her finances.

Mrs. Hellstrom motioned me to a chair at the spotless Formica table. She pulled a pitcher from the refrigerator and got two amber plastic glasses down from a shelf, the same kind Dick had curled his lip at only a few hours ago. I wondered what he was doing about his coffee-stained shirt and his meetings. Probably he had a spare at the office. Or maybe his secretary raced up to Neiman-Marcus to buy him a new one.

I'm not much of a tea drinker and Mrs.

Hellstrom's stuff clearly had come out of a package, but I sipped some in a sociable way. It had been sweetened with a generous hand. I tried not to make a face as I swallowed.

We talked for a bit about Mrs. Frizell, and some of Mrs. Hellstrom's memories of her. "Of course, she was my mother's generation, but Mr. Hellstrom grew up in this house and used to try to play with her son, but he—her son, I mean—wasn't the kind of boy other kids really liked much. But when you think how strange she is, you can't really wonder, can you? Although she's always been a good neighbor, all that junk in her yard and those dogs notwithstanding."

I didn't get a clear picture of what Mrs. Frizell had ever done to merit the good neighbor sobriquet. Maybe it was just that she minded her own business. The conversation went from there to the selfishness of my generation, something I didn't feel able to dispute, but how happy Mrs. Hellstrom was to find young people on the block who did embody the old neighborly values.

"Of course, I think it was wrong for those young people to put the dogs to sleep, but they did leap in to look after Hattie's affairs. And it can't be a lot of fun for them to take on a cranky old lady like her."

"No, indeed," I murmured. "I guess they're kind of stymied, though, by the fact that they can't find the title to Mrs. Frizell's house."

"Title to her house?" Mrs. Hellstrom asked sharply. "What do they want that for?"

401

I tried to look innocent, even naive. "I expect it's for the hospital. They need to provide some kind of proof of her financial situation. They might even need to take out a mortgage, since it looks as though she'll be laid up for quite a while."

Mrs. Hellstrom shook her head helplessly. "What are we coming to as a country? Here's an old lady who worked hard all her life and now maybe she has to give up her house just because of a little fall in her bathroom? It makes you scared to get old, it really does."

I agreed. I'll be forty in a year. I didn't need Mr. Contreras to make me nervous about what happens to elderly, indigent private eyes.

"She didn't give her private papers to you to look after, did she?"

"Oh, no. Hattie isn't the kind to trust anyone with her valuables. The only thing of hers I have is her box of dog things their pictures and pedigrees and stuff. I took it along when we found her that night, because I knew that was what she really cared about."

"I wonder if I could take a look at it." I tried to speak casually.

"Honey, if it'll make you happy you can study every photo in it. It's not much of anything, but she got herself the nicest little box to keep their papers in. Trust Hattie to pay more attention to something for the dogs than to her own records. . . . More tea, honey?"

When I turned it down she bustled into the

front of the house. She was back in a minute, carrying a black lacquer box about eighteen inches long by four deep. It was a beautiful piece, inlaid with a brightly painted picture of a dog resting its nose on the lap of a girl as the two sat under a pear tree. The workmanship was so good that the lid fit firmly inside the box but came out with only a gentle tug. I found myself staring at an out of focus portrait of Bruce.

"I want to get back out to my plants, honey. You can just leave it on the table when you're done looking at it. And be sure to help yourself to more tea if you want some."

I thanked her and carefully started pulling papers from the box. Underneath Bruce's face was a group picture of the other four dogs standing at the back fence. She'd somehow persuaded them all to get up on their hind legs and put their paws on the railing. Although also out of focus, it was a pretty cute shot. Maybe it would cheer her up to have it next to her hospital bed. I put it to one side to take with me on my next visit.

A series of photos of what must have been earlier dogs lay below those two, along with Bruce's Kennel Club paper and papers for other dogs long gone. A handful of yellow news clips told of Mrs. Frizell's glory years when she'd shown black Labs and won prizes for them. No one had ever suggested that she'd done something that disciplined.

Finally, at the bottom of the box, I found a

small bundle of personal papers. The title to the house. And three bonds, each with a face value of ten thousand dollars. Coupon bonds paying seventeen percent, issued by Diamond Head Motors.

41

A New Breed of Banker

I stared at the bonds for a long while, trying to will them to reveal something more than their face value. Or face valuelessness. In February Mrs. Frizell had closed her account at Lake View, transferred her funds to U.S. Met, and bought thirty thousand dollars of Diamond Head paper. Since her letter to Lake View explained that she was going to receive 17 percent interest at U.S. Met, it seemed like a fair bet that the bank had sold her the bonds. And that meant . . . something so ugly I hoped it wasn't true.

Mrs. Frizell's private papers had been safe at the bottom of the lacquered box for some weeks, but I hesitated to leave them there. Since Mrs. Hellstrom thought Todd and Chrissie were sweet, helpful neighbors, she would surely show them the cache, too, if it dawned on them to ask her. I tucked the title and the bonds into my bag, arranged all the canine glory in its proper order, and carefully fit the lid back into its grooves. Just to add to my own reputation for sweet helpfulness, I rinsed the iced tea glasses and left them on the drainboard.

Mrs. Hellstrom was weeding on her hands and knees when I came back out of the kitchen. "You go through all that stuff, hon?"

"Yeah. No wonder her son feels so bitter: all her mementos are about her dogs. She didn't even keep his kindergarten picture. I didn't know she used to train dogs for show, though."

"Oh my, yes." She sat back on her heels and wiped the sweat from her forehead. "I guess that's why they didn't bother me as much as some of the other folks around here. I can remember when that yard was spick-and-span and she had seven or eight Labs out there, all perfectly behaved. It's only been the last few years that she stopped being able to manage them like she used to. Maia Tertz could tell you about it. She used to buy dogs from Hattie, for her family. All her kids have Labs, descended from some of Hattie's old Labs, my goodness, yes, and I suppose her grandchildren too. I don't expect young folks like Chrissie to appreciate that."

"Chrissie seems to like to help people in other ways," I ventured. "I hear she has quite a lot of financial expertise."

"Maybe, honey, maybe, but Mr. Hellstrom and I, we prefer to make our own investment decisions. We don't have that much to lose, so we can't afford to listen to sales pitches."

"I took one of the pictures of her dogs. I

thought maybe it would perk her up to have it next to her bed."

"Now, why didn't I think of that? That's a wonderful idea. Just wonderful. And I always figured you for such a snob—sorry, honey, that just slipped out." She smiled in embarrassment and got back on her hands and knees to continue plucking invisible weeds from around her rosebushes.

As I walked up Racine to Belmont I felt as though I had a big red X on my bag indicating the location of the bonds. I kept a nervous lookout for anyone who seemed to be dogging me too close. A bus was arriving just as I got to the corner. I climbed on to ride the half mile to the Bank of Lake View, just to be on the safe side.

Back in its cool, musty recesses I rented a safe-deposit box. Alma let me use her Xerox machine to copy the bonds and the title. I made two sets of copies. One I folded and tucked in the inside of my jacket; the other I placed in an envelope in my handbag. After putting the originals in the safe-deposit box I went back to Alma's desk. She finished a phone call and looked at me inquiringly. Her warm smile seemed to be wearing a bit thin where I was concerned.

"You know how Lake View brags about being a full-service bank? I wonder if you'd keep this for me." I held out the key to the box.

She shook her head, not even bothering with a smile. "I can't do that, Vic. It's completely against bank policy."

I tapped my teeth with a knuckle, trying to think. "Could you mail it to me?"

She made a face. "I suppose. If you address the envelope and seal it yourself."

She pulled an envelope from a drawer. I helped myself to a handful of scented tissues from the corner of her desk and wrapped the key in them. I addressed the envelope to myself in care of the owner of a bar I frequent downtown, the Golden Glow, and handed it to her.

"Now you have to admit that we *are* a full-service bank. Tell all your friends." She laughed merrily and put the envelope in a tray marked for outgoing mail.

"Will do, Alma; you got my vote."

I'd seen a pay phone next to the ladies' room in the basement this morning on my earlier visit. I went downstairs to call Dorothy Fletcher, a broker I know.

"What can you tell me about Diamond Head bonds?" I asked after we'd exchanged pleasantries.

"Nothing. Want me to look them up and give you a call?"

"I'm not real reachable today. Could I hold while you check?"

She warned me I might have a long wait, but agreed to do it. I ended up watching the walls for nearly a quarter of an hour. Sylvia Wolfe came down to the ladies' room and we exchanged waves. Nothing else disturbed the basement's sepulchral air. As the minutes stretched by I regretted not carrying a book with me. Even a chair would have been welcome.

Dorothy came back on the line as I was counting the number of burned-out bulbs in the basement chandelier. "I hope you're not thinking of buying these, Vic. They're trading at nineteen— off a face value of a hundred, of course. That may sound like a bargain, but they didn't meet their April interest payment and no one here believes they'll be able to do it in October, either. On top of that they're unsecured."

"I see. Thanks, Dorothy—I'll resist the impulse."

I hung up and massaged my calves, sore from standing so long in one place. U.S. Met had persuaded Mrs. Frizell to put her money into a load of junk. Maybe it was time to pay them a visit.

The Bank of Lake View stood just across the street from the el. Rather than hike back home for the Impala, I climbed the rickety stairs and rode downtown. The train was one of the old green models, with windows opened wide to bathe the riders in gusts of hot air. These old-fashioned cars make me nostalgic for my childhood, for trips downtown with Gabriella on the old Illinois Central, her in gloves and a pillbox navy hat with a small veil, me on my knees next to the open window, excitedly reporting on the passing scene. The scrub around the tracks used to house pheasants and rabbits; once I saw a raccoon.

Today there was nothing but pigeons and broken bottles on the rooftops. The only wildlife I spotted was a man with a three-day growth lying next to one of the chimneys. I hoped he was still alive.

I got off at Chicago and walked west to U.S. Met's headquarters. They'd always been a maverick, outside the mainstream of Chicago finance—their location a mile north of the Loop was just a physical manifestation of it. They had built themselves a modern building about ten years ago, though, and it rivaled any of the West Loop architecture for gleaming glory. Only ten stories high, it still had all the green stone, smoky curved windows, and brass inlays of the bigger modern towers to the south.

The owners had been shrewd gamblers on where the city's growth would take place when they put up the new offices—or their politically connected directors had nudged them in the right direction. A decade ago this area had bordered Skid Row. Now it was home to a high-end retail area that abutted the new gallery district. Judging by the lights at the windows, all ten floors were rented out.

I presented myself to an information officer in the corner of the chrome and green lobby. "I have an appointment with one of your bankers, Vinnie Buttone."

She ran a long magenta nail down a phone list. "Your name?"

I let out a tiny breath of relief. I'd been ninety-eight percent sure Vinnie was here, but it was nice to be proved right. "Chrissie Pichea." I spelled it out for her.

She tapped out Vinnie's extension. "Someone's here for Mr. Buttone. Chrissie Pichea." She stumbled over the last name. I was glad I hadn't tried "Warshawski" on her.

She sat silent, perhaps on hold while Vinnie's secretary found out where he was and whether he would want to see Chrissie. He could be anywhere—looking at loan applicants out on a building site, or given U.S. Met's clientele, a juice operation. Fortunately for me he turned out to be in the building and willing to see his sweet, helpful neighbor.

The receptionist directed me to a row of elevators artfully hidden behind some columns. I rode to the fourth floor, checked with the receptionist there, and was sent into the inner recesses of the bank.

The green-and-gold splendor of the lobby was carried out in muted tones in the building's upper reaches: green plush—with a thin pile as befit the junior level of management that trod it, —and walls covered in a gold fabric-board. A few bright prints on the walls drew the eye and made the long corridor seem lighter.

Most of the office doors stood open, revealing a phalanx of sincere young men in shirtsleeves and ties talking on the phone. Vinnie's office, near the end of the hall, was shut. I knocked below the prim black label identifying him as an assistant vice president of commercial lending.

"Chrissie, hi. Come on over here . . . I thought we'd be more comfortable—" I turned at the sound of Vinnie's voice, coming from an open conference room catty-corner to his office. When he recognized me his round face looked glassy with surprise, then shattered into anger.

"You! What are you doing here? I ought to call security—"

"I came to see you, Vinnie. Being as how we're neighbors and we all want to do the neighborly thing for each other on North Racine." I shut the door behind me and helped myself to one of the fake wicker chairs.

"I want that door open. I'm expecting someone, and anyway, I don't want you in the bank."

"You're expecting Chrissie Pichea, but you're getting me." I smiled. "I gave them her name downstairs—it seemed like the easiest way to get up here. You and I have so much to talk about I just didn't think I could wait until tonight."

He looked from me to the door, then at a phone in the corner of the small room. "I'll give you five minutes, then I'm calling the bank security people and you can explain yourself to the Chicago cops. If you haven't bought off *all* of them." He took his heavy gold watch from his wrist and laid it ostentatiously on the table in front of him.

I dug in my bag for the envelope I'd prepared at Lake View and set it down in front of him, parallel to the watchband. "Even though you were hoping for Chrissie and got me, I think you'll be pleased to see this stuff. I believe the

411

two of you have been looking for it. This will save you the trouble of trying to arrange another break-in."

He shot me a venomous look, but opened the envelope. When he'd unfolded the copies of the title and the bonds his face turned glassy again and the color seeped away from behind the skin. He studied them far longer than the four pieces of paper merited.

"The test will be tomorrow," I said brightly. "Got them memorized yet?"

"I don't know why you think I'd be interested in these things," he said, but his voice lacked conviction.

"Oh, I expect because you, or someone you know, came busting into my place Friday night looking for them. Come to think of it, it must have been you—you'd know when I was away. Talk about police—*I* ought to bring them over here. I couldn't figure out what you might want, but when I found these I had to believe I'd hit the jackpot."

He suddenly picked up the papers and ripped them across.

"Not very bright, Vinnie: you must be able to see those are only copies. And now you've *proved* they're important to you." I watched his lips move wordlessly. "Let's talk about the Diamond Head bonds. Did you sell them to Mrs. Frizell?"

He shook his head, still without speaking.

"Did you get Chrissie to sell them to Mrs. Frizell? . . . Am I getting warm?"

412

"I didn't get anyone to sell them to her. I don't know anything about them. I don't even know they're hers: bonds don't have their owners' names on them." His voice gained strength as he spoke; he sounded positively pompous on the last sentence.

"You don't find the fact that they're with her house title suggestive? Or the fact that I discovered them nestled together in Mrs. Frizell's box of most treasured possessions?"

"Yeah, I know you: you'd say anything. Like accusing me of breaking into your apartment just now. But the Picheas are the old lady's legal guardians. If these things had been in her house they would have found them."

I smiled. "They weren't in her house though."

"Where—" he started to blurt out, then stopped before completely betraying himself.

"Where were they? Ah, that's why it pays to get a professional investigator when you're after this kind of treasure. You have to know where to look.

"Let's talk about the investment advice you and Chrissie have been spreading around the neighborhood. Mrs. Tertz, Mrs. Olsen, Mrs. Hellstrom, they all agree you've been coming around filled with helpful hints—how they can beat their CD rates by ten points. I have an ugly feeling that if they'd taken you up on it they'd have some Diamond Head paper too. Was this your own idea, or did the bank send you out to do it?"

He picked up his watch. "You've had your five

minutes. Now I'm going to call security. And I'll be meeting with a lawyer to talk about you slandering me."

I grinned derisively. "Just don't make it Dick Yarborough or Todd Pichea. They've got enough to do these days. Now, if you call security, I'll ring up the feds. They're very interested in your kind of sales help. And they can subpoena bank files, which I can't."

He looked longingly at the phone, but couldn't quite make up his mind to dial. "What do you want, anyway?"

"Information, Vinnie. Just information. I've figured out a fair amount, you know: you peddling Diamond Head's junk, Todd and Chrissie taking over Mrs. Frizell's assets. . . . So they could get rid of the bonds before anyone saw them? Or just mortgage her house and then sell it off so she can't spoil Yuppieville anymore? And I figure Todd's law firm did the legal work when Jason Felitti debt-financed Diamond Head. And since Jason sits on the board here at U.S. Met, he must have got the bank to take on some of the junk. So he gets eager young bankers like you to sell it in your spare time. I see you guys going door to door, kind of like the Girl Scouts."

And where was Dick in this scenario? Surely not asking Todd Pichea to sell Diamond Head bonds to the little old ladies in his neighborhood. I surely couldn't have been in love once with someone who would carry on like that.

"I don't have anything to say to you. It's time

414

for you to leave." Vinnie's voice came out in a hiss.

He didn't try to phone the bank's cops, but he wouldn't talk, either. I kept at him for half an hour, alternately cajoling and painting a picture of his probable future in the federal pen, but he didn't budge. When I finally got up to leave he was still staring ahead, glassy-eyed.

42

Needling the Fourth Estate

Back in the muggy sunshine, exhaustion overwhelmed me. It was only twelve-thirty, but a fight with Dick and hard work at two banks made me want to go back to bed. I still needed to canvass some of my neighbors and try to talk to Murray Ryerson this afternoon before Mr. Contreras and I went off to meet Eddie Mohr. And I wanted to get hold of Max Loewenthal. My body couldn't be allowed the luxury of wearing out so early.

I hiked back to State Street and started down the stairs to the el. The thought of the long trek home from Sheffield seemed too much. I turned around and waved down a cab. The driver, who swayed and pounded the steering wheel in tune to the beat booming from his stereo, had a serene disregard for any other traffic. On the short stretch from LaSalle to Fullerton he managed to get up to seventy. His anger at my request to slow down was so menacing that I slid out when he stopped at the light on Diversey, tossing the amount of the meter onto the seat next to him. His screaming, mixed with the booming of his radio, followed me as I crossed the street to board the Diversey bus.

The ponderous journey west let me slump comatose in a corner. The chance to pull back from the world around me, even for a quarter of an hour, was unexpectedly refreshing. When I climbed off at Racine I wasn't ready to leap tall buildings at a single bound, but I thought I might be able to manage an afternoon of work.

Back at my place I expected Mr. Contreras to come out, either to talk to me about the work in my apartment or remonstrate some more against going to see the old local president this evening. It seemed like a lucky break when he stayed inside his own apartment, but it did make me wonder if he was too upset to want to talk to me. When I saw he wasn't out back fiddling with his garden, I even got a little worried. He'd been looking after himself for a lot of years, though. I had to assume he could do it for one more afternoon.

The workmen for my apartment had come and gone. They'd put electronic fingerprints on all the doors and windows. A note by my front entrance explained how to activate the system. Mr. Contreras had paid the bills for me. That was another thousand dollars I'd have to scramble together in a hurry. I hadn't realized they had to be paid on the spot.

Following the instructions in the manual they'd left, I programmed the little control box next to my front door. If anyone tried to climb in on me now, Chicago's finest should be with me in minutes.

My morning frenzy had left me sweaty and wrinkled, even a little smelly. I took an extra half hour to lie in a cool bath before changing into my jeans.

It was getting on for two now. Murray Ryerson should be back from his usual prolonged lunch with obscure sources. Fixing myself a sandwich with some of last night's leftover chicken, I went into the living room and dialed his number at the *Star*. He answered the phone himself.

"Hi, Murray. It's Vic."

"Whoo, Vic, what a thrill. Let me get my asbestos gloves in case the phone gets too hot to handle."

"Good thinking, Ryerson. The more sarcastic you get, the easier it will be to have this conversation."

"Oh, She-who-must-be-obeyed, to what do I owe the honor of your call? Or is it privilege? After you shouted vile words at me and slammed the phone in my ear last night?"

I ate some of my sandwich while I tried to figure out how to get us away from hostilities and to the point.

"You still there? Is this a new form of torture? You call up and then abandon the phone while I sit shouting into it like a fool?"

I washed down the sandwich with a mouthful of coffee. "I knew this wasn't going to be an easy conversation before I picked up the phone. But someone said something so weird to me this morning that I thought we ought to try to overcome our mutual repugnance and talk."

"Weird, huh? It wasn't a personal comment, like on your disposition or something?"

I grinned to myself suddenly as I remembered Conrad Rawlings's remarks on my ornenness. "Nah. Guys who aren't strong enough to take me don't worry me too much. This little comment had to do with the freedom of the press."

"We all know the truth about that, Warshawski—that the press is free to anyone rich enough to own one."

"So you don't want to hear about it?"

"Did I say that? I'm just warning you not to expect me to go off on a crusade because of something that's bugging you."

"This is where I came in," I complained. "You won't listen to my stories, then you get offended when I won't tell them to you on command."

"Okay, okay," he said hastily. "Tell me about the threat to my livelihood. If I listen intently and make appropriately outraged remarks, will you tell me about going into the San the other night?"

"It's all tied together in one neat little package,

418

babe." I gave him a detailed account of my breakfast with Dick and Dick's relief that Peter Felitti had been able to keep my exploits at Diamond Head out of the paper.

"See? You thought it was me not talking to you that kept you from getting the scoop. Really, it was Felitti talking to your publisher," I finished.

Murray was quiet for a minute. "I'm not sure I believe you," he finally said. "No, no, I'm not doubting the conversation took place. I just question whether Felitti is a heavy enough hitter to keep something out of the papers on request."

"His brother used to be a Du Page County commissioner and he's still on the board of U.S. Metropolitan. Lots of little political connections run through that bank. Marshall Townley could well be approached that way." Townley was the *Herald-Star* publisher.

Murray thought it over some more. "Maybe. Maybe. I'll poke around a little. Why are you telling me this now?"

"Because too many people have been yanking me around the last two weeks. And when Dick Yarborough let that remark fly this morning— that he could suppress any public report about what I'm trying to find out—it made me, well, pretty peeved."

"Pretty peeved, huh? Is anything left of the guy?"

"He still has one working testicle," I said primly.

"You left one? Boy, you must be getting soft, Warshawski. . . . I guess it's time for me to bite. What are you trying to find out?"

I gave him a thumbnail sketch of my fruitless investigation into Mitch Kruger's death, including my meeting with Ben Loring at Paragon Steel. "I've got to believe Mitch had nosed out something that was going on at Diamond Head. Maybe the theft of the copper wire, depending on how important it was to them to keep it quiet. It could have been something else, though. Interest in his meager papers has been running high, but I finally got hold of them last night and there's nothing in them to show he knew about the theft. But there's nothing in them to show he knew about anything else either."

Murray tried wheedling a look at Mitch's papers from me, but I was keeping Eddie Mohr and the connection to Chicago Settlement to myself until after I'd talked to Mohr this afternoon. Murray hadn't been supportive enough lately to get a free blue-plate special.

"Okay, Warshawski," he said at last. "Maybe there is a story in this. Although I can see Finchley's point, that maybe they just don't like you snooping around down at Diamond Head. I'll talk to some people and get back to you."

"Gosh, Mr. Hecht, thanks. If it wasn't for the hard-working, noble press, where would us poor working stiffs be?"

"In the San, where you belong. Catch you later, Warshawski."

420

I finished my sandwich before dialing Max's number at the hospital. Mr. Loewenthal was in a meeting; could his secretary take a message? I didn't want to leave my phone number and play tag with Max all afternoon. His secretary finally allowed as how if I called back at four I could probably reach him.

Thoughts of Max brought Lotty to the front of my mind from the back recesses where I'd been keeping her. I called over to the clinic and spoke to Mrs. Coltrain. Lotty was working with her new nurse in one of the examining rooms—not a good time to interrupt. Mrs. Coltrain assured me she would let her know I'd called.

I walked slowly back to my bedroom. The longer Lotty and I went without speaking, the harder it was going to be to get back together.

I changed the thin T-shirt I'd put on after my bath for a bra and a silk shirt in a dusky rose. A bra is almost as bad as a shoulder holster on a muggy day, but I didn't want my elderly neighbors so startled that they wouldn't talk to me. I started to put on the holster, then realized that meant a jacket, which meant I'd be a sodden wreck before I'd made it across the street. Surely I could walk around my own neighborhood in broad daylight without a weapon. I left the gun on the bed.

On my way back out I started to knock on Mr. Contreras's door, hesitated, then left without trying to rouse him. Peppy had let out a sharp bark as I stood there: if he wanted to see me he could open the door.

It dawned on me that I hadn't seen any Chicago cops patrolling my stretch of Racine today. Maybe Conrad Rawlings was so annoyed by my comments last night that he had withdrawn his protective arm. My pleasure at having my ability to look after myself put to the test wasn't as strong as it might have been. I almost headed back up the stairs for my gun.

43

High-Voltage Marketing Plan

It took Mrs. Tertz so long to answer the bell that I thought she might be out. When she finally came to the door, her face flushed from the heat, she apologized, but said she'd been on her back porch writing letters. "It faces east, so by this time of day we get a bit of breeze back there. I practically live out there in the summer. What can I do for you, dear?"

"I wanted to talk to you about Mrs. Frizell's situation. Do you have a minute?"

She laughed softly. "I suppose. But if you think a wave of your hand will solve Hattie Frizell's problems, it only shows you have a lot of growing up to do. Come on in, though."

I followed her along a minute, highly polished

hall to the kitchen. The air in the house, heavy with Pine Sol and furniture polish, thickened in the kitchen to an unbreathable density. Little beads of sweat were staining the neck of my blouse by the time Mrs. Tertz had the back door unlocked again. I followed her thankfully onto the porch.

It was a wide, pleasant space, with furniture covered in a chintz whose flowers had faded from years of use. A rolling cart held a television, a hot plate, and a toaster oven. When Mrs. Tertz saw me looking at them she shook her head regretfully and explained that they had to be wheeled into the kitchen at night.

"It used to be that Abe and I left them out here all summer long, but there are too many break-ins these days. We can't afford to put walls up to make the porch secure, so we just do the best we can."

"You don't keep a dog still? Mrs. Hellstrom told me you used to buy black Labs from Mrs. Frizell."

"Oh, my. Yes. And my grandchildren are playing with dogs descended from some of those Labs. But you know, it takes a lot of strength to walk a dog that energetic. When our last old boy died five years ago, Abe and I decided we just didn't have the stamina for a new one. But we miss them. Sometimes I wish—but Abe's got arthritis, and my back's not so good. We just couldn't do it. How's Hattie doing? Marjorie told me you'd been by to see her."

"Not well. She's restless, but not responsive. I don't know what will happen to her." A few weeks in bed could be a death sentence for a woman her age, but Mrs. Tertz didn't need me to spell that out.

"One of the worrying things is her finances. She's going to need long-term care if—when— she heals enough to leave Cook County. Chrissie and Todd want to mortgage her house, but they don't know where the title is."

Mrs. Tertz shook her head again, worried. "I hate to think of Hattie losing that house on top of losing the dogs. I don't think she'll last too long if that happens—if she knows about it, I mean. But I can't help you with money for her, dear, if that's what you want: Abe and I just make ends meet every month on our social security as it is. And now with property taxes going up . . ." She clipped her lips together, too worried to talk about it.

I reassured her hastily. "But the scary thing about her finances is how she has her money invested. That's really what I wanted to ask you about. She sold her CDs at her old bank in February, took a loss, of course, because of the penalties, and put the money into some bonds. Very high-yield—but not paying anything these days. You wouldn't know why she decided to do that, would you?"

Mrs. Tertz shifted in her chair. "We never talked about money together, dear."

I eyed her steadily. "Chrissie Pichea and Vinnie

Buttone have gone around the neighborhood offering people financial advice. They may have persuaded her to buy those bonds."

"I'm sure anything Chrissie did was with the best intentions. I know you two girls haven't seen eye-to-eye on Hattie's dogs, but Chrissie's a very good-hearted neighbor. If she sees me struggling with my groceries she always races over to help me get them into the house."

I smiled, trying to keep hostility out of my face as well as my voice. "She probably thought she was doing Mrs. Frizell a good turn, getting her to trade in her CDs for something that would pay much better. Has she ever offered you a similar deal?"

Mrs. Tertz was so loath to discuss the matter that I began to worry that she and her husband had sunk their savings into Diamond Head junk as well. As we continued to talk, though, it became clear that all she wanted to do was protect Chrissie.

"I'm sure Chrissie is a wonderful person," I said earnestly. "But she may not be very experienced with risky investments. I've been investigating financial fraud for almost ten years now. Someone could have—have pulled the wool over her eyes, so to speak—persuaded her they had a great product for old people. And in her desire to help her neighbors she might not have had the experience to see there was something wrong with the product."

It sounded too thick to me, but Mrs. Tertz was

relieved to think that "you girls" only wanted to help each other out. Telling me she'd just be a minute she disappeared back into the murky air of her house.

I wandered to the porch door and looked out at the yard. Either she or her husband shared the neighborhood mania for gardening: the tiny square of grass was lined with weedless flower beds on one side and vegetables on the other. My father had liked to garden, too, but I hadn't inherited a longing to dig around in the ground.

Mrs. Tertz returned after about ten minutes, her face flushed and her gray curls changed into tiny corkscrews by the humidity. She held out a flyer to me.

"I tried to call Chrissie to make sure she wouldn't mind me showing it to you, but I couldn't get hold of her. So I hope I'm doing the right thing."

My throat constricted with tension. That's what I needed all right—for Chrissie to pop in at this moment. Although I'd already tipped my hand to Vinnie Buttone. What difference did it make if Mrs. Tertz called Chrissie?

I took the brochure from Mrs. Tertz's unwilling fingers and flipped through its four sides. She wouldn't let me borrow it, even for the afternoon, so I studied it carefully while she breathed over my arm.

IS YOUR MONEY DOING ENOUGH FOR YOU?

the front cover asked in screaming type.

The inside panel pointed out the woes of people living on fixed incomes.

"Are your savings in certificates of deposit? Maybe your banker or your broker told you that was the best place for your money now that you're past retirement age. No risk, they probably told you. But no return, either. Your banker may think because you're past retirement you don't deserve the same investments younger folks get. But those CDs he sold you aren't going to grow fast enough to cover the cost of expensive nursing care if you need it. Or to take you on that dream vacation if you want it. What you need is risk-free money that provides great returns."

A photo of an old woman in a derelict nursing home bed stared grimly from the left panel, while an elderly couple with golf clubs gazed raptly at the ocean on the right.

"Just as safe as federally insured funds," the copy trumpeted. "U.S. Metropolitan can provide you with investments that pay up to 17 percent—and leave your worries behind."

"Just as safe as federally insured funds," I repeated aloud. "An unsecured bond that isn't paying jackshit and is trading at nineteen dollars on the hundred."

The bitterness in my voice startled Mrs. Tertz, who snatched the flyer from me. "If you're going

427

to be angry about it I just can't let you look at it; it wouldn't be fair to Chrissie."

I tried to smile, but I could feel my mouth twist sideways. "Chrissie may have meant it for the best, but she wasn't very fair to Mrs. Frizell. I do hope not too many of you on the block here bought investments from her or Vinnie. Otherwise the two of them are going to own most of the street before long."

She bit her lips uncomfortably, but told me she thought it was time for me to go. As she shepherded me rapidly through the house to the front door, I could hear her bemoaning the mistake she'd made under her breath. I think she was talking more about letting me into the house than about buying junk bonds. At least I hoped so.

The heat had lifted somewhat by the time I got outside, but my blouse still grew wet across the neck and armpits during the short walk to my own building. The perfect appeal to a recluse with a chip on her shoulder—your banker is cheating you just because you're old. And your new investment is just as safe as federally insured funds.

As I passed Vinnie's apartment door I wanted to kick it in, to violate his home as he had decimated Mrs. Frizell's. I'd been there several times last year; I knew it was filled with high-priced modern art. Almost as good an investment as a federally insured CD. Figure out how to replace that stuff, I thought, panting as I pictured myself trashing it. I actually gave the door a savage kick that left a scuff mark on the paneling. That alone would drive him into a frenzy: he had personally sanded and painted it an eggshell white. The rest of us were content with the dark varnish that came with the building.

Up in my own place I undid the locks, forgetting my new electronic alarm until a high-pitched whistle interrupted me as I gulped down a glass of water. I sprinted down the hall to the front door and punched in the numbers to shut off the system. I hoped I'd been fast enough to forestall a visit from the cops.

I went back to the kitchen and filled another glass under the tap. I drank it more slowly, carrying it with me as I walked to the living room to call Max. I took off my shoes and socks and massaged my toes. The loafers didn't give enough support; my feet ached from walking around in them.

Curling my legs under me, I leaned back in the armchair with my eyes shut. I needed to relax before I talked to Max. Get the image of Mrs. Frizell restlessly moving in her hospital bed out of my brain, let my anger with Vinnie and Chrissie work its way out of my shoulders and fingertips. I've never been too good at that kind of exercise; after a few fruitless minutes I sat up and dialed Max's number.

He had just emerged from one meeting and was on his way to a second, but he agreed to talk to me for a few minutes. I exchanged greetings with him cautiously, in case he was angry with me again on Lotty's account.

"Lotty still won't talk to me. How is she?"

"She's getting better. The crack is starting to heal and you can't see the bruises now." His tone was noncommittal.

"I know she's back at work—I keep just missing her when I call the clinic."

"You know Lotty. When she's scared she gets angry—with herself for being weak. And when she's angry she starts driving herself into a frenzy of action. It's always been her best protection."

I grimaced at the phone; that was my armor as well. "I hear she's hired a new nurse. Maybe that will ease some of the tension for her."

"She stole away one of our best pediatric nurses," Max retorted. "I ought to disown her for that, but it seems to have cheered her up."

Everyone has problems when personal and professional lives cross, not just private eyes and cops. The thought reassured me.

"I've been thrashing around in my own frenzy, trying to figure out what anyone cared so much about that they had to beat up Lotty over it. And it seems as though all I'm doing is pawing the earth, kicking up dirt, and not getting anywhere."

"I'm sorry, Victoria. I wish I could help, but you're out of my areas of expertise."

"Your lucky day, Max. I called specifically because of your expertise. Do you know anything about Hector Beauregard at Chicago Settlement?"

"Noo." Max drew out the word slowly. "My wife was really the one who worked with the group. Since her death I've continued to support them financially, but I haven't played an active role. Hector's the executive director—that's all I know about him. We both belong to a group of directors of nonprofit organizations, and I see him there occasionally. He seems to have expanded Chicago Settlement's finances greatly, bringing in important corporate donors—I've been a little jealous of his fund-raising prowess, to tell you the truth."

"Have you ever thought he might have done something, well, unethical, to raise money?" I rubbed my toes again as I spoke, as if to squeeze the answer I wanted from them.

"Do you have some evidence he's done so?" Max's voice was suddenly sharp.

"No. I told you I'm just pawing the earth. His name is the only unusual thing I've turned up." Besides the spools of copper from Paragon Steel, but how could those be connected to the head of a big charity? Maybe that was how he got big companies to contribute? Sell each other goods they didn't need, then load them on trucks in the middle of the night and sell them on the sly and collect the proceeds? Too farfetched.

"Could a not-for-profit collect money illegally?" I asked.

"Anyone running an institution as strapped for cash as mine has fantasies," Max said. "But whether you could really execute them without the IRS catching on? I suppose you could do something with stock—get it donated at a high price so your donor could claim it on his income tax, then sell it at a low price so you could claim a loss, but still collect the income. But wouldn't the IRS find that out?"

I felt a little catch of excitement in my diaphragm, the lurch that a hot idea can give. "Can you find out something for me? Who's on Chicago Settlement's board?"

"Not if it means one of them is going to get beaten up for being involved in your shenanigans, Victoria." Max voice wasn't altogether jocular.

"I don't think even you will be beaten up. And I hope I won't either. I want to know if—let's see—Richard Yarborough, Jason or Peter Felitti, or Ben Loring sit on their board."

Max repeated the names to me, getting the spelling right. I realized I didn't have the CEO of Paragon Steel—he would be more likely than his controller to sit on an important board. My *Who's Who in Chicago Commerce and Industry* was down in my office, but my old *Wall Street Journals* were in front of me on the coffee table. While Max made impatient noises about needing to get to his next meeting I thumbed through the back issues until I found the story on Paragon Steel.

"Theodore Bancroft. Any of those five. Can I call you at home tonight?"

"You're ready to jump into action, so everyone else has to too?" Max grumbled. "I'm on my way to another meeting and when I get out of that I'm going home to unwind. I'll get back to you in a few days."

When Max hung up I continued rubbing my toes absent-mindedly. Stock parking. Why not bond parking? What if Diamond Head was getting Chicago Settlement to take its junk at face value, then letting them sell it—at a steep loss, but still, they'd have money they didn't have before?

It was a nice, neat idea. But how had Mitch Kruger stumbled onto it? It was way too sophisticated for him. But maybe not for Eddie Mohr, the old president of the local. Time to go see him and ask.

I sat up and pulled my socks back on, thin pink anklets with roses up the side, pretty to look at but not providing much padding for the feet. I slipped my loafers on and went to my bedroom to collect the Smith & Wesson. Going down the hall I caught sight of myself in the bathroom mirror. My silk shirt looked as though I'd slept in it. I pulled it off and sponged myself under the bathroom tap.

I hadn't done any laundry for two weeks. It was hard to find a clean shirt that looked respectable enough to go interrogating in. I finally had to pull a dressy black top from a dry-cleaning bag. I could only hope the shoulder holster wouldn't tear into the delicate fabric—I wasn't going out of the neighborhood without my gun. A black houndstooth jacket sort of made the top into an outfit, and sort of covered

433

the gun. It was cut a little snugly for total concealment.

Mr. Contreras had been so subdued behind his door that I phoned downstairs before leaving to make sure he was really there. He answered on the sixth ring, sounding like a man on his way to face a firing squad, but determined to accompany me. When I got downstairs he spent several minutes fondling Peppy and her nurslings, as if this were their last good-bye.

"I've got to get going," I said gently. "You really don't have to come."

"No, no. I said I would and I will." He finally tore himself from the dogs and followed me into the hall. "You don't mind my saying so, doll, it's kind of obvious that you're carrying a gun. I hope you're not planning on shooting Eddie."

"Only if he shoots at me first." I unlocked the Impala and held the passenger door for him.

"If he sees you're carrying a gun, and only an idiot could ignore it, he ain't going to feel too much like talking. Not that he's likely to say much, anyway."

"Oh?" I steered the Impala onto Belmont, toward the Kennedy. "What makes you think that?"

He didn't say anything. When I glanced at him he turned a dull red under his leathery tan and turned to look out the passenger window.

"Why does it bother you so much, my going to see him?"

He didn't answer, just continued staring out the window. We'd been on the Kennedy for twenty minutes, inching our way past the Loop exits, when he suddenly burst out, "It just doesn't seem right. First Mitch goes and gets himself killed, and now you want to pin it on the president of my local. I feel like I'm betraying the local, and that's a fact."

"I see." I let a semi move in front of me before starting my crawl across lanes to the Stevenson exit. "I don't want to pin anything on Eddie Mohr. But I can't get your old management to talk to me. If I don't speak to somebody connected with Diamond Head pretty soon, I'm going to have to stop my investigation. I just can't get a lever anywhere."

"I know, doll, I know," he muttered miserably. "I understand all that. I still don't like it."

44

Terminal Call

Neither of us spoke again until we left the Stevenson at Kedzie. We were in an area where warehouses and factories jostled residential streets. Kedzie was badly pitted here from the semis that roared along it. We bounced south between two fast-moving sixty-tonners. I kept the Impala close to fifty, gritting my teeth against the jolts and hoping no one had to stop fast.

Mr. Contreras roused himself from his worries

to direct me to Eddie Mohr's house on Albany near Fortieth Street. I managed to exit without being run over. We suddenly found ourselves in an oasis of bungalows with well-tended yards, one of those pockets of tidiness that make the city look like a small, friendly town.

In neighborhoods like these the garages are approached from the alleys that run behind the houses. I pulled up in front, wondering if the Oldsmobile that had been used in the attack on Lotty was out back. I'd like to sneak a look at it before we left. A spotless Riviera sat in front of the house—presumably that was Mrs. Mohr's car. I moved the Impala up behind it.

Mr. Contreras took his time getting out of the car. I watched his unhappy maneuvering for a minute, then turned and marched briskly up the walk to the front door. I rang the doorbell without waiting for him to catch up with me—I didn't want to turn this into an all-night vigil while he decided whether or not he was scabbing by bringing me down to meet the guy.

The house itself was blanketed with thick curtains. It felt like a place empty of inhabitants. After a long few minutes, in which I debated going around to the back or just sitting in the Impala until someone showed up, I caught a movement in the thick shroud next to the door. Someone was inspecting me. I tried to look earnest and sincere and hoped that Mr. Contreras, now standing behind me, didn't look too woebegone for conversation.

A woman of about fifty opened the door. Her faded blond hair was matted in uneven clumps, as though glued to her head by an inexpert wig-maker. She stared at us through protuberant, lackluster eyes.

"We've come to see Eddie Mohr," I said. "Are you Mrs. Mohr?"

"I'm his daughter, Mrs. Johnson. He won't be ready for viewing until next week, but you can talk to Mother if you're old friends of his."

"Ready for viewing?" My jaw dropped slackly. "Is he—he isn't dead, is he?"

"Isn't that why you came? I wondered how you knew so fast. I thought maybe that was your father with you."

Mr. Contreras clutched my arm, his legs suddenly unsteady. "I just talked to him this morning, doll. He—he was expecting us. I . . . He sounded fine to me then."

I turned to look at him, but none of the things I wanted to say were appropriate at such a moment. No wonder he'd been so subdued: he knew I wanted to try to catch Eddie unawares. He may have felt he was betraying the local, but he probably thought he was betraying me too.

"I'm sorry," I said to Mrs. Johnson. "Sorry to intrude at such a time. This must have come as a terrible shock. I didn't know he was ill."

"It wasn't his heart, if that's what you're thinking. Someone shot him. Just as he was walking up Albany. Shot him in cold blood and drove on up the street. Damned niggers. Not satisfied

437

with tearing up Englewood and shooting each other up. They have to come up and kill people in McKinley Park. Why can't they just stay where they are and mind their own business?" Her face turned red with anger, but tears were swimming in the protuberant eyes.

"When did this happen?" I kept my voice gentle, but only by digging my nails into my palms.

"About one this afternoon. Mother called me, and of course I came right over, even though it meant turning the register over to Maggie, which is always a mistake. It's not that she's dishonest—she just can't add or subtract. Chicago schools just don't do the job they did when I was growing up."

It's the little things that worry us at moments of great loss. Maggie at the cash register . . . you can get your mind around it. Father shot dead on the street. . . . No, leave that one alone.

Mr. Contreras was stirring restively behind me, not wanting me to probe like a ghoul. I ignored him and asked Mrs. Johnson if anyone had seen the niggers in question.

"There were only two people on the street— Mrs. Yuall and Mrs. Joyce were coming back from the store. They didn't pay any attention to the car. You don't expect to see someone shot down in broad daylight in your own community, do you? Then they heard the shots and saw Daddy fall over. At first they thought he'd had a heart attack. It was only later they realized they'd been hearing shots."

She stopped talking and turned her head, listening to someone behind her. "I'll be right there, Mother. It's one of Daddy's old friends. He called this morning. Do you want to see him? . . . Excuse me a minute," she added to us, going back into the house.

"This is terrible, doll, terrible," Mr. Contreras whispered urgently. "We can't intrude on these people."

I gave him a tight smile. "I think it would be a good idea if we found out what he was doing out on the street. After all, he had two cars. Why was he walking instead of driving? And why were you calling him to let him know we were coming?"

Mr. Contreras turned red. "It was only fair. I couldn't have you barging in, trying to pin Mitch's death on the union, without giving him some notice—"

Mrs. Johnson came back to the door and he cut himself off in mid-sentence. "Mother's lying down. She's with a friend, but she'd like to know if Daddy said anything special this morning when he talked to you. Can you come on in?"

Mr. Contreras, beet-colored at the idea of talking to Mrs. Mohr while she was lying down, tried excusing himself. I grabbed his arm and propelled him forward.

The bedroom scene was actually as chaste as could be. Instead of the normal pint-sized bungalow room, Mrs. Mohr occupied a master suite. A ruffled duvet hid the bed. Mrs. Mohr was slumped in a large chintz armchair, her feet on a matching footstool. She was dressed for day, in stockings and heels, her face fully made-up, so that the furrows cut by tears and terror emphasized her age. The neighbor sat next to her in a straightbacked chair. A pitcher of iced tea and a glass were at Mrs. Mohr's elbow.

The curtains, done in the same bright floral pattern, were pulled back so that only white gauze covered the windows. A set of French doors led to a patio. Beyond it I could see a swimming pool. A remarkable addition for a South Side home.

"Here are some more friends for you, Gladys," the neighbor said, getting up. "I'm going to go home for a while, but I'll bring some supper over to you later."

"You don't have to do that, Judy," Mrs. Mohr said in the thread of a voice. "Cindy here can take care of me."

Cindy, Kerry, Kim—all those cute, girlish names parents love to bestow on their daughters, which don't suit us when we're middle-aged and grief-stricken. I thanked my mother's memory for her fierce correction of anyone who called me Vicky.

When Judy left I moved over to Mrs. Mohr's side. "I'm V. I. Warshawski, Mrs. Mohr, and this is Mr. Contreras, who used to work with your husband. I'm so sorry about his death. And sorry we have to bother you."

Mrs. Mohr looked at me apathetically. "That's

440

all right. It doesn't matter, really. I just wanted to know what the two of them talked about this morning. It seemed like afterwards he was angry and upset, and I hate to have to remember him like that."

"It looks as though you have a lot to remember him by," I said, indicating the room and the pool beyond with a sweep of my hand. "He seems to have been a wonderful provider."

"It was when he retired," Mrs. Mohr explained. "He worked hard all his life and earned himself a good pension. Young people complain nowadays. Like all those niggers, they just want something for nothing. They don't understand you have to work hard, the way Eddie and I did, to earn the nice things in life."

"Yes, indeed," I said enthusiastically. "I know Mr. Contreras here, who worked with Eddie for—was it thirty years?—would love to put a pool in our backyard, but our co-op board won't let him."

"Come on, doll," Mr. Contreras said indignantly. "You know I don't want to do anything like that. And even if I did, I don't have the money for it."

"You don't?" I said, reproachful. "I thought you worked hard all your life, just like Eddie Mohr. I know you said you could afford a car if you wanted one, although not necessarily a Buick Riviera along with an Oldsmobile."

A shade of alarm crossed Mrs. Mohr's face. "Eddie was the president of the local for a long time. He did a lot for them at Diamond Head, and he got a special—special agreement when he retired. We didn't want to say anything to any of the other men on the floor, because we knew it might not seem fair. We only could afford all this when he retired. They just finished work on the room here and the kitchen two months ago. But there was never anything dishonest about it. Eddie was a very honest man. He was with the Knights of Columbus and he was on the parish council. You can ask anyone."

"Of course." I sat in the chair Judy had vacated and patted Mrs. Mohr's hand in a soothing way, wondering if I was being as big a scab as I felt. "What kinds of special things did he do for them at Diamond Head?"

She shook her head. "Eddie was a decent man. He left his work at work and never bothered me with it. When we were starting out, when it was the two of us with Cindy and her brothers, I had to work too. I baked cakes at Davison's. It's too bad we couldn't have had some of this money back then."

"It's only because the neighborhood went down so much that Dad could afford to do this," Mrs. Johnson said. "Lots of houses standing empty. He could have moved away. He should have moved away. But he wanted to stay here because he grew up here, so he bought the lot behind us and added the pool. He was only helping the neighborhood and then they had to go and shoot him."

In the distance we heard the doorbell ring. Cindy Johnson moved off to answer it, patting her matted hair without seeming to feel it.

Tears welled in Mrs. Mohr's large eyes. She looked past me to Mr. Contreras. "What did he say to you? Or you to him? After he hung up he went back to his den—we turned the old kitchen into a den for him when we put the new one on last winter—and called some people. He wouldn't tell me what the problem was, just went out and left me and I never saw him again. What did you say to him?"

Despite the air-conditioning, Mr. Contreras was wiping sweat from his neck, but he answered manfully. "Him and me—we were never very close when we was working. He hung with a different crowd, you know how that goes. But I heard from one of the boys that he was giving a lot of money to a charity. I never heard of the outfit, but Vic here has some friends who played the piano or violin or something at one of their benefits. I told him we wanted to come talk to him about it. I don't know why it got him so upset, and that's a fact."

"What did he say to you?" Mrs. Mohr asked painfully.

"He thanked me. Thanked me for calling him in advance, I guess was how he put it. If I'd known . . . I sure wish I hadn't made that call."

"You think he went out to meet someone?" I asked Mrs. Mohr.

She plaited and unplaited her fingers. "I . . .

yes, I guess he must have. He said he was going to Barney's—that's a bar, but you can get sandwiches there—that he had to talk to a man and he wouldn't be eating lunch with me."

"Is Barney's where he went when he needed to talk to people privately?"

"Men need a place where they can go and be with other men. You young girls don't always understand that. But you can't keep them tied to your apron strings all day long, it doesn't do your marriage any good. And I know Barney; we grew up together. His father used to own the saloon before him. They've been there on the corner of Forty-first and Kedzie for sixty years now. They serve good sandwiches, good corned beef, none of that packaged stuff they sell you at these fast-food places. It was a good place for Eddie to go. He could shoot a little pool too. He always liked that. But I wish I hadn't let him go today. If I'd kept him here, found out what made him so upset, he wouldn't have been walking down the street when that car drove by. He'd be with me still."

Cindy came back in and bent over her mother. "There's a nigger out front now, Mother. He says he's a detective and he has a badge and everything, but he's not wearing a uniform. Do you want to talk to him? Or do you want me to call the precinct and make sure?"

Mrs. Mohr shook her head. "What's he coming to do? Apologize?"

I felt my face turning hot. "He probably has

444

some questions, Mrs. Mohr. It's probably the same detective who answered the call the night your husband's car was stolen and used to attack a doctor on the North Side."

I got up and went to the front door. As I'd thought, it was Conrad Rawlings. He did not look overwhelmed with delight at seeing me, and I felt my face grow hotter still.

"Well, well, Ms. W. I might have guessed you'd beat me here."

"It's not what you think," I stammered. "I didn't know he was dead. I came to talk to him to try to get a lead on Mitch Kruger."

"That a fact?"

Mr. Contreras, glad to make an escape, had come down the hall behind me. The nerve-wracking experiences of the last half hour made him more belligerent than usual.

"It sure is a fact. I'm tired of watching you cops harass Vic here instead of trying to catch murderers. You never listen to her, so she gets soaked in the canal and then you come around blaming her. Matter of fact, I talked to Eddie Mohr this morning. He was fine then. I told him we was coming down this afternoon and next thing I know he's been shot dead on the street."

"Okay, okay." Rawlings said. "You didn't try to finesse me. What did you want to talk to him about?"

"Money. What about you?"

"Oh, I heard about the shooting and I kind of connected his name with the car that hit the

445

doc. So I thought maybe I'd nose around a little. I'm not as fast as you, Ms. W., but I do try to get there. Tonight was your night for working late; I do remember you telling me that yesterday."

Cindy joined us in the hallway before I could think of something to say that might ease some of the bitterness in his voice. I could kiss him in front of Mr. Contreras, but not in front of Cindy. It would seem patronizing, and make his interview with them too difficult.

"Do you know him?" she asked.

"Yes. He's a friend of mine. A good friend, even if he's a little quick to judge me sometimes."

"I guess you can talk to my mother. But keep it brief. She's had a bad shock today."

"Yes, ma'am," Rawlings said. "I'll keep that in mind. . . . Drive that heap of yours carefully on the way home, Vic. I don't want to hear any of the boys had to pull you over."

45

A New Profession Beckons

"Do you think I killed him, doll?" Mr. Contreras asked when we were back in the car.

His anxiety robbed me of any desire to upbraid him for warning Eddie Mohr this morning. "Of course not. If either of us did, it was me, pushing on the investigation."

"You don't think he was shot by gangs, do you?"

"Nope. Someone got him to go out to Barney's and shot him as he walked home. I just wish . . ." I cut myself off.

"What, doll? What do you wish?"

"I wish I hadn't found Mitch's picture. Of Eddie with Hector Beauregard. And at the same time I wish I knew who he called this morning. Maybe Conrad can find out more than we could, although it's not too likely with Cindy and Gladys thinking of him as a barely articulate lesser ape."

"Conrad, huh? You getting kind of friendly with a cop if you're starting to talk about him by his first name."

I felt myself blushing. "Let's see if Barney will tell us anything."

During the short drive to the tavern I suggested a strategy to Mr. Contreras. He agreed readily, anxious to make what amends he could for his disastrous phone call.

Barney's was a small place, with one room for the pool table and one room for the bar. A handful of old men sat at two of the scarred tables in the bar. Some had drinks, but most seemed to be there for companionship. When they caught sight of strangers in their midst, they stopped talking and stared straight ahead.

A solidly built man in his early seventies got up from one of the tables and went back to the bar. "Can I help you folks?"

We walked up to him, Mr. Contreras taking

the lead. He asked for a beer and drank a little, then offered a comment on the weather, which Barney greeted in silence. Mr. Contreras surveyed the room, studying the men one at a time, while they sat stonily, occasionally directing glances of outright hostility in my direction. It was a men's bar, and whatever the libbers might do downtown to places like Berghoff's, Barney's was going to stay pure.

Finally Mr. Contreras gave a little grunt of recognition and turned to Barney. "I'm Sal Contreras. Me and Eddie Mohr worked together at Diamond Head for more than thirty-five years."

Barney drew back slightly, but Mr. Contreras pointed at one of the tables and said, "Ain't that right, Greg?"

A man with an enormous beer belly shook his head slowly. "Maybe so, but . . . well, light ain't so good in here. Shine some on him, Barney."

The owner leaned behind the counter for a switch and turned on an overhead bulb. Greg looked at my neighbor for a long, doubtful minute. His face cleared suddenly into a big grin.

"That's right, Sal. Ain't seen you since you retired. We've all been getting older, though you look pretty good. You moved north, what I heard."

The other men started moving in their chairs, finishing drinks, murmuring to each other. We belonged, after all. They didn't have to form a posse.

"Yeah," Mr. Contreras said. "After Clara died

448

I just couldn't stay in the old neighborhood. I got me a nice little place up on Racine."

"That your daughter? She turned out mighty nice. I thought your kid was older, though."

"Nah. This here's my neighbor. Vic Warshawski. She was driving me down to visit Eddie this afternoon, so I wouldn't have to take the el. Then we found out he was dead. I guess you probably heard all about that."

"Yup." Barney intervened, anxious to regain control of his bar. "He was just in here not five minutes before. Then they shot him on his way home. Clarence here, his wife saw Eddie die. When the cops and all finished talking to her she came and got him."

A bald man next to Greg nodded portentously. Either Mr. Yuall or Mr. Joyce. Having comforted his wife in her shock, he had hastened back to Barney's to share it with his friends.

"Mrs. Mohr thought he'd come here to meet someone," I ventured, hoping our bona fides were now well enough established for me to speak.

"That's what Eddie said," Barney agreed. "He was expecting to meet some man here for lunch. He waited for an hour and finally decided he'd had enough. He ate a hamburger by himself and left for home."

"Did he leave a message—in case the man he was waiting for showed up after all?" I asked.

"Yeah, he did, Barney," Greg said. "Remember? He said it was some management squirt and he was tired of waiting on management squirts, so if the guy showed up to tell him to call when he really wanted to have a meeting."

"That's right. Him getting shot like that, it went out of my mind." Barney scratched his thin gray hair. "But what name did he say?"

I waited while he pondered. "Milt Chamfers? Or Ben Loring?" I finally offered.

Barney nodded slowly. "I believe it was one of them. Chamfers. I believe that's the name all right."

Greg agreed that Chamfers was the name Eddie had given, but it didn't mean anything to him. He'd apparently left Diamond Head before the new owners took over. No, Eddie had never mentioned Milt Chamfers to him or to any of them.

"That's quite a nice addition Eddie put on his house," Mr. Contreras said, remembering the script we were trying to follow. "I wish I could afford me a swimming pool and a Buick and all. I was at Diamond Head thirty-eight years, not counting the war, but I sure never got me a retirement deal like that."

There was a murmur of agreement around the tables, but Clarence explained that Eddie had come into some money. No, he hadn't known Eddie had rich relatives. Must have been some distant cousin back in Germany remembering his poor American relations.

"Used to be the other way around," one of the other men said bitterly. "Didn't used to be

Americans had to be someone else's poor cousins."

The conversation turned to the usual complaints of the helpless, over the niggers and lesbians and Japs and everyone else who was ruining the country. Mr. Contreras had a shot and a beer to be sociable. We left under cover of a flurry of newcomers eager to discuss Eddie's death. I was just as glad to get out before Conrad Rawlings showed up, anyway. Assuming Mrs. Mohr made him privy to the news that Eddie had been here right before his death.

When we were back outside I stood on the walk, not moving for a minute.

"What is it, doll?"

"What exactly did you say to Eddie when you called?"

The old man turned a dull mahogany. "I said I was sorry. I know it sounds like I sent him out to be shot. You can't be more worried about it than me, doll, so give me—"

"That's not what I meant. After you talked to him he felt upset enough to call—apparently—Milt Chamfers, who agreed to meet him, just as a pretext to get him out on the street so someone could shoot at him. What did you say?"

Mr. Contreras scratched his head. "I told him who you was—a detective, I mean. And that that photo of him that Mitch had, the one from the charity, had you all excited. And that we was on our way down to ask him where he got enough money to support a big downtown charity like that, when I knew he was a Knights of Columbus man from the word go. And I just wanted to give him time to think about it first. I just wish—"

I saw a cab coming, a rarity on this stretch of Kedzie, and grabbed Mr. Contreras's arm to hustle him to the curb.

"Hey, doll, what're you up to?"

"Get in. . . . We can talk when we get someplace a little less exposed."

I asked the cabbie to go along Kedzie until we came to a public phone, and then to wait for me while I made a call. A few blocks down he pulled over to the curb.

I phoned a car rental company I know on the North Side called Rent-A-Wreck. I got their machine, and told it I was desperate for some wheels, that I'd be there in half an hour and hoped they'd be picking up their messages in the meantime. Rent-A-Wreck is a shoestring operation that a couple of women run out of their house, with the cars parked in the backyard. I hoped they were just sitting over dinner, not answering their phone but listening to their calls.

Back in the cab Mr. Contreras and the driver seemed to have come to a happy understanding. Both were Sox fans with the delusions common to all Chicago baseball lovers: while mourning the loss of Ivan Calderon they really thought this was the year the Sox could do it. I gave the cabbie Rent-A-Wreck's address and leaned back against the seat, leaving them to a heated discussion of whether Fisk should step aside for a younger man.

It seemed to me a minor miracle that I was still alive. If Milt Chamfers was going to shoot Eddie Mohr just because he was afraid of what Eddie might say to me, why wasn't he shooting at me? What had Eddie done for Diamond Head that they funded him on such a lavish scale—but that they didn't want him talking about? I didn't think Chamfers was the mastermind, either in paying off Eddie Mohr or in getting him shot. But who stood behind Chamfers—Ben Loring from Paragon Steel? Or Dick's father-in-law and his brother? Or both, maybe.

By the time we got to Rent-A-Wreck on Cornelia, I was fretting with impatience to be moving, to be doing something, although I wasn't sure what. I paid off the cabbie, giving him an extra few bucks with the tip to wait in case no one answered our ring. When Bev Cullerton came to the door I waved to the cab. He honked and drove off.

"Hiya, Vic. You're lucky we were home. Callie and I were heading over to the coffeehouse when we got your message. You trash those fancy wheels of yours? Maybe we could rehab 'em out back."

I grinned. "That's last week's story. I just need to get around town tonight without anyone on my butt. You got something for me?"

"This hot weather everyone wants a car to get

to Door County. We only have one left and she ain't much."

Given the condition of most of Bev and Callie's cars, one that wasn't much was going to be a real clunker. Beggars can't be choosers though. I gave her a twenty as a down payment and took the keys to an old Nova. The odometer was on its second lap and the steering had been devised to train the Bulgarian weight-lifting team, but Bev assured me it would still do eighty if it had to. She gave us cushions to cover the lumpy seats and held the back gate open until we had cleared the alley.

"You want to go home?" I asked Mr. Contreras.

"Now, look here, Vic Warshawski: you are not going to drag me all over Chicago and then dump me at home like you think I was senile and couldn't understand a few English sentences. I want to know why you left that Impala down by Barney's and what all the fuss is. And if you're up to something else tonight you'd better either plan on me coming with you or just sitting in the car till the sun comes up, 'cause you ain't pushing me out of here. Unless you're planning on hooking up with *Conrad.*" The last word was laced with an adolescent ugliness.

"As a matter of fact, I'd be just as happy for Conrad not to catch up with me again tonight." I wrenched the steering wheel hard to the right and pulled over to the curb, where I gave him a thumbnail sketch of the problems I'd been pondering during the cab ride north. On top of those

I was wondering what Vinnie or the Picheas might do now that I'd discovered their slick pitch to the old people in the neighborhood. This was the first chance I'd had to tell Mr. Contreras about it. He was shocked and angry and we got diverted for a bit by a sermon against those who prey on the elderly.

"Vinnie's a spiteful kind of guy," I said when he'd wound down. "Who knows what he might think up to get even. Anyway, I don't know why I'm still walking around if Milt Chamfers would shoot Eddie just so as to keep him from talking to me. I'm worried that you could be in danger, too, just because you've been hanging out with me—calling Eddie Mohr, going with me to see him, all those things."

"Oh, don't worry about me, doll," he said roughly. "Not that I want to die, but if someone shoots me it's not like I didn't have a good life. What are you going to do tonight?"

"I need to find a place with a phone. But what I really need is to get into Dick's office."

" 'The first Mr. Warshawski,' " the old man repeated with relish. "But what for?"

"That's where it all comes together: the Diamond Head bonds Mrs. Frizell bought from Chrissie Pichea; Chicago Settlement; and Diamond Head itself—Dick did the legal work. I just don't see how else to get it without looking at his files. And I don't know how to get in there."

"You can't pick the lock?"

"I lost my picklocks in the San the other night,

but that's not really the problem. A big law firm like that, the juniors are working until all hours. I don't know how to get in without being caught. And I don't know how else to get what I need to know."

He thought it over for some time. "You know, doll, I've got an idea. I'm not saying it's a great idea, and it'd need some work, but you know who gets into places like that without anybody paying any mind to them?"

"Cleaning crews, but—"

"And workmen," he interrupted triumphantly. "They're just part of the furniture to management squirts."

46

New Duds—
But Not from Saks

Mr. Contreras had to go home to feed Peppy and let her out. We decided that I would drop him on Diversey and pick him up on Barry, at the top of our alley. I wasn't very happy with the plan, but had to agree that anyone staking out the place was more likely to be gunning for me than for him.

I spent the next half hour in misery. I couldn't take the car up Racine in case they had someone smart enough to be looking for me regardless of what I was driving. I went the long way around to Barry and sat hunched down in the driver's seat, my gun out, straining my ears for any sounds of violence so that I might race to Mr. Contreras's rescue. When he appeared at the mouth of the alley my stomach heaved uncontrollably; I retched up a mouthful of bile, just getting my head out of the car in time.

Mr. Contreras, torn between excitement and worry, offered me his giant handkerchief to clean my mouth. I used it a little ruefully. Marlowe never let his nerves get the better of him.

My neighbor had brought a couple of faded boilersuits with him, along with an outsize tool box. We dumped the load in the back. I wrenched at the steering wheel and moved out of the neighborhood. Before we did anything else I needed a glass of water and something to eat—other bodily needs that never seemed to afflict the great detectives.

We found an all-night diner on Clark and stopped for sandwiches. As the Near North Side grew ever more yuppified this was one of the few remaining places for cops, delivery drivers, and others on the graveyard shift.

Mr. Contreras excused himself after he'd eaten half his ham sandwich. "I just thought of something, doll. You stay here and act natural."

He was gone before I could protest, leaving me in mixed astonishment and anger. I am definitely not the waiting type. This was my second chance this evening to reflect on how evil I'd been all those times I'd left my neighbor pacing the floor unhappily at night while I jumped from gantries. I'm not sure either my character or my disposition was improved by the reflections.

After he'd been gone five minutes I took the bill to the cashier. I was on my way out to look for him when he came in, a look of such self-satisfied mischief on his face that my ill humor died down.

"Oh, there you are, doll. I thought you was going to wait for me."

"I paid the bill. Someone's just about to pick up the rest of your sandwich. You want to rescue it?"

"Nah. I ate enough. Tell you the truth, my stomach's kind of jumpy. I got us something that'll really help."

I bustled him out to the Nova before he could proclaim it to the diner at large. When we were safely inside the car, he flourished a fistful of paper at me. I tried turning on the overhead light, but that had died during the car's first hundred thousand miles. I pulled out of the lot and stopped under a streetlamp. Mr. Contreras had lifted a bunch of work orders from Klosowski's Emergency Electrical Repair van.

"I saw the door wasn't locked when we went by, and then, while we was eating, I thought, well, why not? They'll look more official than anything we could make up down at your office."

We had decided to take a chance on finding my office still in the clear and go in there to try to manufacture a document that would get us into Crawford, Mead. Mr. Contreras was right: these would be much better than something jerry-rigged on my Olivetti.

"And," he added, his voice squeaking a bit with excitement, "I got you a cap, too—you ought to cover up those curls of yours."

He pulled a Klosowski cap from his back pocket.

"Too bad you didn't find me a false mustache and a beard as well. You know, I think we'd better move on south. Looks to me like someone's heading for the van. This might be his favorite hat."

We parked the Nova on Adams and circled around on foot to come at the Pulteney from the north. After getting in and out unmolested yesterday I was pretty sure we were dealing with people amateurish enough not to associate me with an office, but there was no point in revealing a car we'd been at such pains to get.

The elevator was having one of its rare fits of functionality. I would take it up while Mr. Contreras followed on foot. I gave him the key to the stairwell door with instructions to go hell for leather for the cops if I was under attack, not to leap into the fray.

His jaw set stubbornly. "I ain't the kind of guy who's going to run the other way when a lady's getting beat up. You'd better resign yourself to that."

To my dismay he pulled a pipe wrench out from under the boilersuits. It was his favorite weapon, one that he used with more gusto than ability. I started to debate the point with him, then decided there wasn't time. The likelihood of my being jumped didn't seem that great, anyway.

When the elevator creaked to a halt on the fourth floor, I turned off its light and slid out the door on my knees, propping my left hand on the wall for balance, holding the Smith & Wesson in front of me with my right. The hall seemed clear; I used my pencil flash for a quick survey and didn't see anyone.

The Pulteney management doesn't encourage its tenants to use the facilities: night-lights are unheard of in the hallways. I got to my feet and tiptoed down to my own door. After using the building for twelve years, it was easy to move around in it in the dark.

As I'd hoped, no one was lurking—either in the hall, or inside my place. I had the lights on and one of Mr. Contreras's filched work orders in the Olivetti when he came in—it had taken him a while to figure out how to open the stairwell in the dark.

"So they could have beaten you to a pulp while I was back there fooling around with the darn door. As if I don't already feel bad enough sending Eddie Mohr to his death."

I rested my wrists on the keyboard. "It didn't happen that way. He chose to sign on to some deal with Diamond Head—you didn't make him do that. Your calling him didn't make them shoot him, either: it probably only accelerated the time-table. If we'd seen him this afternoon—"

"You might have talked some sense into him and he'd still be alive. You don't need to be nice to me, doll, just to save my feelings. I can see there's more to this business of talking to people than I've figured out."

I got up from the machine and put an arm around him. "The worst thing you can do in an investigation is slow yourself down chewing over what you did wrong. When the case is finished you can take some time and try to learn from your mistakes. But when you're in the middle of it—you just have to be like the Duke of Wellington—forget about it and go on."

"Duke of Wellington, huh? He's the guy that beat Napoleon, right?"

"The very one." I sat back down at the typewriter. "Tell me something evil-sounding that could go wrong with someone's electrical outlets—something so bad, we can't let anyone watch us while we work for fear they'll fry their eyeballs."

Mr. Contreras pulled one of my client chairs next to the typewriter. "I don't know, doll. All this fancy, modern equipment folks have in their offices, I don't know what they'd have, and tell you the truth, I don't know what could go wrong with it."

"Don't worry about that. The junior legal beagles we're going to run into won't know either. Dick probably has a computer, and his secretary

will have a CRT to the company's big system."
I tried to imagine my ex-husband's office.
"Maybe she has a big printer, because she'll be
printing a lot of forms. Since he's one of the senior partners, she might not have to share it with
anyone."

Mr. Contreras thought about it slowly, drawing
himself a diagram on a piece of scrap paper.
"Okay. Put in something about a high-voltage
short to the cover of the machine—maybe it
knocked an operator out, or blew her across the
room or something."

I typed that in, adding a date and time of call.
Then I made a fake form for Klosowski by using
the header from the work order and a blank piece
of paper in my copier. On Mr. Contreras's suggestion I used that to type in a report of an earlier
inspection of a short in the building's air con-
ditioner that had been traced to R. Yarborough's
office. The whole thing was about as spurious
as I could imagine, but it might get us in the
door.

47

A Short in the System

Despite the hour, a bevy of tireless young lawyers
were fluttering around Crawford, Mead's offices.
We got in through their locked mahogany doors

simply by showing our work order to the night guard in the main lobby and getting him to phone up to the office for us.

No one had told him about a danger in the electrical plant; he looked surly and frightened and threatened to call his boss. We assured him the problem had been traced to one office on thirty—that *our* boss had warned us very sternly against alarming people since we only had to deal with the wiring in one room.

"Don't get us fired, man, okay?" I pleaded.

He grudgingly decided he would keep it to himself and phoned upstairs for us. "But you better give me advance warning if this place is going up in smoke."

"If it goes up in smoke you'll be the only one sitting pretty," I pointed out, following Mr. Contreras onto the elevator.

Once on thirty Mr. Contreras took charge. Even though the Koslowski cap covered my hair and shielded my face, we didn't want to run the risk of someone recognizing me. The worst danger was that Todd Pichea, who knew Mr. Contreras as well as me, might be working late. We needn't have worried, though—as the old man had pointed out earlier, workmen in a professional office are considered about as human as water buffalo, only not as unusual.

Mr. Contreras flourished our work order at a young man in a T-shirt and jeans, stressing the extreme danger of any inexperienced person coming near the dangerous electrons floating around Dick's office. Clutching a massive print-out for security, the young man escorted us as far as the top of the interior stairwell.

"Mr. Yarborough's office is at the end of the hall there. Uh, this key should open his office. If, uh, you don't mind, I need to get back to work. Maybe you can find it yourselves from here. You can leave the key at the front desk when you leave."

"Right," Mr. Contreras said sternly. "And make sure no one comes down here until we give you the all-clear. We're going to cut one of the lines. You may notice the lights dim occasionally, but it's nothing to worry about."

Our guide couldn't wait to get clear of the area. With any luck the whole crew would be scared enough to leave work early tonight. I didn't want some braver soul coming to investigate while I was copying Dick's files.

When I unlocked my ex-husband's office I felt a kind of guilty thrill. It reminded me of the times when I was small and hunted out the drawer where my dad hid his police revolver. I knew I wasn't supposed to touch it, or even know where it was, and excitement and shame would get me so wound up I'd have to put on my skates and race around the block a few times. With an un-easy twinge I wondered if those feelings were what had led me into detective work. I remem-bered my advice to Mr. Contreras—plenty of time for self-analysis later.

Dick rated a suite with a waiting room, a small

sanctum for his secretary, and a large office whose curved windows overlooked the Chicago River. Mr. Contreras busied himself in the waiting area, unpacking some businesslike cables from his toolbox and snaking them across the floor. He had also brought a small power screwdriver, with which he undid a vent along the floorboards, exposing an interesting nest of wires.

"You go on inside and look at papers, doll. If anyone shows up I'll start buzzing away with this guy."

I found myself tiptoeing into Dick's office, as if my steps on his Kerman could raise his hackies out in Oak Brook. The room didn't run to filing cabinets. He had several shelves of the legal casebooks he felt he needed every day, a slab of burled blond wood that apparently was a desk, and an elaborate sideboard housing German ceramics and a wet bar. Teri and their three blond offspring beamed at me from the burled slab.

A door on one side led to a private bath. A second door opened on a shallow closet. A few clean shirts hung there. I couldn't resist looking through them; at the back hung the one I'd flung coffee on. He'd forgotten to take it home for Teri to look after. Or maybe he couldn't bring himself to explain to her how it got that way. I grinned in rather childish triumph.

I tiptoed back across the Kerman to his secretary's office. Harriet Regner had hitched her star to Dick's when he was starting out and had to share a secretary with five other men. She'd been his executive secretary now for ten years and managed a small staff of clerks and paralegals for him. If Dick was involved in something truly illegal, would he trust it to Harriet? I thought of Ollie North and Fawn Hall. Men like Dick always seem to find women so enthusiastic in their devotion that they consider their bosses more important than the law. Harriet would take care of anything questionable herself. The clerical grunts she supervised would handle her routine filing elsewhere.

On that fine logic I approached her filing cabinets. Their blond burl matched Dick's desk, although I suspected in here it was just veneer. Without my picklocks it took a certain amount of force to unlock the cabinets: I had to get Mr. Contreras to come in and blast them with his power driver. I didn't really care, though, if Dick knew I'd been here—I hadn't even bothered to wear gloves. It was one thing to find out what he was up to, and quite another to figure out how to confront him with it. If he thought I'd been burglarizing him it might force his hand.

Once I had the cabinets open, Diamond Head leaped out to greet me. Their affairs occupied an entire cabinet and spilled over into the top drawer of a second. I'd thought I was going to be home free when I found the files. I'd forgotten the amount of paper a law office generated; it was the only way to show they were really working. When Mr. Contreras heard me cursing, he came in to see what was wrong. He clucked sympathetically, but didn't feel able to help. Anyway, he had to man the lookout post.

I skimmed through the material in the first drawer. It dealt with the conditions surrounding Paragon's sale of Diamond Head. Paragon had bought a helicopter manufacturer, Central States Aviation, Inc.; the Justice Department had ruled that they needed to divest themselves of Diamond Head as a condition of the acquisition. That explained why they got rid of the little engine company, something that had been troubling me.

An enormous stack of documents detailed a consent decree between Paragon and Diamond Head. I hovered over them, tempted to read them closely, but I needed to get to material that might explain terms of a settlement between Diamond Head and Eddie Mohr. Carefully keeping everything in its original order I put that stack on the floor next to me and turned to the next drawer.

Here I found the documents dealing with the bond issue enabling Jason Felitti to buy the engine maker. Skeletons from the Felitti family popped out at me in the form of letters from Peter Felitti to Dick. Jason had sold most of his shares in Amalgamated Portage years ago, apparently to finance his political ambitions in Du Page County. He'd used the remainder to acquire a stake in U.S. Metropolitan Bank and Trust.

When he wanted to sell that stake to help finance his acquisition of Diamond Head, Peter put his foot down. Let Jason use debt financing, he wrote to Dick. This was in 1988; Drexel was still riding high. It was relatively easy to find an investment banker willing to issue the debt that would enable Jason to make the purchase.

That same memo explained why Jason wanted Diamond Head to begin with, or at least gave Peter's version of the case. Jason played golf with one of Paragon's outside directors, a political crony who also sat on U.S. Met's board. The crony knew Jason wanted to establish himself as a financial success separate from his brother— why not buy Diamond Head? Since Paragon had to unload it in sixty days, they would take any offer they could get.

All this was fascinating, but not illegal. Not even immoral. It was the next drawer that suddenly revealed what I was looking for.

Jason, a year into his purchase, couldn't meet his debt payments. The airplane industry was in a recession. No one wanted the splines that were Diamond Head's specialty. And even if they did, sales wouldn't begin to cover his interest payments, let alone to repay the principal.

But the pension fund for Diamond Head's work force was currently valued at twenty million. If Jason could cash that in, he could breathe more easily. The catch was, an informal poll of the rank and file showed he'd probably lose a vote on converting the fund to an annuity. But Eddie Mohr, the president of the local, agreed on the union's behalf. In exchange for a cash settlement of five hundred thousand dollars, he signed documents allowing Diamond Head to sell the union pension fund and convert it to an annuity.

But how could they get away with it? There were all those pensioners like Mr. Contreras. Surely they would notice when their checks went down in value. I was about to call out to my neighbor, when I found the answer. The annuity would be structured so that current pensioners would be paid what they presently received. The paying institution would change from the Ajax Insurance Company, which managed the union fund, to Urban Life, an insurance company owned by U.S. Met's directors—which also agreed to acquire a significant amount of Diamond Head junk.

I felt myself gasping for air. Cash in the pension fund without union consent and pay off Eddie Mohr to make it possible. Of course, he was the duly elected representative of the union. The feds might rule that that made it a legal transaction. But Eddie, knowing Mitch Kruger had died sniffing around the deal, might have felt unable to face another old buddy from the shop. When Mr. Contreras called, maybe it pricked his loyalty to the local. Maybe he called Milt Chamfers and told him he just couldn't keep cheating his buddies. I wondered if I'd ever know.

A gold-rimmed carriage clock on Harriet's desk chimed the hour. I looked up with a start: two o'clock and I still had three drawers to go. Mr. Contreras came in to see how I was doing.

"I just got back from scouting around. I think

we've got the place to ourselves now. Need me to do anything?"

"Want to copy some of these documents? I think I've found something pretty hot. Don't stop to read the stuff now; it'll only get you too mad to go on."

He was happy to help out, but had never used a copier before. Harriet's Xerox was so complicated that it took a fair amount of time to get him comfortable using it. It was close to three when I got back to my papers.

I riffled through the remaining files quickly, hoping to find a reference to Chicago Settlement. When I couldn't find anything, I stashed the papers back where they belonged and turned once again to the stack dealing with Paragon Steel. Mr. Contreras finished his photocopying. Laying the copies next to me, he said with a delicate cough that he was going to find a men's room. I nodded absently, forgetting Dick's private john until after he'd disappeared down the hall.

I had just gotten to what looked like a juicy section, dealing with Paragon's obligation to keep Diamond Head functioning, when Mr. Contreras came racing back in.

"Someone's come in, doll. I think it may be the cops. I'd sort of wandered to the front, just giving the place the once-over—"

"Pack up your tools and explain the rest to me later. If they come here, I want them to find you in the act of restoring the vent cover."

He stumbled back to the waiting room. I

shoved the papers back in their folders and jammed them into the drawers any old way. I looked at the photocopies in momentary indecision. If it was indeed the cops and I got searched, I couldn't be found with those on me.

I opened Harriet's side drawer and took out a large manila envelope with Crawford, Mead's return address on the corner. Stuffing my copies into it, I addressed the envelope to myself at my office and sprinted down the hall. I called out to Mr. Contreras as I left not to worry, that I wasn't abandoning him.

Mr. Contreras was right: we had cops. I could hear them at the bottom of the interior staircase planning how to search the upper floors. Panicking slightly, I went from room to room until I found one with outgoing mail in a basket. I slid my envelope into the middle of the stack and walked back up the hall to join Mr. Contreras.

I got there just as one of the patrolmen came down the hall with the night guard from the lobby.

48

Off the Hook

Fred Roper, the night guard, was triumphant. "I knew there couldn't be something wrong with the air-conditioning. Not without them telling me about it when I came on duty."

"It only took you five hours to figure it out," Mr. Contreras said. "What'd you have to do—take off your shoes and socks and think it through with your toes?"

We hadn't actually been arrested yet, just taken to one of the small side offices for questioning. Mr. Contreras's adrenaline level was about high enough to send the Galileo probe hurtling past Mars. I kept hoping he would calm down before the charges against us multiplied—illegal entry and snoopery were bad enough. Although we'd managed to get most of the evidence packed up in time, Mr. Contreras was still rewinding coils of wire when the cops showed up.

His last comment was certainly justified. It miffed Fred Roper no end. He explained for the third time, in detail, how he started getting suspicious when the last of the Crawford, Mead, employees left—around one-thirty—and we were still up there. He finally made up his mind that we might not be up to any good and called his boss. The security firm's night manager phoned the building engineers' night manager, and confirmed that all the appliances and wiring were functioning smoothly. On his boss's instruction, Roper called the cops.

Roper's dull, nasal voice, and his excited repetitions made me want to jump up and strangle him. The police were no doubt using him as a weapon to torment me into confessing.

472

"What were you doing here, anyway?" the senior member of the patrol demanded. "And no more of this shit about you being an electrician and this being your neighbor helping you out. The unions don't operate like that. And your normal neighbors don't carry guns or PI licenses."

Officer Arlington was a thickset man in his late fifties, with a bald spot that he tried to drape his few lingering hairs across. As soon as he'd pushed us into a conference room—before saying a word—he'd taken off his cap and combed his hair.

"No, I know," I said quickly, before Mr. Contreras could step to the mat again. "Mr. Contreras is just trying to protect me, which is really sweet of him. The truth is, well, this is painful to have to talk about to strangers."

"Get used to it, girlie—you're going to see a lot of strangers before you finish telling your tale." Officer Miniver, a younger black man, shared his partner's menacing attitude toward suspects.

"Well, it's like this." I spread my hands in a pantomime of feminine helplessness. "The man whose office we were in, he's my ex-husband. And I can't get him to keep up with his child-support payments. I don't have any money, I can't afford to take him to court—and anyway, how could I win against a big lawyer like him?"

"Lots of ladies can't get their child-support payments, but they don't go breaking into their

473

husbands' offices. What was that supposed to do for you?"

"I was hoping to find, well, evidence, I guess, of his ability to pay. That's what he keeps telling me, that he can't afford it because of his mortgage and his new family and everything in Oak Brook."

"And you needed a gun for that?" Miniver said derisively.

"He's threatened me in the past. Maybe it was foolish of me, but I didn't want to be beaten up again."

"He's a terrible man, terrible," Mr. Contreras confirmed. "How he could treat a sweet girl like Vic here so mean I'll never understand."

I could see neither Arlington nor Miniver's heart was going to break over this. They seemed pleased to think Dick was clever enough to evade his obligations. They asked me a series of questions about our decree and how Dick had managed to avoid paying me anything for years.

In the end, Arlington whistled admiringly. "Guess all that legal education gets you something after all. . . . Too bad you didn't spend your money on a lawyer sooner, girlie, instead of breaking in here. Because you're sure going to have to come up with the dough for one now that we're arresting you."

"Why don't we call Richard Yarborough first? He's the one who has to press charges in the end."

"Yeah, but a guy who won't pay child support

474

sure isn't going to be very understanding about you digging through his personal papers," Arlington said.

"Let him decide that. The one thing I know about Richard Stanley Yarborough is that he hates other people making up his mind for him."

It was four-thirty now. They felt they couldn't possibly bother such an important lawyer in the middle of the night. Anyway, they were panting to take Mr. Contreras and me to the station and stuff us in holding cells for the remainder of the night.

"I do get the one phone call," I said. "And I don't have any scruples about bothering a big man at home. So I'll call him. You can listen in on the extension, but your watch commander won't have to know you disturbed him."

Before either Miniver or Arlington could object I went to the phone standing in the corner and dialed his home. It's one of those mental perversities that I know Dick's number by heart.

He answered on the fifth ring, his voice thick with sleep.

"Dick, it's V.I."

"Vic! What the fuck are you doing calling now? Do you have any idea what time it is?"

"Four-thirty-five. I'm down at your office and a couple of cops want to arrest me for illegal entry. I thought you'd like to put your two cents in first."

There was no extension in the room. Arlington had sent Miniver scurrying down the hall to find a line he could listen in on. I heard a click just then as he came on.

"Damn right I do. What the hell are you doing in my office?"

"I felt so bad about spoiling your shirt this morning that I just couldn't sleep. I thought if I could take it home and wash it for you, you might forgive me. Of course, ironing isn't my strong suit, but maybe Teri would do that."

"Damn you, Vic!" I heard a muffled voice in the background, and then Dick, softly, saying, "No, it's all right, sweetheart. Just a client who's gotten herself in over her head. Sorry to wake you up."

"The lady says you won't pay her child support," Miniver interjected on his line.

"I won't what?"

"Dick, if you keep shouting like that, poor old Teri's never going to get back to sleep. You know, the back payments you owe me for little Eddie and Mitch. But I looked in your Diamond Head file, and found that you had more cash than I ever dreamed of. I haven't been able to buy myself new shoes because every dime I make goes to feeding your two little boys, but if you could spare something out of Diamond Head, well, it would make a big difference."

There was a long silence, then Dick demanded to talk to the officer without my being on the phone. Miniver, to make sure it stuck, had me bring Arlington onto the line. Dick seemed to be asking if I had been searched, because Arlington said all they'd found was a gun.

"He wants to talk to you again." Arlington jerked his head at me.

"You don't have any proof," Dick said peremptorily when I was back on the line.

"Sweetheart, you're always underestimating me. I smuggled it out of the building before the cops showed up. Believe me, I could be showing it to my newspaper friends by this time tomorrow."

He was so quiet I could hear the Oak Brook birds begin to tweet behind him. "You still there, Officer?" he said at last. "You can let her go. I don't think I want to press charges at this time."

Miniver and Arlington were so disappointed at not being able to arrest us that we cleared the building as fast as possible. I didn't want them to dream up some secondary charge, like impersonating an electrician. The police followed us to the Nova, and then tailed me closely until I had passed the LaSalle exit on Lake Shore Drive. They finally got off at Fullerton.

We rode up to Belmont, where I turned into the harbor and cut the engine. The eastern sky was already rosy with the coming dawn.

We grinned at each other, then suddenly both began laughing. We laughed until our ribs ached and the tears streamed down our cheeks.

"What do we do now?" Mr. Contreras asked when he'd recovered from the fit.

477

"Sleep. I can't do anything else without a few hours in bed."

"You know, doll, I'm so . . . I don't know what the word is. I don't think I can sleep."

"Wired," I supplied. "Yeah, but you'll crash pretty soon and then you won't be good for anything. Besides, Peppy needs you. What I think . . ."

I squinted at my watch. Five-fifteen. It was early to call anyone, but I didn't want to go back into our building alone right now. My own apartment should be secure, but if Vinnie was tied into Chamfers at all, he could let a whole gang into the building to waylay me. Or worse yet, my neighbor. I was damned if I was going to cry for help to Conrad Rawlings. That meant I needed to turn to my friends the Streeter Brothers. They ran a furniture-moving business, but did a little security work on the side.

As it turned out, I didn't wake Tim Streeter. He and his brother Tom were already up, getting ready for an early breakfast before starting a moving job. If I could wait until six he'd be able to bring a crew of five over to my building on their way to the move.

I was ravenous. We whiled away the time at the all-night diner where we'd stopped last night. Mr. Contreras, who hadn't thought he was hungry, packed away three fried eggs, hash browns, a side of ham, and four pieces of toast. I stopped after two eggs and the hash browns. I hoped no one was going to jump us: a full stomach isn't the best preparation for battle.

Tim and Tom Streeter showed up at ten after six, whistling lightly and joking with their crew. The Streeter boys are both enormous, topping six-four and muscled to move pianos down five flights of stairs. The three other men weren't exactly tiny either.

Leaving two of the crew out front, the rest of us went around to the back. If someone was hanging out on the stairs there, we'd be able to spot them before walking into a trap. The sun was well up now; it was obvious that the area was clear. We checked behind the garbage cans in the basement entry just to be sure, then went up to my place. No one had penetrated my security system.

We were cautious in moving through the front door into the main stairwell, but it was clear too. I used my flash. Someone had been here last night: they'd left a crumpled McDonald's bag on the floor. And urinated on the stairs. For some reason that enraged me more than the idea of people lying in wait for me.

"It's just punks, cookie," Mr. Contreras reassured me. "You can't let yourself get so wound up over a bunch of punks. I'll come up and clean it for you."

"You go take care of Peppy. I'll worry about this."

Tim asked if I wanted someone to spend the day—they could manage the move with four men if they had to. I rubbed my eyes, trying to think. Exhaustion was beginning to encase my brain in concrete.

"I don't think so. We should be okay during the day. Can I check with you tonight? Would you have someone if we need an extra body in a fight?"

Tim agreed readily—business had been light lately. With the recession, fewer people were buying new places and moving into them. We went downstairs together, to make sure Mr. Contreras's place was clear. I barely had the energy left at that point to make it back up the three flights to my own apartment. I knew I should scrub the stairwell, but couldn't force the extra action on my body. I just remembered to take off the shoulder holster and unhook my bra before collapsing across the bed.

49

When Top Management Talks . . .

My sleep was punctuated by dreams of the worst job I'd ever held, trying to sell *Time-Life* books by phone in the early seventies, except in my dreams I was being pursued by a relentless telemarketer. At one point I thought I'd actually picked up the phone and yelled "I don't want to buy anything now" into it. I slammed it down only to have it start ringing again.

I sat up in bed. It was one-thirty and my mouth felt like a cotton-ball factory. The phone was ringing. I eyed it malevolently, but finally picked it up.

"Yes?"

"Is this V. I. Warshawski? Why in hell did you hang up on me just now? I've been trying to reach you all morning."

"I'm not on your payroll, Mr. Loring. I'm not worried about jumping high enough fast enough to keep you happy."

"Don't give me that crap, Warshawski. You yanked pretty hard on my chain Monday, warned me Paragon's affairs would be in the papers if I didn't talk to you. You can't pull a stunt like that, then leave me hanging."

I made a sour face at the phone. "Okay. Let's talk."

"Not over the phone. You can meet me in Lincolnwood in half an hour if you leave now."

"Yes, but I'm not leaving the city today. You can be here in half an hour if you leave now."

He hated it. All executives hate it when you don't leap the first moment they bark out an order. But I couldn't stray from my base, even assuming my stiff body would start moving. Between Vinnie and Dick something was going to happen soon. I wanted to be here for it.

The conversation ended with my giving Loring directions on how to find my apartment. "And

481

by the way, how did you get my home number? It's not listed."

"Oh, that. I called some people to find out about you and they sicced me onto Daraugh Graham at Continental Lakeside. He gave it to me." The old executive network strikes back.

I staggered into the bathroom to scrub my teeth clean of lint. If I only had half an hour, I needed a workout more than I did coffee. Since I still hadn't replaced my running shoes I put everything I had into my exercises, working a lot more with my handweights than usual. It took a full forty minutes but my brain felt looser, as if it might be willing to do a little work if called on.

I showered and dressed. I dug through the mess on the floor of my hall closet and unearthed an old pair of running shoes. They dated back five or six years and were worn too thin for serious running, but they made getting around easier than the loafers I'd been wearing.

Since Loring still hadn't shown, I made coffee and a snack. After fried eggs at six this morning it was time to get back to a healthier regimen. I sautéed tofu with spinach and mushrooms and took it into the living room with the Smith & Wesson. I didn't seriously expect Loring to attack me, but I didn't want to be really stupid at this point either. I tucked the gun under a stack of papers on the couch and curled up cross-legged next to them.

I was halfway through my tofu when Luke Edwards called to tell me the Trans Am was ready.

He gave me a lugubrious account of the patient's near-death and her survival, due solely to his heroic efforts.

"You can come get it today, Warshawski. In fact, I wish you would—I need the Impala back. I've got someone who wants to buy it."

With a guilty jolt I remembered leaving the Impala around the corner from Barney's on Forty-first Street. With all the truck traffic in and out of the warehouses there, I sincerely hoped Luke's baby was in one piece. I calculated times. If Loring arrived soon I'd be able to leave by four, but I'd have to go south on public transportation—otherwise I'd just have to fetch Rent-A-Wreck's Nova back later.

"I don't think I can make it before six, Luke."

"I got plenty to keep me busy here, Warshawski. I'll be waiting for you."

When he'd hung up I looked at my watch again. It was close to three now—I guess Loring had to prove he could keep me waiting, since I had made him come south. Corporate egos are a much more disagreeable feature of my job than the occasional thug.

I called a friend of mine who was a senior counsel for the Department of Labor, and was lucky enough to find him in his office.

"Jonathan: V. I. Warshawski."

It had been some months since we'd last spoken. We had to go through the ritual of discussing baseball—Jonathan, who'd grown up in Kansas City, had a regrettable affection for the Royals—

before I could ask what I needed to know. I sketched it as a hypothetical scenario: a company wants to convert a union's pension fund to an annuity and pocket the cash. They get the duly elected officers of the collective bargaining unit to sign onto the plan.

"Now, suppose the officers sign on without putting it to a vote of the rank and file. Would the courts see that as legal?"

Jonathan thought a bit. "Tough one, Vic. There've been some related cases under ERISA, and I think they hinge on how the local conducts its business. If the officers make other financial decisions for the local without a vote, I think they'd probably find that it was legal."

ERISA was a twelve-year-old law supposedly designed to protect pension and other retirement programs. It had already generated more volumes of federal case law than the Talmud.

"What if the officers received, well, substantial cash for signing onto the plan?"

"A bribe, in fact? I don't know. If there was evidence of intent to defraud the union . . . but if it was just to convert a pension to an annuity, it's possible ERISA would find it unethical but not illegal. Is it important enough that I should check up on it?"

"It's pretty important, yes."

He promised to look into it by Friday. When we'd hung up I wondered what position Dick was really in. He must have looked into the legal angle before getting Eddie Mohr to sign over the pension fund. Surely he hadn't been so blinded by greed that he'd exposed himself to a federal prison sentence.

My spinach was too cold now to be appetizing. I took the plate back to the kitchen. Presumably the folks at Diamond Head killed Mitch Kruger because he saw Eddie living well and wormed out of him how he'd got the money from the company. And when Mitch came around trying to get them to ante up for him, they conked him on the head and pushed him into the San. Did that mean they *knew* what they'd done was illegal? Or just that they were afraid it might be? People panic at the thought of exposure when they've done something shameful. And if the bosses let their panic be felt by underlings whom they've hired strictly for brute muscle, anything can happen. Still, Dick was walking a mighty fine line here.

I found myself holding the plate, staring abstractedly out the kitchen window, when Loring finally rang the bell. Mr. Contreras was up and about: I could hear his fierce interrogation of the visitor when I opened my front door.

It wasn't until then that I remembered the urine in the corner of the stairwell. The stench was unmistakable, but it was too late to do anything about it now.

Loring's face was set in angry lines when he came in. "Who the hell's that old man? What business does he have questioning me?"

"He's my partner. Part of his job is to check

485

my visitors. People've been stalking me all week—it makes both of us nervous. Coffee? Wine? Tofu?"

"Nothing for me. I don't want to be here and I don't want to prolong it. Your partner, huh? Not much of an operation."

"But you're not here as my business consultant, are you? I need some coffee. I'll be back in a minute."

The pot I'd made with my lunch was cold. It took about five minutes to brew up some fresh stuff. By the time I returned to the living room Loring himself was coming to a rolling boil—always a critical moment in cooking.

"What are you trying to do to me, Warshawski? I run the finances of a major corporation. I dropped everything to meet with the members of our board who could give me the green light to talk to you—and now you're jacking me around just for the hell of it. I might be better off taking my chances with the press."

"No, you wouldn't. And you don't need me to tell you that. I spent all of last night looking at files relating to Diamond Head. I got in at six-thirty this morning and went to bed. I know now—"

"Where?" he demanded. "If you had access to Diamond Head files, why the hell are you screwing around with me?"

"I didn't until last night. Have access, I mean. It was pure luck, in combination with my partner's areas of expertise. I still don't know

486

what your problem is, though. I know now that the consent decree when you bought Central States Aviation meant you had to sell Diamond Head." I sketched out what I'd learned from Dick's papers last night.

"If you know that, you know everything," Loring said. His face was still set in tight lines.

I shook my head. "What's so secret about it? Did you have to sign some kind of defense department clearance that means you can't talk to mere taxpayers about it?"

"No, nothing like that. What do you know about the decree?"

"Not a lot. That you had sixty days in which to sell, and Jason Felitti came to you with a better offer than you thought you'd be able to get if you waited. And then you had to give some guarantees that you wouldn't drive them out of business."

Loring gave a bark of laughter. "I wish! No, you didn't see the real decree. Or you didn't read it very carefully."

"I wasn't as interested in it as I was in—well, some other things. And I only had a few hours with the files."

"What other things?"

"You first, Mr. Loring."

He went to the front window to conduct an interior debate. It didn't take him long: he hadn't come all this way on a business day only to return empty-handed.

"Daraugh Graham warned me about you," he

commented with less animosity. "And I suppose if he trusts you I can too."

I tried to smile in a trustworthy way.

"If you'd read through the whole consent decree, you would see that the Justice Department's care for Diamond Head went way beyond protecting them from us: we had to guarantee their survival by continuing to provide a market for their products. And by continuing to supply them with raw materials."

Loring smiled bitterly as he saw my mouth gape open. "It's not unprecedented. Some other steel companies have gotten stabbed by the same kind of deal. But Felitti had, or seemed to have, good credentials. I mean, everyone in the industry in Chicago knows Amalgamated Portage. We've done business with them for years."

"But Peter Felitti wouldn't tie the family company in with Diamond Head."

"We only discovered that later. But that didn't matter. He was plenty willing to help in other ways: he saw that Jason got debt financing. I suppose most backers assumed Amalgamated Portage would be behind Diamond Head—we did, after all. It wouldn't have mattered, if Jason had been honest."

"So what's he been doing? Ordering supplies from you that he doesn't need and then reselling them on the black market? Why don't you go to the feds?"

"We didn't have any evidence. . . . Is there more coffee? I'm afraid I was a little short earlier."

I grinned at him. "I can make some fresh, but it'll keep you waiting, unless you don't mind coming out to the kitchen."

He followed me to the back of the apartment. I moved the plate of cold tofu to the sink and put water on to boil again. Loring took the papers from a chair and put them on the floor so he could sit down.

"When you showed up on Friday and started flaunting tales of knowing we were bankrolling Felitti, I thought you were working for him, that you might be trying to muscle something extra out of us. But when you called Monday with the tale of the copper spools—then I knew what they were doing."

I poured boiling water into the coffee cone. "You could have hired a detective and had that information a year ago. Why didn't you?"

He shook his head in frustration. "We always had complete audit reports from them. And they had a very reputable law firm behind them. I didn't like it, but I didn't think—"

"A detective would quickly have told you that the senior partner handling the buyout was the son-in-law of Jason Felitti's brother. Then you could have started worrying about conflict of interest."

"Okay. I'll get a detective on the case. What do you charge?"

"Fifty dollars an hour and any expenses that aren't part of my normal overhead."

"You're too cheap, Warshawski. But maybe I'll hire you."

I showed my teeth at him. "And maybe I'll be available."

"Sorry, sorry. I said it wrong. Seriously, I'll talk to the board tomorrow. It's your turn now. What was it you were mostly interested in—this dead man you mentioned the other day?"

"Right." I gave him a thumbnail sketch of Mitch Kruger and Eddie Mohr and what I'd learned last night from my time in Dick's files.

"Jason Felitti was just scrambling," Loring said when I finished. "He was too ignorant to come up with a plan. He got goods from me and stole them, cheated the union out of their pension plan, parked bonds with a charity—all that's just flailing around."

"Yes. Not a criminal mastermind. Not even a bust-out artist, as I originally suspected. Just an incompetent schlep who wanted to prove he was as big as his brother. The problem is, I don't see how I can tag them for murder. And I care more about that than I do about your theft problem. I'm worried about the pension fund too. I don't want innocent bystanders screwed out of their rights."

Loring, of course, only cared about protecting Paragon's interests. He wanted me to drop everything and plan a stakeout that would provide definitive proof of Diamond Head's reselling Paragon raw materials. The way it stood right now I only had evidence that they were loading copper onto trucks in the middle of the night, not whether they were reselling it or whether Diamond Head management was involved.

I let him argue his case while I tried to figure out answers to my own problems, but at four-thirty I showed him the door. "You were so late getting here you've backed up the rest of my schedule. I need to get going. You can talk to me tomorrow after you've spoken to your board."

"Then you'll take the case if they approve hiring you?"

"I don't know. But I can't discuss it until I know whether you're a serious customer or not."

He didn't like it, but when he saw I wasn't going to budge he finally left, wrinkling his face in disgust at the stench on the stairs. I stayed long enough to strap on the Smith & Wesson before heading for the el.

50

Saint Stevenson and the Truck

I stopped on my way out to let Mr. Contreras know where I was going. As a full-fledged partner in crime, he deserved to know. Besides, the fact that someone had been waiting in the stairwell last night made me extra cautious. I wanted him to monitor the building's traffic even more rigorously than he usually did.

491

"Vinnie may be letting thugs into the place. Just keep an eye out. Don't expose yourself unnecessarily—but if strangers go clomping up to the third floor, call the cops. In fact, call Conrad." I gave him Rawlings's home number as well as the number at the station and took off before he could flood me with accusations over my intimacy with an officer.

During the slow el ride south I wondered what I could do about the Picheas and Vinnie and Mrs. Frizell. Even if I proved Vinnie and Chrissie persuaded Mrs. Frizell to buy some of Diamond Head's useless bonds, I wasn't sure the state's attorney would think that rotten enough to remove the Picheas as her guardian. I wondered whether Mrs. Frizell's strange estranged son might be persuaded to take action. Since his main rivals to her affection, the dogs, were out of commission, maybe he would at least want to protect his own measly inheritance.

The el let me out at Twenty-second and Kedzie around five-thirty. It was more than two miles down to Barney's from there, but I longed for a good walk to clear my body. Thunderheads had started to cloud the sun about the time I changed trains downtown, but I thought I could walk fast enough to beat the storm.

After a few blocks in the dust that the trucks were kicking up on the narrow roadway, I began to doubt the health value of the walk. My old Tigers, too, didn't have as much left in their soles as I had hoped. My feet started to hurt. Every time I came to a bus stop I'd wait a few minutes to see if one were coming behind the trucks. Plenty of northbound buses trundled by, but they must have been falling off the end of the earth when they got to Congress: nothing was returning south.

I could just see Barney's sign when the rain broke. I sprinted the last two blocks and rounded the corner onto Forty-first.

The rain and my sore feet made me stupid. A truck was double-parked across the street from me, its engine running. I looked at it cursorily, unlocked the Impala, and started to slide into the driver's seat.

A movement from the truck startled me and I moved faster into the car, reaching for my Smith & Wesson. My mistake was in trying to do both. The door was wrenched open and a pistol thrust against my head while I was still fumbling for my own gun. Careful not to move my head, I rolled my eyeballs as far up as they would go. I was looking at the Hulk.

He didn't speak or move. My stomach heaved. I was glad I'd only put half a plate of tofu into it. That lessened the chance of total humiliation. I heard glass shatter to my right. I jerked around involuntarily and felt the pistol jam into my neck.

One of the Hulk's pals had broken the glass in the passenger side of the Impala and was calmly unlocking the door. He, too, had a gun. When he had it stuck in my side, the Hulk climbed into the backseat. Stupidly enough, the only thing I could think was how pissed Luke was going to be when he saw the broken window on a car he wanted to sell.

"Drive," the Hulk growled.

"Your slightest wish is my command. Where to, O king?" Despite my dry mouth and heaving stomach, my voice came out without a quaver. All those years of practicing breath control to my mother's critical standard paid off in a crisis.

"Down to the corner and make a left," the Hulk said.

I turned left onto Albany. "Back to Eddie Mohr's?"

"We don't want to hear it from you." A piece of metal attached itself to the back of my head. "Right at the corner."

"To Diamond Head, then."

"I said we didn't want to hear it from you. Left on Archer."

We were heading to the plant. Rain was starting to come in through the broken glass, spattering the man to my right, but also the dashboard. Another thing that would peeve Luke.

If they were just getting me to the plant so that they could kill me in private I didn't think I had a prayer. I wished I'd seen Lotty before I came down here. I wished she hadn't spent the last week in fear because of me. And I wished my own last minutes weren't to be spent in terror.

I still had my gun. But I couldn't figure out how to get to it without one of my escorts shooting first. When we pulled up on the tarmac in front of the plant, the Hulk slid out of the back-seat and opened the driver's door. His pal ordered me to kill the engine. I did, but left the key in the ignition. The Hulk yanked on my left arm, wrenching me from the car, while his pal kept me covered. From around the side I could hear the throb of truck engines.

I whirled inside the Hulk's arm, so that his body shielded me from his partner, and kicked hard on his shin. The damned Tigers were too soft.

The Hulk grunted, but kept his hold. "Don't make it harder on yourself than it already is, girlie."

He frog-marched me into the building, his partner covering us. We went down the long hall past the assembly room where the women had been so sympathetic about my uncle. Past the T-intersection that led to the loading bays. On around to the small stretch of corridor that housed the offices. The Hulk pounded on Chamfers's door. A voice told us to come in.

Milt Chamfers was sitting on a chair in front on his desk. Jason Felitti was facing him. Behind the desk sat the big brother, Peter.

"Thanks, Simon," Chamfers said. "You can wait for us outside."

Simon. Why could I never remember his name?

"She had a gun when she was here before," the Hulk said.

"Ah . . . a gun. Have you searched her?" That was Peter Felitti.

It didn't take Simon long to find the Smith & Wesson. His hand lingered longer than was necessary on my left breast. I stared past him stonily, hoping there would be a chance to respond more appropriately in the future.

"Good afternoon, Ms. Warshawski. You did go back to your maiden name, didn't you, after your divorce?" Peter Felitti asked when Simon had closed the door behind him.

"No." I massaged my shoulder where the Hulk had yanked it from the socket.

"No, what?" Chamfers demanded.

"I didn't go back to my own name: I never gave it up. Thank God, of all the imbecile things I did when I was young and in love, I never allowed myself to be called Mrs. Yarborough. Speaking of which, where is the distinguished counselor?"

Jason and Peter exchanged angry looks.

"I wanted to bring him," Jason began, but Peter cut him off.

"I tell you, the less he knows, the better."

"You mean if it gets to court," Jason said. "But you keep telling me we can keep things from going that far."

"So how much of your shenanigans is Dick privy to, anyway?" That was probably the least essential thing to worry about right now, but it seemed important to know Dick hadn't been involved in the attempts on my life.

"We thought you might listen to him," Peter said. "The way you clung to his arm that night at the concert I thought you were still carrying a torch for him. He said you'd never pay attention to him in a million years. It's too bad he was right."

"Carrying a torch?" I echoed. "No one says that anymore. What was I supposed to listen to, anyway?"

"To keep your goddamned snooper's nose out of Diamond Head." Peter slammed the desktop. Its hollow metal top buckled at the blow; he rubbed the side of his hand. "We were managing perfectly well until—"

"Until I came along and found out about the bond parking and defrauding old ladies and stealing raw materials from Paragon. Not to mention fooling around with the pension fund."

"That was perfectly legal," Jason said. "Dick told me so."

"And stealing copper from Paragon? He okay that too?"

"Everything would have been fine if you hadn't felt you had to make a fast buck under the table." Peter spat at his brother.

"It was Milt's idea," Jason whined. "He'd take a cut instead of a production bonus."

Chamfers moved angrily in his chair and started to protest, but shut up at a gesture from Peter.

"You were always such a fucking two-bit operator, Jason. You pissed and moaned because Papa didn't leave you the company, but he knew you were too stupid to run it. Then you pissed for forty years while you screwed around on the fringes of big-time politics, so I helped you get your own company. And now you've fucked that up."

"Whose fault is that?" Jason's round face looked green in the uncertain light. "You had to use your hotshot son-in-law to do the legal work. I could have got it—"

"You could have got it screwed nine ways from Sunday if I'd left it to your Du Page County Board cronies. I'm cleaning up after Warshawski for you, but you know the condition. You stop funneling supplies away from Paragon."

My legs felt wobbly at his words. I grabbed the doorknob behind me for support. It had a little button lock in it. I pressed it home. That wouldn't keep Simon out long, but any fraction of a second would help.

"Cleaning up after me?" I repeated the scary words, trying to tame them. "Come on, guys. Ben Loring at Paragon knows all about this. The city cops know about Chamfers getting the Hulk to knock Mitch Kruger into the canal. Did he also kill Eddie Mohr, Milt? Or did you do that yourself?"

"I told you she knew too much," Jason said. "You should have done something sooner."

"Oh, for Christ sake, Jason. I'm telling you this really is the last time I get involved in your problems."

"Got that right, big guy," I said brightly. "This

498

one is probably going to take the rest of your life to sort out."

"I can see why Yarborough ditched you as fast as he could," Peter said. "If you'd been mine I would have beaten some sense into you."

A cold rage gripped me, straightening my legs. "You might have tried it once, Felitti, but you sure wouldn't have wanted to do it twice."

I noticed the light switch out of the corner of my eye. For the first time since arriving I felt able to think clearly, to plan for action.

Felitti tightened his lips. "You're everything I'm glad my daughters aren't. I just can't see what attracted a man like Yarborough to a—a dyke like you."

It was such a feeble insult and he looked so steamed up saying it that I couldn't help laughing.

"Yeah, laugh," Jason said. "You'll do it out of the other side of your mouth in a minute. Why'd you have to come around here, anyway?"

"Mitch Kruger. He was an old friend of a good friend of mine. And he ended up dead in the canal. If everything you were doing with the pension fund and the bonds was so open, why did Chamfers get so bent out of shape when Mitch Kruger showed up last month demanding a piece of the pie in order to keep his mouth shut?"

"I told you Eddie Mohr would be a weak link," Milt said to Peter. "He claimed he never said anything to any of the boys that would make them think he got his money from the company. But I always had my doubts."

"And what about Eddie Mohr and Chicago Settlement?" I persisted. "Why on earth was he giving money to that outfit?"

"That was Dick's idea," Jason said. "I told him it was a mistake, but he said they'd take a lot of the bonds, only we had to encourage people who'd benefited from the deal to contribute."

"And you've got to admit that the guy preened at getting his picture taken with a lot of downtown money," Chamfers said.

"I see." I smiled. "My . . . uh . . . partner couldn't figure it out—he said Eddie was a Knights of Columbus man all the way."

"Your partner?" Peter demanded. "Since when do you have a partner?"

"Since when are my business affairs any concern of yours?" I pulled down on the light switch and fell to the floor.

"Simon!" they bellowed.

I could hear Simon on the other side try the knob, swear, and put his shoulder into the door. Someone came up behind me, trying to get at the switch. I grabbed him at the knees and pulled hard. He came crashing over at the same time that Simon kicked the door open. I squirmed out from under the body I'd tackled. Staying on my hands and knees, I made it past Simon and out the door.

Simon's pal was rushing in behind him. He grabbed at me as I went past, but missed. I ran down the hall, trying to get back to the entrance. Someone fired at me. I started moving from side to side as I ran, but I was too exposed a target. When they fired again I turned down the T-intersection to the loading bays.

The same subdued industry I'd interrupted last week was taking place on the work floor. A couple of men overhead were steadying a load on a gantry while another couple stood at the open back of a trailer to receive it.

I sprinted past them out onto the bay and jumped to the ground. I couldn't hear anything over the truck engines, to know whether the Hulk was close at hand or not, and I didn't stop to look. I could feel the gravel under the thin soles of my Tigers, could feel my toes wet with sweat or blood. It was still raining. I didn't waste energy wiping water from my eyes, just kept running until I reached the Impala.

"Don't flood now," I gasped at it, turning the key while I slammed the door shut. The engine caught and I reversed with a great squeal of rubber. A bullet tore through one of the back windows. I shoved the car into drive without braking. The gears ground, but Luke's magic fingers on the transmission kept it running smoothly and we leaped forward.

I careened down the drive toward Thirty-first Place. I was almost at the intersection when I saw the lights of one of the semis bearing down on me from behind. I turned right, sharply, so sharply that the car skidded on the wet road. I spun around in a circle, my arms cold with fear, chanting to myself my father's lessons for managing a skid. I straightened out without flipping over, but the truck was now right behind me, almost touching the back of the Impala. I accelerated hard, but he was bearing down on me too fast.

We were running on an access road to the expressway, next to the stilts of the exit ramp to Damen, where pylons lowered the road notch by notch. I could just make out a fence through the rain.

Another semi was coming toward us, its lights flashing, its horn blaring. At the last second I pulled off the road into the prairie grass. I had the door open before I left the road. Just before the Impala hit the cyclone fence I jumped free and rolled onto the grass.

There was a terrible scream of metal on metal as the truck behind me drove through the Impala, knocking it from its path. I scrambled up the cyclone fence, did a belly flop across its pointed top that raked open my shirt and my stomach, and landed on the cement floor beyond.

I made myself get up and start moving again, but red pain was searing my lungs and I was starting to black out. I stumbled over a hubcap and fell down. Lying on my back I watched the semi plow through the fence, heading straight toward me, its headlights pinning me.

I staggered upright. My right foot caught in

a discarded tire and I started to fall back to the concrete. I seemed to be dropping in free-fall: I was landing slowly enough to watch the tractor rush toward me.

Just as I hit the pavement sparks erupted from the cab top. A cannon exploded, making my head vibrate against the concrete. The engine ruptured the cab's grille and a geyser of antifreeze sprayed the night. As I wrenched my ankle free of the tire and dove away I heard a heart-shattering scream. A starburst the color of blood decorated the truck's windshield.

I lay behind a pylon, panting. The exit ramp notched down too low here for a truck to clear, but Simon had been so intent on killing me that he hadn't noticed. The top of the truck had caught the edge of the ramp.

I looked up at the cracked concrete. In the dim night air I could just make out pieces of exposed rebars. Traffic roared overhead. It seemed so queer that people were rushing to and fro above me, utterly oblivious of the violence down here. The world should have paused a moment to catch its breath, make some acknowledgment. The expressway itself should have shuddered. But the pylons, towered over me, unmoved.

51

Just Deserts—
or Whatever—
for the Guilty

I ended up in my own bed that night, although for a while it didn't look as though I'd get there. The trucker who'd been heading toward me had called the cops on his CB once he'd extricated himself from his cab. He had slammed into the side of Simon's trailer as it jackknifed across the road. His own cab had flipped over, but he'd been wearing a seat belt and mercifully walked away from the accident with minor bruises. By later accounts he'd been threatening to sue everyone involved until he saw Simon's pulpy head.

I'd stayed on the pavement under the Stevenson until the cops came looking for me—not me specifically, of course, but the driver of the Impala. I'd been too exhausted by then to move, or to care much what happened next. Shivering in the back of the squad car, I tried giving a coherent story about the evening's events.

The patrolmen gave me a clearer picture of what had happened to Simon. His momentum had been so great that when he rammed the expressway roof it drove the back tires into the ground, exploding them. That explained the cannon shot, which was still ringing in my head. The same force expelled the engine from its blocks, propelling it through the radiator. The cab perched rakishly on its hind wheels while firefighters extricated Simon's remains from the windshield.

After we'd talked, the patrolmen radioed their base and sent someone over to pick up the Felitti boys and Chamfers. The three of them had been waiting in Chamfers's office, presumably for word from the Hulk that I'd gone to my lesser reward.

We'd all ridden over to the Fourth Area together, Chamfers insisting that I was a notorious break-in artist whom they'd surprised in the act. "I'm very grieved over Simon Lezak's death. He was trying to help out, to chase her from the premises when we surprised her—"

"And he got carried away by his zeal and ran over the Impala," I butted in.

"I don't think we'll ever have a clear picture of what happened under the expressway tonight." Chamfers addressed himself to Detective Angela Willoughby, who seemed to be in charge of the interrogation. "Truckers don't carry the little black boxes you get on a 747, so we don't have Simon's last thoughts."

"Hatred and glee would sum them up pretty well; I could see the boy's face in my rearview mirror just before I left the road," I said. "Did you get a statement from the oncoming trucker?

He could probably confirm that Simon was doing his best to run me over."

Willoughby looked at me with flat gray eyes, but didn't say anything. The uniformed man taking notes dutifully wrote down my question and poised his pen over his notebook for our next outburst.

I tried one more time. "Were they still loading Paragon Steel materials onto trucks when your officers showed up? The controller at Paragon might have a word or two to say about that. And I doubt if he'd connect me with Diamond Head's theft ring in any way."

Chamfers and Peter Felitti joined in a chorus of outrage. Who was I—a sneak thief—to question their business operations? When Dick showed up—he was the Felitti brothers' counsel, after all—I began to think I was going to be arrested while the upright citizens went home to bed.

I was certainly the one who looked like a miscreant. Besides the tears in my jacket, the knees in my jeans had broken through when I slid across the pavement in them. My shoes were in tatters, my hair matted to my skull, and I didn't even want to know what my face looked like. Justice may be blind, but she does favor a clean, neat appearance.

The Felittis had called Dick away from some party or other, but he'd stopped at home to change into an austere navy suit. Angela Willoughby was clearly impressed, both by his blond good looks and his imposingly wealthy demeanor: she allowed him to huddle in a corner with his clients.

When he came away he talked sorrowfully to Angela about the evening's disaster. A subordinate had gone overboard in his loyalty to his employers. It was tragic that Simon Lezak had died in action, but fortunate that I'd survived.

I bared my teeth at the last sentence. "Glad you think so, Dick. Your daddy-in-law explain to you how old Simon happened to go overboard? How he jumped me to get me to the plant?"

"Misguided zeal," Dick murmured. "They knew you'd broken into the plant before—they didn't know how far you'd go in an investigation."

I jumped up, or tried to—my muscles responded with a slow crawl—and grabbed his arm. "Dick. We need to talk. They're not telling you the truth. You're going to be blindsided."

He gave me the superior smile that used to infuriate me fifteen years ago. "Later, Vic. I need to get my clients home, and I think you'd be glad to be there yourself."

It was close to midnight by then. Willoughby was just agreeing that the Felittis and Chamfers could leave with Dick, when Conrad Rawlings showed up. I'd told Willoughby at the beginning of the evening that he and Terry Finchley were both involved in the case, but didn't realize she'd actually sent someone to notify him. As it turned out, she hadn't: he'd picked up word from someone at his precinct who'd heard it earlier on the police band.

Rawlings looked around the room. "Ms. W. I thought I told you I was going to be peeved if you went off to tackle thugs on your own without telling me. And I don't even get the story from you in person. Some stranger has to tell me about it."

I put my hands up to pat my filthy curls. "Detective Willoughby—Sergeant Rawlings. I think you met Dick Yarborough a couple of years ago, Sergeant. These other guys are Peter and Jason Felitti and Milt Chamfers. They're going home. The detective here is sorry she had to bother such swell suburbanites.

"The reason I didn't call you to tell you in person was that I was too embarrassed: I got jumped. Went to Forty-first and Kedzie to pick up my car, and the Felitti brothers' pet thug, Simon, was lying in wait for me."

Dick looked at me with bright, hard eyes. "Vic, we don't need to hear that story again. I'm taking my clients home. I can only say I warned you to mind your own business."

"The thing is," I continued, speaking to Rawlings, "the boys here are so pumped up, they've forgotten about forensic evidence."

Dick stopped on his way out of the room.

"Fingerprints, Richard. Neither the Hulk—sorry, Simon the Valiant—nor his sidekick wore gloves. They jumped me at the corner of Forty-first and Kedzie when I was picking up the Impala. Even though the car is a mess, it should be possible to find their prints on the inside. The Hulk sat in the backseat with a gun at my head. The sidekick sat in the passenger seat with another gun stuck in my ribs. That's how we ended up at Diamond Head. They forced me to drive there. Anyway, you should find their prints inside the car."

"You impound that Impala, Detective?" Conrad demanded.

"It's been towed, Sergeant," Willoughby said stiffly.

"You get on your little mike and tell them it's evidence in a murder case. Not to mention aggravated assault. I want that thing at the lab before the sun comes up, Detective. I've been working this case all week now and I'm going to be pretty frustrated if I lose it because we compacted the evidence."

Her expression would have melted steel, but she spoke into her mike. Dick had turned pale during the discussion and had started talking to his father-in-law in a savage undervoice. I couldn't hear the conversation, but it was clearly dawning on Dick that his relatives were landing him on a griddle. He gave me a look I couldn't decipher, so far was it removed from his usual cockiness, and hustled his clients from the room.

While Willoughby busied herself with summoning underlings, Conrad gripped my shoulders and demanded a detailed account of my evening. I'd given him a brief synopsis by the time Willoughby finished issuing orders to get the Impala from the police pound to the lab.

Conrad turned back to her. "You get a doctor to see this suspect, Detective?" Conrad had demanded.

Willoughby lost some of the icy poise that had made her formidable during four hours of questioning. "Her life isn't in danger. I was trying to make sure we didn't have serious felony charges to bring against her."

"Take it from me: we don't. I'm driving her to a doctor. You got a problem with that, I'll give you my watch commander's phone number."

Willoughby was too professional to get into a fight with another detective in front of a suspect. I would have been pissed in her place, too, but under the circumstances I didn't have much empathy to spare for her.

"I really don't need a hospital, Sergeant," I said as we left the station. "I just want to get home and get to sleep."

"Ms. W., I have seldom seen anyone who looked more in need of major surgery. Of course, it could just be your elegant wardrobe. But unless you want a high-speed chase along the South Side on foot, you don't have any choice in the matter, on account of you don't have a car and I'm driving."

He took me to Mt. Sinai, but not even his muscle could get me to a doctor right away—there were eight gunshot wounds and three knife injuries ahead of me. The charge nurse had stood up to tougher pressure than Conrad could muster.

While we waited I asked Rawlings to phone Mr. Contreras, who would be pacing the floor by now—if not taking the law into his own hands. Around three, after I'd fallen asleep on the narrow vinyl chair, I was finally taken into one of the treatment cubicles. Conrad watched anxiously while the harried intern cleaned my abrasions, gave me a tetanus shot, and stitched together the deepest of the cuts in my abdomen. I also had a couple of burns on my back from the antifreeze. In my general misery I hadn't noticed them.

"She going to be okay?" Conrad asked.

The intern looked up in surprise. "She's fine—this is all superficial. If you want to arrest her, Sergeant, she can certainly handle jail with these wounds."

"I don't think we need to do that." Rawlings shepherded me from the room with a packet of pain pills and a prescription for antibiotics. "Still, Ms. W., if you go off on another junket like tonight's without letting me know—I'm not so sure. I might stick you into County for a month to sober you up."

52

Tying Knots

I slept the clock around and woke to find Mr. Contreras in my living room. Even though Conrad had phoned him from Mt. Sinai last night, the old man had kept vigil in the lobby until we finally showed up. It was a little after four then. I went to bed at once, and had no notion of whether Rawlings stayed or not.

Mr. Contreras, who'd kept a set of keys, had let himself in a little after two. "Just wanted to see with my own eyes that you was okay, doll. You feel like telling me what went on last night? I thought you was just getting the Impala."

"That's what I thought too. Didn't Conrad clue you in?" I told him about the Hulk jumping me, and his hideous death under the Stevenson. At the end of the recital, after Mr. Contreras had gone over events enough to allay the worst of his worries, I said I thought our troubles were over.

"The only thing to worry about now is subpoenas, and they'll be hitting us thick and fast. But you can relax your watchdogging. And give me back my keys, please."

"So you can give them to Conrad?" His tone was jeering, but there was real pain in his face.

"You're the only guy who's ever had the keys to my place. I don't go handing them around randomly."

He refused to let me lighten the conversation. "Yeah, but . . . seemed like he was holding you awful close last night. This morning. And he didn't leave here until noon."

"I know you don't like it when I date anyone." I kept my voice gentle. "I'm sorry about that— sorry because I love you, you know, and I hate to hurt you."

He knotted his hands together. "It's just . . . Face it, doll: he's black. African, if you like that better. They'd burn both of you in your bed back in my old neighborhood."

I smiled sadly. "I'm glad we're not on the South Side, then."

"Don't make a joke of it, Victoria. It's not funny. Maybe I've got some prejudice. Heck, probably I do, I'm seventy-seven, you don't change how you was raised, and I grew up in a different time. But I don't like seeing you with him, it makes me uncomfortable. And if I don't . . . Well, you just can't picture how ugly people can be in this town. I don't want you buying yourself a lot of grief, doll."

"I just got through seeing with my own eyes how ugly people in this town can be." I leaned forward and patted his leg. "Look, I know it's hard—to be black and white together. But we're not that far down the road yet. We're two people who've always liked and respected each other, and now we're trying to see whether, well, our attraction is just bad old jungle fever, or has something more substantial to it. Anyway, Conrad isn't black. He's kind of copper."

Mr. Contreras clutched his ears. "I can tell just by you saying that that you like the guy."

"Sure, I like him. But don't crowd me into making any other declarations. I'm not ready for them yet."

He wordlessly handed me my keys and got to his feet.

He tried to shake off the arm I put around him, but I kept a grip on his shoulder. "Please don't cut me out of your life, or take yourself out of mine. I'm not going to say something stupid, like I know you'll come around in the end. Maybe you will, maybe you won't. But you and I have been friends a lot longer than I've known Conrad. It would bring me great pain to lose you."

He mustered a smile from some depth. "Right, doll. I can't talk about it anymore right now. Anyway, I been away from the princess too long. She needs to get out more often while she's nursing."

I felt melancholy after my neighbor left. I'd started an affair with Rawlings because an erotic spark had always jumped between us, and the time had somehow been right last week. But I didn't need Jesse Helms or Louis Farrakhan to tell me the road ahead would be rocky if Rawlings and I got serious about each other.

As I was listlessly poking through the refrigerator Murray called, practically slobbering into the phone in his eagerness for my story. This morning's *Herald-Star* had had a fine photo of the wreckage of Simon's truck and the Impala, but the text was short and ambiguous. The paper didn't want to accuse the Felitti boys of any malfeasance, not with their political connections. They didn't want to take me on, though, since I'd been an important source for them over the years. I gave Murray my version of events: I had nothing to gain and everything to lose by being snappy with him while the Felittis gathered ammunition. When we finished, I sent him to Ben Loring in the hopes that Paragon Steel could provide some hard documentation to shore up my own case.

By then it was almost six. I braced myself and called Luke Edwards to tell him about the Impala. He was furious. The fact that his baby was at the police labs and would be featured as an exhibit in a murder trial only enraged him further. He threatened to take a jackhammer to the Trans Am just so I'd know how he felt. I was on the phone with him for almost an hour. We weren't exactly friends again by the time I hung up, but at least he finally agreed to let me pick up the Trans Am.

"Although a less generous man would keep it as a hostage, Warshawski," came his parting shot.

I also gave Freeman Carter a call. I wasn't sure I wanted him representing me in the trials and suits that lay ahead. Freeman was at home, but he'd heard a pretty complete version of events from some of his old associates. He brought up the representation issue before I did.

"I was too close to that situation, Vic. I let my own anger over what Yarborough was doing to the firm cloud my mind, and I took it out on you—which is inexcusable between a lawyer and a client. But the real problem is a potential conflict of interest. You need someone speaking for you who is unimpeachable, because Yarborough may be firing some pretty big rockets. I'll come up with a few names. And I'll see that the bills don't get out of hand. And after that—I don't know—you can take your time to decide whether you want me to work for you in the future or not."

"Thanks, Freeman," I said quietly. We left matters at that for the present.

I was moving restlessly around my living room, wanting to talk to Lotty, not wanting another painful conversation, when Mr. Contreras showed up unexpectedly. He'd gone to the corner for a pizza, the kind we both like, thick with vegetables and topped with anchovies. And he'd picked up a bottle of the Ruffino I often serve him.

"I know I should've called, make sure you wasn't planning on—on doing anything else for dinner, but I could see you didn't have much food left. And we had a pretty good adventure. I thought we ought to celebrate."

Carol Alvarado showed up unexpectedly when

we were close to the bottom of the bottle. She was taking the graveyard shift tonight, filling in for someone else, she explained, and was just stopping for a minute on her way to the hospital. She'd read the brief story in this morning's *Herald-Star*, but wanted to talk to me specifically about Mrs. Frizell.

She turned down an offer of wine. "Not when I'm going on duty. You remember I told you I thought I might have the answer for Mrs. Frizell?"

So much had happened in the last few days, I'd forgotten our conversation at the hospital. I hadn't thought much of her secretive optimism then, but I made polite noises.

"It was her meds. I talked it over with Nelle McDowell, the charge nurse, and she agreed: too much Valium can have that effect on an old woman—make her restless and at the same time appear senile. And when it's combined with Demerol it's almost a recipe for senility. So we stopped the drugs for seventy-two hours and today she's definitely better—not totally over it, but able to answer simple questions, focus on who's talking to her, things like that. Only, she keeps asking about her dog Bruce. I don't know what we're going to do about that."

"Neither do I," I said. "But it's wonderful news. Now, if only I can get the Picheas out of her life, she can move back home one of these days."

"She's still going to be in a nursing home, or having to convalesce someplace," Carol warned.

"It's way too early to talk about bringing her home. . . . Do you think you could come see her? Nelle says you have a good effect on her."

I made a face. "Maybe. I'm not very fit right now—I've had a couple of rough days in the detection mines."

Carol asked for details on last night's heroics. When I finished she only said, "Gosh, Vic. Too bad they didn't bring you to County instead of Mt. Sinai. I could have patched you up—it would have been just like old times."

I shook my head. "Maybe you leaving the clinic was good for me as well as you. It's time I stopped turning to you and Lotty every time I scrape my knee."

Carol shook her head. "You and Lotty don't understand. Leaning on people who love you isn't a sin. It really isn't, Vic."

"Try telling her," Mr. Contreras jeered. "I been breaking my head on that brick wall long enough."

I punched him lightly on the nose before seeing Carol to the door.

53

Subterranean Homesick Blues

The next morning Mr. Contreras helped me prepare a wicker basket. We lined its bottom with plastic and put a couple of towels inside. The puppies, almost three weeks old, had their eyes open. With their soft, rich fur they looked adorable. We picked the two smallest and put them in the basket. Peppy watched us intently, but didn't protest. By now she spent some time away from her brood each day. Their little nails were scratching her stomach and the joys of maternity were starting to wear off.

At County Hospital, Nelle McDowell greeted me with genuine pleasure. "Mrs. Frizell's making real progress. She'll never win a Miss Congeniality prize, but it's wonderful to see someone come back from the edge the way she has. Come and take a look yourself."

She eyed the wicker basket thoughtfully. One little nose was pushing through a crack. "You know, Ms. Warshawski, I think you may be violating hospital policy. But I'm too busy this morning to have seen you come in. You go on down the hall and talk to the lady."

The change in Mrs. Frizell was remarkable. The sunken cheeks, which had made her look like a corpse, had filled out, but more impressive was the fact that her eyes were open and focused.

"Who are you? Some damned dooder?"

I laughed. "Yeah. I'm your damned do-gooding neighbor, Vic Warshawski. Your dog Bruce got my dog, Peppy, pregnant."

"Oh. I remember you now, coming around to complain about Bruce. He's a good dog, he doesn't roam the neighborhood, no matter what you people say. You can't prove to me he sired your bitch's litter."

I put the basket on the bed and opened it. Two black-and-gold fur balls tumbled out. Mrs. Frizell's face softened slightly. She picked up the puppies and let them lick her. I sat down next to her and put a hand on her arm. "Mrs. Frizell . . . I don't think anyone has told you, but Bruce is dead. While you were unconscious, someone took all your dogs and put them to sleep. Marjorie Hellstrom and I tried to save them, but we couldn't."

When she didn't say anything I went on, "These are two of Bruce's offspring. They'll be able to leave their mother about the time you're ready to come back home. They're yours if you want them."

She was scowling in the fierce way people do when they're trying not to cry. "Bruce was one dog in a million. One dog in a million, young lady. You don't just replace a dog like that."

One of the puppies bit her finger. She admonished it sternly, but with an undercurrent of affection. It cocked its head on one side and grinned at her.

"You might have just a little bit of his look, sir. Maybe just a little."

I left the puppies with her for half an hour and told her I'd be back with them again the next day.

"Don't think I've made up my mind about this;

I haven't. I may sue you for negligence, letting my dogs die. Just keep that in mind, young lady."

"Yes, ma'am. I will."

When I got home I told Mr. Contreras I was pretty sure she would take two of the dogs, but that he'd better get hustling to find homes for the other six. Before he could start trying to argue me into keeping one of them, I diverted him with a plan for Vinnie. As soon as he'd grasped the details, the old man was enthusiastic.

That night he waylayed Vinnie as the banker came in from work, then buzzed my apartment twice to let me know he was ready.

I came down the stairs two at a time. Vinnie's round brown face tightened in dislike when he saw me. He tried to brush his way past me, but I grabbed his arm and hung on.

"Vinnie, Mr. Contreras and I have a deal for you. For you and Todd and Chrissie. So why don't we go down there and talk and try to put all this ugliness behind us."

He didn't want to do it, but I murmured words about the police and the feds and the investigation that was revving up into U.S. Met's role in unloading Diamond Head's excess junk.

He frowned pettishly. "I could sue you for slander. But we might as well go down to the Picheas. He's my lawyer and can tell you where to get off."

"Splendid."

If anything, Todd and Chrissie were even less happy to see me than Vinnie had been. I let them squawk for a few minutes, but Mr. Contreras didn't approve of some of Todd's language and told him so. Todd's jaw dropped—perhaps no one had ever chewed him out at such length before.

I took advantage of the momentary quiet. "I have a deal for you three high-flyers. Call it a plea bargain. Todd, I want you and Chrissie to resign your guardianship of Mrs. Frizell. She's fully alert now, her hip is starting to mend, and she'll be able to come home and manage on her own, with only a little help, in another month. She doesn't need you. And I don't think you can do her any good. So if you resign your guardianship, and if you buy back her three Diamond Head bonds—at face value—I will promise not to say a word to the U.S. attorney about your role in marketing those bonds around the neighborhood. Of course, if you start pushing them again the deal is off."

They all started to speak again, in a chorus that included the fact that I should mind my own business, and anyway, they hadn't been doing anything illegal.

"Maybe. Maybe. But you walked a mighty fine line, promising people that junk was just as good an investment as a federally insured CD. You could be disbarred, Todd, for taking part in something like that. U.S. Met might want to promote you, Vinnie, for your efforts, but they'd probably ditch you when the publicity heated up."

The trouble was, none of them could admit they had done anything wrong. They had talked themselves into the idea that anything that got the results they wanted was by definition legal. I had to hammer repeatedly on the same key to get their attention: I had enough connections to the Chicago media to blow this story sky-high. And when that happened, their bosses would see them as sacrificial lambs.

"Remember Ollie North? You may think he was a hero, but his bosses didn't have any compunction throwing him to the wolves when the spotlight shone their way. And you guys don't have Marine uniforms to strut around in. You'll be on the streets chasing the same jobs fifty thousand other kids are, and those mortgage payments come right on the fifth of the month."

They agreed in the end to my terms, but stubbornly insisted they had never crossed the bounds of propriety, let alone the law. The five of us—Mr. Contreras didn't want to be left out—would meet at the Bank of Lake View at four Monday afternoon. Todd and Chrissie would bring an order from the probate judge showing the termination of their guardianship agreement. And they would have a cashier's check for thirty thousand, to buy back the Diamond Head bonds.

In exchange, I promised not to mention their role in peddling junk when the federal investigators started asking about U.S. Met. Mr. Contreras and I went home exhausted. We drank a bottle of Veuve Cliquot to celebrate.

The next morning I wondered if our jubilee had been premature. The doorbell rang at nine, just as I was trying to see how much of a workout my stomach could take. The voice at the other end of the squawk box announced itself as Dick Yarborough.

He came up the stairs with Teri, who was ready for a photo layout in a navy Eli Wacs trouser suit, her smooth peach skin perfectly made up. Dick had on the suburban executive's weekend costume, a Polo shirt, baggy cotton trousers, and a sports jacket.

"Vic—it is all right if I call you that, isn't it? I feel as though I know you." Teri stretched out a hand in a gesture of intimacy while Dick lingered in the background.

"Yeah, I feel as though I know you too." I ignored her hand. "You two want something special? Or am I a stop-off point on a goodwill tour of the poor?"

Dick winced, but Teri gave a faint saintly smile. She sank onto the piano bench and opened her eyes wide at me.

"This is a really hard visit for me to make. Let's face it: you and Dick were married once, and I know there must still be some feeling between you."

"But I'd put on a lead shield before getting close enough to examine it," I said.

"They say that hate is the other side of love," she announced with the air of someone presenting the law of gravity to firstgraders. "But I

524

know—Dick's told me—that you lost your own father, so I think you can understand my feelings."

"Peter's dead?" I was astounded. "It wasn't in the morning paper."

Dick made an impatient gesture. "No, Peter's not dead. Teri's having trouble getting to the point. She and Peter are very close and she's afraid she may lose him to a long jail sentence if she can't persuade you to drop charges."

I felt my lips tighten with anger. "It's great that they're close. Peter especially is going to need a lot of support over the next several months— maybe even the next twenty years. And knowing his daughter's in his court, believes in him a hundred percent, will only help."

Tears glistened on the ends of Teri's lustrous lashes. Waterproof mascara kept black smears from developing under her eyes. "Dick said you had a strange sense of humor, but I can't believe you think this is funny."

"I don't find anything that's happened in the last three weeks very funny. Two old men were killed because your daddy and your uncle didn't want them squealing about a pension reversion your husband set up. At least one old lady nearly became homeless because of a slick marketing scheme your uncle organized to chisel her out of her life's savings. And I don't feel very happy myself, having been shot at and almost run over."

I fingered the ridges on my stomach through my cotton T-shirt. The bandages covered the cuts, but I kept thinking they were oozing every time I twisted my torso.

"But Daddy explained all this to me. None of this was his doing. The people at the Diamond Head plant misunderstood him and Uncle Jason. They should never have done what they did. Everyone agrees it was wrong. Daddy will prove it in court; Dick can see to that. But it would make our lives so much easier if he didn't have to, if you would agree that it was all a big mistake. I'd hate for Dick to have to attack you in public. And you know, in a case like this, they'd hire investigators to dig up your secrets—talk about your love life, your disregard for the law, all those things."

Fury had me so in its grip, I could barely see. I jammed my hands into my pockets so Dick couldn't see their trembling. "Discovery cuts both ways, sugar. By the time I get done with my case your husband will be lucky to have his legal license, let alone be walking around outside a federal prison."

Dick, who'd never really come into the room, had wandered over to the window during the last interchange. When he spoke it was to the glass; we had trouble hearing him.

"My only role in this case will be as a witness."

Teri and I were both stunned into silence, but she recovered first. "Dick! I can't believe you would be such a—such a traitor. After everything Daddy's done for you! You promised me—"

"I promised you nothing." Dick kept his back

to us. "I finally agreed to come today because you were so hot on the idea. I told you if you could get Vic to listen to you I'd undertake drawing up a proper agreement with her. But I've been trying to get you to understand all night that I cannot represent your father and uncle."

"But Daddy's counting on you.

He finally turned around. "We've been through this a hundred times, but you won't hear it. Leigh Wilton advised me very strongly not to represent them—that the appearance of impropriety would be too great, given my position on the Diamond Head board. I would do them more harm than good. And, Teri, I just don't believe in them. I've talked to enough of their employees the last few days to believe they wanted to kill Vic. Your father set me up: he got me to deliver warnings to Vic under the guise of protecting *me*—keeping her from getting too close to the pension reversion. He must have known I'd never countenance an attack on her life."

Teri sprang to her feet, spots of color blooming under her blusher. "You're still in love with her! I don't believe it."

Dick gave a tired smile. "I'm not in love with her, Teri. I guess I should have said I wouldn't countenance their trying to kill anyone, regardless of race, creed, sex, or inquisitiveness."

Teri's eyes were bright with tears. She ran to the door. "Find your own way home, Mr. Hotshot. I'm not riding with you."

I expected him to race off after her, but he

stood frozen in the room, his shoulders slumped, long after the echo of the slamming door had died down.

"I'm sorry, Dick. Sorry for the bad time that lies ahead for you."

"I was sure you'd brandish your gun in triumph and tell me I have only myself to thank."

I shook my head, not trusting my voice.

"You'd be right. I do have only myself to thank. You've always known how weak I am. Teri . . . if she saw through my—my facade of strength . . . didn't let on. She built me up. Turned me into one of those see-through buildings." He gave a harsh bark of laughter. "It's not that I think of you often, but I did hope over the years when you saw how important I'd gotten you'd be sorry. Not sorry you left me, but sorry you despised me."

I felt my cheeks flame in embarrassment. "I'm a street fighter, Dick. I had to be as a kid just to survive, but I'm afraid I never outgrew it. Someone like Teri suits you better than I do. You'll see; you two will get through this time somehow."

"Maybe. Maybe. Look—it was that damned pension agreement that started all the trouble. Not all of it—that prize asshole, Jason, letting his crew bilk Paragon didn't help any. But trying to keep the reversion secret—two men died over that. And when it comes out—the legal stuff's clean, but it could keep us in court for a decade. I talked to Ben Loring at Paragon this morning.

He's willing to help restructure the agreement, buy out the annuity and refund the plan, if the local wants to vote on it. We'd take it out of U.S. Met and give it back to Ajax Insurance to manage."

I felt my shoulders sag in relief. Mr. Contreras's pension—all the guys in the local—had been worrying me all week. "Can you afford it? I thought most of the money was in Diamond Head junk."

Dick nodded. "Loring'll work something out. And Peter will have to agree to put up some Amalgamated Portage shares as collateral. He doesn't want to, but he'll come around in the end. It'll be his only hope for a plea bargain."

"And you?"

"I don't know. I offered Leigh my resignation. He wouldn't take it. He did agree that we didn't need young Pichea in the firm anymore after this year: that should please you. But—I need a leave of absence from the law, and Leigh supported that—more because he doesn't want me embarrassing the firm than for any other reason, but I'll still be gone six months. If I join an ashram, I'll let you know."

I offered him a lift downtown to the train, but he said he needed to walk, to clear his head. I went downstairs with him.

He took my hand and held it between both of his. "We had some good times together, didn't we, Vic? It wasn't all fighting and contempt, was it?"

I suddenly remembered Dick going with me

529

every weekend to stay with my dad when Tony was dying. I'd forgotten that in the curtain of bitterness I'd draped across the past, but Dick, orphaned at five, adored Tony, and wept openly at his grave.

"We had some important times together." I squeezed his hand, then pulled mine away. "Now you'd better go."

He left without looking back.

54

A Long Way from Home

The next four weeks were a long, slow period of legal discovery, of hiring people to fix up Mrs. Frizell's house, of finding someone to help her once she got home, and arranging with the state to pick up the tab. Carol Alvarado did a lot of the legwork for that.

I called Mrs. Frizell's son, Byron, in San Francisco to let him know how his mother was doing. He was almost as excited by the call as she had been to learn we'd been talking to him.

About the time Mrs. Frizell was ready to come home we found homes for the last of the puppies. Mr. Contreras out-talked me and kept his favorite, an all-gold male with two black ears. He insisted on naming it Mitch.

The same day the old lady returned, Todd and

Chrissie put their house on the market. Even with the recession in real estate we didn't expect it would take long to sell: they had done a beautiful job of rehabbing it, and Lake View has become prime yuppie real estate.

Lotty and I started talking again, but Lotty seemed brittle, almost fragile. We couldn't seem to recover our old, profound intimacy. She was working ferociously, so much so that the flesh was beginning to leach from her bones. Despite her frantic pace, her usual vital spark was missing.

When I tried telling her what had happened to Simon and the other thugs who most likely had attacked her, she refused to listen to me. Her injuries, or her fear, had given her a repugnance to my work. I worried she was feeling a repugnance, a withdrawal, from my whole life. I talked to Carol as well as to Max about her. They were both worried, but could give no counsel besides patience.

"She's forgiven me," Carol said. "She'll come round with you too. Give her time, Vic."

I didn't say anything, but it looked like a more serious problem to me than that.

Probably the most amazing event of that period was the afternoon that Mitch Kruger's son showed up. Mitch, Jr., turned out to be a petroleum engineer, sunburned from months in the Persian Gulf—he'd been in Kuwait helping restart production there. His mother had seen our ad in one of the Arizona papers and sent it off to him in Kuwait City. Mitch, Jr., stopped in Chicago on his way home to find out what we had to say to him.

He thanked us for our efforts in tracking down his father's killers, but added depressingly, "I can't get too excited about it—I hardly remember the guy. I'm glad he had some friends to help him out when he died, though."

When I told Conrad about it later, he laughed. "Don't look so disconsolate, Ms. W. At least the guy thanked you. Hell, ninety percent of the time all I get is hate mail for my efforts."

I was working hard during this time—not just helping build the case against the Felittis and fixing up Mrs. Frizell's home, but also taking jobs for real clients with real money. My first retainer had gone to new running shoes. Still, I spent as much time as our frantic schedules allowed with Conrad.

Mr. Contreras, trying valiantly not to meddle, couldn't hide his discomfort from the sergeant. I was upset by it and tried discussing it with Rawlings.

"At least he's talking to you. My sister heard about you from some busybody on the grapevine and won't let me sully her living room now."

I gasped out loud and Rawlings laughed a little. "Yeah, white girl: cuts both ways. So don't let the old guy worry you."

I tried not to, nor to wonder how long we could stay close before our careers collided, but it was hard just to relax into the relationship.

Despite my barricade of work I found myself

waking time and again from nightmares of my mother's death, dreams in which Lotty and Gabriella were inextricably entangled.

Conrad was with me one night when the unbearable phantoms broke open my sleep. Trying not to wake him, I slid from my bed to the living room and went to the window. I could just make out the corner of the Picheas' house. I wanted to go out in the night and run, run so fast and so far I could break away from my nightmares.

I was trying to imagine a place where you could safely be outside at three in the morning, when Conrad came up behind me. "What's the problem, Ms. W.?"

I put my hands over his arms, but continued to look out the window. "I didn't mean to wake you up."

"I'm a light sleeper. I've been hearing you get out of bed every night we've spent together this month. If you don't want me to stay the night, just tell me so, Vic."

"It's not that." I was whispering, as if the dark imposed silence.

He stroked my hair lightly. We stood silent a long minute.

I hadn't planned on telling him about Lotty or my nightmares, but in the dark, with the warmth of his body against mine, I suddenly blurted, "It's Lotty. I'm so scared—scared she's going to leave me the way my mother did. It didn't matter that I loved my mother, that I did what I could to look after her. She left me anyway.

I don't think I can bear it if Lotty abandons me too."

"So you have to keep everyone around you on pins and needles all the time? Is that it? So guys like me, or even the old man downstairs, don't get enough of a hold on you to leave you in the lurch?"

I held him more tightly, but couldn't say anything else. Maybe he was right though. Maybe that's why I reacted so roughly every time Mr. Contreras, or Lotty, or anyone else worried about my safety. It could even be why I pushed myself to the brink time and again. When my muscles slowed down, would I find other strengths to get me across those chasms? I shivered in the summer air.